Also by Melissa Marr

Wicked Lovely

Ink Exchange

FRAGILE ETERNITY

melissa marr

BOWEN PRESS

An Imprint of HarperCollins*Publishers*

Library of Congress Cataloging-in-Publication Data
Marr, Melissa.
    Fragile eternity / Melissa Marr. — 1st ed.
        p.   cm.
    Sequel to: Wicked lovely.
    Summary: Aislinn and Seth struggle with the unforeseen
consequences of Aislinn's transformation from mortal girl to
faery queen as the world teeters on the brink of cataclysmic
violence.
    ISBN 978-0-06-121471-4 (trade bdg.)
    ISBN 978-0-06-121472-1 (lib. bdg.)
    [1. Fairies—Fiction.   2. Kings, queens, rulers, etc.—
Fiction.   3. Fantasy.]   I. Title.
PZ7.M34788Fr   2009   2008034420
[Fic]—dc22   CIP
                                                    AC

09   10   11   12   13   LP/RRDB   10   9   8   7   6   5   4   3   2   1
❖
First Edition

To Loch, for being my forever and always . . .

ACKNOWLEDGMENTS

This book would not have happened without the insights and passion of Anne Hoppe. Thank you for believing in my characters and for sharing the journey. These books are yours as much as they are mine.

Everything I have in my life—including writing—is possible because I was fortunate enough to find a partner who fills in my empty spaces. Loch, you give me the courage and the faith to try to do more than I thought I could. Thank you for being here with me through the travels, the weird hours, the odd questions, and the overall panic-and-glee roller coaster.

Part of writing is filling the well. My ever-patient son convinced me to journey to far reaches to hang out with puffins. My wise daughter reminded me to take nights off for *Buffy* marathons. For these and so many other reasons, you two remain the center of my universe.

My parents continue to offer support every step of the journey. I couldn't do any of this without the wisdom and love you've given me over the years.

A few of the usual suspects were also invaluable during the past year plus. Jeaniene Frost continues to be steadfast in her role as critique partner and dear friend. Melissa Dittmar saved my sanity and organized my universe. Alison Donalty and Mark Tucker completely spoiled me with yet another fabulous cover. Patrice Michelle offered insightful remarks on the text. Mark Del Franco, Kelly Kincy, Vicki Pettersson, Rachael Morgan, Jason Falivene, Kerri Falivene, and Dean Lorey all shared sanity and words of wisdom. Friends like you are a treasure. Thank you, all.

Gratitude must go also to my wonderful readers. Extra thanks goes to those of you who've taken time to come out and meet me, as well as the readers on www.wickedlovely.com and my own web forum (especially Maria, Jennifer, Meg, Tiger, Pheona, Michaela, and Raven) for indulging my chatter urges.

You have all inspired me to keep trying to do better. Thank you.

PROLOGUE

Seth knew the moment Aislinn slipped into the house; the slight rise in temperature would've told him even if he hadn't seen the glimmer of sunlight in the middle of the night. *Better than a lantern.* He smiled at the thought of his girl-friend's likely reaction to being called a lantern, but his smile fled a heartbeat later when she came into his doorway.

Her shoes were already gone. Her hair was loosened from whatever arrangement it had been forced into for the Summer revels she'd been at earlier that night. *With Keenan.* The thought of her in Keenan's arms made Seth tense. She had these all-night dances with the Summer King every month, and try as he might, Seth was still jealous.

But she's not with him now. She's here.

She unfastened the bodice of an old-fashioned dress as she stared at him. "Hey."

He might've spoken; he wasn't really sure. It didn't matter. Not much did in these moments, just her, just them, just what they meant to each other.

The rest of the dress fell away, and she was in his arms. He knew he didn't speak then, not with sunlight like warm honey against his skin. The Summer Court revel had ended, and she was here.

Not with him. *With me.*

The monthly revels weren't mortal-friendly. Afterward, she came to him, though, too filled with sunlight and celebration to simply sleep, too afraid of herself to stay with the rest of the Summer Court all night. So she came to his arms, sun-drunk and forgetting to be as careful with him as she was on other nights.

She kissed him, and he tried to ignore the tropical heat. Orchids, a small ylang-ylang tree, and golden goddess branches clustered in the room. The perfumed scents were heavy in the humid air, but it was better than the waterfall a few months ago.

When she was here, in his arms, the consequences didn't matter. All that mattered was them.

Mortals weren't made to love faeries; he knew it each month when she forgot just how breakable he was. If he could be strong enough, he'd be at the revels. Instead, he admitted that mortals weren't safe in throngs of unrestrained faeries. Instead, he hoped that after the revels she wouldn't injure him too badly. Instead, he waited in the dark, hoping that this month wasn't the month that she stayed with Keenan.

Later, when speech returned, he plucked orchid petals from her hair. "Love you."

"You too." She blushed and ducked her head. "Are you okay?"

"When you're here, I am." He dropped the flower petals to the floor. "If I had my way, you'd be here every night."

"I'd like that." She snuggled in and closed her eyes. There was no light in her skin now—not when she was calm and relaxed—and Seth was grateful for it. In a couple hours day would break; she would see the burns on his sides and back where her hands had touched him too much and she'd forgotten herself. Then, she'd look away. She'd suggest things he hated to hear.

The Winter Queen, Donia, had given him a recipe for a salve that healed sunlight burns. It didn't work as well on mortals as it did on faeries, but if he put it on soon enough, it would heal the burns within the day. He glanced at the clock. "Almost breakfast time."

"No," Aislinn murmured, "'s time to sleep."

"Okay." He kissed her and held her as long as he safely could. He watched the clock, listened to her even breaths as she fell deeper into sleep. Then, when he could wait no longer, he started to slide out of the bed.

She opened her eyes. "Stay."

"Bathroom. Be right back." He gave her a sheepish grin in hopes that she wouldn't ask any questions. Since she couldn't lie, he did his best to avoid lying to her in return, but they'd been down this road a few times.

She started to look at his arms, and he knew neither of them wanted to have the conversation that would follow—the one where she told him she shouldn't come when she was like this and he panicked at the thought of her being at the loft with the Summer King instead.

She winced. "I'm sorry I thought you meant you weren't hurt—"

He could argue, or he could distract her.

It wasn't a difficult choice to make.

When Aislinn woke, she propped herself up on one arm and watched Seth sleep. She wasn't sure what she'd do if she ever lost him. Sometimes she felt like he was all that held her together; he was her version of the vine that wrapped around the Summer Girls—the thread that kept her from unraveling.

And I hurt him. Again.

She could see the shadowed bruises and bright burns on his skin from her hands. He'd never complain about it, but she worried. He was so breakable in comparison to even the weakest faeries. She traced her fingertips over his shoulder, and he moved closer. In all the weirdness of the past few months since she'd become Summer Queen, he'd been there. He didn't ask her to be all mortal or all faery; instead, he let her be herself. It was a gift she couldn't ever repay him for. *He* was a gift. He'd been essential to her when she was a mortal, and he had only grown more important as she'd tried to keep steady in her new life as a faery queen.

He opened his eyes to stare up at her. "You look like you're far away."

"Just thinking."

"About?" He quirked his pierced brow.

And her heart fluttered exactly as it had when she'd tried to be just friends with him. "The usual . . ."

"Everything will be fine." He rolled her under him. "We'll figure it out."

She wrapped her arms around him so she could tangle her fingers in his hair. She told herself to be careful, to moderate her strength, to not remind him that she was so much stronger than a mortal. *That I'm not what he is.*

"I *want* it to be fine," she whispered, trying to force away thoughts of his mortality, of his transience now that she was eternal, of how very finite he was—and she wasn't. "Tell me again?"

He lowered his lips to hers and told her things that didn't require words. When he pulled back, he whispered, "Something this good can last forever."

She ran her hand down his spine, wondering if he'd think she was weird for wanting to let sunlight into her fingertips as she did so, wondering if it would only remind him of how not-mortal she was now. "I wish it could always be like this. Just us."

There was something she couldn't read in his expression, but then he pulled her to him and she let go of thoughts and words.

Chapter 1

The High Queen walked toward the lobby with a sense of trepidation. She normally required that visitors be brought to her, but in this case, Sorcha would make an exception. Having Bananach roaming the hotel was far too dangerous.

In the past few months, Sorcha had moved the High Court to the edge of the mortal world, taking over a city block and remaking it as her own. Stepping within that block meant one left the mortal realm and entered the edge of Faerie. Her domain stood separated, divided from all else. The rules of the mortal world—their sense of time and place, their laws of nature—were all moot within Faerie, even in this space-between where she'd brought her court.

It was the closest to the mortals' realm Sorcha had taken her court in centuries, but now that the other courts were shifting, Sorcha couldn't stay quite so far removed. Her being in the mortal realm too long was untenable, but living at the edge of mortality wouldn't alter their world. It was the reasonable path. The boy king was enthroned with his centuries-missing queen in the Summer Court. His beloved was holding the Winter throne. And Niall, Sorcha's almost-temptation, had taken the Dark Court throne. None of it was unexpected, but all had changed in barely a blink.

She ran her hand along the stair rail, touching the smooth wood, cherishing the reminder of simpler times—and promptly dismissed the lie of nostalgia. She'd held her court for longer than memory. She was the High Queen. Hers was the unchanging, the heart of Faerie, the voice of the world removed, and she was the Unchanging Queen.

The alternative—her antithesis, her twin, Bananach—stood in the room. She swayed toward Sorcha with a slightly mad look in her eyes. Every stray thought of chaos and discord that could have been Sorcha's found its way to Bananach's spirit instead. As long as Bananach existed to host those feelings, Sorcha was mostly spared the burden of such unpleasantness. It made for an awkward bond.

"It's been a while," Bananach said. Her movements were tentative, hands glancing over surfaces as if she needed to familiarize herself with the world, as if the tactile experience would anchor her to reality. "Since we've spoken. It's been a while."

Sorcha wasn't sure if these were questions or statements: Bananach's grasp on reality was tenuous on her best days.

"It is never as long as I'd like." Sorcha motioned for her sister to take a seat.

Bananach lowered herself to a floral divan. She shook

her head, unsettling the long feathers that spilled down her back like mortal hair. "Nor I. I dislike you."

The bluntness was off-putting, but war wasn't concerned with delicacy—and Bananach was the essence of war and violence, carrion and chaos, blood and mayhem. The Dark Court might be Sorcha's opposing court, but it was Bananach who was her true opposition. The raven-headed faery was neither contained by the court nor divided from it. She was too primal to be within the Dark Court, too conniving to be without it.

Bananach's unflinching attention was disquieting. Her abyss-black eyes sparkled unpleasantly. "I feel less *right* when you are near me."

"So why are you here?"

Bananach tapped her talons on the table in a discordant way: no music, no pattern. "You. I come here for you. Each time, no matter where you are, I will come."

"Why?" Sorcha felt herself caught in the centuries-old conversation.

"Today?" Bananach tilted her head at an angle in her avian way, watching, tracking the slightest movement. "I've things to tell. Things you'll want to know."

Sorcha held herself still; not reacting was usually safer with Bananach. "And why should I listen this time?"

"Why not?"

"Because you're not here to help me." Sorcha wearied of their eternity of discord. Sometimes she wondered what would happen if she simply did away with Bananach. *Would*

I destroy myself? My court? If she knew that answer, if she knew she could kill her sister without damning them all, she'd have done so centuries ago.

"Faeries don't lie, sister mine. Where's the reason in not listening?" Bananach crooned. "You're Reason, are you not? I am offering you Truth . . . is there logic in ignoring me?"

Sorcha sighed. "So acting on what you tell me will presumably cause some sort of chaos?"

Bananach swayed a bit in her seat, as if she suddenly heard a thread of music that no one else could—or would want to—hear. "One can hope."

"Or *failing* to act will cause chaos . . . and you are prodding me to get me to do the inverse," Sorcha mused. "Do you ever tire of this?"

Bananach tilted her head in several small increments and snapped her teeth as if she truly had a beak. It was a version of laughter, a curious gesture Sorcha disliked. The raven-faery peered at her with an intent gaze. "Why would I?"

"Why indeed." Sorcha sat in one of the innumerable water-carved chairs that her staff had scattered throughout the lobby. It was studded with uncut jewels, ruining the comfort of the thing but heightening its raw beauty.

"Shall I tell you then, sister mine?" Bananach leaned closer. Her dark eyes glittered with a sprinkling of stars, constellations that sometimes matched the mortal sky. Today, Scorpius, the beast that killed Orion, was in the center of Bananach's gaze.

"Speak," Sorcha said. "Speak so you can be gone."

Bananach's demeanor and tone became that of a story-teller. She quieted, leaned back, and steepled her hands. Once, many centuries past, they would have been near a fire in the dark for these disagreeable conversations. That was when she liked to come with her mutterings and machinations. But even here, in the near opulence of the mortal-made palace, Bananach spoke as if they were still at a fireside, the words lilting in the cadence of tale-tellers in the dark. "There are three courts that are not yours—the one that should be mine, the court of sun, and the court of frost."

"I know—"

Bananach caught Sorcha's gaze with her own and spoke over her, "And among those courts there is a new unity; a *mortal* walks unimpeded through all of them. He whispers in the ear of the one who has my throne; he listens as the new Dark King and the new Winter Queen lament the cruelties of the boy king."

"And?" Sorcha prompted. She was never sure how long these tales would last.

This time, it seemed a short telling. Bananach came to her feet as if she saw a specter in the room who'd beckoned her closer.

"The boy king has much potential for cruelty. I might like Summer." Her hand stretched out to touch something no one else could see. Then she stopped and scowled. "He won't see me, though."

"Keenan does only what he must to protect his court,"

Sorcha murmured absently, already musing on the point behind her twin's tale: it wasn't the Summer King's propensity for cruelties that mattered; it was the role of the mortal. Mortals shouldn't have voice in the affairs of the Faerie courts. If things were kept properly in order, they wouldn't ever *see* faeries, but Sorcha's objection to mortals being granted Sight was disregarded from time to time.

As if mortals born Sighted weren't more than enough trouble.

But trouble was what Bananach craved. Small troubles led to larger disorder. On this, at least, they agreed. The difference was that one of them sought to prevent disorder and the other sought to nurture it.

Hundreds of moments of seeming insignificance combined to create Bananach's desired results. She had been the voice urging Beira, the last Winter Queen, to smite Miach— the centuries-gone Summer King and Beira's sometimes lover. Bananach was the voice that whispered the things they all dreamt in silence, but generally had the sense not to act upon.

Sorcha was not about to have another small problem evolve into chaos-causing troubles. "Mortals have no business meddling with Faerie," she said. "They shouldn't be involved in our world."

Bananach tapped her talon-tipped fingers in a seemingly satisfied rhythm. "Mmmm. *This* mortal has their trust, all three of the courts-not-yours listen to his words. He has influence . . . and they protect him."

Sorcha gestured for more. "Tell me."

"He lies with the Summer Queen, not as a pet, but as if a consort. The Winter Queen gave him the Sight. The new Dark King calls him 'brother.'" Bananach retook her seat and assumed a somber demeanor, which always troubled Sorcha—with good reason: when Bananach was focused, she was more dangerous. "And you, sister mine, have no influence over him. You cannot take this one. You cannot steal him as you have the other Sighted pets and half-mortals."

"I see." Sorcha did not react. She knew that Bananach waited, holding back something to needle her last reserves of calm.

Bananach added, "And Irial had a pet, a little mortal thing he bound and caressed like she was worthy of being in the presence of the Dark Court."

Sorcha tsk'd at Irial's idiocy. Mortals were too fragile to bear up under the excesses of the Dark Court. He knew better. "Did she expire? Or go mad?"

"Neither, he gave up his throne over her . . . so corrupted was he by her mortality . . . sickening, how he cherished her. That's why the new one sits on the throne that should be mine." Bananach's storyteller's guise was still in play, but her temper was growing uglier. The emphasis of words, that rise and fall of tones she adopted when telling tales, was fading. Instead random words were emphasized. Her covetousness over the Dark Court's throne upset her; her mention of it didn't bode well for her state of mind.

"Where is she?" Sorcha asked.

"She's of no influence now. . . ." Bananach fluttered a hand as if to brush webs from in front of her.

"Then why tell me?"

Bananach's expression was unreadable, but the constellation in her eyes shifted to Gemini, the twins. "I know we've shared . . . much; I thought you should know."

"I have no need to hear of Irial's discarded pets. It's a deplorable habit, but"—Sorcha shrugged as if it didn't matter—"I cannot control the depravity of his court."

"I could . . ." A yearning sigh followed those words.

"No, you couldn't. You'd destroy what little self-control they have."

"Perhaps"—Bananach sighed again—"but the battles we could have . . . I could come to your step, blood-dressed and—"

"Threatening me isn't the way to enlist my help," Sorcha reminded, although the point was moot. Bananach couldn't help but dream of war any more than Sorcha could resist her inclination toward order.

"Never a threat, sister, just a dream I hold dear." In a blur too fast for even Sorcha to see clearly, Bananach came to crouch in front of her sister. Her feathers drifted forward to brush against Sorcha's face. "A dream that keeps me warm at night when I have no blood for my bath."

The talons that Bananach had tapped so erratically took on a regular cadence as they dug in and out of Sorcha's arms, pricking the skin with tiny moons.

Sorcha kept to her calm, although her own temper felt close to surfacing. "You ought to leave."

"I should. Your presence makes my mind blurry." Bananach kissed Sorcha's forehead. "The mortal's name is Seth Morgan. He sees us as we are. He knows much of our courts—even yours. He is strangely . . . moral."

Some whisper of fury threatened to surface at the feel of her sister's feathers drifting around her face; the calm logic that Sorcha embodied was only challenged by the presence of the strongest Dark Court faeries. Neither Summer nor Winter faeries could provoke her. The solitaries couldn't ripple the calm pool that rested in her spirit. Only the Dark Court made her want to forget herself.

It's logical. It's the nature of opposition. It makes perfect sense.

Bananach rubbed her cheek against Sorcha's.

The High Queen wanted to strike the war-faery. Logic said Bananach would win; she was violence incarnate. Few if any faeries could outlast her in direct battle—and the Queen of Order was not one of them. Yet, in that moment, the temptation to try grew strong.

Just one strike. Something.

The skin of her arms had begun to sting from so many small wounds when Bananach tilted her head in another series of short jerky moves. The feathers seemed to whisper as Bananach pulled back and said, "I tire of seeing you."

"And I you." Sorcha didn't move to stanch the blood that trickled to the floor. Movement would lead to pitting her strength against Bananach or angering her further. Either would result in more injuries.

"True war comes," Bananach said. Smoke and haze filtered into the room. Half-shadowed figures of faeries and mortals reached out bloodied hands. The sky grew thick with illusory ravens' wings, rustling like dry corn husks. Bananach smiled. The not-yet-there shape of wings unfolded from her spine. Those wings had spread over battlefields in centuries past; to see them so clearly outside a battlefield did not bode well.

Bananach stretched her shadow-wings as she said, "I follow the rules. I give you warning. Plagues, blood, and cinders will cover their world and yours."

Sorcha kept her face expressionless, but she saw the threads of possible futures as well. Her sister's predictions were more probable than not. "I'll not let you have that sort of war. Not now. Not ever."

"Really?" Bananach's shadow spread like a dark stain on the floor. "Well, then . . . it's your move, sister mine."

CHAPTER 2

Seth watched Aislinn argue with the court's advisors, far more vocal with the fey than she ever was with humans. On the table in front of them, Aislinn had the pages of her new plan, complete with charts, spread out.

When she sat in Keenan's loft, with the tall plants and crowds of faeries overfilling the place, it was easy to forget that she hadn't always been one of them. The plants leaned toward her, blooming in her presence. The birds that roosted in the columns greeted her when she walked into a room. Faeries vied for her attention, seeking a few moments in her presence. After centuries without strength, the Summer Court was beginning to thrive—because of Aislinn. At first, she had seemed uncomfortable with being in the center of it, but she'd grown so at ease with her position that Seth wondered how long it'd be until she abandoned the mortal world, including him.

"If we assign different regions like this—" She pointed

to her diagram again, but Quinn excused himself, leaving Tavish to explain once more why he thought her plan was unnecessary.

Quinn, the advisor who'd replaced Niall recently, plopped down on the sofa next to Seth. He was as unlike Niall in appearance as he was in temperament. Where Niall had highlighted his almost common features, Quinn seemed to strive for some degree of polish and posturing. He kept his hair sun-streaked, his skin tanned, his clothes hinting at wealth. More important, though, where Niall had been a voice that could pull Keenan from his melancholia or dissipate the Summer King's temper, Quinn seemed to fuel Keenan's mood of the moment. *That* made Seth leery of the new guard.

Quinn scowled. "She's being unreasonable. The king can't expect us to—"

Seth simply looked at him.

"What?"

"You think Keenan's going to tell her *no*? To anything?" Seth almost laughed aloud at the idea.

Quinn looked affronted. "Of course."

"Wrong." Seth watched his girlfriend, the queen of the Summer Court, glow like small suns were trapped inside her skin. "You have a lot to learn. Unless Ash changes her mind, Keenan will give her plan a try."

"But the court has always been run like this," Tavish, the court's oldest advisor, was repeating yet again.

"The court has also always been ruled by a monarch,

hasn't it? It still is. You don't *need* to agree, but I'm asking for your support." Aislinn flicked her hair over her shoulder. It was still as black as Seth's, just as it had been when she was a human, but now that she'd become one of them, her hair had golden streaks in it.

Tavish raised his voice, a habit he'd apparently not been prone to before Aislinn joined the court. "My Queen, surely—"

"Don't 'my Queen' me, Tavish." She poked him in the shoulder. Tiny sparks flickered from her skin.

"I don't mean to offend you, but the idea of local rulers seems foolish." Tavish smiled placatingly.

Aislinn's temper sent rainbows flashing across the room. "Foolish? Structuring our court so our faeries are safe and have access to help when they need us is foolish? We have a responsibility to take care of our court. How are we to do that if we don't have contact with them?"

But Tavish didn't back down. "Such a major change . . ."

Seth tuned them out. He'd hear Aislinn recount it all later when she tried to make sense of it. *No need to hear it twice.* He picked up a remote and flicked through the music. Someone had added the Living Zombies song he'd mentioned the other week. He selected it and turned the volume up.

Tavish had a please-help-me look on his face. Seth ignored it, but Quinn didn't. Grumbling, but eager to prove his worth, the new advisor went back over to the table.

Then Keenan walked in the door with several of the

Summer Girls beside him. They looked more beautiful by the day. As summer approached—and as Aislinn and Keenan grew stronger—their faeries seemed to blossom.

Tavish immediately began, "Keenan, my King, perhaps you could explain to her grace that . . ." But his words died after a glimpse at the expression of ire the Summer King wore.

In response to his volatile mood, Aislinn's already-glowing skin radiated enough light that it hurt Seth to look at her. Without even realizing she was doing it, she'd extended sunbeams like insubstantial hands reaching toward Keenan. Over the past few months, she'd developed an increasingly strong connection with the Summer King.

Which sucks.

All Keenan had to do was look her way and she was at his side, papers forgotten, argument forgotten, everything but Keenan forgotten. She went to him, and the rest of the world went on pause at Keenan's look of upset.

It's her job. Court things have to come first.

Seth wanted to not be irritated by it. He'd worked hard to become the person he was now—a person whose temper was under control, whose sardonic streak didn't lead to making cruel remarks. He channeled those discordant tendencies into his paintings and sculptures. Between his art and his meditation, he was able to hold on to peace these days, but Keenan tested that hard-earned progress. It wasn't as if Seth couldn't understand the importance of strengthening the Summer Court after centuries of growing cold, but sometimes it was hard to believe that Keenan didn't over-play minor worries to keep Aislinn's attention. He'd spent centuries assuming that what he thought, or wanted, was of utmost importance. Now that he had the power to go with the arrogance, he wasn't likely to become less demanding.

Tavish motioned the Summer Girls to him and led them to the kitchen. With Niall gone and Keenan trying to reestablish his court's authority, not to mention forge new agreements with the other courts, Tavish had assumed responsibility for helping the Summer Girls learn some degree of independence. Seth thought it was perversely funny that spending hours making sure that a group of beautiful girls was in good spirits was considered work, but no one else seemed to find it humorous. What was impor-tant in the Summer Court wasn't always what made sense to a mortal—a fact of which Seth was regularly reminded.

As Keenan relayed whatever new crisis he'd run into, Seth gathered his things and stood. He waited until Aislinn looked over at him and then said, "Ash? I'm out."

She came to stand beside Seth—near but not touching. It wasn't that she couldn't reach out, but she was still tenta-tive. They'd only been a couple for a few months. Although it was hard to resist the temptation to remind them all that she was *his*, Seth didn't touch her. He stood there, waiting, not pressuring. It was the only way with her. He'd figured that out more than a year ago. He waited; the tension built; and then she leaned against him, folding herself into his arms and sighing.

"Sorry. I just need to"—she shot a worried look at Keenan—"court stuff, you know?"

"I do." Seth had spent more hours than he liked to think about listening to her try to make sense of her new responsibilities, utterly unable to help her. She had a long list of things that required her attention, and he just sat there waiting.

"But we're still on for the Crow's Nest tomorrow, right?" Her tone was worried.

"I'll meet you there." He felt guilty for being selfish, for adding to her worry. He wrapped his fingers in her hair, tugging it gently until she tilted her head back and kissed him. It burned his lips, his tongue, when she was nervous or upset—not impossibly painful but enough that he couldn't pretend that she was the girl he used to know. By the time he pulled back, the burn had faded. She was calm again.

"I don't know what I'd do without you. You know that, don't you?" she whispered.

He didn't answer, but he didn't let go either; holding her in his arms was the best answer he could give her. She would be without him sooner or later: he was mortal, but *that* was a conversation she refused to have. He'd tried to talk to her, but she stopped every conversation with either tears or kisses—or both. Unless they found a way for him to belong in her world, eventually he'd be gone, and Keenan would be the one holding her.

To go from not wanting to make commitments for the next night, to putting everything aside in hopes of convincing Aislinn to trust him, to thinking about forever was unsettling. He hadn't figured himself for the whole getting-married-and-settling-down thing, but since she'd been in his arms and in his life, he'd hated the thought of being anywhere but with her.

The Summer King had walked over to the table and was examining Aislinn's diagrams, notes, and charts. Despite how weird the situation was for all of them, he often made a point of letting Aislinn and Seth have privacy. It was obvious, though, that moving away was not easy for Keenan.

Or Ash.

Quinn cleared his throat as he reentered the room. "I'll walk you out if you're ready."

Seth wasn't ever ready to walk away from Aislinn, but he didn't see the sense in sitting around watching her murmur with Keenan either. She had responsibilities; they both needed to keep those in mind—even if those responsibilities included late nights and parties with Keenan. She had a job to do.

And Seth had . . . Aislinn. That's what he had: Aislinn, Aislinn's world, Aislinn's needs. He existed on the fringe of her world, with no role, no power, and no desire to walk away. It wasn't that he wanted out, but he wasn't sure what to do to be further into her world.

And she doesn't want to talk about it.

"See you tomorrow." Seth kissed Aislinn once more and followed Quinn to the door.

CHAPTER 3

Donia was at her house—*Beira's house*—when Keenan and Aislinn intruded on her. It wasn't her preferred place, but she'd taken to conducting business there and keeping her cottage for personal matters, space only Evan and a few select guards could enter.

And Keenan. Always Keenan.

When Keenan came through the ridiculously carved door—his copper hair shining like a beacon—Donia wanted to go to him, just for a brief moment to pretend that what they shared, that their decades of history entitled her to such easy comfort. It didn't, especially when Aislinn was beside him. Keenan's attention to his queen's every thought and action bordered on obsession.

Would Ash care if I went to him?

To some degree, Donia doubted it: the Summer Queen had been the one to arrange Donia's tryst with Keenan at Winter Solstice. She'd been the one insisting that Keenan did, in fact, love Donia although he'd never said the words. Yet, Keenan wouldn't risk even the briefest display of emotion around Aislinn.

So they all stood awkwardly in the foyer, surrounded by a number of Hawthorn Girls who calmly watched from the church pews that lined the walls. Sasha lifted his head from the floor where he was resting. The wolf glanced at the summer regents briefly, closed his eyes, and resumed sleeping.

Evan, however, wasn't so calm. He eased closer to Donia. "Shall I stay with you?"

Mutely, she nodded. Evan was her closest friend these days; she suspected he'd been so for years before she acknowledged that his omnipresent protectiveness was not simple duty. She'd thought his guarding her was because so many other of Keenan's guards were afraid of her, but when she'd become the new Winter Queen, Evan had left Keenan's court to stay at her side. She reached out and squeezed his hand in silent gratitude.

"The others?" he murmured.

"They stay inside. We'll go out back." She raised her voice then and said, "If you'd like to join me?"

Keenan was beside Donia. He didn't touch her, not even a casual brush of her hand. He opened the door as they approached, as familiar with the house as she was. It was his mother, the last Winter Queen, who'd lived here before. After holding the door for her and for Aislinn, Keenan entered the garden. Snow and ice melted in his wake. *Better that than having the Summer King and Queen inside where my fey are.* Donia wasn't willing to risk endangering her faeries, and while Aislinn might do fairly well at containing her emotions, Keenan was volatile even on his best days.

If she watched long enough, Donia knew she'd see storms crashing in his eyes. When they'd been together, those flashes of lightning seemed mesmerizing. Now, they seemed too bright, too brief, too everything.

"Be welcome here today." Donia gestured to one of the wooden benches scattered throughout the winter garden. They were clever things, fitted together by craftsmen's skills, no screws or bolts anywhere in them.

Keenan didn't move. He stood in her garden, as untouchable as he'd been for most of their relationship, making her feel somehow lacking. "Do you have any guests?" he asked.

"What business is that of yours?" she responded.

I do not answer to him, not now.

Under the edge of the bench, an arctic fox crouched. Only its dark eyes and nose showed in the snowbank. The rest of its body blended with the stark white ground. As Aislinn and Keenan came closer—warming the air around them—the fox darted away to the thicker snows by the high walls that surrounded the garden. Despite Donia's dislike for the last Winter Queen, she enjoyed the winter garden immensely: in this, at least, Beira'd done a wise thing. The garden's walls and roof allowed for a small bit of winter year round—a nourishing sanctuary for her and her fey.

Donia sat on one of the benches. "Are you seeking someone specific?"

Still standing, Keenan gave her an exasperated look. "Bananach was seen near here."

Aislinn laid her hand on his arm to stop his short-tempered words.

"Although I'm sure you are well cared for here"—the Summer Queen smiled blindingly at Evan, who had moved behind Donia—"Keenan needed to check on you. Right, Keenan?"

Keenan glanced at Aislinn, seeking something—assurance, clarity, it was hard to say with them. "I don't want you talking to Bananach."

The ground at Donia's feet grew heavy with snow as her temper stirred. "Why exactly are you here?"

Tiny storms flashed in his eyes. "I was worried."

"About?"

"You." He moved closer, invading her space, pushing her. Even now, when she was his equal, he had no regard for her boundaries. Keenan pulled his hand through his copper hair. And like a bespelled mortal, she stared at it, at him.

"Worried about me or trying to dictate to me?" She stayed as still as winter before the storm breaks, but she felt ice churning inside her.

"War being at your door *is* of concern to me. Niall's furious with me, and . . . I just don't want any of the Dark Court near you," Keenan said.

"It's not yours to decide. This is *my* court, Keenan. If I choose to listen to Bananach—"

"*Do* you listen to her?"

"If Bananach or Niall come here, I'll deal with them, just as I would with Sorcha or any of the strong solitaries . . . or you." Donia kept her tone cool.

She beckoned to the Hawthorn Girls, who'd moved to the doorway.

The ever-silent faeries drifted outside and looked at Donia expectantly. They were the family she'd never expected to find in the cold Winter Court. She smiled at them, but didn't bother to hide her irritation when she told Keenan, "Matrice will show you out. Unless there are personal matters you wanted to discuss?"

The lightning in his eyes flared again, illuminating his face with that strange flash of brightness. "No. I suppose not."

Protective to a fault, Matrice narrowed her eyes at his tone.

"Well, then, if we're done with our business"—Donia kept her hands relaxed, refusing to show him that even now she was tempted to reach out to ease that temper—"Matrice?"

Keenan's anger fled for a moment. "Don?"

She gave in then and touched his arm, hating that it was her—*again*—who had to reach for him. "If you want to see *me*, not the Winter Queen, but *me*, you are welcome at the cottage. I will be home later."

He nodded, but didn't agree, didn't promise. He wouldn't—not unless his real queen had no need of his attention.

Donia hated her for a moment. *If she weren't here . . .* Of course, if Aislinn hadn't become Summer Queen, Keenan would be wooing yet another mortal, in search of the one who'd free him.

At least I have part of him now. That's better than nothing. That's what she'd told herself at first, but as he turned away, accepting Aislinn's hand as they walked, following the Hawthorn Girls back toward the house, Donia had to wonder if it really was better.

That night, Donia walked toward the cottage with the illusion of solitude. In the quiet, Evan undoubtedly trailed behind her. If she concentrated, she'd see the blurring wings of the Hawthorn fey in the shadows, hear the chiming music of the lupine. A year ago those same details would've set terror in her heart. Evan had been Keenan's fey then; and Winter Court faeries had been harbingers of conflict, emissaries from the last Winter Queen, carrying threats and warnings.

So much had changed. Donia had changed. What hadn't changed was how badly she craved Keenan's attention, his approval, his touch.

Frozen tears clattered to the ground as she thought about the impact of that craving on her life. She'd surrendered her mortality in the hope that she was his missing queen. *I wasn't.* She'd watched him woo innumerable mortals in that search as if it didn't hurt each time. *It did hurt.* She'd willingly gone to her death at his mother's hands for helping him find that queen. *But I didn't die.*

Instead she was at the helm of the court that had over-powered and oppressed his own for centuries—and her court wanted it to stay that way. Too much of a climate change too fast wasn't good for any of them. Her court pressed the matter, rustling for a few shows of force to remind him that they were still stronger. While in the dark, when it was just the two of them, Keenan would whisper sweet words of peace and balance.

Always in the middle . . . because of him. And he'd walk away from me for Ash if she'd say the word. . . .

Angry with herself for dwelling on it, for even thinking of it, Donia swatted at the tears rolling down her cheeks. He wasn't hers, would never be truly hers, and she couldn't help but feel terrified of that inevitable truth.

She stepped onto her porch.

And he was there waiting, beautiful face furrowed in concern, hands reaching out for her. "Don?"

His voice held all the yearning she'd felt for him earlier.

All of her clarity faded as he held open his arms. She slipped into his embrace and kissed him, not bothering to keep her ice in check, not caring if it wounded him.

He'll stop.

But instead of pushing her away, he pulled her closer. That awful sunlight he carried in his skin flashed brighter. The snow that had begun to fall around them was sizzling away as quickly as it fell.

Her back was against the door. She hadn't unlocked it,

but it still swung open. At a glance, she realized that Keenan
had melted the lock.

It's not Solstice yet. We shouldn't. Can't . . .

There were welts on her arms where he touched her, blisters on her lips. She tangled her hand in his hair and held
him tighter to her. Frost spread down his neck.

He'll stop. I'll stop. Any second now.

They were on the sofa, and tiny fires burned on the
cushion above her head. She let her winter slip further out.
The room was filled with heavy snowfall. The fires hissed
as they were extinguished.

I'm stronger. I could stop.

But he was touching her. Keenan was here, and he was
touching her. She wasn't stopping. Maybe they could make
it work; maybe it would be fine. She opened her eyes to look
at him, and the brightness blinded her.

"Mine," he murmured between kisses.

Their clothes kept catching fire, smoldering out as the
snow smothered the flames, only to ignite again. Blisters
covered her skin where his hands had gripped her. Frost-
burnt patches of skin were visible on his chest and neck.

She cried out, and then he pulled back.

"Don . . ." His face was grief stricken. "I didn't mean
to . . ." He propped himself up on one arm and looked down
at her bruised arms. "I don't want to hurt you."

"I know." She slid to the floor, leaving him alone on the
smoking sofa.

"I just wanted to talk." He watched her warily.

She concentrated on the ice inside of her, not on how close he still was. "About us, or about business?"

"Both." He grimaced as he tried to pull on his tattered shirt.

She watched him button it up, as if that would help hold it in place. Neither spoke as he fussed with the ruined cloth. Then she asked, "Do you love me? Even a little?"

He stilled, hands aloft. "What?"

"Do you love me?"

He stared at her. "How can you ask that?"

"Do you?" She needed to hear it, something, anything.

He didn't answer.

"Why are you even here?" she asked.

"To see you. To be near you."

"Why? I need more than your lust." She didn't cry as she said it. She didn't do anything to let him know how badly her heart was breaking. "Tell me we have something more than that. Something that won't destroy either of us."

He was a sunlit effigy, as beautiful as always, but his words weren't beautiful. "Don. Come on. You know it's more than that. You *know* what's between us."

"Do I?"

He reached out. His hand was healing, but he was bruised.

That's what we do to each other.

Donia stood up and walked outside, needing not to see the destruction in her home.

Again.

Keenan followed.

She leaned against the cottage. *How many times have I stood here, trying to keep my distance from him or from the last Winter Queen?* She didn't want a repeat of the last time Winter and Summer tried to be together.

"I don't want us to destroy each other like they did," she whispered.

"We're not like them. You're not like Beira." He didn't touch her. Instead he sat on the porch. "I'm not going to give up on you if we have a chance."

"This"—she motioned at the destruction behind her— "isn't good."

"We slipped for a minute."

"Again," she added.

"Yes, but . . . we can sort it out. I shouldn't have reached for you, but you were crying and . . ." He squeezed her hand. "I slipped up. You make me forget myself."

"Me too." Donia turned to face him. "No one else angers or thrills me like this. I've loved you most of my life, but I'm not happy with things the way they are."

He stilled. "What things?"

She laughed briefly. "That might work on your other queen, but I know you, Keenan. I see how close you two are growing."

"She's my queen."

"And being with her would strengthen your court." Donia shook her head. "I know. I've always known. You've never been mine."

"She has Seth."

Donia watched the Hawthorn Girls flitting among the trees. Their wings glistened in the dark. She weighed her words. "He'll die. Mortals do. And then what?"

"I want you in my life."

"In the dark when she's not around. A few nights of the year . . ." Donia thought over the handful of nights when they could truly be together, no longer than a few stolen heartbeats. The taste of what she couldn't have made it so much harder to weather the months when even a kiss was dangerous. She blinked away icy tears. "It's not enough. I thought it would be, but I need more."

"Don—"

"Listen. Please?" Donia sat down beside him. "I'm in love with you. I've loved you enough to die for it . . . but I see you trying to romance her and yet still coming to my door. Charm isn't going to let you have us both under your sway. Neither of us is one of your Summer Girls." Donia kept her voice gentle. "I accepted death to give you your queen—even though it meant losing you, even after years of conflict."

"I don't deserve you." He stared at her as if she was his world. In that look—the same look that she'd fallen for innumerable times—he seemed to hold all of the words she longed to hear. In moments that she collected like treasures, he was her perfect match. Moments weren't enough. "I've never deserved you," he said.

"Sometimes I'm sure of that . . . but I wouldn't love

you if that was entirely true. I've seen the faery king you
can be and the *person* you can be. You're better than
you think"—she touched his face carefully—"better than
I think sometimes."

"I want to be the person I could be with you . . ." he
started.

"But?"

"I need to put my court's needs first. For nine centuries
I've wanted only to reach where I am now. I can't let what
I want—*who* I want—get in the way of what's best for my
fey." He raked his hand through his hair again, looking like
the boy she'd met back when she thought he was a human.

She wanted to comfort him, to promise it would be fine.
She couldn't. The closer summer came, the more he and
Aislinn were drawn together. He hadn't come to see her
but a few times since spring had begun. Today, he'd come
making demands. Loving him didn't mean letting him rule
her—or her court.

"I understand. I have to do the same thing . . . but I want
you, Keenan, not the king." She leaned her head against
his arm. As long as they were careful, not forgetting, not
losing control, they could touch. Unfortunately, touching
him made self-control a challenge. She sighed and added,
"I want to set aside the courts when we are together, and
I need you to accept that my loving you doesn't mean that
dealing with my court is different from any other business
of yours. Don't think that what we share means that my
court is malleable."

He held her gaze as he asked, "And if I can't do that?"

She glanced at him. "Then I need you out of my life. Don't keep trying to use my love to manipulate me. Don't expect me not to be jealous when you bring her to my house and stare at her like she's your world. I want a real relationship with you . . . or nothing at all."

"I don't know what to do," he admitted. "When I'm around her I feel like I'm enthralled. She doesn't love me, but I *want* her to. If she did, my court would be stronger. It's like buds opening in the sunlight. It's not a choice, Don. It's a need. She's my other half, and her decision to be 'friends' weakens me."

"I know."

"She doesn't . . . and I don't know if it'll get any easier."

"I can't help you with this one"—she entwined her fingers with his—"and I hate you both sometimes for it. Talk to her. Find a way to be with her or find a way to be free enough to be truly mine."

"She doesn't hear me when I try to talk to her about this, and I don't want to quarrel with her." Keenan's expression was that of enchantment. Even talking about her distracted him.

Donia looked at him, the same lost faery she'd loved for most of her life. Too often she'd been the one to soften when they were at odds, too often she'd helped him because they'd both wanted the same goal: Winter and Summer to balance. She sighed. "Try again, Keenan, because this is going to end badly if something doesn't change."

He kissed her pursed lips softly and said, "I still dream that it was you. No matter how many times I've looked, in my dreams it's always been you who were meant to be my queen."

"And I would be if the choice were mine. It isn't. You need to let me go or find a way to distance yourself from her."

He pulled her closer. "No matter what happens, I don't want to let you go. *Ever.*"

"That's a different problem altogether." She watched the frost form on the steps beside her. "I'm not meant for Summer, Keenan."

"Is it so wrong to want a queen who loves me?"

"No," she whispered. "But it's not working to want two queens to love you."

"If you were my queen—"

"But I wasn't." She laid her head on his shoulder.

They sat there like that, leaning together carefully, until morning came.

CHAPTER 4

Sorcha had summoned Devlin after breaking her fast. True to form, he was there within mere moments. In their eternity together, her brother had never been anything other than reliable and predictable.

He stood just inside the doorway, silent as she crossed the expanse of the hall. Her bare feet made no sound as she stepped onto the dais and sat upon the single polished silver throne. From here, the cavernous hall was beautiful. There was a symmetry of design that was pleasing to behold. This room—and only this room—did not fold under her will. The Hall of Truth and Memory was impervious to any magic but its own. Once, when the Dark Court resided in Faerie, this was where inter-court disputes were resolved. Once, when they shared Faerie, this was where sacrifices were made. The slate-gray stones held those, and many more, memories.

Sorcha slid her feet over the cool earth and rock upon

which her throne was placed. When one lived for eternity, memory grew hazy at times. The soil helped her keep focus on Faerie; the rock tied her to the truth of the Hall.

Devlin wouldn't move until she was settled. In some ways, her adherence to order and rules was essential to Devlin. The structure helped him keep to the path he'd chosen. For her, order was instinctive; for him, it was a choice he made every breath of every day.

The words were rote, but he said them all the same: "Are you receiving, my lady?"

"I am." She settled her skirt so that the bare tips of her feet were hidden. Silver threads shimmered in her hands and on her cheeks; they shimmered elsewhere that she'd sometimes reveal, but her bare feet stayed covered. The proof of the nature of her connection to the Hall was not something to show her court.

"May I approach?"

"Always, Devlin," she reassured him again, as she had for longer than either of them could recall. "Even without asking, you are welcome."

"You honor me with your trust." He dropped his gaze to her concealed feet. He knew the truth she shared with none other. Reason made clear to both of them that her trust in him was going to be the source of her stumbling someday. Reason also made clear that there wasn't a better choice: trusting him secured his loyalty.

And we haven't fallen yet.

He was her eyes and hands in the mortal realm. He was

her violence in times when such a thing was needed. But he was also Bananach's brother—a fact that none of the three of them ever forgot. Devlin saw their sister regularly; he cared for the mad raven-faery, even though her aims were utterly disorderly. His affection for their sister made it so that no amount of time or service could erase Sorcha's slivers of doubts in his loyalty.

Will he side with her someday? Does he now?

"Dark fey have drawn the blood of one of your mortals . . . on Faerie soil," Devlin began. "Will you judge them?"

"I will." Again, the words were rote: she always judged. It was what Reason did.

Devlin turned to retrieve the accused and the witnesses, but she stopped him with a raised hand.

"After this I need you to visit the mortal world. There is a mortal who walks among three courts untethered," she said.

He bowed. "As you wish."

"War thinks he is key."

"Would you have me eliminate the mortal or retrieve him?"

"Neither." Sorcha wasn't sure what the right move was just yet, but hasty action wasn't it. "Bring me information. See what I cannot."

"As you will."

She refocused on the trial. "Bring them in."

Moments later, four Ly Ergs were brought into the room

by guards under Devlin's command. In the land of mortals, the red-palmed faeries' habit of drawing blood wasn't a concern; out there, most of the depravities that happened weren't Sorcha's concern. However, these four weren't in the mortal world.

Several score of her own court followed the accused into the room. Hira and Nienke, handmaids and comfort to her these past few centuries, came to sit on the stair at her feet. They were clad in simple gray shifts that matched her only slightly more ornate garb, and like her, they were barefoot.

She motioned to Devlin.

He turned so he was angled, not putting his back to her but facing the Ly Ergs and the court attendees. Standing thusly, he could see everyone.

"Does your king know you are here?" he asked the Ly Ergs.

Only one replied: "No."

"Does Bananach?"

One of the four, not the same Ly Erg, grinned. "Lady War knows we act to bring about her wishes."

Sorcha pursed her lips. Bananach was careful—not acting to overtly sanction an attack on Faerie ground, but undoubtedly encouraging it.

Devlin looked to Sorcha.

She gave a curt nod, and he slit the Ly Erg's throat. The movement was steady, but quick enough that it was silent.

The other three Ly Ergs watched the blood seep into the rock. The Hall absorbed it, drinking in the memory of the dead faery. The Ly Ergs had to be physically restrained from touching the blood. It was their sustenance, their temptation, their reason for almost every action they undertook.

Scuffling ensued as the Ly Ergs tried to reach the spilled blood—which both displeased and pleased Devlin. He smiled, scowled, and bared his teeth. It was a brief series of expressions that the court would not see. They knew not to look to Devlin's face when he was questioning uninvited guests.

Sorcha listened to the truths the Hall shared with her: she alone heard the whispered words that shivered through the room. The High Queen knew that the Ly Ergs weren't acting on direct order. "She did not specifically instruct them to come to Faerie."

Her words drew all gazes to her.

The floor rippled slightly as the stone opened and enfolded the Ly Erg into the firmament of the hall. The soil under her feet grew damp, and she felt the silvery veins in her skin extend and burrow like roots into the hall, taking nourishment from the necessary sacrifice to Truth—and magic.

Blood had always fed magic. She was the heart of that magic. Like her siblings, she needed the nourishment of blood and sacrifice. She, however, took no pleasure in it; it was mere practicality to accept it. A weak queen couldn't keep Faerie—or the magic that fed all faeries in the mortal world—alive.

"Your brother's death is an unfortunate consequence of treading in Faerie without consent. You did not come to me upon entering Faerie. Instead you attacked members of my court. You bled one of my mortals." Sorcha looked out at the assembled members of her court, who watched her with the same unwavering faith they always had. They liked the stability and safety she gave them. "Over there, other courts also have rights and power. In Faerie, I am absolute. Life, death—these and all things are at my will alone."

Her fey waited, silent witnesses to the inevitable restoration of order. They understood the practicality of her choices. They didn't flinch as she let her attention slide over them.

"These three intruders struck one of my mortals in my lands. Such a thing is not acceptable." Sorcha caught and held Devlin's gaze as he looked up at her. "One may live to explain their transgression to the new Dark King."

"As my Queen wills, so be it," he said in a steady, clear voice that was in extreme contrast to the gleam in his eyes.

The court attendees lowered their gazes so the sentence could be carried out. Understanding did not mean relishing the bloodletting. High Court faeries weren't crass.

Most of them at least.

With a slow, steady hand, Devlin dragged a blade across another Ly Erg's throat. Here in the Hall, touching the soil and stone, Sorcha knew Truth: the blade wasn't as sharp as it should be and her brother took pleasure at the finality of these deaths. Most important, she knew that he cherished the fact that his action gave her the nourishment that she needed for the High Court to thrive, that this was another secret they shared.

"For our court and at our queen's will and word, your lives are ended," Devlin said as he lowered the Ly Erg to the gaping hole that opened in the stone.

He repeated the action, sacrificing the third faery.

Then he held out his bloodied hand to her. "My Queen?"

With her feet in the soil, she knew that for an instant he wanted her to rebuke him for enjoying the Ly Ergs' deaths. He dared her to chastise him as he stood with spilled blood on his hand. He hoped for it.

The court lifted their gazes to the dais.

Sorcha smiled reassuringly at Devlin and then out at them. "Brother."

The silvered threads in her skin thrummed with energy as they retracted into her skin again. She took his hand and stepped to the already immaculate floor where the remaining Ly Erg stood and looked longingly at the blood on her hand.

"Neither your king nor Bananach can grant consent in Faerie. Follow the rules." She kissed his forehead. "This time you are granted mercy in exchange for carrying word to your king."

She turned to her brother and nodded. Without another word, he led her through her faeries, away from the Hall and into the still of her garden. That, too, was routine. They did as order required, and then she retreated to nature's quiet while he retreated to the mortal plane.

This time, however, Devlin would seek out the errant mortal. This Seth Morgan was an aberration. If his actions had drawn Bananach's attention, he required further study.

CHAPTER 5

When Seth came out of the stacks that afternoon, Quinn was waiting. The guard's expression was falsely friendly.

"I don't need an escort," Seth muttered as he passed the guard and went to check out his newest folklore books.

His objection didn't matter.

Once Seth shoved the books into his satchel, Quinn motioned toward the exit. "If you're ready?"

Seth would rather walk alone, but he had no chance of convincing the guard to disobey orders. The world was dangerous to a fragile mortal. Aislinn insisted the guards look after him at all times. He got it, but it took increasing effort to bite back vitriolic replies and resist escape attempts. *Which is stupid.*

He walked silently past Quinn and kept silent as they made their way to the Crow's Nest, where he found Niall waiting at the street-side door. The Dark King leaned against the wall, smoking a cigarette and tapping his foot in time to whatever music they had playing inside. Unlike Keenan and

Aislinn, Niall had no guards accompanying him or lurking nearby. It was just him—and he was a very welcome sight.

Quinn spared Niall a look of contempt. "He's not of our court anymore."

Niall stood silent as Quinn scowled at him. He'd changed since he'd become the Dark King; the obvious difference was that he was letting his previously close-shorn hair grow. That wasn't the real difference though—when Niall had been with Keenan's court, he moved with a sense of caution, as if being alert to potential threats was essential. It hadn't mattered where they were; even in the safety of the loft, Niall was vigilant. Now, he held himself with an easy comfort. His casual nonchalance said that nothing and no one could harm him—which was true to a large degree. The heads of the courts were vulnerable to only the other reigning monarchs or a few exceptionally influential solitary faeries. Niall, like Aislinn, was nearly impervious to fatal harm now.

Quinn lowered his voice as he added, "You can't trust the Dark Court. Our court and theirs do not mingle."

Seth shook his head even as a smile threatened. Niall's intentionally provocative posture, the way Quinn resituated himself as if for an attack—a few short weeks ago, Niall would have responded the same way to the last Dark King. *It's all relative.* Niall had changed. Or maybe he was always this ready to provoke trouble, and Seth hadn't noticed.

Seth held Niall's gaze as he asked, "Do you mean me harm?"

"No." Niall gave Quinn a deadly look. "And I am far more able to keep you safe than Keenan's bootlicker."

Quinn bristled but didn't speak.

"I'm not going to be safer anywhere else. Seriously," Seth told Quinn in an even voice, not letting either amusement or irritation show. "Niall's my friend."

"What if—"

"Gods, just go away," Niall interrupted as he stalked toward them with a menace that suited him far too well. "Seth is safe in my company. I wouldn't put a friend in danger. That would be *your* king who treats his friends so carelessly."

"I don't imagine our king would approve," Quinn insisted, speaking only to Seth, looking only at Seth.

Seth arched one brow. "*I* have no king. I'm mortal, remember?"

"I'll need to report this to Keenan." Quinn waited for several heartbeats, as if the threat would matter to Seth. When it was apparent that it didn't, he turned and left.

Once he was out of sight, the menace vanished from Niall's expression. "Nitwit. I can't believe Keenan raised him to advisor. He's a yes-man without any moral compass, and—" He stopped himself. "It's not my concern. Come."

He opened the door and they went into the pervasive gloom of the Crow's Nest. It was a comforting sort of dankness—no swooping birds or frolicking Summer Girls. Seth felt at ease there. Back when his parents were still around, he'd spent many afternoons there with his father.

In truth, Seth had practically grown up in the Crow's Nest. It'd changed, but when Seth looked at it, he could still see his mom behind the bar sassing some fool who made the mistake of thinking she was a pushover. *More like a bull-dozer.* Linda was tiny, but what she lacked in size she made up for in temper. Seth hadn't been more than fourteen when he realized that his father's presence at the bar was simply an excuse to be around Linda. He'd claimed he got bored at home, tired of retirement, restless without a job, so he did small repairs at the bar. It wasn't boredom; it was about being nearer to Linda.

I miss them. Seth let the memories come. It was okay to do so here. It was the closest thing to a family home he had these days.

Linda hadn't really taken to the whole mother thing. She loved him; he had no doubt about that, but when she married Seth's dad it wasn't in hopes of settling down and starting a family. The moment Seth was old enough, she had another scheme to go somewhere new. His dad had shrugged and gone along without hesitation.

Or thought to invite me along.

Seth put a stop to that train of thought as Niall led the way to a table that was pushed into the darkest corner of the room. They walked past the diehard drinkers who were already several beers into their afternoon. The mid-day crowd was an odd mix of office workers and bikers and people between jobs or whose seasonal work hadn't hit its stride yet.

They picked a table with some privacy, and Seth unfolded one of the battered menus he'd snatched from the next table.

"It hasn't changed." Niall pointed at the menu. "And you'll order the same thing."

"True, but I like looking at it. I like that it's the same." Seth waved one of the waitresses over and placed his order.

Afterward, when it was just the two of them, Niall gave him an odd look and asked, "Do I seem the same to you?"

"There's more shadows"—Seth gestured at the air around Niall where whispery shapes swayed and spiraled into each other—"around you, and the whole weird-eyes thing is new. Creepier than Ash's too. She gets seas and nice stuff mostly. You? There's weird abyss people."

Niall didn't look happy about that detail. "Irial still has the same eyes."

Seth knew better than to pursue *that* topic. Niall's relationship with the last Dark King was never something to bring up when Niall was already melancholy. Instead, Seth told him, "You seem happier."

Niall made a rude sound that might have been a laugh. "I don't think I'd call it happy."

"More comfortable in your skin then." Seth shrugged.

This time Niall laughed for real, a sound that seemed to cause everyone in the room—except Seth—to shiver or sigh longingly. Without thinking, Seth reached up to touch the stone he wore on a cord around his throat. It was an anti-glamour charm that Niall had given him; arguably it was to protect him from Niall's uncontainable appeal to baser traits, but it had the side benefit of helping Seth resist other faery magicks as well.

Keenan never offered or even told me there were charms. . . . Seth shook his head. It was no secret that the Summer King wasn't going to volunteer to do anything that would make life easier for Seth. If Aislinn suggested something, Keenan cooperated without hesitation, but he never initiated it. When Niall became the Dark King, he'd been free to share all manner of knowledge with Seth.

Niall said, almost casually, "Have you mentioned the charm to Ash?"

"No. You know she would ask Keenan why he hadn't offered me one first . . . and I'm not sure I want to be the reason for yet another fight between them."

"You're a fool. *I* know why he didn't offer you a charm. So do you. And if Ash found out about it, she would know as well."

"All the more reason not to tell her. She's having a rough time with the changes and balancing," Seth said.

"And he'll use every one of those things to his advantage if he can. He's—" Niall stopped with a fierce look.

Seth followed Niall's gaze. A dark-haired faery, with woad-written art on her face and arms like warriors in Celtic battle paintings, stood surrounded by a cluster of six shorter faeries with red-stained hands. The image of a raven shimmered over the top of the female faery's face. Blue-black hair that was somehow also feathers stretched to her waist in tangled snarls. Unlike most faeries, both her faux-mortal face and birdlike features were visible, blinking in and out of dominance.

"Don't get involved." Niall moved his chair back away from the table as she approached.

She tilted her head in a decidedly not-human way. "What a pleasant surprise, *Gancan*—"

"No." Niall's temper snapped out with actual tendrils of shadow, invisible to the Un-Sighted mortals in the club. "Not 'Gancanagh.' *King.* Or have you forgotten?"

The faery who'd spoken didn't flinch; instead she let her gaze slip slowly over Niall. "That's right. Things are cloudy in my mind some days."

"That is not why you chose to not-name me." Niall didn't stand yet, but he had angled his body in a position that would make sudden movement easier.

"Too true." The birdlike faery's posture tensed. "Would you fight me, my *king*? The battles I need are not near enough."

Seth felt the tension grow increasingly thick. The other faeries had dispersed, taking up posts throughout the Crow's Nest. They looked gleeful.

"Is that what you want?" Niall stood.

She licked her lips. "A little tussle would help me."

"Do you challenge me?" He reached out and ran a hand through the faery's feather-hair.

"Not yet. Not a real challenge, but blood . . . yes, I want that." She leaned forward and snapped her mouth with

an audible clack, and Seth wondered if she had an actual
beak.

Niall fisted his hand in her hair and held her head away
from him.

She swayed as if they were dancing. "I could ask after
Irial. I could mention how wounded he is that you refuse
his . . . counsel."

"Bitch."

"That's all I get?" She glared at him. "A word? I come
unbloodied. I come seeking you. I get a *word*? Is this how
you treat me after—"

Niall punched her.

She tried to skewer his still-extended arm with the bone-
white knife that she was now holding.

They were too fast for Seth to follow. What he could tell
was that the faery was more than holding her own. In a few
moments, Niall had a series of cuts that looked mostly shal-
low. He took her legs from under her, but she was up and on
him before she even hit the ground.

In the blur of it, she appeared to have a raven's beak and
talons in addition to the short knife. The screeches from her
beak-mouth were horrific sounds, battle cries that seemed
like they should call the other faeries to her side. Instead,
the faeries who'd come with her sat on tables and stools,
watching silently.

Niall had her pinned briefly in an embrace of sorts—her
back to his chest.

She stayed motionless for a moment. The look on her

face was embarrassing to see: it was not unhappiness but an intimate sort of pleasure. She sighed. "You're almost worth fighting."

Then she flung her head backward into Niall's face with such force that she bloodied his nose and mouth.

Niall didn't release his hold, though. Instead, he loosed his right hand and cupped her head with it. He took her momentum and spun her to the ground. He kept her on the floor with one hand on her head and his body half on top of her. Niall stayed there, his body pinning the motionless faery.

She turned her bloodied face to his, and the two held each other's gazes.

Uncomfortable, Seth looked away and realized that the waitress was standing beside him; she said something.

"What?"

The waitress spoke again. "Niall. I didn't see him leave. Is he coming back?"

With a start, Seth remembered that she couldn't see the faeries. Only he saw the fight. Only he saw them bloodied and tangled together. He nodded. "Yeah. He'll be here."

The waitress gave him an odd look. "You okay?"

"Yeah. Just . . . you startled me." He smiled. "Sorry."

She nodded and moved on to another table.

Behind him, Seth heard Niall say, "My dear?"

Seth turned to see Niall stand and reach down to the faery. "Are we done?"

"Mmmm. Paused. Not done. Never done until you're

dead." She took his hand and, with the liquid grace that characterized so many faeries, she came to her feet. Her eyes were unfocused as she gingerly touched her cheek. "That was good, my King."

The Dark King nodded. He didn't take his gaze away from her.

"I'll come for you tonight," she whispered in what was either a threat or a proposition.

Then she turned her head in a series of short jerky moves, locating each of the six red-palmed faeries unerringly. They moved in unison toward her. Without another word exchanged, the group left as suddenly as they'd arrived.

Niall glanced at Seth. "I'll be right back."

He left as well, and Seth sat there, stunned by the random violence and unsure what to think of it.

Seth realized that another person had seen the fight: a faery, invisible to Un-Sighted mortal eyes, stared at him from across the room. Coarse white hair was bound back into a tiny knot at the crown of his head. His features were sharp, angular in ways that made him seem carved. It was a different sort of sculpture than what Seth created, but in the instant, Seth's hands itched for a block of dark stone to try to sculpt an opposite piece. The pale faery stood staring, and for a moment, Seth wondered if he was alive. He was so inflexible that the illusion of being carved was complete.

Once Niall returned a few minutes later, he was not so blood-covered. His glamour hid the state of his clothes and the cuts on his skin, so the only mortal in the room who saw that anything had changed was Seth.

When Niall sat down at the table again, Seth said, "Do you know him?"

Niall followed Seth's gaze to the side of the room where the statuelike faery still stood. "Unfortunately." Niall removed a cigarette case from a pocket and slid one out. "Devlin is Sorcha's 'peacekeeper,' or her thug, depending on who's doing the defining."

The faery Devlin smiled placidly at them.

"And I'm not in the mood to deal with him," Niall added, without taking his attention from Devlin. "Very few faeries are strong enough to test me these days. She is. Unfortunately, he is too."

Unsure how the day had gone so suddenly tense, Seth shot another glance at Devlin, who was approaching their table.

He stopped, still invisible, and said to Niall, "Trouble comes, my friend. Sorcha is not the only target."

"Is she ever?" Niall flicked open his lighter.

Without being invited, Devlin pulled a chair out and joined them. "Sorcha was once fond of you. That should matter, even to you. What she needs is—"

"I don't want to know, Dev. You see what I am now. . . ."

"In control of your own path."

Niall laughed. "No. Not that. Never that."

Seth wasn't sure what the right move was, but when he started to stand, Niall gripped his forearm. "Stay."

Devlin watched, seemingly impassive. "He's yours?"

"He's my friend," Niall corrected.

"He sees me. He saw *her*." Devlin's tone wasn't accusing, but it was alarming nonetheless. "Mortals aren't to See."

"He does. If you try to take him"—Niall bared his teeth in an animalistic snarl—"any kindness I once felt for your queen or friendship for you will not stop my anger." Then he glanced at Seth. "Go nowhere with him. Ever."

Seth raised one brow in silent question.

Devlin stood. "If Sorcha had meant for me to take the mortal, he'd be gone. She hasn't ordered his collection. I am here now warning you of trouble in your court."

"And reporting back on it."

"Of course." Devlin gave Niall a look that was beyond disdainful. "I report everything to my queen. I serve the High Court in all things. Be alert to my sisters' words."

Then he stood and left.

Niall ground out his first cigarette, which he hadn't smoked, and pulled out another.

"Want to explain any of that?" Seth gestured around the room.

"Not really." Niall lit the cigarette and took a long drag. He held the cigarette in front of him with a bemused look on his face. "And really, I'm not sure I *can* explain it all."

"Are you in danger?"

Niall exhaled and grinned. "One can hope."

"Am I?"

"Not from Devlin. He'd have tried to take you if he was sent here to do so." Niall glanced at the doorway through which the High Court faery had left. "Devlin comes here on High Court business because Sorcha does not often walk among mortals."

"And the faery who attacked you?"

Niall shrugged. "It's one of her hobbies. She enjoys violence, discord, pain. Keeping her in check is one of the many challenges Irial left me. He helps, but . . . I have trouble trusting him."

Seth didn't know what to say to that. They sat in awkward silence for several cigarettes.

The waitress stopped to clean the tables nearest them—again. She stared at Niall with blatant interest. Most faeries and mortals did. Niall was a Gancanagh, seductive and addictive. Until he'd become Dark King, his affection was also fatal to his partners.

"Who was she? The faer—" Seth broke the word off as the waitress came to their table with a clean ashtray. He told her, "We'll let you know if we need anything."

"I don't mind stopping, Seth." She spared him a scowl before turning her attention to the Dark King. "Niall . . . Is there anything you need?"

"No." Niall stroked the girl's bare arm. "You're always good to us. Isn't she, Seth?"

After the waitress walked away, sighing and darting a glance back at Niall, Seth rolled his eyes and muttered, "We ought to pass those charms of yours out to everyone here."

A grin replaced the gloomy expression on Niall's face. "Spoilsport."

"Enjoy it. Enjoy the attention, but reserve your affection for faeries," Seth cautioned.

"I know that. I just need"—the Dark King winced as if the thought hurt him—"I just need you to keep reminding me. I don't ever want to be what Keenan is, what Irial was."

"Which is?" Seth asked.

"A selfish bastard."

"You're a faery king, man. I don't know how much choice you have. And with what just happened with the raven-faery—"

"Don't. I would spare you and myself from your knowing the unpleasant things in my life if you'll let me."

Seth held up a hand in a halting gesture. "Your call. I'm not judging you either way."

"That makes one of us then," Niall murmured. After a still moment, he straightened his shoulders, rolling them like he was testing for motility. "I suppose the true dilemma is where to direct my bastardness."

"Or you know, try harder on the resisting-it thing."

"Sure." Niall's expression was bland as he added, "That's *exactly* what the Dark King is to do: resist temptation."

Chapter 6

Aislinn was feeding the birds when Keenan came in slamming doors and scowling. One of the cockatiels clung to the back of her shirt and poked its beak through her hair to watch the Summer King. The birds were a source of comfort for Keenan. Sometimes, in his melancholy or irritable moods, sitting and watching them was one of the only surefire ways to adjust his temper. The birds seemed to know how valuable they were and acted accordingly. Today, however, he didn't pause among them.

"Aislinn," he said by way of greeting before he walked past her and to his study.

She waited. The cockatiel took flight. None of the other birds came toward her. Instead, they all seemed to be watching her expectantly. The cockatiels' crests were raised. The other birds merely stared at her—or in the direction Keenan had gone. A few squawked or chirped.

"Fine. I'll go see him."

She followed him into the study. The room was one of the two that were Keenan's domain. The other—his bedroom—wasn't one she ever entered, but the study was where they usually went when it was just the two of them. She felt weird going in there without him. The Summer Girls sometimes curled up on the sofa with a book, but they had no interest in keeping boundaries with Keenan. Aislinn did. The closer summer crept, the more she felt a pull toward him—which she didn't want.

Aislinn stood just inside the doorway, trying not to feel ill at ease about being in his space. He kept telling her that the loft was hers as much as his, that *everything* was hers now. Her name was on store accounts, credit cards, bank cards. She ignored them, so he went for more subtle gestures, things that he thought would make her feel at home in the loft. *Little threads to tie me.* It wasn't obvious at first glance that he'd changed the study again, but if she looked around the somber room, small things would be different. She didn't live there, but she spent enough time at the loft that it was a second—*third*—home these days. Her nights were divided among home, Seth's, and the loft. She kept clothes and toiletries in all three places. Her real home, the apartment she shared with Grams, was the only place where she was treated like she was normal. At home she wasn't a faery queen; she was just a girl who needed to do a bit better in calculus.

While she stood tentatively at the door, Keenan sat at one end of a dark brown leather sofa. Someone had set out a pitcher of ice water; condensation was rolling down the sides of it in little rivulets. It puddled on the surface of the slab of agate that served as a coffee table. He tossed away one of the newest pillows, an oversized deep green thing without any ostentatious decorations. "Donia won't see me."

Aislinn closed the door behind her. "What for this time?"

"Maybe over asking about Bananach. Maybe still over this business with Niall. Maybe something . . . else—" Keenan broke off midthought and scowled.

"Did she talk to you at all?" Briefly, Aislinn rested her hand on his forearm before going to the other end of the sofa. She kept her distance by habit, breaking it only for etiquette or gestures of friendship, but every day it grew more difficult to keep that distance.

"No. I was stopped at the door *again*, refused admittance to the house. 'Unless it is official business,' Evan said. For three days, she's been unavailable and now this."

"Evan is just doing his job."

"And enjoying it, I'm sure." Keenan was not very good at rejection of any sort; Aislinn had figured that out back when she was still mortal.

She switched the topic. "It seems odd that she'd be upset over Niall now or over us asking about Bananach."

"Exactly. Once Niall calms down, his holding the Dark Court can be an asset to both of our courts. She's—"

"No. I mean, she seemed calm enough when we left the other day. Not happy but not truly angry." Aislinn hugged a pillow to her like a big stuffed toy. Talk of the intricacies of faery relationships and courts and of grudges between faeries with centuries of history made her feel so very young. Many of the faeries might look—and often act—like her classmates at school, but the whole longevity thing made life far more complicated. Brief relationships spanned decades; long friendships stretched over centuries; betrayals of yesterday and decades and centuries past all cut deeply. It was a challenge to navigate.

"Am I missing something?" she asked.

Keenan watched her with a pensive expression. "You know, Niall was like that. He helped me focus, went straight to the point. . . ." His words drifted away as tiny clouds shifted in his eyes, a promise of rain as yet unfulfilled.

"You miss him."

"I do. I'm sure he's a great king. . . . I just wish it wasn't of such a vile court. I handled things poorly," he said.

"We both messed up there. I ignored things that I should've reacted to, and you—" Aislinn stopped herself. Rehashing Keenan's deceits and the consequences for Leslie and for Niall yet again wasn't going to help. "We both made mistakes."

Leslie's being caught in the heart of the Dark Court was Aislinn's fault too. She'd failed one of her closest friends—and she'd failed Niall. Aislinn shared the weight of the responsibility for the actions of the Summer Court. It was why she was trying to work on a closer relationship with Keenan: they had joint responsibility, and if she was going to bear the guilt for his less palatable actions she needed to know what they were in advance.

And stop them if they're awful.

"And they made bad choices. We aren't the ones responsible for that." Keenan couldn't have said it if it was a lie, but it was an opinion. Opinions were shaky territory with the faeries-don't-lie rule.

"We aren't absolved either. You kept things from me . . . and they paid the consequences." She had not entirely forgiven him for his using Leslie or Niall, but unlike Donia, Aislinn had no choice but to get along with the Summer King. Unless one of them died, they were bound together for eternity or until they no longer held the Summer Court— and faery rulers tended to hold their courts for centuries. That was pretty close to an eternity.

Eternity with Keenan. The thought terrified her still. He wasn't particularly inclined toward an equal ruling status, and she wasn't experienced at dealing with faeries. Prior to her transformation into a faery monarch, her primary method of "dealing" was avoidance. Now, she had to rule them. He had nine centuries ruling without his full power. It was hard to say that she should have an equal voice, but the alternative—responsibility for the consequences but not involvement in the decisions—wasn't a solution.

And since she'd become their queen, the summer faeries had become important to her. Their welfare mattered; their happiness and safety were essential. It was as instinctual as the need to help Summer grow to strength, but that didn't mean everyone else should be sacrificed for the progress of Summer. Keenan didn't get that.

She shook her head. "We're not going to agree on this, Keenan."

"Maybe"—Keenan looked at her with such open affection that she could feel the sunbeams under her skin responding— "but at least you aren't refusing to speak to me."

Aislinn moved farther back into the corner of the sofa, her message implicit in the movement. "I don't have a choice in the matter. Donia does."

"You have a choice. You are just . . ."

"What?"

"More reasonable." He didn't hide the smile that came as soon as he said it.

The tension that had been growing inside of her dissipated at his easy smile. She laughed. "I've never been as *un*reasonable as I've been the past few months. The way I've changed . . . My teachers have commented. My friends, Grams, even Seth . . . My mood swings are awful."

"Compared to me, you're quite unflappable." His eyes were sparkling: he knew how volatile she'd become. He'd been the target of her temper more than anyone else.

"I'm not sure it counts as being reasonable if *you're* the measuring stick." She relaxed again. During all the weirdness over the past few months, he'd found ways to make her lighten up. It was a big part of what had made it bearable to be the Summer Queen. His friendship and Seth's love were her mainstays.

Keenan's smile was still there, but the plea in his eyes was serious as he asked, "Maybe *you* could talk to Don? Maybe explain to her that I miss her. Maybe you could tell her that I am sad when I can't see her. Tell her that I need her."

"Shouldn't you tell her?"

"How? She won't even let me in the door." He frowned. "I need her in my life. Without her . . . and without you being—I'm not good at things. I try, but I need her to believe in me. To not have either of—"

"Don't." Aislinn didn't want him to follow that thought any further. The peace between the courts was new and tenuous. It was better if Donia and Keenan were at peace with each other, but talking to Donia alone made her anxious. They'd become friends of a sort, not as close as Aislinn had initially hoped, but close enough that they'd spent afternoons together at first. That had ended when spring began. *When things with Keenan changed.* They could avoid talking about it, but it took constant effort for her and Keenan not to touch each other.

"I can try, but if she's upset with you, she might not be willing to talk to me either. Lately, she's bailed every time I've tried to make plans with her," Aislinn admitted.

Keenan poured them both glasses of water while he talked. "It's because Summer is growing stronger, and Winter is weakening. Beira got surly every spring—and that was when I was still weak."

Keenan held out a glass to her—and she froze.

It's just water. And even if it were summer wine, it

wouldn't affect her like it had the first time. She pushed away the thoughts.

"Ash?"

She started, caught off guard by his uncommon usage of her shortened name. She pulled her attention from the glass and glanced at him. "Yeah?"

He ran a thumb over the outside of the glass as he held it up higher. The liquid was crystal clear. "It's safe. My intentions are not to harm you. *Ever*. Even before, I didn't wish you harm."

She blushed and took the glass. "Sorry. I know that. Really."

He shrugged, but he was so easily hurt by her moments of panic. She suspected he felt them sometimes, as if their sharing the court was creating a bond neither of them was prepared for. No one else in the court could see through the facades she erected—only Keenan.

Friends. We are friends. Not enemies. Or anything else.

"I'll talk to Don," she told him. "No promises. I'll try, though. Maybe it'll even be good for us. . . . She's been so short-tempered with me the past few weeks. If it's just a spring thing, maybe it'll be good to talk."

He took her hand and squeezed it gently. "You are good to tolerate the positions I put you in. I know that this is not yet easy for you."

She didn't let go of his hand, holding on to him with the strength she had gained when her mortality was replaced by this otherness. "I'll only tolerate so much. If you keep another secret like you did with Leslie"—she let the sunlight that lived in her skin slip out, not a loss of temper but a show of her growing control over the element they shared— "it would be unwise, Keenan. Donia was what made freeing Leslie possible. You failed me. I don't want that to happen again."

For almost a full minute, he didn't answer; he just held on to her hand.

When she started to pull back, he smiled. "I'm not sure this threat is having the result you'd like it to. You're even more alluring when you're angry."

Her face flushed as the words she *should* say and the words she could say weren't the same, but she didn't break her gaze. "I'm not playing, Keenan."

His smile vanished, and he let go of her hand. A serious look came over his face. He nodded. "No secrets. That's what you are asking of me?"

"Yes. I don't want to be adversaries—or play word games." Faeries twisted their words to allow themselves every possible advantage.

The faery before her spoke quietly, "I don't want to be adversaries either."

"Or play word games," she said again.

The wicked smile returned. "Actually, I like word games."

"I'm serious, Keenan. If we're going to work together, you need to be more open with me."

He had a challenge in his voice when he asked, "Really? That's what you want?"

"Yes. We can't work together if I have to wonder what you're thinking about all the time."

"If you're sure that's what you want." His voice was wavering between teasing and intensely serious. "Is it, Aislinn? Is that what you truly want of me? You want my total honesty?"

She felt like she was walking into a trap, but backing down was not the right approach if she was to be his equal. She forced herself to look him in the eye as she said, "It is."

He leaned back and took a sip of his water, watching her as he did so. "Well, so you don't need to wonder . . . I was thinking—just now—that sometimes we get so caught up in the court stuff, Donia, Niall, your classes . . . It's easy to forget that nothing I have would be mine were it not for you, but it's never easy to forget that I still want more."

She blushed. "That's not what I meant."

"So *you're* going to play word games now?" There was no denying the challenge in his voice this time. "You can decide when my honesty is welcome?"

"No, but—"

"You said you wanted to know what I'm thinking; there weren't conditions. No word games, Aislinn. Your choice." He sat his glass on the table and waited for several heart-beats. "Have you changed your mind so easily? Would you prefer we have secrets or not?"

Aislinn felt the edge of terror approach her, not in fear of physical safety, but in fear that the friendship they'd been building was tumbling around her.

When she didn't speak, he went on. "I was thinking that no one else could've handled *any* of the things you have. Even adjusting to being fey . . . Not one of the Summer Girls adjusted so quickly. You didn't mourn or rage or cling to me."

"I knew about faeries. They didn't," she protested. She hated the faery inability to lie more and more as he spoke. It would be easier to lie and deny how painlessly she had become fey. It would be easier to say that she wasn't adjusting to her new life far faster than she'd ever thought. It would be easier to say she was struggling.

Because then he wouldn't be doing this to me.

He'd given her space, given her time. He'd been a friend and not even approached the boundaries she'd set.

Run. Run now.

She didn't.

And Keenan moved closer, invading her space. "You know it's more than that. I *know* now that it was right that I didn't find my queen all these years. Waiting for you was worth everything that I thought I couldn't endure."

He had a hand in her hair now; sunlight slid down her skin.

"If you were my queen, *truly* my queen, our court would be stronger still. If you were mine, without mortal distractions, we'd be safer. We'd be stronger if we were truly together. Summer is a time to rejoice in pleasures and heat. When I'm around you, I want to forget everything else. I love Donia. I always will, but when I'm near you—" He stopped himself.

She knew what he was not-saying. She felt the truth of it, but that part of her wasn't something to give over to her court's health. Had he known they'd feel this way? Had he known that her insistence on approaching queenship as a job and not a relationship was going to limit their court's growth? She didn't want to know the answer.

"The court is stronger than it's ever been in your lifetime," she murmured.

"It is, and I'm grateful for what you've given our court. I'll wait as long as I must for the rest. That's what I'm thinking about. I suppose I should be thinking about the list of things we have to do, but"—he leaned closer, holding her gaze—"all I can think right now is that you're here with me where you belong. I do love Donia, but I love my court too. I could love you as we're meant to love one another, Aislinn. If you'd let me, I could love you enough that we'd forget everything but each other."

"Keenan . . ."

"You asked for honesty."

He wasn't lying. He couldn't. *It doesn't matter.* His telling her these things didn't, couldn't matter.

Aislinn could feel the sunlight that lived somewhere in the center of her. It stretched out to fill her skin to bursting. She was responding to Keenan's brief touch with an intensity that she'd felt only with Seth—which was wrong.

Is it? A traitorous voice whispered inside her. *He's my king, my partner. . . .*

She put a hand on Keenan's chest, intending to push him away, but sunlight pulsed between them at the contact. Their bodies were a giant conduit; sunlight looped between them like a stream of energy that grew stronger as it slipped through the barrier of skin.

His eyes widened, and he drew several unsteady breaths. He leaned toward her, and she felt herself leaning into him. Her arm was bent at the elbow so that—although she still had a hand on him as if to push him back—they were chest to chest, her arm pressed between them.

And he kissed her, something he'd only done when she was mortal. Once, she had been lost under the dizziness of too much summer wine and too many hours dancing in his arms. The second time was a taste of seduction when she was telling him to leave her alone. But this time, the third time, he kissed her so gently that it was barely a brush of lips. It was a question as much as a kiss. It was affection, and somehow that made it worse.

She pulled away. "Stop."

Her word wasn't much beyond a whisper, but he still paused. "Are you sure?"

She couldn't answer. *No lying.* She could taste the ripeness of summer in the words, a promise of what she could have if she came just a moment closer.

"I need you to move back." She concentrated on the meaning of those words, on the feel of the sofa, on the spines of the leather-bound books she could see on the wall behind Keenan—on anything but him.

She lowered her hand from his chest.

Slowly. Just concentrate on what matters. My life. My choices. Seth.

Keenan pulled back as well, watching her intently as he did so. "The court would be dying if it weren't for you."

"I know that." She couldn't move any farther away. There was nowhere to go; the sofa arm was already digging into her back.

"I would be useless without you," he continued.

She clutched the pillow in her lap like it was a shield she could hold between them. "You held the court together for *nine centuries* without me."

He nodded. "And it was worth it. Every torture was worth it for where we are now and for where we could be if you accept me someday. If we had the time to just be together as we should be . . ."

For another too-long moment, she stayed still, trying to find the words to diffuse the tension that had sprung up. This wasn't the first time he'd been so expressive in his words, but it was the first time he'd reached out to touch her skin in anything other than casual affection. The combination was too much.

"Space?" Her voice broke on the word.

He moved back farther. "Only because you ask it of me."

She felt lightheaded.

Keenan gave her a strained smile.

She stood on unsteady legs and walked to the door. She

pulled the door open and clutched the doorknob until she was afraid she'd break it. It took more self-control than she'd have liked, but she caught his gaze. "This changes nothing. It *can't*. You are my friend, my king, but that's . . . all you can be."

He nodded, but it was a gesture that indicated that he heard her, not that he agreed, which was abundantly clear as he said, "And you are my queen, my savior, my partner— and that's everything."

CHAPTER 7

Aislinn walked aimlessly through Huntsdale. Sometimes she didn't feel able to be around Seth; that happened more and more of late with thoughts of Keenan lingering on her mind. She'd been thinking about the things Keenan had said and the way she felt when he reached out toward her, and she was afraid. His separation from Donia would make him more insistent on being with her. They were already too close with summer's approach, and she didn't know what to do about it.

Part of her wanted to talk to Seth, but she was terrified that he'd go away. No matter how often he whispered that he loved her, she still worried that she'd mess it all up, and he'd leave. Sometimes she wanted to run from the world of faery problems; how could she expect him not to want the same thing? Seth had to share her with her court and her king. If she told him that Keenan was pressuring her—and that she was tempted—would that be the final straw?

Seth gave her space, but he noticed when she was upset and she wasn't sure what she would say if he asked her why. *My king, my other half, he's decided to change the rules. And I barely refused.* She wasn't up for that conversation, not any time soon. She would be. She'd tell him. *Just not yet. Not until I know what to say.*

She wanted to talk to someone, but her only other friend who knew about the faeries, Leslie, had left town and refused to discuss them; telling Seth meant admitting to being tempted by Keenan; and her other confidant to things faery, Keenan, was the problem. Aislinn was faced with the unpleasant realization that her own circle of friends was far smaller than it had ever been. She'd never had a huge number of friends, but between the months where she was falling for Seth and trying to call it platonic and the changes with being a faery monarch, she'd drifted from the few friends she'd had. She still talked to Rianne and Carla at school, but she hadn't hung out with either of them in months.

After a glance at the time, she called Carla.

Carla answered almost immediately. "Ash? You okay?"

"Yeah. Why?" Aislinn knew why: she never called anymore.

"I just . . . nothing. What's up?"

"You free?"

Carla was silent for a beat. Then she said, "Depends on why you're asking."

"Okay, I was thinking I've been a lousy friend lately. . . ." Aislinn paused.

"Keep talking. You're on the right track. Next part is?"

"Penance?" She laughed, relieved that Carla was making light of it. "What's the price?"

"Ten per game? Meet you there?"

Aislinn turned down the next street to head toward Shooters. "Spot me a few balls?"

Carla snorted. "Penance, sweetie. I've been eying a new video card, and you're going to bankroll it by the time the night's done."

"Ouch."

"Yep." Carla's laugh was joyful. "See you there in thirty."

"I'll get a table." Then, in a decidedly improved mood, Aislinn disconnected. She knew that several of her guards followed behind at a discreet distance. Tonight, she didn't want to see them, though. Shooting pool with a friend wouldn't fix a thing, but it felt closer to the normal life she still missed.

With that in mind, she walked the half dozen blocks to Shooters. The H in the sign was out, so it read SOOTERS— which was far better than when the first s had been out.

It had been weeks since she'd even stopped in. Guilt hit her again—and fear that she'd no longer be welcome. The regular crowd at Shooters worked hard and relaxed with equal enthusiasm. They were all older than she was—some old enough to be Grams' long-ago classmates—but they didn't draw age or class or race lines at Shooters. It was a place where everyone was welcome as long as they didn't start trouble.

Before everything changed, Denny, a pool hustler somewhere in his twenties, had taken her on as a project of sorts. Denny handed her lessons off to his friend Grace when he felt like working a mark, and between their combined tutelage, Aislinn had become a pretty decent shot. She'd never be able to run tables like he did, but that sort of mastery came from shooting every day. Most of the regulars were cool to talk to or shoot with, but it was Denny and Grace whom she'd truly missed.

When she went inside, she saw Denny right off. He was at a table with Grace. When Grace looked up and saw her, her face folded into a smile. "Hey, Princess. Long time, no visits."

Denny took his shot before he lifted his eyes from the table. "Out without either of the Princes Charming?"

She shrugged. "Girl time. I'm meeting Carla."

"Grab a cue or a seat." Grace's voice had a cigarette-and-whiskey rasp to it that contrasted with her body. She sounded like a woman who should be a lithe singer in a vibrant scarlet dress, breaking hearts and inciting lovers' quarrels, but Grace was a different sort of trouble. Wearing black boots, faded jeans, and a man's button-up shirt, she was all muscle and just as able to handle any fights as the men in the room. She took immense pride in the fact that her Softail Custom was outfitted with more chrome and louder pipes than Denny's.

"You want to shoot teams when Carla gets here?" Denny circled the table to reach his next shot. He'd tied his hair back, but the loose ponytail was already coming undone and falling into his face.

"Only if I get Carla," Grace said. "Sorry, Ash, but the two of them together would kill us."

Aislinn cracked a grin. "She already set stakes. Ten a game."

"So, twenty then, for teams?" Denny cleared two balls in a complicated shot that Carla could explain by way of geometry and simple angles, but which Denny executed as a matter of precision and practice. Aislinn had neither geometry nor sufficient practice.

"Or ten still, even splits." Grace opened a bottle of water.

"We might break even, if you have Carla," Denny said. Then he finished clearing the table.

"Or not," Grace muttered.

He grinned. "Or not."

Something bluesy kicked up on the jukebox; Aislinn had been there often enough to recognize classic Buddy Guy. Across the hall, murmured conversations rose and fell among the clack of balls. Cries of defeat and victory broke into the familiar hum of Shooters. *It's good to be here.* She'd spent too much time with faeries; hanging out with friends was the change she needed.

By the time Carla arrived, Aislinn could almost convince herself that life was as it had been before. Not that before had been perfect, but sometimes it seemed like things had been a lot clearer then. Contemplating eternity, a job she had no idea how to do well, and a relationship that was heading toward uncrossable lines—it wasn't relaxing.

But Carla was there, Denny and Grace were there, the music was good, and the laughter was easy. The rest of the night was reserved for friends and fun.

"Game," Carla crowed. She did a little victory shimmy that made Denny look away and Grace smirk.

"Somebody's keeping a secret," Aislinn murmured to Denny.

Denny narrowed his eyes. "Leave it alone, Ash."

Grace and Carla were chatting as Grace racked the balls. Aislinn put her back to the table and kept her voice low. "Age is relative. If you—"

"No, it's really not. Maybe someday when she's had a chance to live a little more . . . but she hasn't, and I'm not going to steal that chance." Denny glanced at Carla as he sat back on one of the stools against the wall. "You two have years to enjoy your freedom before you settle down. I'm already at the point of wanting that."

"So how old is too old?"

He grinned. "Don't get prickly. Seth's not too old for you. A year or two isn't a big deal."

"But . . ."

"But I'm almost a decade older. It's different." Denny pushed away from the stool. "Are we going to shoot or do each other's hair now?"

"Jerk."

He grinned. "Yet another reason you shouldn't encourage me."

"Whatever." She smiled back at him.

As they played, Aislinn thought about Seth—*and about Keenan*—and she wasn't sure if she agreed with Denny. *Is he right? Is more than a few years too much?* Part of her thought he was right. Being with Seth never felt like there was any question of maturity or wisdom or any imbalance. With Keenan she felt like she was constantly stumbling.

She pushed aside her thoughts and concentrated on the game. Carla and Grace made a great team, but Denny was more than their match. They all played for fun; he played for money most weeks.

"Hey, dead weight," he called, "your shot."

Carla laughed. "Ash is just trying to help me out, aren't you?"

"It's as good an explanation as any for the easy shot you missed earlier. . . ." Denny smiled as he gestured to the table.

She didn't miss that one, but she missed more than her share over the next few hours. It was the least complicated evening she'd had in a while—no unspoken issues or worrying about every word she said and each move she made. It was exactly what she'd needed.

When she got home later that night, Aislinn wasn't surprised that Grams was waiting up for her. There might be guards that trailed her these days, and that whole never-let-faeries-know-we-see-them thing was pretty much a moot point now, but Grams still treated her like she was a normal girl. *Well, as normal as I ever was.* Home was the place where she could be small and afraid. It was where she was chastised for forgetting to add milk to the grocery list if she used the last of it. It was a haven . . . but that didn't mean that the rest of the world was left at the door.

Aislinn walked into the living room. Grams sat in her favorite chair; she had a cup of tea in hand. Her long gray hair was still plaited but not up.

The braid was longer than Aislinn could stand her own hair ever being. As a child Aislinn had thought Grams was really Rapunzel. If the faeries were real, why not Rapunzel? They lived in a tall building with windows overlooking a strange world. Grams had let her hair grow even longer back then, and it was ashy blond. Aislinn had asked her, once, about her theory.

"But wouldn't I be the witch keeping you safe? Trapping you up here in our tower?"

Aislinn had thought about it. "No, you're Rapunzel, and we're hiding from the witch."

"And what happens if the witch finds us?"

"She'll steal our eyes or make us dead."

"So if we leave our tower?" Grams turned everything into a quiz. Everything was about them, and wrong answers meant staying inside longer. "What are the rules?"

"No looking at the faeries. No talking to faeries. Nothing to attract faeries' attention. Ever." Aislinn counted the big three rules off on her fingers as she said them. "Always follow the rules."

"Exactly." Grams had hugged her then. Her eyes were shimmering with tears. "Breaking the rules will let the witch win."

"Is that what happened to Momma?" Aislinn tried to see Grams' face, hoping for clues. Even then she knew that Grams didn't always answer the whole way.

Grams snuggled her more tightly. "More or less, baby. More or less."

Moira wasn't a subject they discussed. Aislinn looked at Grams, the only mother she'd had, and hated that she'd be so long without her. Eternity was a long time to be without family. Grams, Seth, Leslie, Carla, Rianne, Denny, Grace . . . everyone she'd known before Keenan would die. *And I'll be alone. With just Keenan.* She couldn't speak around the ache in her heart.

"There was a special program on the complications of the unexpected weather shift." Grams motioned to the television. She was big on paying attention to the weather now that Aislinn was the embodiment of summer. "A bit on the flooding problems and some theories about the cause of the sudden environmental shifts . . ."

"We're working on the flood thing." Aislinn kicked off her shoes. "The speculation is harmless though. No one believes in faeries."

"They were talking about how the polar bears are—"

"Grams? Can we not do this tonight?" Aislinn flopped down on the sofa, sinking into the cushions with a comfort she never felt at the loft. No matter how much Keenan tried, that wasn't home. That wasn't where she felt herself. This was.

Grams clicked off the television. "What happened?"

"Nothing. Just . . . Keenan . . . we had a discussion—" Aislinn wasn't sure of the words she needed. She and Grams talked about dating, sex, drugs, drinking, everything really, but it was usually in the abstract. It wasn't up close and detailed. "I don't know. I went out to Shooters with Carla after. It helped, but . . . tomorrow, the day after, next year— what am I going to do when I don't have anyone but him?"

"So he's pressuring you already?" Grams didn't waste time. She never had been one for subtleties.

"What do you mean?"

"He's a *faery*, Aislinn." The loathing wasn't even close to hidden.

"So am I." Aislinn didn't like saying that sentence, not yet, maybe not ever. Grams accepted her, but she had a lifetime of fear and hatred against the very thing Aislinn now was. Her daughter died because of them.

Because of Keenan.

"You're not like them." Grams scowled. "You're certainly not like *him*."

Aislinn felt the first few tears of frustration burn in her eyes. She didn't want to let them fall. She didn't have enough control yet, and sometimes the weather reacted to her emotions even when she didn't want it to; right now she wasn't sure she could control both her emotions and the sky. She took a calming breath before answering, "He's my partner, my other half. . . ."

"But you're still good. You're honest." Grams came over to the sofa. She pulled Aislinn close.

Aislinn leaned into the embrace, let Grams baby her.

"He's going to push you to do what he wants. It's his way." Grams stroked Aislinn's hair, threading her fingers through the multicolored strands. "He's not used to being rejected."

"I didn't—"

"You rejected his affection. That smarts. All faeries are prideful. He a faery king. Women have been giving themselves to him since he was old enough to notice them."

Aislinn wanted to say that Keenan wasn't interested in her just because she said no. She wanted to say that he was interested in her because of who she was. She wanted to say that their friendship was evolving, and they just needed to find a way to make it make sense. But she wasn't sure if any of that was true. There was a part of her that believed he was simply reacting to her refusal of his attention or to centuries of thinking that queen equated to bedmate. There was another, less comfortable part that believed that because they were partners the compulsion to be more than friends was only going to grow stronger. *That* part was terrifying.

"I love Seth," she murmured, clinging to that truth, not admitting aloud that loving one person didn't mean not noticing anyone else.

"I know that. So does Keenan." Grams didn't pause in the rhythmic motion of her affection. She always knew how to nurture without smothering. It was something no one else had ever done—not that there'd been anyone else. It had been them, just the two of them, forever.

"So what do I do?"

"Just be you—strong and honest. The rest falls into place if you do that. It always has. It always will. Remember that. No matter what happens over the . . . centuries ahead of you, remember to be honest with yourself. And if you fail, forgive yourself. You'll make mistakes. The whole world is new, and they have all had so many more years in it than you."

"I wish you were going to always be with me. I'm scared." Aislinn sniffled. "I don't know that I want forever."

"Neither did Moira." Grams did pause then. "She made a stupid choice, though. You . . . you're stronger than she was."

"Maybe I don't want to be strong."

Grams made a small noise that was almost a laugh. "You might not want to, but you'll do it anyhow. That's what strength is. We walk the path we're given. Moira gave up on living. She did some things that were . . . dangerous to herself. Slept with strangers. Did God-knows-what when she . . . Don't get me wrong. I got you out of her mistakes. And she obviously didn't do anything that made you born as an addict. She didn't end your life or give you to *them* either. She let me have you. Even at the end, she made some tough choices."

"But?"

"But she wasn't the woman you are."

"I'm just a girl. . . . I—"

"You're leading a faery court. You're dealing with their politics. I think you've earned the right to be called a woman." Grams' voice was stern. It was the one that she used when she talked about feminism and freedom and racial equality and all of those things that she'd held to like some folks hold to a religion.

"I don't feel ready."

"Honey, none of us ever does. I'm not ready to be an old lady. I wasn't ready to be a mother either time—to you or to Moira. And I surely wasn't ready to lose her."

"Or me."

"I'm not losing you. That's the only gift the faeries ever gave me. You'll be here, strong and alive long after I'm dust. You're never going to want for money or safety or health." Grams sounded fierce now. "Almost everything I could want for you *they* gave you, but only because you were strong enough to take it. I'm never going to like them, but the fact that my baby is going to be fine after I'm gone . . . It goes a long way to making me forgive them for all the rest."

"She didn't actually die in childbirth, did she?" Aislinn had never asked, but she knew the stories didn't add up. She'd heard Keenan and Grams talk last fall.

"No. She didn't."

"Why didn't you ever just tell me?"

Grams was silent for a few moments. Then she said, "You read a book when you were little, and you told me you knew why your mother left you. You were so sure that it wasn't her fault, that she was just not strong enough to be a mother. You said you were like the girls in the stories whose mothers died so they could live." Grams' smile was tentative. "What was I to do? It was a little bit true: she wasn't strong enough, just not the way you meant it. I couldn't tell you she chose to leave us because she was mostly faery when you were born. In your version, she was noble and heroic."

"Is that why I'm this? Because she wasn't human when I was born? Was I ever all the way mortal?"

This time, Grams was still so long that Aislinn wondered if they were going to have a repeat of the silences that always came when there was talk of Moira. Grams sat and stroked Aislinn's hair for several minutes. Finally, though, she said, "I've wondered, but I don't know how we'd know that. She was barely mortal when you were born. Add that to what-ever makes us have the Sight . . . I don't know. Maybe."

"Maybe she was the queen he was looking for. Maybe you were too. Maybe it's why we have the Sight. Maybe it could've been anyone in our family. Maybe when Beira'd cursed him and hid the faery whatever-it-was that was to make someone the Summer Queen . . . it could have been *any* of us. If Moira had taken the test . . . I wonder if she'd have been the queen. I wonder if I would've still ended up a faery. If she wasn't really mortal when I was born—"

Grams interrupted Aislinn's increasingly fast flow of words. "Wondering about *what-if* doesn't help, Aislinn."

"I know. If she was a faery . . . I wouldn't be alone."

"If she had chosen to accept being a faery, I wouldn't have had you to raise either. She wouldn't have left you behind."

"She *did* leave me. She chose to die rather than be a faery. Rather than be what I am now."

"I'm sorry." Grams' tears fell into Aislinn's hair. "I wish you didn't know any of that."

And Aislinn didn't have a response. She just lay there, her head in Grams' lap, like she had so many times as a little girl. Her mother had chosen death over being a faery. It didn't leave much room to doubt what Moira would've thought of the choices Aislinn had made.

CHAPTER 8

Seth wanted to be surprised when he saw Niall waiting inside the Crow's Nest the next day, but he wasn't. Their friendship was one of the things Niall held fast to, and Seth, for his part, wasn't objecting. It was like discovering that he had a brother—albeit a twisted and moody older brother—no one had bothered to tell him about.

Seth spun a chair around and straddled it. "Don't you have a job or something?"

The Dark King lifted a glass in greeting. A second glass sat on the table. He gestured toward it and said, "Poured not by my hand or of my cup."

"Relax. I trust you. Plus I'm already *in* your world"—Seth lifted the glass and took a drink—"and not planning on walking out of it anytime either."

Niall frowned. "Maybe you should trust less freely."

"Maybe." Seth leaned over and grabbed a clean ashtray

from the next table and slid it to Niall. "Or maybe you should chill out."

In one corner, the band was doing their sound check. Damali, one of Seth's semi-regular partners before-Aislinn, waved. Her copper-tinted dreads were midway down her back when he'd seen her last. They weren't much longer, but they were dyed magenta now. Seth nodded and turned his attention back to Niall. "So, you feeling the need for a lecture or being overprotective?"

"Yes."

"Talkative and maudlin today. Lucky me."

Niall glared at him. "Most people are intimidated by me these days. I'm the master of the monsters that Faerie fears."

Seth arched a brow. "Hmmm."

"What?"

"This whole 'fear me' thing doesn't work for you. Better stick to the brooding." Seth took another drink and looked around the Crow's Nest. "You and I both know you could order all of their deaths, but *I* know you wouldn't do it."

"I would if I needed to."

Seth didn't have an answer to that—it wasn't a point of argument—so he switched topics: "Are you going to be gloomy all afternoon?"

"No." Niall glanced at the far corner. This early, there was an open dartboard. "Come."

"Woof," Seth said, but he stood even as he said it, relieved to move on to *doing* something.

"Now, why don't my real Hounds obey so quickly?" Niall had apparently decided to try to lighten up. He smiled, weakly, but still it was a smile.

Seth went over and pulled the darts out of the board. He wasn't serious enough about the game to carry his own. Niall, however, did carry his own. He had been a faery-but-not-king for too long. As a king, he wasn't prone to reacting to steel, but that was a very recent change. A lifetime habit didn't let go so easily. He opened his case; inside were bone-tipped darts.

While Seth selected the straightest of the steel-tipped darts for himself, Niall watched with a bemused expression. "It's not toxic anymore, but I still would rather it not touch my skin."

"Cigarettes aren't toxic to you either, but you certainly don't hesitate there."

"Point. The darts shouldn't bother me," Niall agreed, but he still made no move to touch the darts in Seth's hand.

With a comfort he rarely felt around the denizens of the Summer Court, Seth turned his back to the King of Nightmares and eyed the board. *Home. Safe.* The fact that Niall's presence in his home of sorts only added to his sense of security was not lost on him.

"Cricket?"

"Sure." Seth didn't see the benefit in pretending he was up to playing something more serious. He wasn't good enough to give Niall any challenge on his best days, but that wasn't what throwing darts was about anyhow. It was a way to pass the time, a task for focus.

They played three games in almost complete silence, and even though he was obviously distracted, Niall won them all with his usual ease. When Niall had aimed and thrown his third and final dart, he said, "I hope you forgive better than you shoot."

"What's up?" Seth couldn't stop the wave of worry that rose at the Dark King's carefully neutral tone.

Niall spared him a glance as he retrieved his darts. "Unfinished business. Trust me."

"I don't want trouble."

"I'm the Dark King, Seth, what trouble could there possibly be?" Niall grinned, finally looking almost happy. "They're here."

And for a heartbeat, Seth didn't want to turn. He knew he'd see them—his girlfriend and his competition for her affection—when he turned. He didn't like to see them together, but his self-control was short-lived. Even though it meant seeing her with Keenan, Seth couldn't resist looking at her. He never could, even when she was mortal. Aislinn was smiling up at Keenan; she had a hand resting lightly in the crook of his arm. She'd begun to adopt more of the faeries' formal mannerisms in public.

Niall spoke in a low undertone: "Don't ever think he can be trusted. He counts the days until you are out of his way, and he has time on his side. I know you love our—*the*— Summer Queen, but yours is a losing battle, especially as you're not fighting. Cut your losses before they destroy you, or fight back."

"I don't want to give up." Seth looked at Ash. He'd thought the same thing more than a couple times lately. "But I don't want to fight anyone."

"Fighting is . . ." Niall started.

Seth didn't hear the rest of the words: Aislinn had looked up and caught Seth's gaze. She left Keenan and started across the room.

Casually, Keenan turned to talk to one of his guards as if her absence wasn't painful. *It is though.* Seth knew that; he had studied the Summer King's reactions, watched them change as winter ended. Keenan would keep Aislinn nearer him always if he could.

Just like I would.

Niall gave Seth a pitying look as Aislinn approached them. "You're not listening at all, are you?"

All the air in Seth's lungs seemed to vanish.

Is it her *or what she is?* He'd wondered that more and more. He'd never really done the relationship thing before Aislinn, so trying to figure out what was normal was a challenge. Was the escalation of fascination normal? Or was it because he was in love with someone who wasn't human anymore? He'd done enough reading of old folk stories the past months to know that humans could rarely resist a faery's allure.

Is that what's happening to me?

But Aislinn was slipping into his arms then. When she brought her lips to his, he couldn't care less about why he was fascinated by her, or if Niall's warnings were true, or what Keenan intended. All that mattered was that he and Aislinn were together. Sunlight soaked into his skin as she wrapped her arms around him.

He held on to her tighter than he would've before—*when she was human*. He couldn't grasp her tightly enough to ever hurt her, not now that she was faery.

Her hands slid up his spine, and she let a trickle of sunlight into her skin as she touched him. Such boldness in public was uncharacteristic.

He broke their kiss. "Ash?"

She pulled back a little more, and he shivered at the loss.

Like the sun being taken away.

"Sorry." A light blush colored her cheeks.

He didn't have any faith in his ability to formulate a sentence yet.

"I love you," she whispered against his lips.

"You too." Seth promised. *Always.*

She nestled into his arms with a little sigh. She wasn't a queen, wasn't a faery, wasn't anyone but his Aislinn then.

"You okay?"

"I am now."

Not a minute later, though, she tensed. Although Aislinn couldn't see Keenan, she obviously knew that he stood behind her. Whatever connection they had was growing stronger, and it wasn't making life any easier.

For his part, Keenan's expression hinted at confusions he wouldn't voice. Aislinn's residual humanity, her ability to switch from ruler to just a girl, seemed to baffle Keenan. Seth had watched him try to make sense of Aislinn's refusal to distance herself from the human world. It was a strength: the people she saw benefiting from her dedication to rebuilding Summer's strength inspired her to do more. But it was also a weakness: time with mortals reminded her of the unpleasant differences between mortal and fey and kept her aloof from her faeries. That distance was the source of a rift in the court, a vulnerability that caused more than a little rumbling.

Added to that were tensions from Aislinn's refusal to be a "proper queen" and Keenan's ongoing relationship with Donia; the court was stronger, but it was not healed.

Seth knew it would change with time—especially as the mortals Aislinn loved aged and died—but Keenan was openly dissatisfied by any weaknesses that could endanger Aislinn. The strengthening faeries' frustrations with their monarchs' choices made Keenan worry about what would happen as those faeries grew bolder. That worry for Aislinn was one of the few things that Seth appreciated about the Summer King. Keenan did treasure Aislinn. He wanted to keep her safe and happy.

He also wants to keep her to himself.

"You ought to step away, Keenan. I see what you're doing. I've watched you play these games for centuries."

Niall's voice was suddenly smoke and shadows. "Try thinking about what others need for a change."

"I don't believe what I do now is any of your business."
Keenan maneuvered so that he was farther from Aislinn
and facing Niall. In doing so, the Summer King had put his
back to the brick wall—assuring that no one could come up
behind him.

"If you hurt Seth"—Niall shot a smile at Seth—"it will
be."

"He isn't of your court."

Derision dripping from his voice, the Dark King said,
"Only an ass would think that matters. Leslie is lost to me.
Your queen's *friend*, and you let her be corrupted—"

"By the Dark Court, *your* court, Niall." Keenan glanced
at Aislinn, at Seth, at the various mortals in the room. In
the dim alcove where they stood, the conflict wasn't attract-
ing any attention yet.

"It is my court, and with all I've learned from the two
twisted kings I've loved and lived for, it won't ever bow to
yours. Don't try me, Keenan." Niall stalked toward Keenan,
closing the distance, menace clinging to his skin. "Hurt
Seth and you *will* answer to me."

Keenan didn't speak.

"Tell me you hold no ill will toward him, Keenan."
Niall's voice had dropped to a low growl that Seth hadn't
known resided in his friend. Beside the Dark King, the abyss
maidens took form and swayed; their bodies were tongues
of black flame, twisting and undulating. Seth knew they

were capable of devastation if let loose, but he wasn't sure if that was a good or bad thing. In a part of himself he tried to keep hidden, there was rage at Keenan and excitement at the thought that Niall would slap Keenan down. *Which isn't cool.* Seth kept those urges in check these days. He'd worked hard at becoming the person he was now. He didn't indulge in fights or one-night stands; he didn't get stupidly drunk or set out to try things just because they were forbidden. He was calm—even when it wasn't his instinctual reaction.

"Niall?" Seth let go of Aislinn and stepped around the abyss dancers. "Chill."

"He doesn't speak, does he, Seth?" Niall had curled his hands into fists.

"I know where I stand." Seth knew Keenan had mixed feelings. He hadn't acted to injure Seth, but it would be a surprise if he hadn't considered it. *At length. Probably with Tavish advising him on the risks.* Seth wasn't going there, though; it didn't help things. "I don't need to hear his answer."

"Ash does." Niall's posture was still, but shadows rippled out from him onto the brick wall behind Keenan. The black bars could solidify into a cage. "Back away, Seth. Please."

Seth moved farther from the small space where the two kings stood glaring at each other. After seeing the conflict with the raven-faery, Seth was aware that standing between these two was a bad idea. *Mortals are too fragile.* The thought disgusted him, but it was true. *I am too easily broken by them. By* all *of them.*

"Keenan wouldn't hurt Seth," Aislinn murmured. She came over and took Seth's hand. "I wouldn't forgive that, and he knows it."

Niall spared her a censorious glance. "Really?"

Sunbeams flickered around her as she became irritated with Niall. "Yes, *really*."

They all paused at a commotion in the doorway. Summer Court guards were attempting to refuse entrance to a group of heavily decorated faeries. It didn't work. Gabriel, the Hound who was the left hand of the Dark Court, sauntered in. With him were six other Hounds—including Chela, Gabriel's rough and strangely sweet mate—and Gabriel's half-mortal daughter Ani. The tread of Gabriel's feet reverberated through the floor. The wave of fear the Hounds brought in their wake rippled across the room.

And Seth was once more grateful for the anti-glamour charm Niall had given him. He might be breakable, but he was not susceptible to the Hounds' fear, to any of their glamours. Donia had given him the Sight, but that only allowed him to See them. Niall gave him protection from the way they could toy with his emotions.

"Gabe," Seth said, not sure if the Hounds' arrival was good news or not. They weren't known for counseling caution or calm. "Good to see you . . . I think."

Gabriel laughed. "We'll see."

Chela winked. "Mortal."

Niall didn't look away from Keenan. "You hurt Seth,

and I will not forgive you. He's my friend, under the Dark Court's protection."

"Keenan is not going to hurt Seth," Aislinn interjected. "And our court keeps him safe already. He doesn't need you."

Keenan gave a bland look to Niall and then asked Seth, "Do you offer fealty to the Dark Court, Seth Morgan?"

"No."

"Do you offer it to the Summer Court?"

Seth felt Aislinn tense beside him. "No, but I wouldn't turn down friendship with either if it's offered."

"There's a cost. . . ." Keenan's guileless expression was disingenuous, a sort of lie. "Pain, sex, blood, there are many horrible prices the Dark Court can demand. Are you going to be willing to pay what *they* ask for to buy protection?"

"Seth?" The worry in Aislinn's voice was real. She was the only one in the room who might believe that Keenan was trying to help Seth.

In offering his court's friendship, Niall had thrown an unasked-for lifeline, not a trap. Seth got that. *Even if she doesn't see it.* A court's friendship was more than just Niall's friendship: it meant that those who swore fealty to that throne would act as if he were one of their own. It meant he'd have many of the benefits of belonging to a court without the obligations or duties. Considering how vulnerable he was, it meant he had strength to call upon—from a court that many of the solitaries, the High Court, and the

Summer Court feared. Even if it didn't irritate Keenan, it would be appealing.

"It's cool," Seth assured Aislinn. "Niall is my friend."

"The friendship of not just the Dark King but the Dark Court is offered, to be paid with blood and no other coin," Niall said. His eyes held fear that Seth would reject his offer.

"Accepted." Seth stretched his wrist out in front of him and waited. He didn't reach toward Niall or the Hounds. The details of what would follow were utterly unclear to him. Most everyone there could draw blood without a blade, but they also all carried weapons of some sort. It was doubtful that anyone other than Niall would bleed him, and even if they did, Seth trusted that Gabriel and Chela—the two next highest-ranking dark faeries—would be cautious with his safety.

Only Keenan means me harm.

"I trust you," Seth said—to Niall, to the Hounds.

"I am honored." Niall leaned in and lowered his voice to say, "But Dark Kings really *don't* resist temptation very well."

Then, with a wicked grin, he turned and slammed his fist into Keenan's face with enough force that the Summer King's head hit the brick wall with a loud thud.

In a breath, the faeries all became invisible.

Aislinn rushed to Keenan's side as he crumpled and fell. The Hounds surged forward to stand like a wall of menace alongside Niall.

The abyss dancers shimmied.

And Niall licked his knuckles. "Sealed and paid with blood. The rules don't say it has to be *your* blood, Seth."

CHAPTER 9

Aislinn put herself between Keenan and Niall before the thought to protect her king had even finished forming. "Stop."

"You don't want to try me right now." Niall turned his back on her and started to walk away.

She followed. On some level she understood that her temper was propelling her to act foolishly, but it didn't matter. Her king was wounded at this faery's hand. She had to strike out at anyone who would attack their court; she had to crush anyone who would weaken them.

Niall's action isn't about the court, though. Niall and Keenan hadn't resolved their conflicts, and Niall believed that Keenan was a threat to Seth. *This is personal, not court.* Logic tried to interfere with impulse. *But Keenan is hurt.*

She took hold of Niall's arm. The smell of sizzling skin

was instant. Her sunlight had flared brighter than she realized.

Niall didn't flinch. Instead he drew his arm—and therefore her—tight to his body. Her fingers were pressed against his chest, burning small holes in his shirt. Instead of pulling away from her, he held her close enough that she had to tilt her head back to look at him. Once she did, Niall said, "My court would like more conflict with yours . . . and I"—he smiled—"I have to wonder if they're right."

"Let go." She tugged her hand and concentrated so she was no longer injuring him.

He gripped her wrist. "Any blood would've done the trick, but I wanted his. I'm not in violation of any laws for doing it. And, really? I suspected I'd enjoy it more this way"—he looked beyond her and grinned at Keenan lying prone on the ground—"and I did."

Then he released her.

She backed away carefully. "You hurt him."

"And you injured me. The difference, Aislinn, is that I'd do it every day if I could find justification. Would you?" Niall didn't sound like the same faery who'd helped her get used to her new role as Summer Queen, and he surely didn't sound like the faery who'd wooed Leslie. Those faces were gone, and what stood in front of her was a faery that rivaled the worst of the ones she'd hid from as a child.

Her sunlight barely in check, she glared at him. "I'm not the one starting fights."

"Shall I start one? Really start the conflict they crave? My court whispers and chants tales of what we could do while your court is still weak. It grows hard not to listen." His dark dancers swayed around him like shadows come to life. Gabriel and several other Hounds stood waiting.

This could get uglier than we can handle.

They hadn't brought a lot of people with them. She wasn't expecting trouble. Sure, there were rumblings of discord, but faeries were always in small dissentions. The court rulers kept that in check. Niall had been one of the good guys. Donia was one of the good guys. The two courts that had caused trouble for hers were both led by faeries who'd been confidants—*and more*—to Keenan. He'd trusted that their past would protect the Summer Court. He knew they were out of sorts, but he hadn't thought it was severe enough to lead to any true problems. *It's not the way faery courts work, Aislinn,* he'd assured her. *We aren't so quick to strike out,* he'd promised. And she'd believed him—until now.

"Do I frighten you, Ash?" Niall's voice was a low whisper, as if they were the only two people in the room. "Do I remind you of why you thought we were monsters?"

"Yes." Her own voice came out shaky.

"Good." He glanced to the side of her, where a wall of shadows had formed. Outside that wall lay the only faery there, other than her, who could tear down those shadows, but she wasn't sure how to, and Keenan was unconscious on the ground.

As if the detail were of only casual interest, Niall added,

"Your king never learned to fight. He had me and all the rest to do it for him."

The wall of shadows grew and enclosed the two of them in a bubble. She pushed against it; the texture was simultaneously feathery and slick. *New moon. Hunger. Fear.* The touch of it made her shiver. *Need. Drowning under black waves of need. Teeth.*

She jerked her hand away and forced herself to focus on the conversation. "Why are you doing this?"

"Protecting the mortal *you* love?" Niall shook his head. "I won't have Keenan break him too, and you've proven that you won't defend your friends from him. You're good for your court, but your mortals . . ."

"*Your* court did that to Leslie."

"And you could've saved her. If you'd offered her your court's protection before he took her—" He broke the sentence off with a growl. "You failed her just as you'll fail Seth."

"I made mistakes, but I would *never* hurt Seth. I love him." Aislinn felt her own temper getting less stable. Niall had trapped her, struck her king, and intimated that Seth was vulnerable because of her. Earlier she'd hurt Niall by accident, lack of control, but now . . . now, she wanted to hurt him. *Severely.* Her temper was flaring, and in that moment, she saw no reason to try to control it. The air inside the shadow bubble was growing blisteringly hot. She could taste acrid desert air, sand against her lips.

"Strike me, Ash. Go ahead. Give me leave to let my court

loose on yours. Convince me that I should let them torture your frail Summer Girls. Invite me to permit them to draw rowan blood," he whispered in a tone meant for bedrooms and candlelight. That was the nature of the Dark Court, though—violence and sex, fear and lust, anger and passion. He reached out and caressed her cheek as he added, "Allow me to give in to their desires."

Irial was less dangerous to us. That was Niall's weak spot— Irial. *Stop treating him like a friend. Don't think of him like a mortal.* Her mind tangled trying to figure what move made sense here. So much she'd learned about faeries was no longer useful. She'd long since surrendered the ability to live by most of the rules Grams had taught her. One rule was still helpful though: *If I run, they'll chase.*

She came closer, advancing on him. "The last Dark King thought to tempt me. Here. In this same place . . ."

Niall laughed, looking almost joyous for a brief flash, but that pleasure was gone as quickly as it had arrived. "If he'd truly tried, he would've had you. He didn't try you, Ash . . . you were a momentary distraction, a quick flirt. Irial's just that way."

"Keenan says you're like Irial—a *Gancanagh.* He didn't explain that to me before," she admitted, not proud of her king's deceits or the results, but willing to be honest. "Are you still? Are you addictive?"

"Why? You want a taste?"

Something feral waited. She saw it under the thin veneer of civility that was still Niall. It wasn't a surface she wanted to crack. Logic warned her away, but she didn't heed it. "So we really should start treating You like Irial. . . ."

"No"—Niall put his hand on her shoulders and pushed her until she was crushed between the wall of shadows and him—"you should remember that Irial didn't really want to hurt Keenan. I do. I only need an excuse. Will you give me one, Ash?"

The feel of that wall behind her body was overwhelming. Dangerous temptations whispered on her skin; things she would rather not consider came rushing to her mind. *Keenan under my hands. Mine. Not just a taste, but drowning in him.* It wasn't a Dark Court faery she wanted, but it was Dark Court energy that made her mind go places it really shouldn't. Dark Court temptations made her think of the faery she wanted, not the mortal she loved. Her heart felt too fast in her chest as the shadows pulled her under her fears and lust.

"I want—" She bit down on her lip, not speaking those words, not admitting that she thought of Keenan in that instant.

"I know what you want, Ash. What *I* want is to wound him." Niall looked through the shadows at Keenan. "I want him to cross lines that would justify attacking him."

"Justify?" She tried to push away from the shadows that were cradling her.

"To myself. To Donia. To Seth."

"But . . ."

"My court wants it. It's a big part of why they embrace

me as their king. . . . It's why Bananach flaunts herself in my chambers every moment she can. She comes to me, blood-ied and hungry for whatever anger I have." Niall looked at Seth, who pushed futilely against the shadow barrier. "Seth wants you. He loves you. Keep him safe from Keenan . . . or I'll have more than reason to let loose the perversions and cruelty of my court."

She looked through the barrier. Seth was saying some-thing, but his words were blocked by the smoky wall. His expression, however, wasn't. He was livid. Her very calm Seth was anything but peaceful.

"If *Seth* would forgive me, Ash, I would use you as my excuse to provoke your king." He squeezed her shoulders. "You hurt Leslie by your stupidity. You hurt me."

He pushed her into the shadow wall until she thought her heart would fail. Terror surged through her, sliding into her stillest corners and prodding all her fears and doubts to fruition. *Alone. Not good enough. Weak. Stupid. Destroying Seth. Wounding my court. Failing my king.*

"I'm sorry. I never wanted Leslie to be hurt. You know that. . . ." She forced her mind to focus, calling on the warmth inside of her, the peace of summer sun that was her own strength. It wasn't enough—not against a faery king who knew what he was doing. "I know you aren't really this cruel. You're a good person."

"You're wrong." Niall's gaze darted to Gabriel and the other Hounds, who were shadowy outlines outside the cage Niall had erected around the two of them. Then, finally, he pulled her away from the wall of darkness. "Ask your Summer Girls if I am a white hat. Ask Keenan when he rouses. Ask yourself if your fears of me are well founded. You're all alone with a monster, Aislinn . . . and your lusts, your fears, your angers are like blood-lures."

But I am not *alone.* That simple statement made the difference. There was a person on the other side of the wall who loved her, and there was a faery who was a part of her. Seth gave her courage; Keenan gave her sunlight. She let herself draw her own and Keenan's sunlight into her skin; that familiar warmth chased away the thick shadows that had invaded her body. "I need to go. Drop the wall."

"Or?"

Without any thought beyond making the Dark King bend to the Summer Court, she shoved that sunlight forward, pushing it into Niall's skin. Languor and satiation, bodies musky with summer's sun, a sirocco's biting winds— all of it surged into him. *Fair pay for the shadows.* It was the full weight of summer's pleasure with a tinge of pain. "We are stronger now. Don't provoke him . . . or me."

His hands were still restraining her, but he closed his eyes.

She thought she'd made her point. She thought of telling him that they wished things hadn't happened as they had. She truly wanted peace between the courts. It was only a few heartbeats of hope and guilt, and before she could decide, he opened his eyes. The maw of the abyss watched her from inside him.

"You're thinking like a mortal, Aislinn." He licked his lips. "Or maybe you're thinking like Keenan—flashy displays of power don't intimidate me."

She took a fumbling step backward, trying to pull away from him.

"Even if Seth wasn't my friend, I wouldn't try to seduce you. I would, however, reach out and break those delicate bones of yours." He was chest-to-chest with her. "I am the Dark King, not some young pup to be impressed by a display of temper. I lived with Irial. I learned to fight alongside Gabriel's Hounds."

Niall squeezed until she felt how breakable she still was—to him, to another faery ruler.

Seth pressed against the shadows again. His hand was on the outside of the barrier. If he could force his way through it, he could touch her, but he couldn't cross the shadows. The frustration on his face was awful to see. As she looked at him, fear plain on her face, Seth cursed. He shook Keenan, but the Summer King was unresponsive.

Several Hounds waited around Keenan. They neither helped nor interfered with Seth's attempt to rouse him. Other Hounds stood at the door barring any faeries who tried to enter.

"You can be a good queen and a good person, Aislinn. Don't let your belief in Keenan lead to hurting Seth, or I will exact the cost of every hurt you've been forgiven." Niall released her and simultaneously lowered the wall.

She fell to the floor.

With seeming indifference, Niall walked past the mortal he'd been defending, past the king he'd once served, past his own faeries.

Seth stopped him. "What in the hell are you doing?" He felt the last bit of calm he'd worked so hard to build inside of him fleeing. "You can't—"

"Seth. Don't." Niall gripped Seth's arm. "The Summer Court needed a reminder that I am not theirs to command."

"I'm not talking about the court. That's *Ash*. You hurt *Ash*."

"Listen very carefully." Niall looked at Seth as he spoke, each word clipped and precise. "She is un-broken. Frightened, but that's not a bad thing. If she were truly hurt, you'd be nursing her, not lashing out at me. You know that as well as I do."

Seth had no answer to that. Arguing would be a lie, and—as he did with Aislinn—Seth tried to never lie to Niall.

Two shadow dancers pressed against Niall; their bodies were almost as tangible as living beings. One male stood behind Niall. His diaphanous body was extended, elongated so that his arms draped over Niall's shoulders. His hands met over Niall's ribs. The second shadow dancer was beside Niall; she held one hand flat over his heart, centered above the hands of the first shadow dancer. Absently, Niall reached up and caressed the entwined hands.

"She followed me," Niall reminded him. "I am who I am,

Seth. I spent centuries wearing the Summer Court's leash. I won't be anyone or anything other than myself again. I gave her the chance to walk away, and she threatened me."

"Because you knocked out Keenan . . ."

Niall shrugged. "We all have choices to make. She chose to try me. I chose to point out her follies."

"What you did was jacked up."

"She is physically uninjured." Niall frowned, but his voice softened. "I don't want discord with you, my brother. I did what needed done."

"Whatever happens. Whenever . . ." Seth knew he couldn't ask for any promises. Aislinn had eternity as a faery queen, a ruler who didn't exactly approve of Niall's court. All Seth could say was, "I want her to be safe."

"And Keenan?" Niall's voice was emotionless. "Do you fault me for injuring him?"

Seth paused as he tried to find the words to answer. Niall waited, still but for the steady rise and fall of his chest under the hands of the shadow dancers. A few breaths later, Seth caught and held Niall's gaze. "No. I want her safe. I want you safe. And I don't want him to ever get away with manipulating or hurting either of you."

Niall sighed in obvious relief, and the dancers vanished, retreating into whatever void they lived in. "I'll do what I can. Go see to her."

And Seth had to face her—his beloved, the one he couldn't have saved, the one who was cradling someone else. She had been in danger, and he had been useless to her.

What happens when it isn't someone like Niall? What would I do if Niall had hurt her? He was mortal-weak.

Keenan wasn't any help either, Seth reminded himself. The difference, of course, was that Keenan could go after Niall, and if he had been conscious, he would've done so when she was trapped.

Sometimes being human sucks.

CHAPTER 10

"Are you sure you should move?" Aislinn cradled Keenan's head in her lap. He seemed more embarrassed than injured, more upset than angry.

The imprint of her lips on his forehead and his cheeks glowed faintly in the dimness of the room. It made her feel guilty, this proof that she'd touched him. It wasn't an intimate kiss. It wasn't new. They'd discovered that her kiss healed him when she'd still been a mortal awaiting the test to be Summer Queen. But, in the wake of their recent kiss and in light of the shaming thoughts she'd had about him when she was captive to Niall, she felt embarrassed.

Keenan sat up and pulled away from her, forcing more distance between them than normal. "I don't need coddling."

"Are you okay? Dizzy?" she asked.

He sat on the floor beside her, but out of reach. He glared

at Seth. "Seth must be thrilled."

She froze. "Don't do that. Don't blame Seth for Niall's anger."

"Niall punched me *for Seth*." He didn't stand yet, and she was pretty certain it was because he wasn't sure he could.

"And I went after Niall *for you*."

Keenan smiled—cruelly. "Well, then."

She glanced over at Seth, who had stopped midway across the room. He wasn't likely to approach when he could tell that she and Keenan were arguing. *He* never treated her as anything less than an equal. "If you'd seen Niall . . . what he . . . when—"

Keenan was the one who froze this time. "When he *what*?"

"Niall is stronger than me." She crossed her arms over her chest. "If Niall wanted to hurt me, he could've. There wasn't anything I could do to stop him."

"Did he hurt you?" He was suddenly closer, running his hands over her arms, reaching toward her as if to pull her to him.

And I want him to. It was instinct. It was also unnecessary: she was fine.

"Stop. I'm bruised, but that's all . . . and that was my fault as much as his." She blushed. "I lost my temper. He tried to walk away, but you were hurt and I was . . . furious."

She recounted what he'd missed.

"And what did you feel against the shadows?" Keenan's

tone wasn't hurt or angry now. It was a challenge, the same challenge he'd raised in their prior conversation. "What did you lust for?"

She ducked her head. "That doesn't . . . I'm not . . . telling you. That wasn't real. It was just a result of some perversion of—"

The words stopped, lies unable to be spoken.

"What you feel for me is *not* a perversion, Aislinn. Is it so hard to admit that? Can't you give me that much?" He pushed, as if hearing her say it would change anything, as if that admission mattered as much as the Dark King striking him, as if their personal situation was of tantamount importance.

It isn't.

"You already know the answer to that—and it doesn't change *anything*. I love Seth." With that, she stood and crossed the room. She tried to tuck that whole uncomfortable topic away as she went toward Seth.

He wasn't happy either; it was plain on his face.

"He okay?" Seth asked grudgingly as they sat down at a battered table the guards had commandeered for them.

"His pride's not, but his head seems to be."

"You?" Seth didn't push or hover. He trusted her enough to know she would've come to him if she needed something.

"Scared."

"Niall's . . ." He shook his head. "I don't think he'd hurt you. Not really, but when you were in there, I wasn't really sure. You looked scared when he pushed you against that cage thing. What *was* that?"

"Dark Court energy, like my sunlight and heat or Don's ice. Niall's is other stuff. Fear, anger, and lust. Dark Court things. Like Niall causes."

"Lust?" Seth repeated.

She blushed.

And Seth said the words she wouldn't: "But not for Niall."

He glanced at Keenan, and she saw the sadness in Seth's eyes. Then he reached out and took Aislinn's hand.

No pressure. Even now. He trusted her.

The band had started as they sat there; Damali sang something about freedom and bullets. Her voice had an intensity that could carry the band good places, but the lyrics were dismal.

Silently, Keenan joined them at the table. He didn't look any happier than she felt—or than she suspected Seth felt—with them all being there together.

When the song ended, Seth looked at him and said, "You okay?"

"Yes." Keenan pressed his lips together in a cross between a grimace and a smile.

The next song began, sparing them from further attempts at civility.

Typically Aislinn wasn't girlfriend-y in public, but she moved over to sit on Seth's lap. He slid his arms around her and held on. Somehow, despite the noise of the band, it

felt like a silence between them. It wasn't anger, but it was
weighty all the same. They both knew things were more
precarious than either of them liked.

Across from her, Keenan caught her gaze before he left.
It wasn't a look she could—*or wanted to*—understand.
Hurt? Angry? It didn't really matter. All that she knew was
that there was a tugging sensation, a compulsion to follow Keenan if he went too far from her side. Usually, if
she ignored it long enough, it dulled—or maybe she simply
stopped noticing it so much—but those first few moments
after he left were horrible. It was growing worse each day. It
was like refusing to breathe when she'd just surfaced from
too long underwater, like telling her heart to stop its rapid
rhythms when she'd been kissed almost long enough.

Seth brushed his fingertips over her cheek. "Everything's
going to be okay."

"I want it to be." She leaned in to Seth's touch. It was
better to just be honest. Seth was her anchor, the only thing
that made sense most days.

I really can tell him anything. He gets me. She felt foolish for keeping things from him. *Again.* He'd believed her
when she first told him about faeries. He trusted her; she
needed to work harder at returning that unwavering trust.

Seth could read her—not through some strange faery
bond but because he knew her. It wasn't why she loved him,
but it was part of it. His calm, his honesty, his art, his passion, his words—there were more reasons to love him than
she thought possible. Sometimes, it was hard to understand

why he'd choose to be with her.

"Do you want to talk about it?" he asked.

She glanced over her shoulder at him. "I do. Just . . . not here, not right now."

"Right. I'll wait. Again." Seth's earlier frustration flashed on his face for a moment. "Maybe you should go rescue him from Glenn."

"What?" She didn't want to go rescue anyone; she wanted to stay in Seth's arms. She wanted to find a way to tell him something inside her was messed up. She wanted to fix everything.

"Glenn's on the bar tonight. You know he's going to hassle Keenan if one of us isn't over there, and I don't think Keenan would appreciate my presence just now."

"It was Niall, not you. Keenan should know that."

Seth ignored this and said, "Go save your king, Ash. His pride's already wounded, and he's a prick when he's feeling insulted."

Keenan came back first. He handed a beer to Seth. "Aislinn didn't need to follow me."

"We didn't think you needed to be hassled by Glenn," Seth said.

The Summer King looked stiffer than usual. He didn't like the Crow's Nest, but he wouldn't say that. He went where Aislinn wanted him to, did what would make her happy. If it wasn't the same way Seth felt, it might irritate him.

Who I am kidding? It still does.

Keenan sat on the chair, studiously watching the band. They weren't awful, but they didn't merit that sort of attention. Damali might, but the rest of the band was average at best.

Seth wasn't up to trying to pretend things were all right. "I don't know what happened between you two before tonight, but I can probably guess. . . ."

The look Keenan gave him confirmed Seth's fears.

"Right. Here's the thing. If she chooses to give you more than her friendship, it'll suck for me. Probably how you feel now."

Keenan was motionless, but it was much the same way that caged lions became motionless—sizing you up for weakness. For all their feigning humanity, faeries were something Other. Aislinn was Other, and the longer she was with them, the further away from mortal normalcy she'd be.

And from me.

It was easy enough to forget that they weren't human, but Seth was learning to remind himself. Other wasn't bad; it just wasn't the same rules. Keenan seemed more human after so long among them, but if it wasn't for Aislinn's insisting that Seth stay in her life . . . well, neither Seth nor Keenan had any illusions there.

He's thought about it. That objective disregard for Seth's safety flickered in Keenan's words sometimes. *So I can hear it.*

"I see it," Seth said. "You watch her like she's your universe. She feels it too. I don't know if it's a summer thing or what."

"She is my queen." Keenan spared a glance for Seth, and then he resumed watching the band. If Seth thought Damali was actually that interesting to Keenan, he might worry for her.

"Yeah. I got that a while ago. I know you haven't been real forthcoming on making it easier for me either."

"I've done everything she's asked or suggested."

"With her few months of experience in your world? Real helpful, that." Seth snorted. "But I get it. I don't particularly enjoy helping you either. I will if she asks it of me."

"So we understand each other." Keenan nodded, still staring at Damali. His attention had caused her to shine: her vocals were spot on.

"I hope we do." Seth let all the anger he'd kept in check plain in his tone then. "But just to be clear—if you take advantage of her or manipulate her into something she doesn't want, I'll gladly use whatever influence I have."

In other circumstances, Keenan's look of derision would be funny; it was equal to the affronted expression that Tavish wore all the time. "You think you can outwit me?"

Seth shrugged. "I don't know. Niall knocked you out to assure my safety. Donia isn't seeing you, last I heard. Chela and Gabe seem fond of me. I'm willing to try if I need to." He poked at his lip ring as he weighed his words. "If she makes a fair choice, that's one thing. If you use whatever this faery bond is to try to control her, that's altogether different."

Keenan's smile was far from human then. He looked every bit the ageless creature he was—utterly emotionless in his voice and guise, sitting in a mundane room like an ancient god among the rabble. "You do realize I could have you killed. By morning, you could be nothing more than a pile of charred ashes. Your very presence weakens my court. After centuries of waiting, I am unbound, but my queen is weakened by clinging to her mortality—because of you. She is drawn away from what would strengthen me—by you. I don't have any logical reason not to want you dead sooner than you already will be."

Seth leaned forward so his words wouldn't be overheard. "Are you going to order my death, Keenan?"

"Would you kill for her?"

"Yeah. *For* her, especially if it was you"—Seth smiled—"but not as a way to win her attention. That's weak, and she deserves better than that."

"She'll mourn you sooner or later. The worry over you saddens her. The maudlin focus on your brief life span distracts her. It would strengthen my court if you were gone already and she were truly my queen. . . ." Keenan's words faded as he looked at Seth with an unreadable expression on his face.

"If you have me killed, she'd find out, though. Would *that* strengthen your court?" Seth looked away to watch Aislinn walk through the room toward them. She frowned as she saw them but didn't rush or do anything obvious.

He turned back to Keenan, who was lion-still again, watching Aislinn too.

The Summer King spoke quietly, "No. Your death by my word would upset her. Tavish recommended it, despite the complications, but I think the dangers to my court outweigh the benefits of your death. I cannot order your removal—tempting though it may be. It would push her further away."

Seth's heartbeat sped. Suspecting your death had been discussed so coldly was one thing; hearing it confirmed was entirely different. "Is that why you don't do it?"

"In part. I had hope that I could be with Donia, at least for a while. Instead, Aislinn and I are both worried over the lovers we can't keep. It's not the way Summer should feel. Our court is about frivolity, impulse, and that dizzy blur of pleasure. It's not love I feel for Aislinn, but our court would be stronger if she were mine. Every instinct I have pulls me toward her. It drives a wedge between Donia and me. We all know that if you weren't in the way Aislinn *would* be mine."

Seth watched the Summer King watch Aislinn. His mouth was dry as he prompted, "But?"

With effort, Keenan pulled his gaze away from Aislinn. "But I don't kill mortals . . . even those who stand in my way. For now, I'll deal with the way things are. It won't last forever." He sounded a little sad as he said it, but Seth wasn't sure if Keenan was sad that Seth was in the way or that he *wouldn't* always be in the way. "So I'll wait."

Later, Seth would ponder it, but just then, Aislinn slid into his arms.

Aislinn motioned toward Damali. "She's good."

They both murmured assent.

"It makes me want to dance." She swayed in his lap. "Do you want to?"

Before Seth could reply, Keenan reached over and touched her hand. "I'm sorry, but I need to leave."

"Leave? Now? But—"

"I'll see you tomorrow." He stood slowly, moving with the faerie elegance that seemed to announce their Otherness. "The guards will be outside to escort you . . . wherever you go tonight."

"Seth's," she whispered. Her cheeks flushed.

Keenan's expression didn't change. "Tomorrow then."

And then he was gone, moving faster than mortal eyes—even Sighted ones—could follow.

CHAPTER 11

Seth wasn't surprised when Aislinn became restless a few songs later and wanted to walk. She'd been that way before she became a faery. That was one of the things that hadn't changed—like keeping things from him. She'd always had to keep secrets, and her first instinct when she feared rejection was to continue to do so. Understanding why she was secretive didn't mean accepting it, though. They'd only gone a block or so when he asked, "Are we going to talk about what's bothering you?"

"Do we have to?"

He raised his brow and stared at her. "You get that I love you, right?" Seth leaned his head against hers as he said it. "No matter what."

She paused, tensed, and then her words tumbled out too fast. "Keenan kissed me."

"Figured that." He kept an arm around her as they resumed walking.

"What?" Her skin flickered as her anxiety spiked.

"He was being weird. You were weird." Seth shrugged, but he didn't alter his pace. "I'm not blind, Ash. I see it. Whatever this tie is between you two is getting worse as summer comes."

"It is. I'm trying to ignore it, but it's not easy. But I will. Are you *mad*?"

He paused, weighing his words before telling her. "No. Not pleased, but I expect it of him. It's not about what he did. Tell me what *you* want."

"You."

"Forever?"

"If there were a way." She held tight to his waist like he was going to vanish if she let go. It hurt. His skin was mortal, and hers wasn't. "There isn't, though. I can't make you *this*."

"What if I want that?" he asked.

"It's not something you should want. *I* don't want to be *this*. Why would—" She slipped in front of him and looked up at him. "You know I love you. I love only you. If I didn't have you in my life . . . I don't know what I'm going to do when you"—she shook her head—"but we don't have to think about this. I told him no when he kissed me. I told him that I love you, and he's only my friend. I resisted him when I was mortal, and I'll do it now."

"But?"

"It's like a pressure inside me sometimes. Like being away from him is *wrong*." She looked desperate, like she wanted him to tell her the lies that she was trying to tell herself. "It'll get easier with time. It has to. This being-a-faery thing is new. And his being unbound is new. It's just . . . it *has* to get easier with time or practice or something, right?"

He couldn't tell her what she wanted to hear. They both knew it wasn't getting easier.

She looked down and lowered her voice, "I asked Donia . . . before. About you becoming *this*. She told me it was a curse, and she couldn't do it, and neither could I . . . or Keenan. Keenan didn't change me or the Summer Girls. Neither did Beira. That was something Irial did. It's not something we can do."

"So . . . Niall . . ."

"Maybe. I don't know." She leaned into his embrace, but her words weren't ones he wanted to hear. "But maybe it's better this way. You getting cursed so we can be together isn't cool. What if you hate me someday? Look at Don and Keenan. They're stuck dealing with each other forever now, and they fight all the time. Look at the Summer Girls. They'll wither away without their king. Why would I want that for you? I love you . . . and being this . . . My mother died rather than be a faery."

"But I want to be near you always," he reminded her.

"But you'll lose everyone else, and . . ."

"I want forever with you." Seth lifted her chin so he was able to look directly into her eyes. "The rest will fall into place if I can be with you."

She shook her head. "Even if I didn't think it was a bad

idea, *I* can't make it happen."

"If you could . . ."

"I don't know," she admitted. "I don't want to have power over you, and I don't trust Niall, even if he could . . . and . . ." She was getting more and more upset as she spoke. Sparks flickered from her body. "I do want you with me, but I don't want to lose you. What if you were like the Summer Girls? Or—"

"What if I wasn't? What if I die because some faery is stronger than me?" Seth asked. "What if you need me and I can't be there because I'm mortal? Being only halfway in your world makes me vulnerable."

"I know. Tavish says I should set you free."

"I'm not a pet to be released into the wild. I'm in love with you, and I know what I want." Seth kissed her, hoping his emotions were as clear in his touch as he was trying to make them in his words. The sun sparks tingled against his skin—electricity and heat and some weird energy that mortal words couldn't name.

Forever. Like this. It was what he wanted; it was what she wanted too.

He pulled away, half drunk on her touch. "Forever together."

She was smiling then. "Maybe there's another way. We can . . . Tell me we'll be okay either way?"

"We will," he promised. "We'll figure it out."

He kept one arm around her as they started walking again. It *would* be okay. The Summer King claimed that his objection was to Seth's mortality, to his pulling Aislinn away from her court. If Seth were a true part of the Summer Court, there would be no room for objection—but even as he thought it, Seth knew it wasn't that simple. *It could be.* He'd never wanted anything as much as he wanted forever with Aislinn. He just needed to find a way.

"Riverside?" She glimmered then, her entire body pulsing with sunlight, and he held on to her, his own fallen star. "There's music tonight."

He nodded. He didn't ask how she knew: it called to her. Large gatherings of her faeries were like beacons to her now.

"Can we run?" In her eyes endless blue lakes were shimmering. She might claim to not like being a faery, but part of her liked some of it very much. If Aislinn could set aside her fear of who—*what*—she was now, she'd be happier.

He nodded, and then he held on to her. His feet barely touched the sidewalk, glancing off the earth like they were flying. If he let go, he'd crash horribly, but he wouldn't let go of her, not now, not ever.

When they stumbled to a stop at the bank of the river, she was laughing at the joy of speeding over the earth, at the freedom of who she was and what she'd become.

A band was set up alongside the banks. One of the singers was a merrow. She languished in the water, chirping orders at others on the shore. Her skin was tinted moss green, slightly phosphorescent in the dark. She wore a silver cape over a kelp-strand dress that revealed far more than it covered. From the waist down her body was a scaled fish-tail, but somehow even that looked elegant. Behind her, a trio of male merrows lolled about with kelpies, but unlike her, the other merrows were hideous. Their faces were those of catfish, whiskered mouths gaping open as they watched their sister with a protectiveness that made Seth wonder if the Dark Court faeries really were the ones to fear. Water-dwelling faeries were creepier.

But then she started to sing, and her brothers joined in on a chorus, and Seth forgot that they were anything other than glorious.

It wasn't a language he knew. It wasn't even a proper song, just them preening a little. Every cell in his body seemed to struggle to find a way to align with that music. His breathing found their rhythm. It wasn't glamour; his charm protected him from that. They were just that good.

He and Aislinn stood silently, lost in the sound and the feel of the music. The notes lifted them, stealing their secrets, their souls, and spinning them into the air and water where pain was gone. There were no worries. There was no fear. It was every perfect moment filling him until his skin couldn't contain it.

Then the music stopped.

The spell broke; gravity returned to his spirit and anchored him to the earth. Their music was like that, lifting you away from the world only to drop you without warning. The drop ached; the absence was like a physical blow.

"They're amazing," Aislinn whispered.

"More than." Seth looked away from the merrows. The only time he and Aislinn could find a space to sit was between songs. When the music began, it was either stand transfixed or dance. He suspected that Aislinn could resist the pull of the songs, but he couldn't. Faery music was all-consuming.

They'd taken only a couple steps when a skogsrå caught Seth's attention. Of all the fey creatures he'd met, skogsrås were among the most unsettling. They existed to tempt; it was their sole purpose. Backless and hollow inside—literally and figuratively—skogsrås' allure was in their neediness. That space was a hungry emptiness both mortal and faery found difficult to resist. Without the charm Niall had given him, Seth wasn't sure how he'd overcome the temptation.

The skogsrå, Britta, blew him a kiss.

Aislinn tightened her hold on his hand but didn't comment.

Seth didn't react. He nodded but made no encouraging gestures. The music nights were held in areas declared neutral territory for the event, so the skogsrås would all be bolder. Truth be told, Britta would probably be bold regardless of where they were. Any faery strong enough to be solitary but linger where there were several courts in conflict was not to be dismissed lightly.

Britta walked toward them. Neutral ground meant they were all equal here. Seth liked that, but the tension in Aislinn's body made clear that right now she wasn't liking it.

A few steps away, Britta tripped, and without thinking, Seth caught her. In doing so one of his hands slid over the space where her back should be. Even though the thin shirt she wore covered most of that void, he still felt the tug of that empty space.

"Nice save, love." She kissed his cheek with a familiarity that was not earned. Then she looked at Aislinn. "Queenie."

As she sauntered off, Aislinn murmured, "I'm never going to get comfortable around some of them, am I?"

"You will," he reassured her. "We both will."

"Things weren't easier before, but it seemed like they made more sense." She rested her head against him.

"It'll all make sense again. You're new to this," he said.

She nodded, and he suspected that it was because she couldn't answer without trying to twist her words into a misdirection so she sounded less afraid than she was. He was afraid too. If he told her the things Keenan had said, if he told her how much she really hurt him when she forgot her strength, it'd push her away when he wanted to pull her closer. He wanted closer to her, but until she figured out who she was and he found a way to become not just a mortal caught in a world of faeries, distance was inevitable.

Then the merrows began singing in earnest. Musicians joined in from along the river's edge and from in the trees and farther away in the darkness where mortal eyes couldn't see them. Thrumming beats and lilting piping, sounds that weren't made by any instruments mortals had, and voices rising and falling like the fingers of water lapping the shore—pure music was all around them.

Aislinn sighed in contentment. "It's not all bad, is it?"

"Not at all." He felt the music, the purity of it, like it was a tangible thing. The world of Faerie wasn't perfect, but it was so much fuller sometimes. Their casual music was more intense, more enthralling than the music that even the best human musicians could make. No one choreographed the movement of the dancers who interpreted the notes with their bodies; no one directed the musicians who blended together in the darkness.

"Come with me." Aislinn led him to a dead tree.

In the boughs, three ravens perched. For a heartbeat, he was certain their gazes were affixed on him, but Aislinn tugged his hand and he followed, as consumed by her as he was by the music. He thought his heart would beat right through his chest when she let go of his hand. His back was to the singers, but the music swirled around him. In front of him, she was a vision that rivaled their music. She touched a bit of a vine that was twined around the skeletal tree. It grew under her hand, rustling and extending until a hammock-like chair dangled from a branch.

Then she let go of the vine and took his hand again.

As long as he was touching her, seeing her, lost in her,

he could move. The music still held him, but she was more than faery magic. Love can give a person strength to break through glamours and magicks.

"Curl up with me?" she asked.

"With pleasure." He sat back into the vine-net and held his arms open for her.

CHAPTER 12

When Bananach arrived, Donia was sitting in a window seat on the fourth floor watching the stars appear in the sky. It was one of her favorite times of day, when the colors that streaked across the sky faded. Things were neither bright nor dark, but caught somewhere between. That was how life had felt for so long: it could get better or worse. She'd hoped it would get better, but tonight War stood at her gate, seeking her out.

Donia watched Bananach stroll up the path, pausing to grip one of the spiked fence posts. The arrowlike tops of the posts were knife-sharp. Bananach didn't squeeze hard enough to truly wound herself as she stood staring at the house.

Why are you here?

Donia hadn't spent enough time studying the strong semi-solitary faeries. She'd had no reason to do so. But in the past few months, she'd been observing them as much as she could, reading Beira's files of old correspondence with various solitary fey and with the heads of other courts. The Dark Court, in many ways, made far more sense to her than the other courts. Keenan's Summer Court was a fledgling court now. They were still forming an identity. Despite the long history of the court, it was being made new by the recent discovery of Keenan's lost queen. Sorcha's High Court was reclusive and unwilling to interact with anyone outside her realm in any but the most minimal ways. The Dark Court was an elaborate network of criminal enterprises. During Beira's time, Irial had sold whatever drugs were in vogue. His fey had ties to celebrated crime and petty enterprises. He himself owned a string of adult clubs and fetish bars that catered to almost every kink. Some of that had changed when Niall took over the Dark Court. Like Irial, the new Dark King did not cross some lines, but he had more of them. Bananach, however, had no lines. She had only one goal, one purpose—the chaos and bloodshed of war.

As Donia stared down at War through the dingy window, the amoral, single-minded faery stood, eyes closed, and smiled.

Behind her, Evan tapped lightly on the door. "Donia?"

He entered, filling the dusty room with the woodsy scent that clung to him. "Aaaah, you see already that she is here."

Donia didn't look away from the window as Evan came to stand at her back. "What does she want of us?"

"Nothing we want to give her." Evan shivered.

Donia didn't think that having her faeries, even her Head of the Guard, around was a wise move. War would overcome any solitary guard—and often entire platoons—without effort. It was better to not set temptation before her. It was better to avoid contact entirely, but that wasn't an option today.

Donia said, "I'll see her alone."

Evan bowed and left as Bananach came racing up the stairs.

Once in the room, the raven-faery settled herself in the center of the rug. She sat cross-legged as if at a campfire—dressed in bloodstained fatigues, perfumed with the scent of ashes and death—and patted the floor. "Come."

Donia watched the more-than-slightly-mad faery carefully. Bananach might appear friendly in this moment, but War didn't come calling for no reason. "I've no business with you."

"Shall I tell what business I have with you then?" Bananach gestured around the room, and screams rose from the silence that reigned over Donia's domain. Faery and mortal voices intertwined in a raucous cry that forced tears to Donia's eyes. Smoky faces hovered and blinked out in the room. Bleeding corpses trampled by faery feet appeared—only to be replaced by grotesque misshapen limbs reaching through windows. Those images gave way to montages of past battles in fields where the grass was stained red and homes burned. Flickering among these were glimpses of mortals sickened by plague and famine.

"Lovely possibilities come to us." Bananach sighed as she looked at the stark corners of the room where her rendered images flashed to almost-life. "With you on my side, so much can be done sooner."

The red-stained grass vanished as a new image appeared: Keenan stretched out under the faint image of Donia. They were on the bare floor where they'd once made love. As Donia watched, she saw herself on the floor entangled in Keenan's arms. The image wasn't real, but it gave her pause.

> *He was frostburnt; she was blistered.*
>
> *She spoke to him, said words she had said over and over, words she'd once swore never to tell him again. "I love you."*
>
> *He sighed a name not hers. "Aislinn . . ."*
>
> *Donia rose.*
>
> *"I can't do this, Keenan," she whispered. Snow squalls rolled into the room.*
>
> *He followed her, pleading forgiveness yet again. "Don . . . I didn't mean . . . I'm sorry. . . ."*
>
> *Her illusory doppelgänger buried her hands in Keenan's stomach, stabbing him.*
>
> *He fell.*

Sunlight flared, briefly blinding her even though it was illusion.

"You are just like Beira," Bananach's words came out as a sigh. "Just as tempestuous, just as ready to give me my chaos."

Donia couldn't move. She sat staring at the shimmering vision of herself with hands red with Keenan's blood.

"I worried, feared you'd be different." Bananach crooned the words. "Beira took so much longer to reach the point of striking the last Summer King. Not you."

The red-handed Donia stood over Keenan, watching him bleed. He had rage in his eyes.

"That hasn't happened." Donia called every reserve of Winter's calm to the forefront. "I have not hurt Keenan. I love him."

Bananach crowed. It was an ugly sound, breaking the peace of Donia's home. "A thing I am grateful for, Snow Queen. If you were cold inside, you wouldn't have the cruelty of Winter that we need to get things in place."

"Why tell me this?"

"Tell you what?" Bananach's head tilted in small increments until the angle of it was grotesque.

"If you tell me what it will take to start your war, why would I do it?" Donia crossed and uncrossed her ankles. She stretched, briefly letting her eyes drift shut as if she was nonplussed by the horrors Bananach brought in her wake. It wasn't very convincing.

Battle drums rose like a wall of thunder around them.

Screams pierced the rhythms of that drumming. Then the sound ended abruptly, leaving only the melancholy music of bagpipes, purer for the chaos that had preceded them.

"Perhaps I want you not to stab the kingling." Bananach grinned. "Perhaps that would stop my lovely destruction. . . . Your action can lead to the same upheaval Beira's killing Miach caused."

"Which action?"

Bananach snapped her jaw with a decisive clack. "One of them. Perhaps more."

Donia winced as the illusory figures continued their conflict. Her doppelgänger was struck again and again by a sun-and-rage-filled bleeding Summer King. Then, the scene looped back to the moment where Keenan said Aislinn's name, but this time Donia struck him until he stretched motionless on the floor.

"There are so many lovely answers to your question, Snow." Bananach crooned the words. "So many ways you can give us bloody resolutions."

Again the scene unfolded.

> She spoke to him, said words she had said over and over, words she'd once swore never to tell him again. "I love you."
>
> He sighed. "I love you, but I can't be with you."

Donia couldn't look away.

Once more the scene began.

She spoke to him, said words she had said over and over, words she'd once swore never to tell him again. "I love you."

He sighed a name not hers. "Aislinn . . ."

"I can't do this, Keenan," she whispered. Snow squalls rolled into the room.

He struck her. "It was just a game. . . ."

This time they both struck out at each other until the room was filled with steam. In the steam, corpses appeared again, growing seemingly more solid as the moments passed. In the center of the carnage, Bananach stood like the gleeful carrion crow she was.

"Why?" It was the only word left to Donia. "Why?"

"Why do you freeze the earth?" Bananach paused, and when Donia didn't reply, she added, "We all have a goal, Winter Girl. Yours and mine are destruction. You accepted this when you took Beira's court as your own."

"That's not what I want."

"Power? Him to suffer for hurting you?" Bananach laughed. "Of course it's what you want. All I do is find the threads in your actions that will give me what I want. I *see* them"—she waved at the room—"none of these are my possibilities. They are all yours."

CHAPTER 13

The next week seemed almost normal for Aislinn: things with Seth were right again, Keenan hadn't pushed her boundaries, and court things seemed calm. She couldn't continue ignoring Keenan, and it was becoming almost physically painful to stay so much away from him, so Aislinn had decided to simply pretend that the awkwardness of last week hadn't happened. She might've been avoiding being alone with Keenan the past couple of days, but aside from a few very pointed glances when she called Quinn or Tavish into a conversation they didn't truly need to be a part of . . . and okay, maybe a few very transparent moments of sudden needs for "girl bonding" with the Summer Girls, Keenan pretended not to notice her evasiveness. He merely waited as she held her faeries to her like a shield. She enjoyed time with them, Eliza especially, but that didn't explain away her need to go dancing in the park the moment Keenan came too near.

Totally obvious. It was apparent to everyone, but no one had mentioned it. Aside from Keenan and Seth, no one had enough comfort with her to do so. She was their queen, and right now, that gave her an extra bit of privacy.

They all see that something is up though. They are unsettled by it. She had promised herself that she would be a good queen. Upsetting them all was not what a good queen should do.

With a bit of a tremble in her hand, Aislinn tapped on the study door. "Keenan?" She pushed it open. "Are you free?"

He had her charts spread out in front of him on the coffee table. Music played softly in the background—one of her older CDs, actually, Poe's *Haunted.* She'd picked it up at the Music Exchange one afternoon with Seth.

Keenan looked at her and then made a point of looking beyond her. "Where's your safety team?"

She closed the door. "I gave them the afternoon off. I thought I could be around you . . . that we could talk."

"I see." He looked back at her charts. "You have a good idea here, but we're not going to get very far with the desert area."

"Why?" She didn't bother commenting on his subject change. She wasn't entirely sure she wanted to talk about it either, but they needed to.

"Rika lives there. She was one of the Winter Girls." Keenan frowned. "Far too much like Don. She has issues with me."

"You say that like it's surprising." She stood next to the sofa, nearer him than she should be, but she wasn't going to let whatever weirdness had happened control her.

"It is." Keenan leaned back on the sofa, propped his feet up on the coffee table, and folded his hands. "They act like I set out to hurt them. I *never* wanted anyone hurt . . . except Beira and Irial."

"So they should just forgive and forget?" Aislinn had avoided this topic for months. She'd avoided a lot of topics, but sooner or later they had to sort it all out. Eternity was an awfully long time to let things simmer. "We all lost so many things when you chose—"

"We?" he interrupted.

"What?" She pulled a chair over and sat down.

"You said, '*We* all lost so many things.' You were including yourself with the Summer and Winter Girls."

"No, I . . ." She paused and blushed. "I did, didn't I?"

He nodded.

"I *am* one of them. We, all the ones you chose, lost a lot." She ducked her head, her hair falling forward like a curtain she could hide behind. "It's not like I didn't gain some amazing things too. I get that. Really."

His expression was unusually closed to her. "But?"

"But it's hard. Being this. I swear I'm never going to get my feet to stay under me. Grams is going to die. Seth—" She stopped herself from even uttering that sentence. "I'll lose everyone. I'm not going to die, and they are."

He lifted a hand as if to reach for her, and then lowered it. "I know."

She took a couple calming breaths. "It's hard not to be angry about that. Your choosing me means that I lose the people I love. I'll be around forever, watching them age and die."

"It means I lose the person I love too. Donia will only be in my life as long as your heart is elsewhere," Keenan admitted.

"Don't." Aislinn cringed at hearing him say such things so casually. "That's not fair . . . to *anyone*."

"I know." He was as still as she'd ever seen him. The sun was rising in the oasis she could see in his eyes. "I never wanted it to be the way it's been. Beira and Irial bound my powers, hid them away. What was I to do? Let summer die? Let the earth freeze until all the mortals and summer fey perished?"

"No." The reasonable part of her understood. She knew that there weren't many choices other than the ones he'd made, but she still hurt inside. Logic didn't undo sorrow or fear or any of it, not really. She'd just found Seth, and he was already drifting out of her grasp. *He'll die.* She thought it. She couldn't say it, but she thought it more than once in a while. Years from now, centuries from now, she'd still be this, and he'd be dust inside the earth. *How can I not be angry?* If she weren't a faery, she wouldn't be facing a future without Seth.

"So what would you have done differently, Aislinn? Would you have let the court die? If Irial bound *your* powers, could you shrug it off and let humanity and *your court* wither and die?"

In Keenan's eyes she could see a dying star, a dark orb with a few desperate pulses of flickering light. As she stared, speechless, she saw tiny stars all around that dying sun; they were already lifeless in a growing void. She didn't mean to love her court; if he'd told her months ago that she'd feel like this toward them, she wouldn't have believed him. She'd felt a fierce protectiveness toward them, though, from the moment she became their queen. The Summer Court needed to grow stronger. She was trying to take what little experience she had and her research of politics and governments to help them grow stronger. She was trying to slowly press back against the imbalance that Donia's court still held. Her court, her faeries, the well-being of the earth— these were more than choices. She believed in them. Feeling as she did now, could she have done differently had she been in his position? Could she have let Eliza die? Could she watch the cubs all freeze to death?

"No. I wouldn't have," she admitted.

"Don't think for a moment that I wanted what has happened to the Winter Girls and the Summer Girls." He moved then, leaning forward on the edge of the sofa, and caught her gaze. "I've spent longer berating myself for what I've had to do than you will ever know. I wanted"—he looked at her as more stars, barely flickering in the void, formed in his eyes—"each one to be *you*. And when they weren't, I knew I was condemning them to a slow death if I didn't find you."

She sat silently. *He was my age when this started. Making those choices. Hoping.*

"I'd give them all back their mortality if I could, but even that wouldn't repair what they've lost." Keenan started stacking the papers on the coffee table. "And even if I could make them mortal again, I wouldn't be willing to risk offering that same thing to *you* for fear of it remaking Beira's curse, so even then I'd be left with the weight of knowing that I've taken the mortality of the one who saved me. You're my savior, and I can't make you happy."

"I'm not—"

"You are. And it puts us in something of an awkward relationship, doesn't it?"

"We'll get it sorted out," she whispered. "We have forever, right?" She tried to lighten her tone, to soothe him. This wasn't the conversation she wanted to have at all, but it was the one they'd needed to have for a while now.

"We do." He had resumed the motionless posture he'd had when the conversation began. "And I'll spend it doing whatever I can to make you happy."

"That's not what I was . . . I mean . . . I'm not looking for you to do something to 'make up' for what had to be. I just . . . I'm scared of losing them. I don't want to be alone."

"You aren't. We'll be together for eternity."

"You're my *friend*, Keenan. That thing that happened

the other day? It cannot happen. It shouldn't have happened." She was so tense, muscles clenched so tightly that she couldn't relax her body to unfold her legs from underneath her. "I need you . . . but I don't love you."

"You wanted me to touch you."

She swallowed against the lie she wanted to whisper and admitted, "I did. Once you reached out your hand, I didn't want anything else."

"So what do you want me to do?" He sounded unnaturally calm.

"Don't reach out." She bit down on her lip until she could feel her already cracked skin bleed.

He pulled his hand through his copper hair in frustration, but he nodded. "I will try. That's all I can say and still be truthful."

She shivered. "I'm going to talk to Donia tonight. You love Donia."

"I do." Keenan looked as confused as she'd felt. "That doesn't change what I feel when I see you or think of you or am near to you. You can't tell me you don't feel the same way."

"Love and desire aren't the same."

"Are you saying that all I feel is simple desire? Is that all you feel?" His arrogance was back, as surely as it had been when they first met and she was rejecting his advances.

"It's not a challenge, Keenan. This isn't me running."

"If you gave us a chance—"

"I love *Seth*. I . . . he's my heart. If I could find a way to have him with me for always without being selfish, I would. I'm not going to pretend that I don't feel a pull to be near you. You're my *king*, and I need you to be my friend, but I don't want a relationship with you. I'm sorry. You knew that when I became your queen. Nothing has changed. It's not going to as long as I have him, and I want . . ." She paused. Saying the words she'd been thinking felt so final, but she said it: "I want to find a way to make Seth one of us. I want him with me forever."

"No." It wasn't a reply: it was a king's command.

"Why?" Her heart thudded. "He wants to stay with me . . . and I want to—"

"Donia thought she wanted to be with me forever too. So did Rika. And Liseli . . . and Nathalie . . . and . . ." He gestured around the room, empty but for the two of them. "Where are they?"

"It's different. Seth's different."

"So would you have him be as the Summer Girls? Would you see him die if he left you?" Keenan looked angry. "You just finished telling me that you resent me for changing you. So do many, many others for my changing them. No. Do not pursue this."

"He *wants* this. We can make it work." Aislinn heard him voice the same fears she'd had, but she'd hoped that Keenan would tell her she'd worried foolishly, that there was a way.

"No, Ash. He thinks he does, but being changed would put him in thrall to you, make him your subject. He wouldn't truly want that. Neither would you. I believed the Summer Girls wanted to be with me forever. Many of them believed it too. The Winter Girls believed it enough to suffer for my mistakes. Let it go. Faerie never offers a mortal what they truly seek, and cursing a loved one . . ." The Summer King looked far older than her in that moment. "It's not called a curse because it's beautiful, Aislinn. If you love Seth, you'll treasure him while he's in your life and then let him go. If I'd had other choices—"

Aislinn stood up. "That's what you expected all along, isn't it? Him to go away not long after I changed. You knew I'd feel like this toward you."

"Mortals aren't meant to love faeries."

"So agreeing to my terms wasn't any big deal, right? Seth and I will fall apart and you . . . you'd just . . . No."

Keenan stared up at her, and she thought back to Denny's comments on experience and age and admitted to herself that Denny had had a very good point. If Keenan didn't let up, what would that mean for her? He'd spent most of nine hundred years romancing girl after girl. They all succumbed.

And none of them were his queen.

His look was sorrowful, but his words weren't any gentler. "It's better to love someone and know they go on to happiness than to destroy them. Cursing someone you love is not a kindness, Aislinn. I regretted it each time."

"Seth and I are different. Just because Donia's pushing you away doesn't mean it can't work for me. It could still work for you two. You can sort this out."

"I wish you were right—or that you accepted that I am. Why do you think Don's pushing me away, Ash? Why do you think Seth wants to be cursed? They see what you refuse to admit. You and I are inevitable." Keenan's smile was rueful. "I'm not wrong, and I won't help you make a mistake like this."

She all but ran from the room.

And like she had when she was still mortal, she needed the help of the faery who loved Keenan. Donia's forgiving him for whatever mistake he made would convince him that love could make things right. Then maybe he'd help her. At the very least, he'd stop pursuing her if he had Donia's love. Donia *had* to be with Keenan.

Everything will be fine once Donia takes him back.

The trip to Donia's house was a blur. It wasn't until Aislinn stood alongside a quiet street on the outskirts of town that she admitted how many kinds of fear she felt— not just of what would happen if Donia rejected Keenan for good, but of what would happen when Aislinn went inside the Winter Queen's gorgeous Victorian estate. They had a tentative friendship, but that didn't mean that Donia couldn't be terrifying. Winter hurt, and Donia's home was always Winter.

Winter fey moved soundlessly through a thorn-heavy garden; icy trees and sun-capped shrubs made the yard look out of place among its verdant neighbors. As Aislinn had walked down the street, she'd seen dogs lazing on stoops, a girl sunning herself in languid bliss, and more flowers than she'd seen growing outside in her entire life. Beira's death and Keenan's unbinding had brought a balance that was letting life flourish. But in this yard, the frost would never melt; mortals passing on the street would still look away. No one—mortal or fey—crossed the Winter Queen's frigid lawn without her consent. Consent she'd denied Keenan. *What am I doing here?*

Keenan needed Donia; they loved each other, and Aislinn needed them to remember that. Once-mortals could love faeries.

As Aislinn crossed the yard, the frost-heavy grass thawed under her feet. Behind her, she heard the crackling as the ice re-formed instantly. This was Donia's domain. It was where she was at her strongest. *And where I am weakest.* After centuries of Beira declaring it as her seat of power, this place existed both inside the lines of Faerie and in the mortal realm, a thing that Keenan had been—and was still—unable to accomplish.

Her skin prickled uncomfortably as she walked through that icy world. Aislinn was an interloper, and Winter was as unpredictable as Summer. Donia might deny it, but Aislinn had spent her life cringing at the ravages of the seemingly endless snows. She'd seen bodies dead and frozen on side streets; the lifeless expressions of pain were things she'd not forget. Aislinn had felt the pain of that ice wielded as a weapon when she and Keenan stood against the last Winter Queen.

That wasn't Donia, Aislinn reminded herself, but it did

no good. Something about the very opposition of their courts made Aislinn want to clutch Keenan's hand in hers, but he wasn't there.

As Aislinn stepped onto the porch, one of the white-winged Hawthorn People opened the door. The faery was soundless in her movement. She did not speak as Aislinn came through the doorway and shivered in the chill that pervaded the room. She did not speak as she glided through the dim house.

"Is Donia available?" Aislinn's voice echoed in the stillness, but there was no answer.

She hadn't truly expected one: the Hawthorns were silent. It added to how unsettling they were. They never wandered far from Donia's presence and typically only left the Winter Queen's home if it was necessary to stay at Donia's side. Their red eyes glowed like hearth coals amidst their ash-gray countenances.

The girl led Aislinn past several other quietly watchful Hawthorns who were lingering in the main hall. A fire crackled in one of the rooms they passed; the spitting and popping of logs was the only sound other than the fall of Aislinn's feet on the aged wood of the floor. The Winter Court could move with an eerie stillness that made the back of Aislinn's neck prickle uneasily.

At a door that was closed, the Hawthorn stopped. She made no movement to open the door.

"Do I need to knock?" Aislinn asked.

But the girl turned and drifted away.

"That's helpful." Aislinn reached out a hand just as the door opened inward.

"Come in." Evan motioned her into the room.

"Hey, Evan."

"My queen would speak to you in private," he said, but he followed that with a friendly smile, crinkling his face into an expression that eased Aislinn's tension a bit. Like the Hawthorn People, his berry-red eyes stood out, but where the Hawthorn were tinted like ashes of a dying fire, rowans like Evan were the image of fecundity. His gray-brown barklike skin and dark green leafy hair spoke of trees that moved across the earth untethered. They were creatures of Summer, of her court. It soothed her to see him.

But he was leaving already, and Aislinn was alone with Donia and her wolf, Sasha.

"Donia," Aislinn started, but there suddenly weren't words she could think of to go any further.

The Winter Queen did not make matters easier. She stood watching Aislinn. "I assume *he* sent you."

"He would prefer talking to you himself." Aislinn felt like a small child in the vast unwelcoming room, but Donia hadn't offered her a seat or made any move to sit down herself, so she stood. The rug under their feet was almost threadbare, muted green, and somehow still seemed opulent. Aislinn suspected it was more suited to a museum than daily use.

"I had Evan refuse him entrance." Donia paced away from Aislinn, keeping an exaggerated distance.

It made her anxious that the Winter Queen felt compelled to stay out of reach.

"Can I ask why?"

"You can." Donia seemed unusually unapproachable.

Aislinn forced her irritation and a twinge of fear away. "Okaaay. I'm asking."

"I don't want to see him." Donia smiled, and Aislinn shivered.

"Look. If you want me to go, just tell me. I'm here because he asked and because I like you." Aislinn folded her arms over her chest, as much to keep herself from fidgeting uneasily as to keep from reaching out to smash one of the delicate snow globes that lined a shelf on the wall. They weren't the sort of thing she'd expect Donia to have, but right now didn't seem like the best time to ask about them. Something about Donia's behavior was off, and Aislinn felt herself responding to an unspoken threat.

"Your temper is more obvious as Summer's strength grows." Donia's chilling smile was steadfast. "Like his. You even look like him with that glow pulsing under your skin."

"Keenan is my friend." Aislinn bit down on her lip and curled her fingers tighter into her folded arms, not in nerves but for tiny bits of pain to ground herself.

The Winter Queen walked farther away. She paused at the window and traced her finger over the glass, covering it with frost flowers. She didn't look at Aislinn as she began to speak. "It's like a wound, loving him. He's everything I ever dreamed of. When we are together"—she sighed, a cloud of freezing air that left tiny icicles clinging to the drapes—"I don't care that he could burn me up. In that moment, I'd welcome it. I'd say yes even if it ended me."

Aislinn's temper fled, and she blushed, unprepared for this sort of conversation with Donia.

Donia didn't turn from the glass as she continued, "I've wondered if that's why Miach and Beira were so unable to coexist. I see it, history ready to repeat itself. Don't think I am unaware, Ash."

The Winter Queen turned her back to the window. She leaned against it, framed by the icy lace with which she'd decorated the glass and drapes.

"I'm not judging you. I *want* you to be with Keenan," Aislinn insisted.

"Even if it's a mistake?" Donia's tone wasn't one Aislinn could read. It verged on taunting. "Even if it's history repeating? Even if the consequences are horrific? Would you have us start a war to protect your heart?"

Aislinn couldn't answer. She hadn't really thought much about the fact that Keenan's parents were the Summer King and Winter Queen.

"I wonder now if Beira's killing Miach was unexpected. Summer Kings are so volatile. Winter can be so much calmer." As Donia spoke, a chair of ice formed under her. The edges weren't smooth, but ragged like waves frozen in mid-break.

Aislinn didn't mean to, but she laughed. "Can be? I've

seen the temper in you. Summer *can* be calm too. Whatever
you two have just isn't . . . and I don't think calm is what
either of you would want. I saw him after Solstice. There
were frostbites on his skin, but he was happy."

"You would see those marks, wouldn't you?" Donia gave
her a look that wasn't friendly at all. "Every time I think I
have him out of my system, and then he's sweet or wonderful . . ." She looked wistful. "Do you know what he did?"

Aislinn shook her head.

"He had a gardening company remove the hawthorn . . .
that awful plant that was the scene of every test. It's gone
from here and from the cottage. Not killed, but replanted
away from me." Tiny ice drops clicked as they shattered at
Donia's feet.

"That's sweet. . . ."

"It *is*." Donia's face was a mirror of the feelings Aislinn
often felt for Keenan—the bittersweet mix of affection and
frustration that assailed her more and more—and Aislinn
hated that they had that in common. She hated that they
were in this conversation.

They stayed there, neither going any further, until Donia
said, "It's not going to change my mind. I know he thinks
he might love me, but he thinks he might love you too."

*I wish I could lie. Right now I really wish I could lie to
her.*

"I don't want . . ." Aislinn faltered. She tried again, "We
aren't . . ." The words weren't wholly true: she couldn't pro-
nounce them. Finally, she said, "I am with Seth."

"You are, but he's mortal." Donia didn't look angry. "And Keenan is your king, your partner. I hear it in his voice when he says your name. He never sounded like this about anyone else."

"Except you."

The Winter Queen nodded. "Yes, except me. I know that."

"He wants to see you. He's upset, and you need to—"

"No." Donia stood. "You're in no position to tell me what I *need* to do. My court has held sway over the earth longer than either of us can imagine. They've watched Keenan suffer under Beira's boot for centuries." Donia was motionless, but her eyes were snowblind. "They do not give up power easily, but I ask it of them. I require them to accept that Summer must have more than a few brief days."

"Then you see why you need to work things out."

"So Summer can grow stronger."

"Yes."

"And that's meant to motivate me?" Donia laughed. "The Summer Court despised me for failing to be you. They weren't there to comfort me when I tried to give him his court and failed. . . . Tell me, Ash, why should I care what goes on in your court?"

"Because you love Keenan, and he loves you, and we can have peace if you two sort out whatever you're angry about this time."

"You have no clue who your king truly is, do you?" Donia sounded bemused. "Even though your mother died to avoid being trapped in his court and you've lost your mortality for him, you're still blinded. I'm not. What stands between us is his arrogance and . . . you, Ash."

"I don't want to be between you. I want Seth to be in my life, only Seth. If I could I'd still be mortal and . . . I wish you had been Summer Queen."

"I know. It's part of what keeps me from hating you." Donia smiled, almost affectionately.

"I don't love him," Aislinn blurted hurriedly, as if afraid the words weren't going to be pronounceable, as if it could be almost a lie. "I'm furious with him regularly and . . . I *want* you and him to be together."

"I know that as well."

"Then just be with him."

"I won't be your shield, Ash." An edge of scorn threaded through Donia's voice.

"My . . . ?"

"You can't hide behind me to make sense of whatever you two are trying to sort out." Donia flexed her fingers almost absently, and hoarfrost crept over the walls. Crackling ice covered sconces and faded wallpaper.

"You two had plenty of problems before me." Aislinn felt her skin warming, an inevitable reaction to the dropping temperature in the room. Her own energy tried to push the chill from the air nearest her.

"We did." Snowflakes floated gently to the ground around Donia. "But they were all based in him seeking *you.*"

"I didn't ask for this." Aislinn was advancing on Donia. She needed Donia to see Keenan, needed her to understand. It was what they all needed. "You have to—"

"Don't dictate to me, Aislinn." The Winter Queen sounded perfectly calm. Her stillness was that of newly fallen snow, untouched, undisturbed.

"I didn't come here to fight you." Her sunlight was a weak shield in the Winter Queen's home. *Her palace.* Call it what she would, that's what it truly was, her palace, her seat of power. *And not where I should be.*

"Maybe that was a mistake." Donia's fingertips were points of ice. "Summer began early this year *because I allowed it.*"

"And we appreciate that."

Donia toyed with the ice in and on her hands, clicking the shards together. "Yet you come into my home as if you are stronger, as if what *you* want matters more, as if your court has a voice in my domain. . . ."

Aislinn's temper flared, a blink of sunlight in the icy room, but she still moved back. "I didn't mean it that way. We didn't. I just don't see why you have to be unreasonable."

"Unreasonable? Because what *Summer* seeks must be a good idea?"

Aislinn couldn't answer. It seemed obvious that a stronger Winter Court wasn't the right answer. Hadn't they all thought that? Donia had faced almost certain death at the last Winter Queen's hands because she had thought that, but as they stood there, it seemed clear to Aislinn that Donia's stance had changed.

"If I strike you, he will be furious, despite your insults." Donia took a step forward. "What would he say? Would it keep him from coming to my door, dragging out this hell he puts us through? Would it put things as they should be?"

"I don't know . . . as they 'should be'? What does that mean?" Aislinn wanted to run. Donia *was* stronger; the Winter Court was still stronger.

"This thing between us isn't as simple as it was before you and I became regents. If we fight, our courts are in discord. My court wants that"—Donia caught her gaze and held it—"and I've thought about it. I've imagined it, driving this ice into your sunlit skin. I've thought about striking you. I would resolve this foolish attempt to pretend we're all friends here."

"Donia?" Aislinn watched her warily. As with Niall, the faery Aislinn thought she'd known was replaced with something feral, someone who could—*and would*—injure her. Aislinn stood alone with the Winter Queen in her palace.

"I like you. I remind myself of that often, but there are other factors. . . ." The Winter Queen's words faded away. Snow drifted around her feet. "The Summer Court is not welcome in my Winter."

Despite the ice covering the walls, despite the chill in Donia's voice, Aislinn's temper finally slipped out of her control. "We have no voice in your court, but you can dictate to us?"

"Yes."

"Why should we—"

And Donia was beside her before the words could come out. She put a hand on the center of Aislinn's stomach and pressed ice-tipped fingers into Aislinn's skin. The ice melted as it pierced Aislinn, but as fast as that ice melted, more extended, cutting deeper into Aislinn's stomach. Bits of it broke off and embedded inside her.

Aislinn screamed. The pain was instant, burning holes inside of her, and Aislinn wasn't sure which was from the stabbing and which was from the ice. *Am I going to die here?*

"Why should you listen to my desires?" Donia murmured. Fingers still red with Aislinn's blood, Donia put her hand on Aislinn's chin and tilted her head so they were eye-to-eye. "Because I am stronger, Ash, and you both need to remember that. This balance you want only comes if *I* allow it."

"You stabbed me." Aislinn thought she might vomit. Her body felt clammy. Pain from the ice inside her skin vied with pain from the punctures in her stomach.

"It seemed prudent." Donia's expression was all too similar to the last Winter Queen's: utterly unapologetic and unmoved by the horrific thing she'd just done.

"Keenan will—"

"Be angry. Yes, I know, but"—Donia sighed, an icy cloud of breath that made Aislinn cringe—"your wounds are mild. They won't be next time."

Aislinn put a hand to her stomach, but it was a weak attempt to stop the blood that trickled from the row of holes in her skin. "Keenan and I could retaliate. Is that what you want?"

"No, I want you to stay away from me." Donia handed her a lacy white handkerchief. "Don't come back here until I invite you. *Any* of you."

And with that, Evan came into the room to help Aislinn to the door.

CHAPTER 14

Aislinn didn't lean on Evan as he walked her out of the house. She didn't clutch his arm for stability as she stumbled on the steps. She kept a hand cupped over her wound, as if holding it would lessen the pain.

I am the Summer Queen. I am stronger than this.

It hurt, though. Donia had pierced skin and muscle, and those muscles moved with each step. There was no way to walk without pain. Each step made her want to cry.

That doesn't mean they need to see it.

Faeries loitered in Donia's yard; whisper-white Scrimshaw Sisters drifted over the snow like ghosts. A Hawthorn Girl perched in the boughs of an ice-draped oak. Her scarlet eyes glistened like frozen berries. Something with tattered wings sat beside her. A glaistig stood with her cloven feet in an old-fashioned gunfighter's stance. They all watched Aislinn as she left their queen's palace.

They heard.

In the moment when Donia had struck her, Aislinn had screamed. The sensation of being stabbed wasn't the sort of thing one takes silently. They'd heard her cry out, and now they could see her blood-wet shirt around the cup of her hand.

I am not weak. I am not defeated.

Midway down the edge of the walk, Aislinn pulled herself straight. "You can go."

The rowan's expression was disinterested; the watching faeries were equally nonplussed, but Aislinn wasn't going to give them the satisfaction of seeing her as weak. She lowered her hand and walked to the end of the flagstones. She paused against the pain, leaning on the iron gate that marked the end of the Winter Queen's yard, but in that pausing she reached into her pocket and withdrew her cell phone. Then she pulled a glamour over her bleeding and far too pale body and stepped onto the sidewalk.

Just a little farther.

She made it a block before the tears started to slide down her face. Without even looking at the phone, she pressed and held a button. When he answered, she didn't let him speak. "I need you. Come get me."

Then she hung up and slid to the sidewalk. Her eyes weren't closed, but they were near enough to it that she was worried. *It's not a serious injury. She said so, and faeries don't lie.*

She stared at the ravens that had settled on a ledge on the building across from her, and she pressed another button and held the phone to her ear. She smiled at hearing Seth's voice, even though it was just a recording. At the tone, she said in as clear a voice as possible, "I'm not going to make it for dinner tonight. Something's come up . . . I love you."

She wanted him to come to her, but she was bleeding on the street—a target unable to defend herself against capture or further assault—and he was a mortal. Her world wasn't safe for him. It wasn't safe at all.

Mortals walked past her. They were murmurs of sound and movement against the quiet she found inside her and held on to. Down the street she heard a bus stop. The din of people coming and going grew louder for a few moments. The ravens cried out, their hoarse calls blending into the sounds of the mortal world around her. She leaned her head back against a building, not concerned with the soot and dirt, but with the fact that the cement and brick were warm against her skin. Warmth was what she needed. *Warmth will fix it*, she thought about that in a tumble of words that sounded like a cadence in her mind. *Warmth, heat, summer, sunlight, hot, warmth, heat, summer, sunlight, hot.* He would bring those things.

She shivered. In her mind, she could see the fragments of ice that Donia'd left inside her skin. Slivers of Winter were buried inside her body. A lesson, that's all it was: a lesson and a warning. *Not fatal.* But she wasn't sure. As she sat there in the street, she wondered if she was hurt worse than Donia'd intended. *Warmth, heat, summer, sunlight, hot, warmth, heat, summer, sunlight, hot.* She thought them like a prayer. He would come. He would bring heat and sunlight.

Warmth, heat, summer, sunlight, hot. I am not that injured. I am not. She was. She felt like she was dying. Being a faery was to mean living forever. It wouldn't if he didn't come for her. *Warmth, heat, summer, sunlight, hot. I'm going to die.*

"Aislinn?" Keenan was lifting her. His skin was solid sunlight, and she burrowed tighter into his arms. He was speaking, telling someone something or other. It didn't matter. Droplets of sunshine fell like rain on her face and soaked into her skin.

"Too cold." She was shaking so hard that she thought she might fall, but he held her to him and then the world blurred.

When she woke, Aislinn was not in her bed at home—or in her bed at the loft or in Seth's bed. She looked up at the snarl of vines over her head. Although she'd never seen them from this angle before, she'd stood in the doorway and marveled at the way they twined around Keenan's bed.

"What are they?" She knew he was in the room; it wasn't necessary to look for him. He wouldn't be anywhere else, not now.

"Ash—" he started.

"The vines, I mean. They're not anywhere else in the loft. Just . . . here."

He came to sit on the edge of the ridiculous red-and-gold-brocade thing that covered his far-too-large bed. "They're called 'Cup of Gold.' I like them. I'm sorry we had discord."

She couldn't look at him; it was stupid to feel embarrassed, but she did. The conversation with Donia replayed in Aislinn's mind, as if reexamining it would make it somehow different. The fear came just as quickly. *I could've died.* She wasn't sure if it was true, but when she'd been alone and bleeding, she'd wondered it. "I'm sorry too."

"For what? You weren't asking for anything I didn't expect." Keenan's voice was as warm as his tears had been when he lifted her from the ground. "We're going to work everything out. For now, what matters is that you are home, safe, and once I know who—"

"Donia. Who else?" Aislinn lifted her head up and held his gaze. "Donia stabbed me."

"Don?" He paled. "On purpose?"

Aislinn wished she could lift one brow the way Seth did. "Stabbing isn't usually an *accident*, is it? She pushed ice into my stomach with her fingertips. Cold enough to make me sick . . ." She started to sit up and felt those tiny wounds resist. It wasn't a sharp pain like the stabbing was, but even the duller sensation brought tears to her eyes. She leaned back. "Obviously this faery healing thing is overrated."

"It's because it was Donia." Keenan's tone was even, but the rumble of thunder outside belied his attempts at calm. "She is our opposite, and she is a queen."

"So . . . now what?"

Keenan blanched again. "I don't want war. It's never the first choice."

Aislinn let out the breath she'd been holding. War wasn't something she wanted either, especially not with her court so much weaker than the Winter Court. The thought of her faeries feeling this sort of pain filled her with terror. There'd already been enough upheaval in Faerie with the changing of power in three courts. "Good."

"If it were anyone but Donia, I'd gladly kill over this." He brushed back Aislinn's hair, letting a little extra sunlight into the gesture. "Seeing you there . . . she's attacking my queen and therefore my court."

Aislinn didn't object to his comfort, not now. The feel of that cold inside her body was too recent. For a brief moment, she wished they were close enough that she could ask him to lie down and hold her. It wasn't sexual, or even romantic; it was the idea of having sunlight spill over her. *Warmth, heat, summer, sunlight, hot.* She blushed guiltily as she thought it, though. It would mean something else to him, and she wasn't going there.

"I could help." He looked embarrassed as he gestured at her stomach. "I would've before, but I know how you are about your . . . space . . . especially since . . ."

She plucked at her shirt. It wasn't her bloodied one. "How did I get this on then?"

"Siobhan. She changed your blouse after I checked your wound. She was here, though—when I checked it. She stayed here."

Aislinn took his hand in hers and squeezed. "I trust you, Keenan. Even if you had"—she blushed—"changed my clothes."

And it was true. She might feel uncomfortable with their closeness and be discomforted with his attentiveness, but she didn't think he'd maneuver her into anything she didn't want or violate her. She'd thought that of him when she didn't know him, but in her heart of hearts she believed differently now. *Donia was wrong.*

"So how?" she prompted.

"Just sunlight. Like what you've done for me, but *more.* It'll heal almost as slowly as if you were . . ." His voice faded at the word.

"Mortal. It's okay to say it. I know what I am, Keenan." She realized they were still holding hands and squeezed his again. "If I were mortal, I'd be dead right now."

"If you were mortal, she wouldn't have struck you."

"I'm not so sure. If you cared about the Summer Girls like . . . this, would she have hurt them?" Aislinn hadn't thought Donia so cruel, but as she lay in Keenan's bed with four icy cuts in her, it was hard to hold on to that belief.

At first, Keenan didn't answer. Instead he stared beyond her at the Cup of Gold vine that was twined around the posts of the bed. Blossoms opened up, revealing deep purple star-lines, and tendrils stretched toward him.

"Keenan?" she prompted.

"I don't know. It doesn't matter, though. Not right now."

"What does matter?"

"That she struck my queen." Something new shimmered in the depths of his eyes: swords wavered and flashed.

Perhaps it should frighten her, that glimpse of rage in her king's eyes, but it comforted her. The other emotions she thought she also saw there, the possessiveness and fear and longing, those were the frightening ones. "But you came for me. I'll heal."

He pulled his hand away from hers, tentative now. "Can I make you well?"

"Yes." She didn't ask what he needed to do; that would be a type of doubt, and right now neither of them wanted that doubt in the room. They were friends. They were partners. They could figure the rest out. They had to.

He is why I'm alive right now.

The ice inside would have kept her wound from healing if he hadn't removed it. In time, the loss of blood would've killed her.

Keenan folded back the heavy comforter, taking the decadently soft sheet with it.

She was injured, but still, she felt the awkward tension building. She had an uneasy suspicion that the discomfort wasn't going to be one of pain, but of pleasure.

"Can you lift up your shirt? I need to see the cuts." His voice was shaky, either from fear or something she didn't want to think about.

The door to the rest of the loft was open. They didn't have closed-door privacy, but no one would come near the room with them in it. Their court would accept their not-dating if they continued this way, but it wasn't the preference. That was no secret.

Silently, she lifted the edge of her shirt so her stomach was laid bare to him. White gauze covered the place where the cuts were. "This too?"

He nodded, but he didn't offer to help. He had his hands clasped together, and he refused to look directly at her.

She peeled back the tape and bandage. Dark plum bruises surrounded the red centers of four cuts. They weren't much more than an inch wide, but they went deep into her. Donia had widened and extended the ice on her fingertips as she drove it into Aislinn's skin.

"This won't hurt," Keenan murmured, "but I suspect it'll be . . . uncomfortable in another way."

She blushed brighter this time. "I trust you."

Without another word he pressed his palm over the frostbitten cuts. The touch of his skin to hers was electric. In his eyes, waves crashed against a deserted beach under a perfect sunrise.

She felt the jolt of pleasure and drew her breath in sharply.

He didn't look away as the sunlight soaked into her body through those tiny incisions; he held her gaze and told her, "You healed Beira's frost with a kiss. I could heal you faster that way, but I can't . . . not like this. I want to, Ash. I want to use the excuse to kiss you here"—he glanced at her bare stomach—"I want to take this trust you're giving me right now and use it to get lost in each other, but I can't. Not with you being mine-but-not-mine. Healing this way is slower, but better. For you and . . . everyone."

"That's probably wise." She took a shaky breath. Her heart was beating out a dangerous rhythm; tiny bits of bliss surged through her entire body as the sunlight melted away whatever cold had lingered. And all the while, he watched her with awe in his eyes. It was a look she usually ran from, but in that moment, there was nowhere to run.

Look away. She couldn't. All she could do was stare at him.

The sunlight grew stronger. She gripped his wrist and shivered, not with cold but with bliss at the electricity zinging in her skin and bones. There was no way to deny that it was sexual. The only touch was his hand on her bare stomach, but it was almost as sexual as what she shared with Seth.

Keenan drew in deep breaths, a steady rhythm that she tried to use as a meditative focus.

"You should stop . . ."

"Should?"

"Yes," she whispered, but she didn't pull his hand away, didn't let go of his wrist. Her skin was alive with sunlight. *His sunlight. Our sunlight.* A sigh slipped from between her lips as a pulse of sunlight stronger than all the rest combined slid from his palm to her skin. Her eyes fluttered closed as wave after wave of pleasure rolled through her body.

Rustling flowers stretched toward the light they were casting in the room.

Then he took away his hand.

Glancing down, she felt like there should be a burned imprint of his touch. There wasn't. There were still four tiny cuts, but the bruising was mostly gone.

"Are you okay?" she asked him softly.

"No." He swallowed, looking just as vulnerable and confused as she felt. "I don't want to be without her *and* without you. She refuses me because of what I feel for you. You both ask me to make choices that go against what I believe I *should* do. I could be happy with either of you, yet I am miserable and weakened by what we are right now."

"I'm sorry." She felt guiltier than she'd ever felt with him.

"Me too." He nodded. "I'd sooner die than see you hurt, but I don't think I could ever strike out at her. You're my queen, but she's . . . I've loved her for what feels like forever sometimes. If you really wanted me like"—he brushed his fingers over her still bare stomach—"this, I'd say good-bye to her. I knew that I'd need to do that when I found my queen. *She* knew. We accepted it. A king should be with his queen. I feel that. Every time I touch your skin, I feel it. It's like—"

"Inevitability," she finished in a whisper. "I know, but I don't love you. I shouldn't have agreed to the healing thing, should I?"

"You were injured. I didn't tell you it would feel . . ."

"Like sex?" She blushed. "Did it feel like that when I healed you?"

"Not as much, but those were small injuries and it was winter then." His hand was not quite touching her but near enough that she could feel the heat beckoning her closer. He didn't so much as flex his fingers, though. "I wasn't to love someone who wasn't my queen. It was to be you I loved, not her, and you . . . you were supposed to love me."

Tears slipped down her cheeks, and she wasn't sure if they were from shame or pain. "I'm sorry." She kept saying it. "I need space from you. I'm sorry . . . I just . . . I'm sorry."

Keenan sighed, but he stayed almost-touching her. "I had to try. Our being together would simplify everything."

"But I don't love you. Donia does. If I could trade places with Donia, I would. I'd walk away from our court if I could. If it would fix everything. . . ."

"You're stronger than I am then. I want it all: court, queen, and love. Your being my queen gave me my court but"—he pulled away—"not you. Not yet. This rush of being unbound has made me foolish. I just need to stay away from you until we make sense of the compulsion to be closer. Maybe we need to keep the guards near us, or not stay in the loft together, or . . . something."

"Will you help me make Seth—"

"No. Never that. I can try harder to give you *now*, but I

won't curse Seth. Even if I didn't want you. In time, Aislinn, we'll explore this thing between us. We *are* inevitable. For now, though, I'll walk away." He turned toward the door. "I'm not sure how to make us stay apart, but for as long as you have Seth, I'm going to try to be with Don."

"So what next?"

"I confront Donia about stabbing you, and hope that it isn't too late." He looked as injured as she felt as he pulled the door closed behind him.

She stared at the door, and then she let herself cry. She was safe. *And alive.* Everything had been so overwhelming, so confusing; her entire life had changed, and she was messing up as much as not. Seth wasn't happy. Keenan wasn't happy. Having someone she thought was a friend stab her was beyond what she could handle calmly.

She cried herself to sleep.

When she woke, Seth stood in the doorway of Keenan's bedroom, not crossing the threshold to actually enter the room. "Is there something you were going to tell me?"

She blinked, clearing sleep from her eyes.

"Tavish wouldn't tell me what was going on. The girls were either silent or tearful and hugging me," he continued. "All they said is that you were in here. If you were here because you're with him, I don't think they'd be crying."

"Seth—" She started to sit up and winced. She put a hand on her stomach.

"You're hurt." He was beside her. "Did he—"

"No. Keenan wouldn't hurt me. You know that."

"So who?"

She brought him up to date, telling him everything except how she felt when Keenan healed her, and added, "I guess rapid healing doesn't take away all the tenderness." She showed him her still slightly bruised stomach. "It's mostly fine, but sore. Faery healing and all . . ."

He sat on the floor beside the bed. "So he healed you. Like you've healed him? With a kiss?"

"Not a kiss. Just his hand." She blushed, and that blush said everything she hadn't spoken.

"Tell me it wasn't a big deal, Ash." His voice was low and pain-filled. "Look at me and tell me that it wasn't intimate for either of you."

"Seth—"

"Tell me I'm not losing more of you to him every fucking day." He held her gaze, looking for answers that she didn't have. He closed his eyes and lowered his forehead to the mattress.

"Seth, I'm . . . I needed healing. You couldn't . . . but I mean . . . I'm sorry. But we talked. He's done pushing. We're going to find a way to sort it out."

"For how long?"

"As long as you . . ." she started, but she couldn't finish the words.

"As long as I'm here? As long as I'm still alive?" He stood

up. "And then what? I know how he looks when you touch his skin. I know this wasn't . . . this isn't casual. And I couldn't help you. Again. I wasn't even strong enough for you to call me."

He shook his head.

"I'm sorry." She reached out her hand.

He took it.

"I talked to him . . . about you. Changing things." She felt tentative as she said it, but she wanted him to know she was trying to find a way. *If I live long enough.* Lately, it felt like threats were everywhere.

"And?" Seth looked hopeful for only a moment.

"He said no, but—"

"Just like that. Niall's right about him. He'd rather I wasn't in your life, Ash. And someday, I won't be. He'll have everything, and I'll have nothing left." He stopped himself, forced his expression to one that lied to her. Then he leaned down and kissed her forehead. "You know what? You don't need this right now, not when you're hurt. I'm going to head out."

"Seth. Please?" Her heart thudded horribly. This wasn't what she wanted: seeing Seth look like this hurt almost as much as the stab wound did. "I'm trying."

"I'm trying too, Ash, but I . . . it's like having heaven and then finding it slipping away. I just need a little space right now. Let me have that." He let go of her hand and left.

And she was alone, injured and lying in a bed she didn't belong in. Outside the door, innumerable faeries waited on her every command, but the two people she most needed had both turned away from her.

Chapter 15

Seth didn't look at or respond to the faeries in the living room. He didn't honestly know if they spoke. Quinn stood and followed him to the door.

I can't deal with him right now.

Seth crossed the street into the park where they held their revelries. The grass was trampled down in a big circle, the whole of it pressed flat like those pictures of crop circles. Rowan-people milled through the darkness of the falling evening. Summer Girls sat in little groups talking among themselves or twirled like small dervishes around the park. A few of the cubs had a drum circle going. It wasn't entirely clear whether the vine-covered Summer Girls danced to the drumbeats or if the lion-maned faeries played to the dancers' rhythm.

Here, in the Summer Court's park, the world of Faerie looked beautiful.

"You don't need to follow me. I'm perfectly safe in the

park," Seth said without looking over his shoulder at Quinn.

"Will you stay in the park?"

"Not forever." Seth sat on a bench that was made from a twist of vines. Some faery artisan had shaped the vines into a braid as they grew. Now, they were a flowering seat. It was one of the myriad amazing things he could see with the benefit of faery Sight.

See illusions. Or maybe see truths. He didn't know. At the edge of the park, a group of six ravens settled in an oak tree. The sight of them gave him pause, but Tracey, one of the gentlest of the Summer Girls, took Seth's hands in hers. "Dance?"

She was already swaying with his hands in her grasp. She was reed thin, but she was still a faery—which meant that she could pull him to her even if he resisted. Tendrils of vines snaked out to draw him closer.

"I'm not really in the mood, Trace." He tried to extricate his hands from hers.

"That's why you should." She smiled as she tugged him to his feet. "It helps you be not sad."

"I just need to think." He had enjoyed the few times he'd spent empty hours dancing with the Summer Girls or listening to them talk. It was like the parties he'd lost himself in. *Before-Ash.* That's how life was divided: *Before-Ash and With-Ash.*

"You can think on your feet too." She pulled him away from the bench, inside the ring, and once his feet touched that soil, he was lost.

He could see the stone sculptures and the fountain as she led him into the circle. He could see the knowing grins on the cubs' faces as the tempo of the music changed. Seeing didn't change anything, though. He saw all sorts of things in his life, but he was powerless to remake them as he wanted them to be.

Vines entwined his waist as Tracey came closer to him; fleeting touches of her hands and hair made her seem all the more ethereal. There was nothing he could grasp and hold; nothing was solid.

"You need to let me leave." He said the words although his feet were moving still. "I need to go, Trace."

"Why?" Her wide-eyed expression seemed guileless, but he knew better. The Summer Girls weren't as unaware as they appeared. Frivolous? Prone to random bursts of glee? Amorous? Definitely. But they also had agendas. They'd lived centuries, waiting for their queen, watching their faery king struggle. You don't live that long under adverse circumstances without developing agendas of your own—or learning how to use people's perceptions to support your illusions.

"Tracey"—he backed away from her—"I'm upset."

She followed, twirling to him, and the music switched to a samba beat. "Stay."

"I need to—"

"Stay." She reached up and tore away his charm, leaving him vulnerable to her glamour.

The chain slithered like a living thing as she dropped the

stone into her top. He stared at the flower petals that were raining around them.

"Stay with us. It's where you belong." Tracey tugged him into her arms.

Some brief awareness pressed on him: he needed that stone. This wasn't right, but the thought was no more lasting than the brush of butterfly wings. The world shifted. All he felt was joy. This was where he wanted to be. Somewhere inside he knew that he shouldn't stay here, but the Summer Girls had taken such pains to teach him to dance the ways they liked, and the cubs were playing so beautifully, and the earth was humming under his feet.

"Yes. Let's dance," he said, but they already were.

Too soon, Tracey kissed his cheek and twirled away, and then Eliza was in his arms. "Rumba?" she asked.

The music switched, and his body moved in time with the beat that reverberated through the soil. He could barely pause long enough, but he did, pulling off his boots so his skin could feel the rhythm.

The moon was high overhead. A girl undulated in the fountain.

Not a girl. A faery. Like Ash.

"Come dance with me, Seth," she beckoned.

Siobhan let go of his hands. *When did Eliza become Siobhan?* He stepped into the fountain. The water soaked his jeans, soothing his sore feet as he reached out for her. The contact was shiveringly good. *I could drown in her.* Logic pushed at him, warning, reminding him that she was made of water. He really could drown in her.

"Are you going to hurt me, Aobheall?"

She pressed her lips to his ear. "Get free of this place, mortal. Their plan doesn't bode well for you tonight."

The fountain spray was a thick curtain around them, blocking clear vision from the others. The sound of the cubs' drumming filtered through the crash of water.

"Call for help," she said.

"Call?"

"Who would come for you, Seth? If you needed rescue, who would save you?" She pressed her body to his as she spoke. "I can't. The girls? The cubs? Our king? Who would make you safe from the whims of Faerie?"

"Niall. Like a brother." He pushed a button on his phone. The water didn't touch him as he did so, only her, Aobheall. He held the phone in his hand but didn't lift it to his ear.

"Where are we, mortal?" Aobheall murmured.

"Fountain." He felt stoned, drifting further into some reality that would keep him untethered.

"And how long have you been in our arms?"

"Forever."

"Damn it, Seth." The voice was from the phone.

"Would you stay here, Seth? Or would you walk out of the park?"

"Stay forever." He couldn't pull away from Aobheall. *With her, with them.* He could see them beyond the veil of water. *Ash's Summer Girls.* They'd take care of him. He remembered being sad before he was in Tracey's arms.

He wasn't sad now. "With you."

Seth was still in the fountain when Niall arrived.

The Dark King stepped into the water, and for a moment, Seth was struck by a wave of emotions completely at odds with his true feelings. Niall was a god. Seth looked at him and couldn't remember ever wanting anyone quite so intensely.

Then Niall lifted Seth's hand and pressed something into it. "You seem to have misplaced yours."

The touch of the charm to his skin cleared Seth's head. He realized he was soaking wet and standing in the fountain with Aobheall—and lusting on his best friend.

"You"—he took Aobheall's hand—"are kind."

Her laughter was the sound of crashing water. "Not truly, Seth. If I were kind, I would've suggested you call Niall before I had my chance to dance with you."

"For a faery, you are kind," Seth amended.

"Come dance with me if you need to forget. I'll hold that charm for you, not forever, but for as long as we negotiate in advance." Aobheall turned away and slid her hand down Niall's face. "And *you* are still always welcome in my fountain."

Niall smiled. "I am in your debt."

She laughed again. "And when haven't you been? I like keeping you there."

The Dark King kissed her. Shadows shifted into the water droplets. Instead of multicolor rainbows, the arc that formed was shimmering bands of gray and silver studded with bursts of light. As Niall kissed Aobheall, her form dissipated, and she became a part of the water falling in her fountain. The sound of her final sigh lingered for a brief moment.

Niall stepped out of the fountain and into the park. "Seth?"

Silently, Seth followed him. The Summer Girls weren't dancing; the cubs had stopped playing; the rowan were motionless. None of the Summer Court denizens were eager to have conflict with Niall. Well, maybe a few of them were, if the looks on their faces—especially Siobhan's—were honest. In truth, Seth suspected that more than a couple of the Summer Girls still sought Niall out, but that wasn't something Seth wanted to know.

"Tracey?" Niall called.

She spun to him and held out her hands. The vines on her skin shrunk away from Niall, but she didn't. Niall took both of her hands in his.

"You really oughtn't do this again." Niall stepped on the tendril of a vine snaking from her ankle toward Seth. He ground it under his boot. "Seth is my brother now."

"We like Seth. He was sad and leaving us . . ." Tracey reached a hand toward Seth.

Niall caught her wrist, stopping her from touching Seth. "So you took his charm to make him feel better?"

Tracey nodded. Several others, including Siobhan and Eliza, came to stand beside Tracey.

"He was happier," Eliza said. "What does it matter *why*?"

"You could be happy with us. Stay with us, and you'd be near Aislinn too," Tracey murmured to Seth. "We don't want you to leave us too."

"The queen is just struggling." Siobhan's words were to Seth, but she stared at Niall as she spoke. "That happens sometimes when people want things that confuse them. You shouldn't leave her behind."

"I wasn't leaving. I was . . . I just need some space." Seth glanced across the street. The windows of the loft were open. Plants from inside and outside crowded into them. *Wanting closer to her. To them.* He didn't want to explain his feeling to anyone, not his friend, not the Summer Girls. Somehow his business had become public; too many people knew things that should be private. A burst of anger filled him at the thought. "I'm not . . . I'm just *done* with dealing with this right now."

He turned and started walking. Either Niall would come with him, a rowan guard would follow, or one of the glais-tigs would take the task. *No leaving me un-watched.* He didn't choose to be a subject of Faerie, but he was. Court affiliation or not, he was under their control. *I did choose it when I chose her.* Right now though, with the image in his head of Aislinn resting in Keenan's bed, that realization wasn't much comfort.

Niall was silent as they walked to Seth's train. He was silent as Seth filled the kettle and measured the tea. He was even silent as Seth fed Boomer. Faeries could do patience far

better than Seth could; even with years of practicing meditation, Seth's calm felt too easily rattled.

He poured the boiling water from the kettle into the
small teapot Aislinn had found for him in some shop. *When
she was a mortal.* Seth pushed that thought away. She wasn't
mortal. She wasn't going to be ever again. Waiting for things
to get better wasn't good enough. Things could stay as they
were, or they could move forward.

Seth sat down across from his friend. "Even Tracey is
stronger than I am."

"You're a mortal." Niall held his still empty cup. "If you
hadn't lost your charm—"

"I didn't lose it."

"Point." Niall took the teapot and poured their cups. "It's
difficult I'm sure . . ."

"You have no idea." Seth's snort of laughter even sounded
bitter to him. "You've never *been* human. You're all so damn
perfect, so strong, so . . . everything. That's what Ash
needs."

"Don't go there," Niall cautioned. "Nothing you could
follow that with is wise."

"What would have happened if Aobheall was in a different mood?"

"The girls didn't mean you harm. Not really. If Ash
wasn't so distracted right now—" Niall stopped himself.
"If you need out of our world, I will help you. Maybe you
should consider going."

"That isn't what I want." Seth sipped his tea. He felt like

Aislinn was slipping away, and he wasn't sure how much longer he'd be able to stay in her world as a mortal. She didn't call him when she was hurt because he was too vulnerable. The conflict between the courts was growing. It felt like he needed out or in; being halfway between worlds wasn't a viable plan.

Seth sat his cup down and told Niall, "I want to be a faery."

Niall looked appalled. "No, you don't."

Seth poured another cup of tea. "I'm not interested in dying or in leaving her. I'm not strong enough to stand against the weakest faeries. I can't resist a glamour . . . I need to be a faery."

Niall stared at him. "This is a bad plan, my friend. Trust me."

Seth paused then. *My friend.* A faery's use of such terms was a gift, not done lightly, not to be ignored. "I value your friendship, Niall, and I trust you completely. That's not at question."

Niall's tense expression relaxed a bit.

Then Seth continued, "But I won't change my mind just because you disagree. You know me better than that. Help me?"

Niall got up and paced. "I'm tempted. Despite knowing it would be selfish of me, despite knowing it would destroy you if I helped you do this thing, despite how much I care for you . . . I'm still tempted."

"You're losing me." Seth dumped the ashtray he'd set

out for Niall. He might accept his friend's smoking, but the stench of cigarette butts disgusted him. "Explain."

"Two courts can work together to create a curse like Irial and Beira did—but I won't curse you. The only other choice is going through Sorcha, and there would be a cost there as well."

"What kind of cost?"

"With Sorcha? Probably my becoming a bit mortal, you becoming a bit twisted . . . Balance. Exchange. That's her deal." Niall paused; his stillness seemed almost as jarring as his pacing had been. "She could shift essences. I would assume some of your mortality, making me unfit to be Dark King. I would be done with the burden that Irial foisted off onto me, and you would assume some of my . . . nature."

"So you win. You get out of here, and I get to—"

"No." Niall walked to the sink and rinsed his cup.

"It's my choice," Seth said.

"History is filled with people rushing into disaster for love of one sort or another. My history is filled with the results of such deplorable choices." Niall walked to the door. He looked haunted and strangely afraid of Seth.

"So you made mistakes; that doesn't mean I would."

"Not me, Seth. The people whose lives I ruined." Niall opened the door. "I won't be a part of your mistake. Enjoy the time you have with Ash, or move on. Those are your only choices."

Seth sat staring at the door after Niall left. *My only choices.*

Neither of those choices was good enough—but Niall had given Seth another choice.

Sorcha. The High Queen is the answer.

Now Seth just needed to find her.

CHAPTER 16

The commotion at the door was to be expected. Donia felt the waves of heat pulsing against her from the pew where she sat just inside the entryway. Across from her, on the seats and backs of other church pews, faeries waited attentively. It wasn't quite popcorn-at-the-movies, but it wasn't far from it. Sasha wasn't there; such amusements were befuddling to the wolf. The faeries, however, were rapt.

"I *will* come in," Keenan repeated for the third time.

"Unless my queen consents, you will *not*." The rowan stood before the door, as imposing and resolute as he had been when he guarded Donia under Keenan's command. None of them had forgotten that he had once pledged his fealty to the same Summer King to whom he was denying entry.

"Don't force me to do this, Evan."

Evan didn't flinch, although Donia did. The idea of Evan being hurt filled her with fear. If it wouldn't undermine Evan's authority, if it wouldn't undermine her own, she'd tell him to stand down, but letting Keenan walk in freely when she'd ordered otherwise was unacceptable. If she didn't intend to speak to him, she would call reinforcements, but that too was unacceptable. She needed to talk to him, but he needed to grasp that her door was not open to him. The implied statement of only token resistance, the insult of having only one guard—*of that guard especially*—at the door would not be lost on Keenan.

It was, like so much in Faerie politics, a game of sorts.

Once more Evan objected, "She has been clear that you are to be stop—"

The thud and hiss of burned wood was startling, albeit also inevitable. The door was completely incinerated. Evan was charred, but not fatally so. *It could've been much worse.* The Summer King could've started with violence instead of giving Evan the chance to back down. He could've killed Evan. He hadn't. His restraint was a gift of sorts to her.

Keenan stepped over Evan's prone body and stared at Donia. "I've come to speak to the Winter Queen."

Behind him, one of the kitsune, Rin, darted out to check on Evan. The fox-faery glared at Keenan from behind a spill of stark blue hair, but Rin's animosity faded the moment Evan gripped her hand. Several other kitsune and a number of lupine faeries watched. They were standing and sitting and crouching expectantly. They'd make a stand against the Summer King, but Donia wasn't willing to see any of them injured to prove a point. She'd trusted Evan—agreed with him even—that he needed to deny Keenan admission.

That was as far as she felt like going.

"I don't recall you having an appointment," she said as she turned and walked away, knowing that he'd follow. She wasn't airing their quarrel in front of her faeries or going to allow them to feel the pain of his temper.

Keenan waited until they were outside in the garden. Then, he grabbed her arm and spun her around so she had to look at him. All he said was, "Why?"

"She upset me." Donia pulled free of his grasp.

"She *upset* you?" His expression of confused outrage was one she'd seen innumerable times over the years. That didn't make it any easier. "You stabbed my queen, attacked my court because she *upset* you."

"Actually you upset me. She simply added to it." There was no inflection in her words. She kept her face free of emotions as well. Those dangerous feelings were sunk into the well of cold within her.

"Do you want war between our courts?"

"Most days, no." She took another step to the side, looking at the snow around her feet as if the whole conversation was of little interest to her. For a moment, she thought the ruse would work—on one of them at least. "I just want you to stay away from me."

Then he slipped close enough that her resolve faltered. "What happened, Don?"

"I made a choice."

"To challenge me? To prove your court is stronger? What?"

Ice extended from her fingers. He glanced at them—and exhaled. It melted.

He took her hand in his. "You stabbed Ash. What am I to do about that?"

"What do you want to do?" She curled her hand around his, holding on to him as tightly as she dared.

"Forgive you. Strike you. Beg you not to do this." His smile was sad. "My court . . . my queen . . . they are almost everything to me."

"Tell me you don't love her."

"I don't love Aislinn. I—"

"Tell me you won't try to convince her to share your bed."

"I can't say that, and you know it." With his free hand, Keenan absently reached out to the tree behind her and ran a hand over it. Tiny buds appeared under the ice. "One day, when Seth is gone—"

"Then you need to stay away from me." Donia could barely see him through the snow that was falling around her. "I don't regret stabbing her. If your court continues to disregard my dominion, she will only be the first of many I'll strike. Most of them aren't strong enough to survive that."

"I'll try to convince her *one day* . . . but 'one day' is not right now." He eased even closer to her, mindless of the snowfall, melting the flakes and nearly blinding her with the sunlight that shined from his skin. The soil at her feet had become swampy as the heat from his body melted the thick crust of ice. It refroze under her feet, but in that moment it was the Summer King who was stronger. His rage gave him an edge over her. "Listen to me for a minute. You're the only one I've ever cared for like this. I dream of you when I'm not with you. I wake with your name on my lips. I don't need to stay away. She wants him, and I want you. When she told me that you stabbed her, it broke something in me. I don't ever want to be at war with you. The idea of striking you terrifies me."

Donia stood motionless. The tree bark pressed into her skin. Keenan's hand was gripped in hers.

"But if you touch my queen again, I'll set that all aside. It'll kill me inside, but she's mine to keep safe. Don't make us have to go there." He pulled his hand from hers and ran his fingers through her hair, and just as quickly as his temper had flared, it faded. He cupped her face. "Please?"

"It's not just about her. You insult my sovereignty whenever you march in here making demands. No one does that. No other ruler. Not a one of the strong solitaries." She put her hands on his chest and let the ice in her hands extend just far enough to break his skin. "You have used up every mercy I had."

He leaned closer, and she couldn't stop the instinct to retract the ice before it seriously wounded him. He smiled as she did so and said, "After all we've overcome to get this close, are you giving up on us now?"

She brushed her lips over his, briefly enough that it couldn't really be called a kiss. Then she exhaled until ice clung to his face and clothes. She couldn't stab him, not yet at least, but she could strike him.

"I love *you*, Don," he whispered. "I should've told you years ago."

Hearing it finally was a bittersweet thing, but that's what it was to love him—painful and beautiful all at once. It had always been that way. Her heart sped and felt like it would break at the same time. She sighed and gave him the words back: "I love you too. . . . That's why we need these things resolved. I'll slaughter your court if we keep going this way."

He grinned. "Don't bank on that."

Then he kissed her, not just a brush of lips as she'd done, but a kiss that scalded her tongue. The tree burst into full bloom. The garden flooded around her. A riot of flowers shot out of the earth.

She was mud-covered as he pulled back.

"I've had centuries to fight Winter with next to no power. I'm unbound now with all of that experience. If we are to be at odds, you might want to remember that." He held her as close as he had during the few nights they'd had together. It was controlled, a show of power; none of his heat touched her. "But I don't want to be at odds. As long as he's in her life, I'll stop. I tried. I had to. It's what's best for the court— but she's not mine to have yet."

Her breath and his mingled into a hiss of steam. "I don't want only part of you during the few years I have you."

He tucked an orchid in her hair. It shouldn't thrive

here, but it did. "I'm not giving up on us or on peace between our courts. I love you. I'm done pushing Aislinn. The strength of Summer's made me stupid. She wants to be with Seth, and as long as she is, I can have more time with you. I'd have forever with you if it were my choice." He kissed her gently. "I don't love her. She and I talked already."

Donia looked away. "I pushed her toward you. I just made a mistake when I let myself think that you'd be mine for a few years . . . she's your match. I'm not."

"Maybe someday, but right now . . . I was carried away by the first summer. It's a heady thing, but I can redirect that energy. Let me have the dream of us for as long as we can. That's what the court needs—a happy king, a king who can't stop dreaming of being lost in someone who wants to be just as lost. Tell me you'll let me get lost in you."

She gave in. *I always do.*

"I will." She pulled him closer. They were mud-caked and as tangled up as they could be without hurting each other. "But that means that until he's gone, you're mine only. I don't want to see you here with her."

"Or meddling in your court. I know. Your court, your rules. No meddling or manipulation." He gave a wry grin at the surprised expression she wore. "I *was* listening, Don. I'll apologize to Evan, follow your rules—and you'll stop stabbing members of my court?"

She smiled. "For now."

"I'll settle for it," he whispered against her lips. "For now."

"Even if you are mine, even if this thing with Ash is not between us, I still need you to understand that I am not your subject. You cannot try to influence my court." She needed that made clear. It wasn't simply his relationship with his queen that was the problem. There were two issues before them.

"I loved you when you were a mortal. I loved you when you were the Winter Girl who existed to oppose me, telling tales of how awful it was to trust me." He sprinkled kisses over her throat and collarbone between words. "I'm not here now because you are the Winter Queen, but despite that, I'll do my best. And when I slip . . ."

"I won't show you any mercy just because I love you." She meant it and was grateful that faeries couldn't lie because for the first time in longer than she wanted to recall, they were being completely open with each other. "But I will try to keep my heartbreak from making me vengeful when Seth dies and you—"

He stopped her with a kiss, and then whispered, "Can we not talk about the end of us? We're at the beginning today. I'm yours. Wholly without reservation. I won't try to interfere with your court. Can you kiss me now?"

She smiled. "I can do that."

It wasn't like any other kiss they'd shared. It wasn't about trying to consume each other, or comfort, or tinged with sorrow. It was slow and careful—and over far too soon.

He leaned against the tree and stared at her with the love she'd dreamed of forever written plainly on his face. "In a few months, I'll be able to spend several days in your arms, but right now"—he carefully stepped farther away—"I've reached the edge of my self-control . . . which I'm *admitting*. You see? We can do this. We can be together."

"On Solstice"—she let a tiny shower of snow fall over them—"there won't be any stepping away."

"Solstice can't come soon enough." He darted forward and kissed a snowflake from her lips, and then he was gone.

He's a fool. She smiled to herself. *He's* my *fool, though. For now.* Eventually, he'd be in Aislinn's arms—*that,* Donia was near certain of. When Seth was gone, Donia would need to let go of Keenan. It might mean moving away from Huntsdale for a few decades when that happened, but until then, she had reason to hope.

Maybe Bananach's visions of war were wrong. She and Keenan had only needed to move forward. War's visions—like Sorcha's reputed far-seeing—were about probabilities, not certainties.

And those probabilities just changed.

CHAPTER 17

Aislinn woke by midday. She was alone in Keenan's room. Her clothes were laid out on an ottoman that someone had brought to sit beside the bed. A tray with breakfast foods sat on the bedside table. Before she dealt with food or dressing, though, she called Seth—twice—but he didn't pick up.

She called Keenan.

"How are you?" were his first words. He sounded calm, friendly, like nothing had happened.

She sighed in relief. "Better. I'm better."

"There's food"—his voice was tentative then—"beside the bed. I had them bring new trays every half hour so it'd be warm for you."

"I could warm it. Sunlight, remember?" She felt relieved that they were able to talk, that they could feel comfortable with each other. "Where are you?"

"The orchards outside the city. It's beautiful here. They're healthy now."

"So you're there because . . . ?"

"I just wanted to give them a little extra attention. Check on them." Warm currents thrummed in his voice. He rarely sounded so at peace.

The depth of his joy at seeing the earth thrive again wasn't something she could quite reach, but she shared it to a lesser degree. She'd known less than two decades of bitter cold; he'd known centuries of it—and had felt responsible for not being able to end it. The truth of that was epiphanic. "That's where you go when I'm in school, isn't it?"

"To the orchard? Not always." His tone grew evasive.

"But other places like it." She uncovered her plate. It wasn't cold, but it wasn't steaming hot either. She let a little heat into her fingertips and warmed the plate and its contents.

"Yes."

"Why didn't you tell me?" She took a bite of the omelet— spinach, cheese, and tomato—one of her favorites.

"It's something I'd rather do on my own. I didn't want to offend you by telling you that you weren't welcome."

She paused, unable to say she wasn't a little hurt. "Why?"

He didn't answer right away, and when he did, his voice was hesitant. "When I was bound, I used to see these places, the struggling trees and fields fighting to produce food for the mortals and the animals. I'd try. Little trickles of sunlight. That was all I had. It wasn't much, but it was something. I have more now."

"I could help someday."

"Maybe. Right now, I don't . . . it's private. I've only ever shared it with one person."

"Donia."

"Yes," he admitted. "She was mortal the first time. Afterward, I took her to some of the places over the years when I needed to talk to her, but I didn't tell her why I went there. . . . I went to her today. We talked."

"And?"

"We're going to sort it all out. We'll work around the pull between us. It'll all be manageable. We just can't let ourselves forget."

"I'm sorry."

"Whatever we do, it's going to be something we both agree on. I held hope that our friendship would grow, that you'd choose to be with me, but . . ."

She took a deep breath and asked again, "Will you help me find a way to change Seth?"

"No." Keenan paused. "We're still learning, Aislinn. The approach of full summer for the first time in either of our lifetimes is intoxicating. It'll get easier for you and for him."

"Promise?" She worried her lip.

"And we'll get stronger."

"Go tend your orchard. I'm going to go try to reach Seth again."

"Tell him I'm sorry too . . . for what it's worth. I'm done pushing you," Keenan added. "Summer's about passion,

Aislinn. It's what we are. Take yours with him, and I'll enjoy my time with Don."

After he disconnected, Aislinn smiled. Even with the pressure of summer, they could all find a way to make this work now that she and Keenan were in accord.

Aislinn ate, dressed, and left the loft. She needed to go find Seth so things could get set right, but when she crossed into the park, she stopped in horror.

The Summer Girls were all bleeding or moving with broken limbs. Their own vines choked them. Rowan guards were set afire. Aobheall in her fountain was solidified into a sculpture. Her mouth was open in a soundless shriek. Smoke lay low in the air, twisting up from the decimated trees and from the bodies of the rowan. Aislinn could taste it. Ashes rained down like gray snow.

One woman, a raven-haired faery, walked through the destruction. A carved bone knife was strapped to her thigh, the white of it standing out starkly against gray camouflage pants. A tattered black cloak, damp with fresh blood, fluttered as she moved. Aislinn was struck by the oddity of a cape over military fatigues until she realized that it wasn't a cloak at all: the woman had feather-hair that fell down her back and seemed to thicken to form dense wings as Aislinn watched her.

"Pretty pictures all for you," the faery said. She made a sweeping gesture across the air in front of her. Unfamiliar patterns were painted on her arms with woad, ash, and blood.

Aislinn looked at her faeries. She'd thought she hated them just a few months ago; she still feared them sometimes. It wasn't hate or fear of them she felt just now though: it was terror and heartbreak.

The faery slid an arm around Aislinn's waist. "It's for *all* of us, really."

"What have you done?" Aislinn whispered.

Tracey was dancing, but one arm hung at an unnatural angle as if it'd been torn from the socket.

Aislinn shoved the raven-haired faery away. "What have you done to my faeries?"

"Nothing." She waved her hand again and the park looked as it should: the Summer Girls and the rowan and Aobheall were all fine. A fire burned in the clearing, though, flames wavered in the center of the circle where the Summer Court typically held its revels. It wasn't a small campfire but a raging blaze.

"Shall I tell you a story, my little queen?" The faery had eyes like Irial and Niall—eternal black—but hers shimmered with a hint of madness. "Shall I tell about what-ifs and what-nows?"

"Who are you?" Aislinn backed away from her as she asked, but she was near certain who she was—Bananach, the essence of war and bloodshed. It couldn't be anyone else.

"Once upon a time, the world was mine. It was a lovely place. Chaos danced with me, and our children ate the living. Far-Dorcha himself dined at my table." Bananach squatted down in front of the fire. It was midday, but the sky was dark with ash and smoke.

Is that an illusion too? Aislinn wasn't sure what to do. Faeries' glamours shouldn't work on her. *Why does hers?*

"Bananach?" Aislinn asked. "That's your name, right?"

"It is a name I use." She tilted her head at an odd angle and glanced at Aislinn. "And you are the ash-girl, the missing Summer Queen, the one who would bring peace."

"I am." Aislinn could feel the heat of the fire as it grew wider still.

Bananach's expression became hopeful: eyes wide, lips parted. "I could like you if you would step willingly to the pyre. Let them blame each other. . . . It's a little thing really. It mightn't even hurt. Sunlight and fire, much the same."

Aislinn trembled. "No. I don't think so."

"I would dance to your screams. You wouldn't be alone," she said cajolingly.

"No." Aislinn stood very still, sensing from Bananach's predatory gaze that sudden movement might be unwise. "I think you should go."

"Don't you want me to answer your questions, little ash-girl? I know much."

"Is there a right response?" Aislinn's words weren't wavering, but she felt certain that the faery knew how intimidating she was. Hoping she wasn't making a mistake, Aislinn added, "Tell me what you will."

The word *will* felt awkward, but *want* was too open and *can* was too limited. Semantics was one of the weird parts

of dealing with centuries-old creatures. Aislinn hoped she'd
phrased it right this time.

The raven-faery brushed her hands on her pants and
stood. "Once, after chaos but before *you*, I advised. I could
make war games as a tableau for monarchs on the edge of
war. I can show the what-ifs when we are near the preci-
pice."

Aislinn stared, speechless for several moments. The
ash in the air felt like it had coated her tongue, prohibit-
ing speech. None of the other faeries saw Bananach. They
weren't reacting at all—to Bananach or to the fire that had
grown immense in their park.

Bananach sauntered through the center of the pyre;
flames brushed against her like the hands of grateful sup-
plicants. "You see my what-if dreams. . . . We draw nearer
the war, little ash-queen. You made that happen."

The flames surged toward Bananach, following in her
wake, singeing her feathers. "You give me hope, so I give
you fair warning. You and I are in balance now. Follow your
path, and I will owe you. I've missed my discord."

As Bananach paused in front of Aislinn, the caustic scent
of burned flesh and feathers mingled with the soothing
scent of burning wood. It was a disturbing combination—
almost as disturbing as the chaos that suddenly spread
throughout the Summer Court faeries as whatever illusion
the war-faery had woven drifted away in the smoke.

They all saw Bananach then, saw War standing face-
to-face with their queen. Guards rushed to Aislinn's side.

Summer Girls clustered together. Aobheall beckoned them to her fountain.

Bananach cackled, but she didn't flinch.

She wouldn't.

The war faery leaned close to Aislinn and whispered her words against Aislinn's cheek. "Shall I break them? Snap the bark people. Make kindling for your pyre, ash-girl?"

"No."

"Shame." Bananach sighed. "You give me a gift, a war on our horizon . . . and we will need fodder for the bloodbath to come . . . still . . ."

In a blur of feather and limbs, she kicked and punched and stabbed several guards. She stopped then, as suddenly as she'd begun to move. Most of the guards were coming to their feet; some were battered but still standing. One wasn't moving.

Bananach looked at the sky. "It grows late, and I have others to see. My king will expect me to come soon."

And with that, the war faery left them in the park reeling in disorder and panic.

Keenan. Niall. Donia. Where was she going? War. Aislinn didn't want war. The idea terrified her. *Too many reminders of death and what I have to lose.* She thought of Grams and Seth and her mortal friends. Grams was under constant watch; so too was Seth. She'd lose them eventually. Mortals died—but not now, not soon. She'd barely begun to discover the beauty that the earth could offer now that the long years of endless winter were past. This was her world. It was a world that should teem with life and possibilities, even if those possibilities were sometimes finite.

She was in love; she was loved; and she was part of something incredible. Many mortals and faeries were. All of that would be destroyed if there was a war. With no worry over the consequences of angering other courts, with no restraints, with rulers and guards too busy to respond to small indiscretions . . . aside from the reclusive High Court, the mortal and faery worlds would be dealing with two—*or possibly three*—Faerie courts in opposition, as well as solitaries who'd no doubt take advantage of the chaos. Aislinn felt sick thinking of it—and desperate to talk to Seth.

She needed to hear his voice; she needed to hear him tell her he forgave her. They'd had a lot against them, but they could work past it. They had so far. He was the cord that kept her together. His faith gave her strength when she thought she couldn't bear up under a challenge; that was the core of what made him irreplaceable. The passion and the romance were incredible, but the center of it was that he made her want to be a better person. He made her believe she could do the impossible. She *could*, with him in her life. They'd only been officially together a few months, but she knew he was the only one she'd ever love like this. He was it, her forever.

She called him again—and still had no answer. She left another voice mail, "Call me. Please? I love you."

With a glance around the park, she found the rowans on duty, saw them collecting their faeries and steering them

toward the loft. They were efficient even in their injured
state.

She called Keenan and said, "I met Bananach. . . . We
are mostly uninjured, but I need you to come home. Now."

CHAPTER 18

With effort, Seth ignored both Aislinn's and Niall's calls all day. Niall had stopped in. They'd shared a tense cup of tea that ended when Seth asked, "Where does Sorcha live?"

Niall set down his cup. "She's unreachable to mortals. Hidden."

"Right, I've heard that. *Where?*" Seth kept his voice fairly steady, but he knew that his irritation was obvious to Niall. "Just take me to her."

"No."

"Niall—"

"No." The Dark King shook his head, stood, and left.

Seth stared at the door in irritation. Aislinn wouldn't help if she knew; Keenan wouldn't help. Niall wouldn't even discuss it. That left Donia or research.

He flicked open his cell and pressed number six. One of the Scrimshaw Sisters answered the Winter Queen's phone. "Mortal?"

Seth shivered at the husk-dry voice. "Can I speak to Donia?" he asked.

"Not tonight."

He closed his eyes. "When?"

"She's busy. I'll take your message."

"Ask her to call me?" He began collecting his folklore books—including volumes he'd acquired from Donia and Niall. "Whenever she can?"

"The message will be conveyed," the Scrimshaw Sister rasped. "Good-bye, mortal."

Seth grabbed a legal pad from his bin of miscellaneous things and sat down in the middle of the stacks of books. "Research, it is."

When the phone rang several hours later, Seth scrambled for it, hoping it was Donia. It wasn't. But he hoped, against logic, that it might be help when he saw Niall's number.

Instead, the Dark King reiterated, "It's a mistake."

"It's not." Seth hung up on him. He didn't want to hear what anyone else thought. He didn't want to hear Aislinn's explanation that it wasn't possible or Niall's guilt-heavy objections. He knew what he wanted: he wanted to be a faery, to have eternity with Aislinn, to be strong enough to be safe in the world where he now lived. Being human wasn't cutting it. He didn't want to be weak or finite or easily overwhelmed. He wanted to be *more*. He wanted to be her equal again.

He just needed to figure out how to find Sorcha and

then convince the High Queen to help him.

No problem. Seth scowled. He could just imagine she'd be willing to pass that gift out without hesitation. *Sure, I'll give you eternity, little mortal.*

He looked at the books he'd searched and found useless. He looked at the few notes he'd made. *Reclusive. Logical. Does not mingle with the other courts. Devlin.* It wasn't helpful.

His careful control of his temper slid away. He stood and swept everything from the counter. It was a satisfying clatter.

Better than meditating.

He was in love, healthy, had plenty of money, a friend who was like a brother . . . but because he was mortal, he could lose it all. Without her, he'd have to sever ties with all faeries. There would be no more riverside concerts. There would be no more magic. He'd still have the Sight: he'd see everything that he couldn't actually have. Losing Aislinn meant losing everything.

If she left him, it didn't matter if he was healthy. And if she didn't leave him, he wasn't strong enough to be in her life and be safe. And even if he was strong enough, he'd grow old and die and she'd move on.

The books were all over the room. None of them had answers.

Everything is wrong.

He walked into the kitchen.

It's useless.

Every dish he owned, except the two teacups and the tea-pot Aislinn had bought him, went smashing into the wall. Then, he punched the wall until his knuckles were blood-ied. It didn't help, but it felt a helluva lot more satisfying than anything else he could think to do just then.

Come evening, Seth had cleaned away the evidence of his loss of temper. He'd reordered the house and his feelings. Being without her wasn't something he wanted to even con-sider. There had to be an answer—but he didn't have one.

He'd find it, though. He wasn't going to lose everything. *Not now. Not ever.*

He sent Aislinn a text—"need space. ttyl"—and then paced around the house. Its size didn't usually bother him, but today it felt constricting. He didn't want to go out, to see faeries and pretend all was well. He knew what he didn't want, what he did want—everything but how to make it happen. Until he came up with some sort of a plan, being around faeries—seeing what he wasn't—felt like cruelty.

So when one of the court guards knocked on the door to ask if Seth was staying in or going out, Seth said, "Go home, Skelley."

"You sure you don't want to go grab a drink? Or we could come inside . . . not for long, but in shifts . . ."

"Space, man. That's what I need tonight," Seth said.

Skelley nodded. He stood there for a moment longer, though. "The girls didn't mean harm. They just"—he paused as if the words he needed weren't quite familiar—"are fond of you. It's like your serpent."

"Like Boomer?"

"He makes you happy by his presence?"

"Yeah." Seth cracked a grin at that. "Boomer being here makes me happy."

"You make the girls happy with your presence." Skelley looked so earnest that it was hard to find him anything but kind as he stood in the iron-heavy railroad yard, even though he likened Seth to a pet snake. "They were worried you'd go away like Niall did."

Seth wasn't sure if he should feel comforted that Skelley was trying to soothe him or insulted that he was being compared to a pet boa constrictor.

Or both.

Mostly, he was amused. Carefully keeping his amusement from his face, he gave Skelley a nod. "That is . . . interesting to know."

The exceptionally thin guard had a gentle streak. Most of the guards wouldn't come to the door talking about feelings. Skelley was an anomaly. "You are liked in the court," he added. "Our queen is happy by your being with her."

"I know that." Seth lifted a hand in a wave at the other guards at the edge of the yard. "But right now, I need to crash. Go relax or whatever."

"We'll be here."

"I know." Seth closed the door.

A few restless hours later, he'd tried to sleep. It didn't work: he was too keyed up. He tried to burn energy:

push-ups, sit-ups, pull-ups on the bar in the walkway. It was futile. *I need air.*

He looked at his clock: just past midnight. The Crow's Nest was still open. In a matter of minutes he was dressed and lacing his boots. His cell buzzed as another text came in. He looked at it: "CYT?"

Am I ready to see her tomorrow?

Usually, it wasn't a question. He didn't think it had ever been a question. *Would she know about the park? Would she ask about Niall? Would she want to talk about Keenan?*

He wasn't sure he'd be ready to deal with any of that. He wanted a plan, a way to reach Sorcha, a way to make things better; talking to Aislinn about everything that wasn't right didn't feel like the best answer. He didn't respond to her message. He wanted to; he wanted to call her right then. Instead, he laid the phone down on the counter.

If I don't have it, I can't call or answer.

Resolved, he walked toward the Crow's Nest. He saw three guards following him, but he refused to acknowledge them. The knowledge that he was babysat so incessantly was more than he could handle just then.

One guard came inside the Crow's Nest, found it free of faeries, and left. Seth knew that they watched both doors. That was the closest to distance he'd be getting.

It's not enough.

After almost an hour sitting by himself, Seth admitted that he was sulking. He hadn't really been thinking about a plan. He'd seen friends, people who didn't come around as much since he and Aislinn had started dating, but he didn't talk to them.

Damali was there again, not singing, but just hanging out. He caught her eye and smiled, and she came over with two beers, hers mostly empty already. "You free now?"

He shook his head. "Just for conversation, D."

"Damn." She whistled. "I thought they were screwing with me. The scrawny chick or the surly guy?"

Seth took the beer she held out. "She's not scrawny."

Damali laughed. "Whatever. She treat you right?"

Does she? He took a drink and avoided the question. "You sounded good the other night."

The look Damali gave him wasn't judgmental or pitying. It was very . . . human. "That wasn't even close to a subtle dodge. You need anything?"

"Just company." Seth had known Damali long enough that he didn't need to pretend. "Things are weird, and I needed air tonight."

She gave him an assessing gaze. "*That* is why I don't do the relationship thing. You used to get it. No getting caught in someone's strings. No regrets. We had fun when you weren't like this."

"I'm happy being tangled up this time, D."

"Yeah. You look like it." She drained her bottle. "Want another?"

When he left a few beers later—without Damali—Seth wasn't in any better spirits. If anything, he felt worse. *All the down and none of the buzz.* Drinking didn't help. It never had.

As he walked, he wondered if he was about to go from worse to really awful. The guards he'd been so eager to leave behind were gone—but not at his request. The raven-faery who'd attacked Niall was following Seth instead, and she wasn't pretending to be stealthy. She walked close enough behind him that he could hear her singing battle hymns to herself.

He knew she should frighten him, and on some visceral level, he was afraid. He didn't have guards or his cell phone. *No sense worrying about what I can't change.* He stepped into the railyard. The tracks and abandoned cars were the ideal security for a mortal dealing with Faerie. His home sat on a small lot at the edge of the railyard. Most faeries stopped at the railroad tracks; this one didn't. She followed him almost to his door. A few yards from the house were wooden chairs he kept in his garden.

He pulled out his key and turned to look at the raven-headed faery.

She sat down in one of the chairs. "Sit outside with me, Mortal?"

"I'm not sure that would be wise." Seth unlocked the door, but he didn't go inside.

She tilted her head far to the side to peer at him. It was a very inhuman gesture. "Perhaps it could be."

"Perhaps." He stayed on his stairs, just outside the now open door. He'd only need to take one step to be inside.

Would it matter? After how fast he'd seen her move when she attacked Niall, Seth was near certain that he couldn't move inside before she reached him—and that she was strong enough to come in anyhow. He considered his options: there weren't any. If Niall himself had struggled with her, a mortal stood no chance.

"Somehow I doubt that having anything to do with you is wise," he said.

The faery crossed her legs and leaned back in the chair. "I like doubts."

And this is why I have guards. But Seth remembered her fighting with Niall, and he suspected that even if the Summer Court guards were there, they couldn't save him if she meant to do him harm. He wondered if she'd killed them— and would him.

"Does your king know you're here?" he asked.

She cackled, a sound that should come from a raven's beak. "Bold child. I'm sure he will . . . eventually. But he is never soon enough to change my paths."

Seth's fear spiked, and he went inside the house. "He's offered me your court's protection. I've accepted."

"Of course. He has a fondness for you, doesn't he? The new Dark King has always liked his mortal pets, not so bad as the last king . . ." She moved toward him with an exaggeratedly slow stride like a film reel advancing one frame at a time.

Seth wished he had his phone in hand. Niall couldn't get there fast enough, but he'd know that it was this faery who'd—*what? killed me?* Seth looked inside: he could see his phone. He took another step backward into the train.

"Well, we shan't tell *him* our business." The faery shook her head like a disapproving parent. "He'd only tell you no if he knew."

He took another step backward. "Tell me no to what?"

She paused mid-step. "Seeing her Royal Tediousness. That's what you want, isn't it? But they'll all tell you no." She sighed, but it wasn't a sorrowful sound. It was longing, and Seth didn't want to know what she was longing for. "Naughty boy trying to talk to the Queen of Reason. She knows of you. Sent her dirty hands to see you. Faerie's all a-titter over the roaming mortal."

At that, Seth stopped as well. "Are you trying to help me?"

The raven-faery resumed pursuing him. She stood only a couple arms' lengths away now; she continued to move with calculated slowness. "But they stand in our way. How can you follow your dreams if they keep you on a leash? Telling you no. They're like that. Taking away choices. Treating us like children."

She was in front of him then. Up close, he could see that the feather-hair falling down her back was singed in places. Shadowy wings blinked in and out of existence. Ashes had dried into patterns on her arms and cheeks. She looked like she'd come to his yard fresh from a battleground.

"Who are you?" Seth asked.

"You may call me Bananach."

He took another step and picked up his phone. "Why are you here?"

"To take you to Sorcha." She nodded as she spoke.

"Why?" He didn't look at the phone as he slid his thumb to the key that would ring Niall's cell.

"Don't. I'm not going to bleed you unless you make it necessary. Doing *that* would make it necessary." The madness in her words and expression had suddenly gone, and she was all the more frightening for it. She gave him a serious look. "We all have dreams, Seth Morgan. For the moment, yours and mine line up. Consider yourself fortunate that your use to me does not require me to injure you today."

Then she stepped past him into his home.

Seth paused, finger still resting on the key that would call Niall. "You're offering to take me to Sorcha?"

"You seek her. Niall won't help you. The ash-queen won't give you what you want. Winter will refuse you. . . . Reason can help if she deigns to do so. Your changing will help me. I've been whispering words to get us here, Seth. Telling secrets to Winter." She stopped and cooed at Boomer. The boa was resting atop one of his heated rocks. She didn't look his way as she said, "Gather your traveling things."

He knew enough by now to realize that she spoke the truth as she saw it.

And as I see it.

The things Bananach said were true: neither Aislinn nor Niall was willing to help him in his pursuit of being a faery. The High Queen could make it happen.

Bananach stood making kissy noises at Boomer—who was undulating in a way Seth had never seen. Then she glanced back at him. "Ask your question. The window is short."

Seth held Bananach's gaze and asked, "You'll take me directly to Sorcha and not harm me?"

She corrected, "I will deliver you *unharmed* to Sorcha. You must be more specific in your words if you're to do me any good. Suppose I'd had someone else harm you as we travel? Precision is the key to strategy. You have the boldness, but not the precision. I need you to be both brave and calculating." Her gaze was assessing. "You'll do. The ravens tell me that, but you must listen well to Sorcha's wisdom. Tedious she is, but Reason will aid you in what we need."

"We? Why *we*?"

"Because it serves my purpose." She opened Boomer's terrarium and lifted the boa. "Answering you further does not."

"Right." He swallowed against a suddenly dry mouth.

From outside the door, Skelley called, "Seth, are you well?"

Bananach held a finger to her lips.

"I am." Seth didn't open the door. The guard couldn't stand against Bananach—and Seth wasn't sure he wanted her to leave. She had answers. She could take him to Sorcha.

Skelley was silent. "Do you need company?"

"No, I think I have what I need." Seth glanced at the faery, who stood sentinel-still watching him. "I just needed a moment alone to find it."

Skelley said his good-bye through the still closed door, and Seth turned to Bananach. "I don't know how you know what I need, but I want to see Sorcha."

The raven-faery nodded somberly. "Call your queen to tell her you're leaving. You can't go there. Not tonight. Not with me. They wouldn't welcome me in their home. And if they saw me—" Bananach made a happy sound Seth felt embarrassed to hear before she added, "Nasty, bloody fun, but it'll wait for another day."

Some residual bit of logic told Seth that he had ventured much too far from the path of good sense.

You can still say no, he thought. *Right now. Tell her you were wrong. Tell her to leave. Maybe she'll listen.*

But that same logic reminded him of how much farther Aislinn seemed to drift each day, of how helpless he was against the weakest faeries, of how short a time he'd had with her as a mortal.

He pushed "**1**" on his cell.

When the voice mail picked up, he started, "I'm leaving tonight, and—"

Bananach suddenly stood in front of him then, invading his space, whispering, "Tell her nothing else."

Seth looked away from the faery. He knew better than to trust her, but he did obey her. He spoke into his phone. "And I'll call . . . later. I just need to go now. I don't know when . . . if—I need to go."

He disconnected.

"Good boy." Bananach uncoiled Boomer from around her arms and handed the snake to him. Then she opened the door. "Hold tight to my hand, Seth Morgan. Reason doesn't wait for us. We must go before the pieces move."

Seth wasn't at all sure what the raven-faery meant, but he took her hand and went into the night with her. He locked the door. A heartbeat later they were far from the railyard, past the guards, and in a street that took a good half hour to reach on foot. She moved faster than Aislinn, and Seth stood trying not to retch.

Boomer shivered a bit from where he was coiled around Seth's shoulders.

"Smart lamb," Bananach murmured as she patted Seth's head.

Several ravens fluttered into the broken windows in the building across from them. They tilted their heads to watch him. Bananach tilted her head in the same gesture, in time with the black birds.

He forced the nausea back. "Where is Sorcha? I need to see the High Queen."

"Hidden." Bananach strolled away, and he ran after her.

She'd offered him his answer, and he wasn't going to let the opportunity escape him—regardless of the risk.

Better to take a chance on forever than wonder "what if" later.

CHAPTER 19

Aislinn was a little surprised that Seth wasn't at her door that morning—and a lot disappointed. The meeting with Keenan and Tavish and a handful of other faeries last night had run into the early hours, but she'd come home afterward in hopes of seeing Seth. They usually grabbed breakfast together before school at least twice a week. Today should've been one of those days.

Invisible to the world, Quinn and a small group of guards were waiting along the street downstairs. She caught Quinn's eye and smiled. They'd developed an accord on the whole privacy bit. It was hard enough to explain Keenan's omnipresence to her friends—and to Seth's friends. If she had a whole *group* of mostly male strangers shadowing her everywhere, there'd be no chance of explaining them away. Unless they were at the Crow's Nest or faery-only places likes the Rath, her guards stayed invisible.

Seth's walking speed was a slow lope, so she usually left

extra time in the morning so they could go slowly. Without him beside her, she walked at a brisk pace.

I could run.

She tried to shake off the uneasy feeling: Seth had been late a few times. Maybe he'd be at the Depot already. He hadn't said he'd meet her, but surely he wasn't that upset still. Seth wasn't temperamental like her. He was reasonable.

Everything will be fine.

She'd forgotten to charge her phone, so she couldn't call him.

The uneasy feeling wasn't letting up. She turned into a lot and around the side of a building—out of sight of mortals—and donned a glamour so as to be invisible to all but faeries and Sighted mortals. Then, she ran.

It felt amazing to move that fast; her body tingled with the sudden freedom. There were parts of being fey that thrilled her far more than she could ever have imagined. The speed at which she could now move was one of them. The downside, of course, was that she was where she needed to be in a few brief heartbeats. It was useful, but it was also over too fast. Being a faery skewed her sense of time. She hadn't yet tried to come to terms with the alternate time that existed in the removed part of Faerie, in Sorcha's demesne, but until she had to meet the High Queen, she wasn't interested in pondering that particular paradox. For now, she'd been having enough trouble thinking about how finite everything mortal was, how brief a time she'd have with Seth and Grams.

She stopped in front of the Depot. The coffee spot was crowded. A number of people she knew were there, filling the tiny tables and leaning against the walls. Aislinn was glad they couldn't see her as she went inside. She rushed through the main room into the smaller rooms: Seth wasn't there either. Her sense of unease grew.

Maybe he's at school. It was possible. Sometimes he met her there before he went to the library or to sketch at the park. If not, it meant that he was upset enough to not meet her, to not want to talk about things. Panic tightened her lungs. *What if he won't talk to me?*

He was the only one who'd ever accepted her as she was, for who she was, with both sides of her new life. Grams tried. Keenan tried. Only Seth truly knew her; only Seth understood her completely.

Still unseen by mortal eyes, she crossed the street and rushed to Bishop O'Connell High School. Not caring how stupid it was, she became visible in between steps. Quinn, behind her, made a disapproving sound, but he wouldn't say anything. He wasn't the sort to comment on faeries' arrogances.

Aislinn glanced back at the guards.

Quinn said, "We'll be here."

She nodded and went inside. For a few moments, she stood there, but the familiar sounds of her classmates' voices were disquieting. These were the people she was to protect, but unlike her fey, they had no idea that she stood between them and a potential war that could devastate the earth. She watched them and listened to snippets of conversation that were so far removed from her now as to be in another language. This was the world she had never truly belonged to—the world her friends lived in, a world where economics exams and prom were life or death, a world where a fight with a boyfriend was even worse. She paused. Some things were the same. *Seth being upset is still that important.* She might not be prom bound, but the faery revels offered her more than enough dancing. Econ still mattered—in very practical ways. And Seth . . . he was everything.

The best time to see him was now. Without another moment's hesitation, she turned and walked right back out the door she'd just entered. She'd go see him. *Maybe he overslept. Or maybe he didn't want to talk. So he can at least listen.* She wasn't going to let this fester. She'd go to him. They'd talk it out. He was essential to her.

So she ran—through the streets, across the railroad yard, and to his door. She heard the guards trailing behind her, but she didn't stop to speak to them. *Let them think I'm impulsive.* All that mattered was reaching Seth.

A few minutes after she'd left the school, she turned her key in Seth's lock and pushed it open. "Seth?"

There were no lights on, no music playing. The teakettle sat on the burner. Two unwashed teacups were on the counter. It looked like Seth had gone out suddenly. He didn't usually leave his cups or dishes unwashed.

"Seth?" Aislinn walked back to the second train car and into the bedroom.

It was early morning, and the bed was already made. He'd left too quickly to wash his cups, but not too quickly to make his bed. She leaned over the side and plugged her phone into the spare charger. As the phone came to life she saw the voice mail notice. He had called.

She was relieved—until she heard it: "I'm leaving tonight, and—" He stopped, and Aislinn could hear another voice faintly—*a girl*—but couldn't make out what she said. Then Seth's voice was back. "And I'll call . . . later. I just need to go now. I don't know when . . . if—I need to go."

Leaving? She replayed it twice more. It still didn't make any sense.

He sounds excited.

She absently ran her hands over the new comforter they'd picked out and listened again. Aislinn heard the voice, whispering very softly in the pause in his words.

He left.

She'd trusted him with secrets that she'd never shared with anyone. When Keenan and Donia were stalking her, she'd opened up to Seth. She'd broken every rule she'd lived by, that her mother and Grams had lived by.

Tears were stinging her eyes, but she blinked them away. "What just happened?"

She couldn't stand being in the bedroom, in the space that was just theirs, any longer. She left the room and went to check Boomer's heat rock. The snake wasn't coiled in his terrarium.

Boomer's gone.

"Seth'll be back." Aislinn looked around the empty house.

Aislinn wanted to run, but it was Seth she ran to when she was lost—and he was missing.

"Where are you?" she whispered.

She couldn't make herself leave yet. She washed her hands and then cleaned the couple of dishes. It wasn't as if she really thought he'd walk in the house while she stood there washing his teacups; she just couldn't bear leaving. When she went to put them away, she discovered that the other dishes were all gone, except the two teacups and the teapot she'd bought him. *Why did he take everything? Why didn't he take the teapot I got him?*

Something is wrong. It wasn't like Seth to just vanish.

She looked around and found broken dishes in the trash. Someone had broken them and cleaned up. If not for Boomer's absence and the excitement in Seth's voice, she could believe that he was in danger.

He took Boomer with him.

Her emotions felt too close to the surface, and since she'd become the Summer Queen, that wasn't something she could let happen, not with emotions like these. She'd seen the result of Keenan's mood swings—miniature tropical storms trapped in small spaces, a sirocco on a city street—and she'd helped contain the consequences of those emotional upheavals. Her presence calmed him. Even after nine centuries as Summer King, he still slipped, but his storms weren't the overwhelming nightmare she felt pulsing inside of her.

She didn't have the control to deal with any of those emotions on her own.

Outside the train, a mist wafted like the fog coming in from the sea, but there was no sea near Huntsdale. The fog was her fault. She felt it, her confusion and fear and anger and hurt swirling faster and faster.

Seth left.

She walked to the door and pulled it closed behind her.

Seth is gone.

Her steps through the city were propelled by sheer will. She was in a haze. Guards spoke. Faeries paused as she passed them. None of it mattered. Seth was gone.

If Bananach or anyone else wanted to hurt her, this would've been the time to do it. She was aware of only the constant repetition of his message in her ears as she played it over and over.

By the time she reached the loft, all she knew of life was reduced to one fact: Seth had left.

She opened the door. The guards were talking to Keenan. Some noise about her being reckless was filtering from their mouths. Others were speaking more noise. The birds were chattering. It was all meaningless.

Keenan stood in the middle of the room; all around him, birds swooped among the trees and vines he kept in the loft. The sight of it usually made her feel a loosening of tension. It didn't this time.

"He's gone," she said.

"What?" Keenan didn't glance away from Aislinn or move toward her.

"Seth. He left." She still wasn't sure if she was more frightened or more hurt. "He's gone."

Without a sound, the room emptied of everyone but Aislinn and Keenan. Tavish, the Summer Girls, Quinn, several rowan—they all slipped away.

"Seth *left*?"

She sat down on the floor, not bothering to walk the rest of the way into the room. "He says he'll call, but . . . I don't know where or why or *anything*. He was upset with me, and now he's gone. When he left the loft the other night, he said he needed space, but I didn't think he meant this. I keep calling. He's not answering."

She looked up at Keenan. "What if he's not coming back?"

CHAPTER 20

Seth stood with Bananach in one of the older graveyards in Huntsdale; it was an oasis set off from ruined buildings and graffiti-decorated walls. It was a place he'd come with friends, a familiar space where he and Aislinn had spent hours walking among the dead. Today, the sense of comfort he usually felt there was replaced with trepidation.

"This is it? The door is *here?*" he asked.

"Some days. Not always." She motioned him forward, past a pair of crooked stones leaning together. "Today it is here."

Between the Sight and the charm-impeding glamour, Seth could see the barrier that stood in front of them. He'd seen barriers elsewhere—at the park by the loft, at Donia's house and cottage, and at the Rath. There were still others shimmering around places where a lot of faeries frequented or nested. But none of the barriers he'd seen were this substantial. The others were misty, like smoke or fog that he could slip through. Contact with them felt uncomfortable as he crossed them, so much so that if he didn't know they were there—or that faeries were real—the barriers would deter him from crossing. It was what they did: kept humans out.

This was different in every way. Neither smoke nor illusion, a veil of moonlight hung from higher up than he could see and touched the earth. The solid fall of it bespoke weight, like thick velvet drapes. He reached out a hand to touch it. He could not push through.

As Bananach moved forward, the barrier rippled out in tiny disturbances as if she had fallen into still water. Then she jabbed her taloned hands into the moonlight veil and parted it. "Come into the heart of Faerie, Seth Morgan."

The voice of caution—a warning that he was on the edge of a decision that would change everything—hummed in his mind. He could see faeries walking through a city that hadn't been visible when the veil was closed. Behind a barrier thicker than any he'd seen in Huntsdale, an entire world was hidden. Something about it was wrong. Logic insisted he pause, consider the dangers, weigh the consequences— but Sorcha was in there. She had the ability to solve his problems. If he could convince her to help him, he could be with Aislinn for eternity.

With Boomer draped around him like a scarf, Seth crossed the veil.

Bananach cackled. "Brave little lamb, aren't you? Walking into a cage without but a moment's pause. Trapped little lamb."

Seth put a hand on the moonlight veil: it didn't part. He tried to push his fingers through it as she had done. It was as steel. The murmured fears in his mind grew to cacophonic levels.

He turned back to her, but she was already walking away. Faeries were moving out of her path, not quite running but obviously fleeing. Bananach strode down a street that could've been in any city, but somehow *couldn't* be in any of them. It was an area that had clearly been a regular human city before, but everything seemed a degree off of normalcy. Buildings were stripped of most metals and had earthy replacements: hardened vines with perfumeless blooms clung to buildings in lieu of fire escapes; wooden poles supported awnings; rock and mineral slabs were shaped into fences and frames.

He glanced behind him and could no longer tell where the veil was. The graveyard and the rest of the city he knew were hidden as surely as this part of the city had been hidden when he was surrounded by the familiar gravestones and mausoleums. He tried to convince himself that this wasn't any more unusual than the things he'd seen since Aislinn revealed the faery world to him.

It wasn't just the earthiness that seemed surreal. The entire place had an atmosphere of order and precision. Alleys were bright and immaculate. A group of human-looking faeries played soccer in the street, but they were serious as they did so. No shouts or loud voices could be heard anywhere. It was akin to walking into a theater showing a silent film—but with a layer of Daliesque oddity to it.

Bananach paused at the entryway of an old hotel. Pale gray stone pillars stood on either side of a doorless opening. Burgundy drapes were held back with gilt leaves. It looked old Hollywood, except it wasn't. Instead of a red carpet, a long roll of emerald moss extended out from the doorway.

The raven-faery stepped onto the moss.

"Come, Mortal," she called. She didn't look his way to see that he followed; she simply expected he would obey.

And Seth didn't see many choices. The veil he'd crossed was impermeable. He could continue standing in the street, or he could follow her farther.

I didn't come here to run away at the gate.

Hoping he wasn't making a mistake, he crossed over to the moss carpet and into the bright doorway.

The hotel lobby was filled with faeries talking in small groups, curled into chairs reading, and in a few cases staring silently at focus objects. Books were stacked in orderly piles on side tables. A white-veiled man was dusting a faery who'd apparently been meditating for some time.

Glancing neither left nor right, Bananach walked past them into a sterile-looking corridor. The faeries who'd noticed her tensed. Some slipped away. Whispered words twisted into an overall breathy hiss in the still of the room as Seth passed among them. Their Otherness was more pronounced than the Summer and Dark Court denizens. Many of them looked almost mortal, but they radiated a stillness that felt alternately rapacious and dismissive. It was frightening.

The raven-faery seemed oblivious. Her feather-hair fluttered like pennants trailing behind her as she swept through hallways, went up and down stairways, and took sudden turns. He felt and heard the low sound of battle drums throughout the building. Pipes and horns wound through the thunder of the drums. The noise sent his pulse racing in dread, but he continued to follow Bananach.

The tempo of the music increased as they raced through empty spaces, building to a fierce cadence that would burst a heart if it tried to keep pace. Then it stopped mid-beat just as Bananach put her hand, flat-palmed, on a closed door and murmured, "There you are."

She opened the door into a vast ballroom. The floor was cut blue marble. Tapestries and art that belonged alongside the most revered masterpieces lined the walls. Some art was framed by pieces of silver that had been left in their natural threadlike state; others were held by simple wooden frames; still more were in what seemed to be glass frames. Vine-wrapped marble pillars stood at regular intervals in the room, supporting a star-scattered ceiling. Seth knew they couldn't be real stars, but he gaped at the illusion all the same.

While he stood awed by the stars and the art, Bananach put herself in front of him and said, "I brought you a lamb."

Reluctantly, Seth took his attention from the wonders around him to look at the faery who sat on a stiff-backed chair in the empty expanse of the room. She was the one who could save him—or crush his every dream. Her hair was like fire: flickering shades of heat shifted in and out of sight as he tried to watch her. Her skin was the same as the moonlight veil he'd crossed to enter Faerie, as if she herself had been formed of that cold light. Yet, as he watched, her skin shifted too. It became as dark as the depths of the universe. She was shadow and light, flame and coolness, white and black. She was both sides of the moon, all things, perfection.

The High Queen. Sorcha. It could be none other. She sat in her empty ballroom, pondering a game board, surrounded by nature and art.

He reached up to grip his charm and ran his thumb over it as if it were a worry stone. Even wearing it, he felt pulled to revere her. The temptation to drop to his knees and offer her his soul was the same sort of insistence a body felt to draw breath. It was automatic and near impossible to resist.

"A lamb?" The High Queen's gaze passed over him with the attentiveness of a hummingbird, pausing and darting away. She returned her eyes to the board in front of her. The game looked to be something akin to chess but several times larger and with six sets of gemstone pieces.

"All of his wet parts are still inside." Bananach reached over and stroked Seth's head. "Do you remember when they brought us sacrifices?"

Sorcha picked up a translucent green figure with a sickle-looking weapon in its hand. "You shouldn't have brought him here. You shouldn't even be here."

Bananach tilted her head in that disturbing birdlike gesture. Her voice was singsongy as she asked, "Shall I keep
him then? Shall I carry him back through the veil, take him
from the field of play? Shall I leave him on the right regent's
threshold; tell them I brought him to the door from inside
your demesne? Shall I, sister mine, take the lamb?"

Seth paused as something unreadable flickered in
Sorcha's eyes. He'd only just arrived here, so he couldn't
imagine where Bananach could leave him or what she could
say that would cause trouble. *The only regents who know me
are Ash, Don, or Niall, and I could explain*—the thought
stopped as clarity hit: she wouldn't be leaving him alive at
anyone's door. If Sorcha didn't allow him to stay, he was
about to die.

He looked around, as if a weapon would suddenly be
lying in reach. There wasn't anything. Sentences from the
lore he'd read rushed to mind in a jumble. *Hawthorn and
Rue, thistle and rose . . .* He knew there were herbs and
plants that offered protection. He kept a number of them
in his train and often with him. He began rummaging in
his pockets. *Words . . . vows . . .* What could he offer not
to die? Bananach had promised to deliver him safely *to*
Sorcha, but nothing beyond that.

Sorcha held the figure aloft before setting it in a square
adjacent to the one it had been in when she lifted it. "Fine.
He can stay."

The raven-faery pressed one taloned hand over his chest, her fingers curling in ever so slightly, as if she'd pierce him with her fingertips. "Be a good boy now. Make me proud. Make our dreams come true."

Then she turned and left.

For a few heartbeats, Seth stood and waited for Sorcha to speak. He'd heard enough about her—not in direct revelations but passing comments that painted her as impeccably proper and uptight—that he thought he should wait for her to speak.

She didn't utter a word.

Boomer shifted, sliding down Seth's arm and lower until the boa was resting at Seth's feet.

Still the High Queen sat silently.

Now what?

Waiting her out was unlikely. He glanced at the doorway through which Bananach had just left and then back at the High Queen. She wasn't looking at her puzzle board now; she gazed into the distance, as if she saw things in the empty air.

Perhaps she does.

After several still moments, he figured he'd try to speak. "So, you're Sorcha, right?"

The look she gave him was not cruel, but it wasn't inviting at all. "Yes, and you are?"

"Seth."

"The new queen's mortal consort." She lifted another

game piece absently. "Of course you are. Not many mortals would know my name, but your queen is—"

"She's not my queen," he interrupted. Somehow that particular clarification felt important just then. "She's my girlfriend. I'm not anyone's subject."

"I see." She lowered the violet carving and straightened the voluminous skirts she wore. "Well then, Seth who is not a subject, what brings you to my presence?"

"I want to be a faery." He looked at her without flinching.

Sorcha moved the game board away. A flicker of what might be interest flashed over her face. "That's a bold request . . . and not one to answer without contemplation."

She could fix everything. She has the power to do it.

An elaborate tapestry was pushed aside, and another beautiful, seemingly emotionless faery appeared from behind it. He could've been one of her game pieces: perfectly still and inhuman. As Seth looked at him, he realized that this was the same faery who'd watched Niall fight with Bananach in the Crow's Nest.

"Devlin," she murmured. "I believe my new mortal needs a resting space for the time, and a reminder of the dangers of impertinence. Would you tend to that while I ponder things?"

"It is my honor." The faery bowed slightly, and then he calmly reached out and gripped Seth's neck.

Devlin lifted Seth by the throat and squeezed, applying

pressure to his windpipe.

Seth couldn't breathe. He struggled, kicking out at Devlin, but everything went dark and he fell into unconsciousness.

CHAPTER 21

"You all right?" Carla asked Aislinn softly as they waited for Rianne to come out of the restroom. She took a while to apply the makeup her mother forbade her to wear to school. "Sick?"

"No."

"Do you want to talk? You look . . . *off.*" The words were hesitant, but they were still there. Carla had become mothering with both Aislinn and Rianne.

"Seth and I—" Aislinn started, but a sob threatened at the thought of finishing that sentence. She stopped the words before the tears at the end of that admission could fall. Saying it aloud in this world made it too real. "He's not . . . here. We had a sort of fight."

Carla hugged her. "It'll be okay. He loves you. He's been waiting around for you forever."

"I don't know." Aislinn tried not to look at the faeries who stood invisibly in the hall. "He took off or something."

"Seth?"

Aislinn nodded. It was all she could do. A part of her wished she could talk to Carla, to Rianne, to someone, but the person she talked to was missing—and telling Carla all about it would mean skirting the truth or admitting truths that Aislinn couldn't quite handle. Mortals really didn't belong in the world of faeries.

"He's gone." She looked at Carla and at the faeries behind her and whispered, "And it hurts."

Her friend made comforting noises, and her faeries stroked their hands over her hair and face. Once that would have terrified her, but now their touches comforted her. The faeries were hers. They were her reason now, her focus and her responsibility. *I need them.* And they needed her; they weren't going to ever leave her. Her court needed her. That truth was a comfort as she went through the motions of the school day yet again.

Faeries weren't often in the school. The metal and plethora of religious symbols made them uncomfortable. Yet, throughout the day, her faeries surrounded her. Siobhan sat beside her in an empty desk during study hall. Eliza sang a lullaby during lunch. The soft cadence of her words was matched by affectionate brushes of faery hands as her guard and other assorted faeries came by without any reason but to show her they cared. *This is my family.* Her court was more than a collection of strangers or strange creatures. Their love didn't make all the pain go away, but it helped. *They* helped. That sense of being cosseted in her court's embrace was a salve on her injured heart—and it was all that helped.

After school, Aislinn didn't race to see Keenan, but her steps as she went up the stairs to the loft were hurried. Being there, surrounded by her king and court, made her feel a sense of security she lacked outside the building.

She still went to school, and she still spent some nights at home with Grams, but in the eighteen days since Seth had vanished, her attempts to reenter her old life had stopped. She didn't see or call her friends. She didn't go anywhere alone. She was safest with Keenan. Together, they were stronger. Together in their loft, they were safer.

After the first couple days, he'd learned not to ask any awkward questions about how she was doing or how she felt or—worst of all—if Seth had called yet. Instead he gave her tasks to keep her distracted. Between schoolwork and court business and the new self-defense training, she'd been exhausted enough that she slept at least a few hours every night.

Sometimes, Keenan mentioned in passing that he'd not had any progress on finding Seth. *But we will,* he promised. It was only slow because they'd been cautious in their inquiries. *Letting Seth's absence become public could endanger him,* he'd explained. *If he's left us, he's vulnerable.* It made things slower than she wanted, but endangering him—*is he already in danger?*—wasn't an option she liked at all. Whether he left her by choice or not didn't matter. She still loved him.

All they'd learned so far was that he'd gone to the Crow's Nest and spent hours with Damali, a dreadlocked singer he'd once sort-of dated. The guards hadn't seen him leave; a tussle with several Ly Ergs who'd captured one of the younger Summer Girls had called their attention away. When they returned to the Crow's Nest, Seth had slipped out, but Skelley had spoken to him afterward. *He was safe in his home,* Skelley repeated. *I don't know how he left. He's never done so before.* Seth left stealthily; he took Boomer; he sounded excited. The evidence didn't add up. *Did he go willingly?* The only reason to believe he hadn't was that it seemed out of character.

Does it though?

Seth didn't do relationships. He'd never been in one before her; he was increasingly tense about her bond with Keenan; and he'd sounded fine when he called. He didn't sound quite right, but telling someone good-bye over voice mail was weird. *Maybe he went to see his family.* She'd spent hours thinking it through, ordering faeries sent to various locations, having them check ticket receipts at the bus and train station. None of it made her feel any better—or brought answers.

Seeing Keenan was all that eased the ball of tension she felt. Today though, when she walked through the door of the loft, he greeted her with a sentence she wasn't sure she wanted to hear: "Niall would like to speak with you."

"Niall?" She felt both fear and hope at the thought of talking to him. She'd tried to contact him the day after Seth had first vanished, but he'd refused to see her.

Keenan's usually transparent emotions were tamped

down so tightly that she couldn't get any sense of what he was feeling. "After you meet with him, we can go over Tavish's notes and have dinner."

She was unable to breathe around the tightness in her chest. "Niall is here?"

The look on Keenan's face was a brief blur of fury. "In our study. Waiting for you alone."

Aislinn didn't correct him as she once would've; the study was hers too now. This was her home. It had to be. *Immortal only if I'm not murdered.* She'd not thought about the finite and infinite until she'd become a faery, but since the change, the idea of reducing forever to just another heartbeat terrified her. The recent threats from Bananach, Donia, and Niall made the possibility of ending seem too real. There were those who could take everything away— and one of them was waiting on the other side of the door.

Knowing Keenan stood a moment away helped, but the trepidation she felt at seeing Niall was still awful. In the first rush of changing, she'd still felt terror, self-doubt, worries— all the stuff she'd hid over the years when she saw the faeries but had to keep her Sight secret. Fear for her safety had faded. It was back now, stronger than it had ever been before.

"Do you want me to come in?" Keenan's offer was without inflection.

"If he said 'no' . . . if he has information and didn't tell me because . . ." She gave him a pleading look. "I need answers."

Keenan nodded. "I am here if you need me."

"I know." Aislinn opened the door to go see the Dark King.

Niall sat on the sofa looking as comfortable as he had when he'd lived there. It was familiar enough to ease the tension Aislinn felt—but his expression of contempt wasn't.

"Where is he?"

"What?" Aislinn felt her knees go weak.

"Where. Is. Seth." Niall glared at her. "He's not been home; he's not answering my calls. No one at the Crow's Nest has seen him."

"He's . . ." All the calm she'd been struggling to feel slipped away.

"He's under my protection, Aislinn." Niall's shadowy figures appeared and perched behind him in postures of judgment. One male and one female sat on either side of Niall; their insubstantial bodies leaned forward attentively. "You cannot keep him away from me just because you don't like—"

"I don't know where he is," she interrupted. "He's gone."

The shadowy figures shifted in agitation as Niall asked, "Since when?"

"Eighteen days ago," she admitted.

The look on his face was censorious. He stared at her for several moments, not speaking or moving. Then, Niall stood and walked out of the room.

She ran after him. "Niall! Wait! What do you know? Niall!"

The Dark King spared a hostile glare for Keenan, but he didn't stop. He opened the door and left.

Aislinn attempted to follow, but Keenan restrained her as she tried to pass him, before she could reach out to take hold of Niall.

"He knows something. Let go—" She pulled free of Keenan. "He *knows* something."

Keenan didn't try to touch her again or close the door. "I've known Niall for nine centuries, Ash. If he walks away, it's not wise to follow. And he's not our court now. He's not to be trusted."

She stared into the empty hallway beyond their loft. "He knows something."

"Maybe. Maybe he is simply angry. Maybe he's off to pursue a suspicion."

"I want Seth home."

"I know."

Aislinn closed the door and leaned on it. "Niall didn't know he was leaving. It's not just me he left."

"Niall will seek him out too."

"What if he's hurt?" she asked, giving voice to the fear she tried to hide even from herself. It was easier to believe he'd left her than that he was injured and unfindable.

"He took the serpent. His door was locked behind him."

They stood there in silence until Keenan gestured toward the study. "Would you like to go over the notes Tavish had collected for us? Or do you want to hit something?"

"Hit something first."

Keenan smiled, and they went to one of the exercise rooms to hit the heavy bags and speedballs that hung there.

Later, after she had hit the bag until her stomach muscles ached to the point that she felt like she'd be sick if she pushed further, Aislinn grabbed a quick shower in the bathroom attached to her bedroom. Until recently, she hadn't felt like it was hers. It was a place to sleep and store a few things, nothing more, nothing less. That had changed after Seth left. She'd withdrawn into the room several times just to hide away from the world—only to retreat from there to roam the whole of the loft, where her faeries were. She needed them, needed to be around them.

That didn't mean she wasn't startled to find Siobhan sitting cross-legged in the middle of the massive canopy bed. The spiderweb drapes that hung like walls around the bed were fastened back, pinned by rose thorns that jutted from the posts of the bed. Surrounded by the fairy-tale setting, Siobhan looked like a princess from one of those animated movies Grams had never approved of watching. The Summer Girl's hair was long enough that tendrils of it brushed the duvet that covered the bed. The vines that twisted like living tattoos around her body rustled as the leaves shifted toward Aislinn.

She's too pretty to be human. Unnatural—Aislinn pushed away the old prejudices, but not before the rest of that thought was there—*just like I am now. Not human.*

"We are sad that he's gone." Siobhan's voice was whispery. "We tried to make him stay."

Aislinn stopped. "You what?"

"We danced, and we even took away his charm stone." Siobhan pouted, seeming falsely young as she did so. "But Niall came and took him from us. We tried, though. We tried to keep him with us."

Yelling at Siobhan wasn't going to help. Despite the posturing of vapidity, Siobhan was clever. Some days, she was unnerving for it. Mostly, Aislinn thought the Summer Girl was loyal to their court—just not so loyal that trusting her was a safe bet.

Aislinn tightened her robe belt and sat down, not on her bed but on the stool in front of the dressing table. "Niall took Seth from the park. Did he take the charm stone?"

Siobhan smiled slowly. "It was he who gave it to Seth, so he'd not leave it with me, would he?"

"Because the charm made Seth . . ." Aislinn lifted a beautiful olive-wood brush, but she didn't do anything with it.

"Impervious to our glamour, my Queen." Siobhan came over, took the brush, and began brushing Aislinn's hair. "It kept him safe from any illusions a faery might press onto him."

"Right. And Niall gave it to him, but you took it." Aislinn closed her eyes as Siobhan methodically pulled the knots from her hair.

"We did," Siobhan confirmed.

"Did *you*?" Aislinn opened her eyes again and held

Siobhan's reflection in the mirror.

The faery paused in her brushstrokes and admitted, "No. I wouldn't upset Niall that way. If you asked it of me, I'd cross him, but unless I must . . . We've been dancing together for centuries. He was the one who taught me what it meant to be not-mortal. When my king turned his attention to the next mortal . . ." She shook her head. "No, I wouldn't upset Niall unless my regents required it."

"I didn't know he had a charm stone," Aislinn whispered. "Did he mistrust me that much?"

"I don't know, but I am sorry that you are sad." Siobhan resumed brushing.

Aislinn's eyes filled with tears. "I miss him."

"I know." Siobhan shook her head. "When Keenan turned his attention away from me . . . We all tried to replace Keenan. I sometimes thought I had." She looked down for a second. "Until he left too."

"Niall. You and he were something more—"

"Oh, yes." Siobhan's expression left no doubts. "Eternity is a long time, my Queen. Our king was often distracted, but until you were found, Niall had a purpose in our court. He hid his darkness with dizzying bouts of affection. I took the lion's share."

She walked over to the wardrobe, opened it, and pulled out a dress. "You ought to dress for dinner. For the king."

Aislinn stood and went over to the wardrobe. She ran a hand along the outside. The tableaus of faery revelries carved into the wood didn't make her pause anymore. The opulence of the room didn't either. Keenan had found these things in an attempt to make her happy; he'd decorated the room lavishly, but she couldn't deny that she liked it—or the dresses inside the wardrobe.

"I don't want to dress up," she said.

Siobhan's princess-perfect face was a vision of contempt. She crossed her arms over her chest. "Wallow. Weaken us as Bananach scouts our perimeter. Distract our king with your selfishness. Keep him from finding happiness with you or with the Winter Queen."

"That's not—"

"He stays away from Donia in order to be by your side when you need him, yet you still refuse to see him as you should—as your true king and partner. He's willing to sacrifice his new chance with her in hopes that you'll move on. Yet you weep and hide, and he worries and mourns. Both of you saddened is unacceptable. Our court requires laughter and frivolity. This melancholy and denial of pleasure weakens the very core of who you are—and weakens us as a result." Siobhan closed the wardrobe with a slam and, in the next heartbeat, turned a plaintive gaze on Aislinn. "If your mortal isn't here to share laughter and pleasure, if our king is denied his joy at loving the other queen, if you are both so maudlin, we grow weak and sad. Your laughter and bliss filters into all of us, as does this wallowing in despair. Go to dinner with our king. Let him help you smile."

"But I don't love him." Aislinn knew the words sounded weak, even as she said them.

"Do you love your court?"

Aislinn looked at her, the faery who'd had the courage to tell her what she very much didn't want to hear. "I do."

"Then be our queen, Aislinn. If your mortal comes home, you can deal with it, but right now, your court needs you. Your king needs you. *We* need you. Take pleasure in the world . . . or send our king to Winter so he can have pleasure. You keep him at your side but give him nothing to smile about. Your pain is hurting all of us. Accept what you can take of the pleasure he would offer."

"I don't know how," Aislinn said. She didn't want to move on, but she admitted—to herself, at least—that she treasured Keenan's comfort. She looked at Siobhan, well aware that her confusion was plain in her expression. "I don't know what to do."

Siobhan's voice gentled as she said, "Choose to be happy. It is what we have all done."

CHAPTER 22

For the next four days, Seth waited in Sorcha's hidden city. After Seth's initial meeting with the High Queen, Devlin had deposited him in a spacious set of rooms, complete with an elaborate terrarium where Boomer was happily ensconced. It wasn't bad—but for the one critical detail. *I left Ash five nights ago.* He wished now that he'd answered her calls or texts the day he'd gone. His phone didn't work here. He had no signal at all.

That was really all he lacked: contact with Aislinn. Everything else seemed to appear before he could want it. Meals arrived in his room, and he broke the injunction against accepting faery food. He'd made his choice: he wasn't leaving the world of faeries. Short of death, this was the path he'd be on. The first moment when he ate the food that was most likely delivered and prepared by faeries felt momentous—like acceptance of a change, like the physical commitment to a new path. He'd wished Aislinn were beside him when he ate the strange meal of unfamiliar fruits and paper-thin pastry, but then again he'd wished she were with him every moment of every day.

He spent most of his time in his quarters, but he'd roamed a bit. After the first day, he realized that he always ended up back at his rooms once he'd thought of it—so he experimented. He had only to think it and take three corners, and no matter how far he'd walked, he was in the hallway that led to his doorway.

A few faeries watched him; a few mortals smiled at him.

Inside his rooms, he'd been given art supplies aplenty—but he couldn't focus. Sitting around wondering about the High Queen's decision wasn't ideal for creating. He'd meditated. He'd sketched some. He'd read in fits—books of law and discourse, treatises in the *Workings of Faerie*, several dense essays in the *In the Companie of Subterraneans*. He'd walked aimlessly. He searched for new insights in the books he found. He was in a building with rooms holding nothing but books: everything he could dream of was at his fingertips.

Everything but Ash.

If it wasn't for missing her, he suspected he'd be happy in the space Sorcha had allotted him. It was set up as if for an artist. One wall was all glass so the light that filtered into the room was wonderful. Beyond that window-wall was an immense garden. Within the room, he had easels, paints, inks, canvas, paper, and in a side room, he had some supplies and tool options for his metalworking. *Everything but inspiration.* Sketching the garden from within a cell wasn't tempting.

The restlessness he'd been fighting the past four days took him to the immense window again. This time, under closer inspection, Seth realized that within the window was a door of sorts. He pressed a half-moon shadow on the glass and the window split to open outward, allowing him access to the garden. As he entered it and looked past the flowers and trees, he saw the ocean, a vast desert, arctic plains, grasslands, mountains . . . Inside his room, he could only see the garden, but when his feet touched the earth outside his room, something unreal filtered into his vision.

Or real.

As he concentrated on the ocean, he could taste the briny air. Years ago, he'd lived by the sea. *Linda loved that.* His father wasn't much for the water, but Seth and his mother had relished it. She'd found motherhood much easier when she felt freer. The sea breeze made her feel that way. Seth could taste it in the air, that familiar salty tang. It seemed too real to be an illusion.

The entire universe is at Sorcha's hands.

Seth could see why she didn't come live inside the main part of Huntsdale or any other city when she had utopia hidden in this space. Donia had the small corner of Winter year-round; Keenan and Aislinn had their park; but Sorcha seemed to have an entire world behind her barrier. Seth couldn't quite see why anyone would leave here willingly. It was perfect.

He stopped himself. He had to stay focused so that when she allowed him to speak, he could try to convince her that he belonged in the world of faeries. Donia had listened when he spoke; she'd given him the Sight. Niall listened when he spoke; he'd offered brotherhood. Faeries seemed to respond favorably to sincerity and courage. Blind adoration, on the other hand, wasn't persuasive—not that he had anything logical to offer as a point of debate. He didn't want to be a finite mortal in a world of eternal faeries. He hoped she'd be sympathetic when she finally chose to listen to his request—and that she'd let him speak to her soon. He wasn't sure how long he would be asked to wait or if he could leave if he was tired of waiting.

Am I a prisoner?

He had no answers, nor anyone to ask. Sorcha's court wasn't like the Summer Court with its constant chatter and laughter. It was . . . calm, and not very embracing.

The exception to that was a faery whose body seemed to be cut of the night sky. Each day she'd paused to offer to share her studio supplies if he ran out.

"You could come to my studio. You could create," she said.

"That's kind," or "I appreciate it," he would say, carefully avoiding any form of "thank you" each time. He'd learned enough of their rules to know to avoid empty words.

"No speaking past the threshold," she repeated each day. And then she'd left without pause. Knowing she was an artist made her seem almost comforting, almost familiar—but for the flickers of distant starlight radiating out as she moved. She cast white shadows on the walls. It made no sense, not logically, but Seth had given up on expecting faeries to adhere to the rules of mortal logic or physics.

Today, when they exchanged their daily comments again, he decided to follow her, but he'd only gone a few paces when he ran into Devlin. The emotionless faery hadn't been around since the night he'd choked Seth. Now he stood like a physical barrier in the hall. "Olivia walks where you cannot."

Seth watched the starlit faery round a corner and vanish from sight. "You going to strangle me again?"

Devlin didn't smile. His posture and movements bespoke strict military training, steel-straight spine and every muscle ready. "If my queen requires it, or if it's in my court's best interests, or—"

"Following Olivia on that list?"

"If you follow Olivia into the sky, you'll freeze to death or suffocate. It would be unpleasant either way." Devlin maintained his military-straight posture. "Mortals aren't designed for sky walking."

Sky walking? Suffocate? Freeze?

Seth stared down the hall where Olivia had long since disappeared. "'Into the sky' literally?"

"She works with a different medium than you do. It's a rarity born of her mixed heritage." Devlin relaxed briefly; his expression was one of awe. "She weaves starlight. Tapestries of filaments so transient they melt each day. The sky isn't a place for fragile mortals. Your body requires breath and warmth. Neither is possible there."

"Oh."

"She would've woven a portrait of you, but the consequence would not be one most mortals like."

"It would kill me," Seth confirmed.

"Yes, her portraits are sometimes anchored longer with mortal breath. Breath for art. Balance." Devlin's voice had a fervor Seth recognized: it was madness perhaps, but it was madness over Art.

Somehow that revelatory moment of passion made Seth feel more at peace.

"Sorcha requests you attend her," Devlin said.

Seth quirked a brow. "Attend her?"

The taciturn faery paused. He stared at where Olivia had vanished several moments past. "You might be better off following Olivia. My queen is—like your queen and like Niall—required to consider the well-being of her court first. You are an aberration and thus in a rather untenable situation."

Seth glanced at Boomer in his immense terrarium, assuring again that the boa was contained, and then closed the door to his room. "I've been in an untenable situation for months. This is about fixing that."

"Bartering with faeries is not a wise plan," Devlin said.

"Art isn't the only thing worth being consumed for."

"So I've heard." Devlin paused and gave Seth a look of blatant assessment. "Niall cares for you, so I will hope you're as clever as you think you are, Seth Morgan. My sisters are neither kind nor gentle."

"I have no desire to fight them."

"I didn't mean in a fight. Their taking notice of a mortal has rarely been a good thing for the mortal, and you are very much drawing their attention." Devlin spoke the words in an extremely low voice. "Come."

The weight of the faeries' gazes felt different as Seth followed Devlin through the hallways. It was unsettling to see them stop mid-sentence, mid-step, mid-breath as Seth passed. Like walking with Bananach, following Devlin involved a series of twists and turns through the building. They went up and down stairwells, in and out of rooms that appeared to be the same ones. Finally Devlin paused in the middle of a nondescript room that Seth was sure they'd just left. *It has a strange doorway.* Seth looked behind him for the door, and the room was suddenly filled beyond capacity with faeries.

All staring.

"Turn and face me, Seth Morgan," Sorcha said.

As Seth turned, the other faeries vanished; the *room* vanished; and he was alone in a vast garden with only her. To one side, flowers twined around one another to the point of chaos. Enormous blue orchids seemed to be choking daisies that tried to push between snarls of blossoms. On the other side of the path, orderly arrangements of roses and birds of paradise were growing at equidistant intervals from flowering cactus and blossoming cherry trees.

Seth looked behind him. The faeries, the room, the building, they were all gone. It was garden and forest and ocean as far as he could see. Sorcha's hidden city wasn't a simple area behind a barrier. A whole world existed here.

"It's just us," the High Queen said.

"They vanished."

She gave him a patient look. "No. The world was reordered. That's how it works here. What I will is what *is*. Most everything here is controlled by my thoughts and requirements."

Seth wanted to speak, to ask questions, but he couldn't. Even with his charm securely fastened around his throat, he felt like he was caught in a glamour stronger than anything he could've imagined. Sorcha, the High Queen, was speaking to him in a fantastic garden . . . in the middle of a hotel.

The High Queen looked at him and smiled.

His phone buzzed. He held it up. Messages scrolled over the screen. As it was still blinking messages, he got a voice-mail indicator too. He stared at his phone, at one message in the center of the screen—"where r u"—and then he looked around him.

"It is not like over there. No mortal rules or trinkets function unless I think them useful. Things here are at my will alone," she added.

Seth knew *exactly* where he was. He lowered his arm, holding the phone tightly as he did so, and caught the High Queen's gaze. "This is *Faerie*. Not like just that you're a faery, but . . . this is it. I'm in another world. It's not like Don's house or the park. . . ."

Sorcha didn't smile, not truly, but she was amused.

"I'm in *Faerie*," he repeated.

"You are." She lifted the hem of her skirt and took three steps toward him. As she did so, Seth could see that her feet were bare. Tiny silver tendrils spoked from between her toes and over the tops of her feet. It wasn't the illusion of silver. It wasn't tattoos like in the Dark Court, or living vines like on the Summer Girls. Thread-thin silver was inside her skin, part but not-part of her.

He stared at those silver lines. If he looked closely, he could see silver tracery on the whole of her skin; faint outlines of veins showed under and through her skin.

"You are in Faerie"—Sorcha took another step—"and you'll stay here unless I determine elsewise. In the mortal realm, there are several courts. Once upon a time, there were only two. One left to find the depraved things they sought. Other faeries followed . . . a few were strong enough to create courts of their own. Others could have but chose to exist as solitaries. Here, there is only me. Only my will. Only my voice." She dropped her hem so her skirt covered her silver-twined feet. "You won't call anyone. Not from here or without my permission."

Seth paused. His phone had transformed into a handful of butterflies that took flight from his palm.

"There will be no communication between my court and theirs. I would prefer you behave properly." Sorcha glanced at his hand and the phone re-formed. "The decisions made here are mine alone. I have no co-ruler. I have neither successor nor predecessor. Your once-mortal queen's happiness doesn't matter here. Ever."

"But Ash—"

"If you are here, you are subject to my will. You sought me, came to my presence, stand in a world that innumerable mortals have dreamed of and died for. Nothing comes without cost in Faerie." Sorcha was nonplussed by his concerns. Her face was a silvered mask, no more flexible than a costume. She extended her hand palm up.

He gave her the phone.

"Why should I listen to your plea, Seth Morgan? What makes you special?"

Seth looked at her. She was perfection, and he was . . . not. *What makes me special?* He had been trying to figure that one out for most of his life. What makes anyone special?

"I don't know," he admitted.

"Why do you want to be changed?"

"To be with Aislinn." He paused, trying to find the right words. "She is *it* for me, the one. Sometimes you just *know*. No one, nothing will ever mean even half as much as she does right now. And tomorrow she'll mean even more."

"So you ask for eternity because you love a girl?"

"No," Seth corrected. "I ask to become a faery because I love a faery queen, and because she deserves to have someone who loves her for *who* she is, not *what* she is. She needs me. There are people—*good* people—I love and I'm a liability to them because I'm a mortal. I'm fragile. I'm finite." He felt himself saying things aloud that he wasn't sure he'd even been able to articulate to himself before, but here with Sorcha in front of him, he knew the right words. "I am in this world. People I care about, the woman I love, friends in all three of the courts . . . This is where I belong. I just need you to give me what it takes to stay with them and be strong enough not to fail them."

Sorcha smiled. "You're a curious mortal. I could like you."

He knew not to say "thank you" so he said only, "You are kind."

"No, that I am not." She looked for a quick moment as if she might laugh. "But I am intrigued by you. . . . If you are to be changed, you'll spend one month of every twelve here with me."

"You're saying yes?" He gaped at her. His legs felt weak.

She shrugged. "You please me . . . and you have the potential to benefit Faerie, Seth Morgan. This is not a gift given lightly. You are binding yourself to me for as long as you live."

"I'm already bound in other ways to two other faery rulers, and fond of a third." He tried to push back the fear that was creeping over him. He wanted this, but it was still terrifying. It was eternity they were discussing. He closed his eyes and tried to concentrate on breathing, on calm spaces in his mind. It took away the edge of panic.

Then he said, "So what do I need to do? How's it work?"

"It's a simple thing. One kiss and you'll be changed."

"A kiss?" Seth looked at her; there were two other faery queens who could demand a kiss without making him uncomfortable. Kissing Aislinn was something Seth never tired of doing, and Donia . . . he didn't think of her that way, but he liked her as a person. *Plus it would irritate Keenan if I kissed Donia.* He smiled at that thought.

The High Queen, however, held absolutely no sexual or romantic appeal. She reminded Seth of the statues in the antiquities sections of art books, austere and unyielding. Even before Aislinn was the Summer Queen, she was passionate; Donia might be winter incarnate, but cold was not the same as temperate.

"Is there another way?" he asked. A kiss seemed a strange request, and while faeries were clever, they also didn't lie. Seth knew that questioning was not only expected, but also lauded.

The High Queen's expression didn't change, not even a flicker of an emotion crossed her face, but when she spoke, her voice hinted at amusement. "Were you hoping for a quest? A seemingly impossible task that you could relay to your queen afterward? Would you like to tell her that you found and slayed the dragon for love of her?"

"A dragon?" Seth weighed his words carefully. "No, not so much. I just don't think Ash would be cool with me kissing you, and faeries aren't always very forthcoming about the ins and outs of things."

"We aren't, are we?" Sorcha sat down on a chair that was almost as elegant as she was. Wrought of silver, it was all graceful lines that had no visible beginning or end, like Celtic knotwork made tactile. It also hadn't existed in the moment before she sat in it.

"So, is there another way?" he prompted.

Sorcha smiled at him, a Cheshire cat's grin, and for an instant he expected the rest of her to vanish. Instead, she fluttered a fan she slid from her sleeve, a demure gesture at odds with her now obvious amusement. "Not that I'm inclined toward. A kiss for your new monarch. It seems only fair to ask what you don't want to give."

"I'm not sure 'fair' would be the right word there."

The fan stilled as she asked, "Are you arguing with me?"

"No." Seth was pretty sure Sorcha was intrigued, so he didn't back down. "Debating, actually. Arguing would involve anger or fear."

Sorcha crossed her ankles, resettling her old-fashioned skirts and exposing the silver threads that crept up her ankles. "You amuse me."

"Why a kiss?"

A spark of something dangerous slid into the High Queen's voice as she asked, "Do you think she'd mind that much? Your Summer Queen?"

"It wouldn't make her happy."

"And that's reason enough for you to not want to do it?"

"It is." He tugged on his lip ring, hoping briefly that he wasn't telling her the exact things she wanted to hear, but increasingly certain that Sorcha found appeal in the idea of Aislinn's displeasure.

This no-lying-to-faeries thing is a bad plan. He wasn't particularly fond of having a moral code just then. *She'd lie to me if she were able.*

Sorcha answered in a whisper-soft voice, "The simple things are perhaps the most difficult."

Then she held out her hand in an invitation he suddenly wanted to refuse. Despite having been surrounded by faeries the past few months, her unnaturally elongated too-thin fingers creeped him out. *She could crush me with that delicate hand.*

"This will make me like you? I'll be a faery after?"

"You will, for all but one month of true fealty spent in my realm each year." Sorcha hadn't moved anything but that bone-thin hand and even that was unwavering. "During that month, you will be mortal."

He couldn't quite get his feet to move, but his mind told him he needed to. Retreat or proceed, those were the choices. "One kiss for eternity with Ash."

At that, Sorcha's calm faltered. "Oh, no, I don't guarantee *that*. One kiss in exchange for faery longevity. You'll be held to faery law: lying will be beyond your capabilities; your word will be a vow. Basic glamour will be yours to wield. You'll be one of us in almost every way, but cold iron and steel will be not be toxic to you because you will retain a touch of your mortality. As to your queen, Summer Court faeries are a fickle lot—volatile, untidy in their emotions. I cannot promise you eternity with her."

She wiggled her fingers then, beckoning him. "Come now. If you'll accept the deal you're seeking . . ."

Seth took a step toward her. "And I'm still me? When I'm out there and here? I'm not your subject out there either?"

"Correct," she confirmed. "Examine my words, Seth Morgan, and choose now. This isn't an offer that will last if you walk away from me today."

Am I forgetting anything? He'd read enough on faery contracts to know that they always looked better than they were. Mortals had been bargaining and losing through loopholes for as long as they'd had dealings with the fey. He'd been paying attention when Aislinn sorted through faery politics; he'd borrowed books from Donia; he'd talked to Niall. The key was in precision.

One month a year, a kiss, and eternity with Ash.

He couldn't see any way that this was a bad bargain. *Except* . . . "Are all the months I owe you in a row?"

When Sorcha smiled this time, it was actually breathtaking. Here, then, was the faery queen he'd expected to see. That glimmer of emotion softened her faery perfection, and he saw in her that same wicked, lovely temptation that Aislinn and Donia exuded.

"No. One month of fealty in my presence, and then you leave Faerie and return to the mortal realm for eleven months there." She let a glamour fall over her until she looked like every dream he'd ever have—perfect and untouchable and somehow deserving of worship for it. "You may, of course, petition me to stay here for those eleven months as well."

Seth reached up and gripped the charm Niall had given him. He squeezed until he thought the smooth stone might cut into his skin. It was little, if any, use in this moment. "Don't hold your breath for that."

"Do you choose to accept my offer, Seth Morgan?"

He shook his head as if to clear the spider webs that seemed to be wrapping around him as she spoke. "I do."

"It's your choice. Come to me if you would choose this. Do you choose to accept this, Seth Morgan?"

He came closer, letting himself be pulled toward her by tendrils he couldn't see. Intangible fibers wrapped around him; they would weave him to her, assure him a place in a world of purity, protect him from the taint of mortality when he was outside Faerie.

And she is *Faerie. She's* everything.

"I do choose this," he said for the second time.

"To be subject to a faery queen is to give every breath at her command. With no hesitation, you offer your fealty and presence here in Faerie for a month each year as long as you draw breath?"

He was kneeling on the earth in front of her, touching her perfect hand. In her eyes, moonlit slivers beckoned. He'd be destroyed by them if he erred. He let go of the charm he'd been clutching so he could reach out to her.

My queen.

"Will you give me your last breath if I ask it of you? Do you choose to accept what I'm offering you, Seth?"

He shivered. "I will. I do. I *choose* this."

"Then give me my kiss, mortal."

Sorcha waited. The Summer Queen's mortal knelt at her feet, clutching her hand, and unable to shake free of her residual glamour, despite his charm, despite her gentleness. She held her appeal in check, but this mortal was meant to be hers. She'd seen it when he first stood in front of her, boldly asking for the gift of immortality. She saw it now when she looked to the future. Seth Morgan belonged to her, to her court, to Faerie. He mattered—and he needed to be not just a faery, but strong as few faeries were.

As he faltered, she debated the wisdom of how she'd chosen to make this so. It was of her own self she was giving. He had no need to know that or to know what a rarity it was. Simply because she could engender a transfer didn't mean she often did so. Mortals simply didn't become faeries, not without being bound to the faery who'd shared an essence with them. There were two ways to do so—as a loved one or as chattel. If he came to her more out of pure selfishness, she'd offer him only selfish use. If he offered more selflessness than self-gain, she'd return that generosity.

"A kiss to finalize our bargain, to unmake your mortality . . ." Sorcha didn't let her hopes into her voice. She wanted him to be worthy of what she was giving to him;

she believed him to be so. He could still turn away; he could fail her in this moment.

"You're not her," he whispered. "Only should kiss her."

"Be strong, Seth." She kept her glamour in check. "If you want this, you must give me my kiss."

"Give you a kiss." His words weren't slurred or unclear, but they were slower.

Sorcha couldn't reach out. She couldn't take his will-power. The choice was his; it was always theirs. "Seal the bargain, or reject the offer."

His eyes were unfocused; his heartbeat was rapid. Then he quirked his metal-decorated brow, and she saw a spark of something unexpected.

"Yes, my queen." He held her gaze as he turned her hand palm up. Then, he gently kissed her palm. "Your kiss."

For a moment, Sorcha didn't react at all. Here was a bold one. Mortals strong enough to resist the temptation of the Unchanging Queen were a rare treasure. Bananach had been right; her own visions of what might be were true: this mortal was different.

Wars are fought over lesser things.

She aided him to his feet, holding his hand in hers as his body began to sway under the first crush of the change. "Our deal is binding."

He pulled away. "Good."

She had intended to leave him drunk on a kiss, lost under a narcotic touch that would lessen the pain. *He ought not have to suffer for being clever. It's not unfair to offer a kindness to my subject.* When Keenan had changed his mortal girls, they had almost a full year to adjust. Seth had only a month—and within Faerie. The first wave of change would be harsh.

She didn't allow her subjects to suffer unnecessary cruelty. It was irrational. "Give me the charm."

She was his queen now: Seth obeyed.

Then the High Queen donned a glamour to look like his *other* queen. "Seth? Come here."

"Ash?" He stared at Sorcha in confusion.

She held her hands out. "Let me help you."

"I feel *wrong*, Ash. Sick," he muttered, weaving slightly on his feet as he tried to look around. "Where'd you come from? Missed you."

"I've been here all along," Sorcha told him.

Few truths were more complete than that revelation.

"Need to sit down." He stretched a hand out for a wall that was not there.

Sorcha stroked his face. "Mortals have no business playing in this world. Sometimes they attract the wrong attention. . . ."

"Just trying to keep *your* attention." He leaned his forehead against hers briefly and then pulled back with a puzzled look. "You're not this tall."

"Shhh." Then she kissed him while his mortality was pushed out by the new faery energy coursing into his body. She let her own calming breath slip into him. It wouldn't take away all the pain, but it would help. Sorcha could

remake the world in Faerie, but she couldn't change everything. Pain, pleasure, sickness, longing, there were things
that even the High Queen couldn't affect.

Sorcha found herself hoping that the Summer Queen
was worthy of this mortal-no-more's passion and sacrifice.

Because he's my subject now.

And like any good queen, Sorcha did what was best for
her subjects whether they asked it of her or not.

CHAPTER 23

Donia waited at the fountain on Willow. This late at night the mortal saxophone player was long gone, and the crowds of children who had frolicked in the water were tucked into their beds somewhere. Matrice, one of the Hawthorn People, perched in a tree nearby. The white-winged faery was one of the only fey in the area. Her tattered wings fluttered like ripped spider webs as she sat watching the sky on the edge of a branch. On the ground at the other end of the courtyard, Sasha crouched attentively. Somewhere farther out, several glaistigs roamed the perimeter.

Donia wanted answers, and of the four faeries she could ask, only one seemed likely to be helpful. Sorcha was unquestionable; Keenan was silent; Bananach was mad. That left Niall. After Seth's sudden disappearance and the whispered rumors coming from Faerie, Donia had little reason to doubt that Seth was in Faerie, a place from which mortals—and more than a few faeries—didn't return.

The High Queen was inflexible, cruel in ways that sometimes made the Dark Court look meek. *Or maybe I'm swayed by my own fears. . . .* Summer's rising strength made her melancholy. Winter had no business being out in the increasing heat of the season, but inviting Niall into her home felt like a betrayal of Keenan. Even now that their chance at a real relationship—however brief—was gone, she couldn't bear the thought of hurting him.

Niall arrived, alone and moving with the fluid grace of shadows stretching over the earth. His stride bespoke the same easy arrogance as his predecessor; his hand held a lit cigarette, a habit he'd adopted along with the responsibility of the court. Violence and temptation, he was the embodiment of the court he'd once rejected. The hint of it had been there when he was with the Summer Court—it was a part of why Keenan had kept him near, in her opinion—but the comfort he had with his own shadows was new.

Niall said nothing as he sat on the bench beside her.

"Why is Seth in Faerie?" she asked by way of greeting.

"Because he's a fool." Niall scowled. "He wanted to become fey. Bananach took him to Sorcha."

"Do you think Sorcha will keep him? Or turn him or—"

Niall cut her off with a look. "I think Sorcha has a habit of stealing away Sighted mortals, and Seth is likely in trouble."

"And Keenan?" She didn't stumble over the question, even though it stung to ask about him just then. She'd had her hopes raised, heard him tell her he loved her, and mere days later, he told her good-bye. Solstice was approaching, but she wouldn't be in his arms.

Niall ground his cigarette on the underside of his boot before answering her. "Seth's been missing and unfindable by all of the Summer Court. There's no way Keenan can't at least suspect where he is . . . especially as I expect that Ash told him of Seth's desire to change."

Idly, Donia let snowflakes fill her palm and shaped them into a small statue of the lone kelpie that lazed in the fountain. Niall sat silently in the dark beside her, waiting for her to steer the discussion. He wasn't pushy, even now that he was the head of the court the faeries feared almost as much as they feared hers.

Things had started shifting when Beira died. They'd changed as Keenan grew stronger. They'd gone off-kilter when Irial stepped down from his throne. Everything had become tentative. Not for the first time since she'd realized where Seth must be, Donia wondered if telling Aislinn was better or worse for the impending conflicts. If Aislinn knew, she'd go after Seth and into a conflict the Summer Court would lose. If she knew where he was, Aislinn would be furious with Keenan for hiding the truth—which would further weaken the Summer Court. Yet, not telling her seemed cruel and would inevitably drive another wedge between the Summer Court and the Winter Court. She'd not forgive Donia or Niall or any of them should she learn that they all knew where her beloved Seth was. And if he were killed in Faerie . . . the consequences of Aislinn learning that everyone had kept silent could be disastrous.

"Should we tell her?" Donia asked.

Niall didn't need to ask for clarification. "I'm not sure. She's grown closer and closer to—" He stopped and gave her a tender look.

"I know."

Niall lit another cigarette. The cherry glowed a warm red in the almost lightless night. "If we do, it'll complicate things. Ash will want to pursue him. Bananach tells me things are already poised for true violence."

Donia tried to separate her own desire for Seth to return to Aislinn from her awareness that war could follow Aislinn's knowing. The consequences of conflict with Sorcha were unfathomable. Then again, the consequences of Aislinn learning that the Winter Court and Dark Court both knew weren't pretty either.

Or of learning that Keenan knows.

Niall sighed. "I don't know. I'm going to see Sorcha. I'll see how he fares, retrieve him if I need to. It's probably past time to go visit Faerie anyhow. . . ."

Donia crushed the snowy sculpture she'd been making and let the flakes drift to the ground where they melted immediately. "We aren't her subjects."

"Sorcha's not like us, Donia. She's without our possibilities for change. She's the essence of Faerie." He stretched his legs out in front of him and crossed his ankles. "If the stories are true, she's the first of us. If she came here, we'd all be her subjects. If we went back to Faerie, we'd be her subjects. Showing her respect is the least we should do."

"I've read her books, Niall. I'm not sure if we'd *all* be her subjects if we went there. *Your* court was her opposition."

"Centuries ago, Don." Niall's shadow-maidens danced beside him in glee, belying the meekness of his words. They writhed in the bluish haze of Niall's cigarette smoke. "Right now, your court is stronger. Mine isn't able to oppose her."

"I don't know. Somehow, I suspect you'd fare better than you're admitting."

Niall's lip curved into a smile, and despite their history of conflict—his working with Keenan and her working against their goals—she felt a loosening of the tension inside her. He seemed happy. Over centuries longer than she'd drawn breath, he'd been sorely abused by Keenan, by Irial, by Gabriel's Hounds. It was soothing to see him lighter in heart for a change.

"You are kind," he said. "If Sorcha spent much time here, it wouldn't matter what we know now. She re-creates the world as easily as we breathe. Once, forever ago, I used to stay near her when Miach was my king, but after Keenan was born"—Niall shrugged as if it wasn't a loss, although his near-reverent tone revealed the extent of what Sorcha's presence had obviously once meant to him—"duty called. Miach's court needed me. Tavish and I held what order we could until Keenan was old enough to escape Beira's house. She let him have his visits to his father's court, but . . . a court needs ruling. We did what we could."

Donia was silent, thinking about the years Keenan spent in Beira's home, about the court without a true king, about Niall trying to rule a court not his. That wasn't something either of them needed to talk about just then. She redirected the conversation. "How long do you think Seth's been there?"

"For him? A few days. Not long enough for Seth to panic, but . . . out here, it's been weeks. I've arranged what I need here to go see him. I won't have him injured if I can protect him."

Donia nodded. "Bananach came to see me." Until that moment, she hadn't been sure she would tell him, but instinct was a critical part of ruling. Hers told her that Niall wasn't a part of Bananach's machinations.

"And?"

"She showed me the future." Donia folded her arms over herself. "I thought we had a chance, but then this happened. She showed me . . . I am not unlike Beira."

"It's only a possible future," he reminded her.

"If war is coming, I don't want to be the cause of it," she whispered. Being the Winter Queen didn't mean that all of her doubts and worries had faded. If anything, it meant that the consequences of her doubts and worries could be catastrophic.

I am not Beira. I will not be the cause of a return to ugliness.

It was Niall's voice that was ugly. "Why do you think I restrain myself against him? I have the power to strike him. You have the power to do so. Yet we don't. I don't want peace, but war is not what's right for my court now. If it was . . ."

Donia shuddered at the cruelty in Niall's voice then. "So why do you let Bananach run free?"

"I don't. I try to keep her leashed enough to prevent all-out war. Why do you think Irial saddled me with . . . I'm trying to do the same thing you are: find a balance that doesn't weaken my court. Unlike you, I want to strike him. I don't forgive as you have, yet war is not what's best for our courts."

"So we don't tell Ash about his suspecting—or possibly knowing—where Seth is." Donia hated it, but the discord that would result from Aislinn knowing Keenan misled her would put all of them in an even more untenable position. And the anger Keenan would have for Donia or for Niall would be dangerous to the already tentative peace.

Niall nodded. "And you let him go."

"I'm trying," she whispered. Uttering those words hurt like a physical pain. To come so close to the love she'd dreamed of and lose it was worse than if she'd not known it was within her reach. "Given time, Ash will accept him. Given time and a few wise choices, perhaps we can still avoid war."

"There was a time when this was what I planned and hoped for—Keenan with his missing queen, happy, strong. It was all that mattered." Niall looked bereft. His shadow-maidens stroked his shoulders soothingly.

"Me too." She thought—but didn't say—that it was still

what she wanted, not the being with Aislinn part, but his happiness. *Even now.* Despite everything, that's what she wanted. She only wished that his happiness didn't mean her sorrow.

They sat in companionable silence for a few minutes, until Donia looked at him and said, "I would prefer that Bananach is contained, but if there is war, Winter will hold to the past."

Niall was mortal-slow as he turned to look at her. "Meaning?"

"Meaning my court will ally with the Dark Court." She stood, letting the snow she'd held in her lap fall to the ground, and waited for him to join her. "Whether it be against his court or the High Court. I want peace. I want . . . a lot of things, but in the end, I need to do what's best for my court."

"If I could let war reign just long enough to make him suffer"—Niall smiled, looking so deadly in that instant that it was hard to remember that he hadn't always been the Dark King—"I would be sorely tempted, but fighting Sorcha . . . none of us wants that, Donia."

"I'd rather fight Sorcha than Keenan." She laid her hand on Niall's shoulder. "Seth is an innocent. Would you let her harm Seth? If you had to side with Keenan to protect Seth, would you?"

"Yes, though I'd much rather fight against him."

"But for Seth?"

"He is as my brother," Niall said simply. "Sorcha will not

keep him against his will."

Donia felt herself swaying slightly. This much time in the heat was wearing on her. "You need to go to Faerie."

"And if it's not Sorcha we need to fight? Would you stand against Keenan?" he asked.

"Not happily, but I will if need be." She held his gaze. "No matter which way we act, Seth's being in Faerie complicates everything."

"Which is precisely why Bananach took him there," Niall murmured. Then, he took her arm and escorted her from the courtyard with a comfort that felt familiar. It wasn't time to dwell on the past, on the losses that she should've accepted years past. It was time to prepare for the future— deadly though it might be.

CHAPTER 24

Aislinn stood nervously outside the door to the formal dining room. Lately she'd had dinner every night with Keenan. Some nights, other faeries joined them; sometimes, a number of the Summer Girls were with them; but tonight, it would be just the two of them.

Choose to be happy. That's what Siobhan had said, and Aislinn had been repeating it like a mantra since that night. For weeks, she'd been attempting just that: not giving up but trying not to wallow either. It wasn't working.

She took a deep breath and opened the door.

Keenan was waiting—which wasn't unusual. She knew he'd be there. What was unusual was the change in the room. Candles were lit everywhere. There were also tapers in the wall sconces and fat pillars on tall silver and bronze stands.

Aislinn crossed to the table and poured herself a glass of summer wine. The decanter was old, something she'd not seen before.

Keenan didn't speak while she sipped her wine.

She looked not at him but at the candle flames flickering in the draft that came through the room. She didn't want discord between them, especially not as he was her lifeline as of late, but she had to know how much Keenan had hidden from her. She asked the question she'd been pondering since Siobhan's lecture: "Did you know Seth had a charm to protect him from faery glamour?"

"I've seen it."

"You've seen it." She let the words drag out, let the silence build, let him have the chance to say something to ease her hurt at not telling her this.

He didn't apologize. Instead he said, "I expect Niall gave it to him."

Her hands tightened on the wood of her chair until it started to splinter into her palms. "You didn't mention it . . . because?"

"I had no desire to mention anything that could drive you further from me. You know that, Aislinn. I wanted you as my true queen. You felt it too." Keenan came and stood beside her. He loosened her hands from the chair. "Will you forgive me? And him? . . . And yourself?"

Tears were streaming down her cheeks again. "I don't really want to talk about any of this."

And Keenan didn't point out that she'd brought it up, or that not-talking wasn't a solution, or any of the things he could've said. Instead, he said, "All I want in this moment is to help you smile."

"I know." Aislinn lifted a napkin from the table and studied the embroidered sunbursts that wound into vines.

"It'll get easier," he continued. He was like that since Seth left, constantly reassuring her.

She nodded. "I know, but right now it's still awful. I feel like I've lost everything. Just like it was for you every time one of the Summer Girls refused the test . . . and when each Winter Girl risked the cold. Either way, each time they came to that point, you lost."

Keenan's expression was guarded then. "Until you."

They stood there in awkward silence for several moments until Keenan sighed. "This conversation is not making you any happier, Aislinn."

"It's not the . . . romantic stuff that I miss . . . I mean, I do." She paused, trying to figure out how to explain this to a faery who—for all his years—didn't seem to have any true friends. "Seth was my best friend before he was anything else. He was the only one I could talk to when you and Donia were . . . when you picked me."

Keenan waited.

"Best friends don't leave without a word," Aislinn said. Now that the words were there, they started bubbling out, and she was saying the things she'd been hiding inside. "I don't need a boyfriend. I don't need a mate or partner or any of that. I need my friends. Leslie's gone. I can't talk to my other friends about anything in my life. Donia *stabbed* me . . . not that we were close, but I thought we were becoming friends. And now, my best friend has left me."

"And you feel alone." Keenan came closer but didn't intrude in her space. "So let me be your friend. That's what you offered me when you became my queen. The approach of summer has added something else to it, but that's . . . I *need* you to be happy, Aislinn."

She nodded, and then she said the words that she wished she didn't have to, "It's been weeks without a word. I don't think he'll be back, but I can't let go."

"Let me be your *friend*, Aislinn. That's all I'm suggesting today. If the rest happens or doesn't, we can deal with that part later. No pressure, just an open door." He held out his arms for an embrace. "For now, just let me be here for you. We need to try to move forward instead of standing here weeping and waiting."

She let him hold her. Her sigh caught between pleasure and remorse as he stroked her hair, letting sunlight slide down the strands until she was languid, at peace as she rarely was these days.

"It'll be okay. One way or another, things will be okay in the end," he promised.

She wasn't sure if he was speaking opinion or truth, but for now, she let herself believe him.

Happiness is a choice.

CHAPTER 25

Another month passed without word. Summer was in full strength. Graduation had come and gone, but Aislinn only knew this because her diploma was waiting at her house one afternoon.

"I'm sorry I missed it," Aislinn told Grams. "If you'd wanted . . ."

"It's okay, sweetie." Grams patted the sofa.

Aislinn went to her. It felt like each step was through too-thick air. "I'm trying. It feels like the sun is choking me some days. And Seth . . . I still don't know."

"It'll get easier. Being this will get easier. I can't say I understand, but"—Grams took Aislinn's hand—"you are stronger than you know. Don't forget that."

Aislinn had her doubts. She felt like she was crawling out of her skin. The earth wasn't merely stretching after its long slumber under Beira's oppressive winter weight; it was trying to find outlets for decades of pent-up energy, and she was the conduit. Each dawn brought her closer to the other half of that heat—her king, her friend, her not-lover. She knew it wasn't a logical thing, the way she tracked his movements. It wasn't even a romantic thing. It was simple need. It embarrassed her. Lust was to be tied to love; with Seth, it had been. With him, she'd felt friendship, love, trust. With Keenan, she had friendship and a sort of trust, but there was no real love. There was something missing.

Grams sat silently beside her. The only sound was the steady tick of a cuckoo clock on the wall. It should be peaceful, but Aislinn still felt like running. Everywhere she went, she felt a pressure inside that she couldn't escape.

Except with Keenan.

Then Grams broke the silence. "If Seth can't handle what you are, that's his loss."

"I'm the one who's lost," Aislinn whispered. "Everything feels wrong without him here."

"But?"

"He's been gone for two months, and Keenan—"

"Is deceitful, Ash." Grams kept most of the censure from her voice.

"Sometimes. Not always."

"He's a conniving bastard, but he'll be in your life forever—" Grams sighed. "Just be sure you're careful with how much you let him in. Or how fast. Don't let this summer thing or your hurt make you foolish. Sex isn't ever the same as love."

"I'm not . . ." Aislinn looked away. "We haven't. I've only . . . with Seth."

"You wouldn't be the first one who fell into a new bed out of loneliness or longing, sweetie. Just be sure you're ready for the consequences if you do." Grams stood then. "Let's get some food in you. I can't fix it all, but I still have comfort food."

"And advice."

Grams smiled and motioned toward the kitchen. "Fudge or ice cream?"

"Both."

Later that night, while Aislinn was curled up beside Keenan watching a movie, she thought about what Grams had said. He wasn't a bastard, not always, not to her. He was ruthless in pursuit of what he thought was best for his court, but he was also considerate and gentle. She'd seen him with the Summer Girls. He cared for them. He cared for the rowan, and not just as subjects, but also as individuals. He was impulsive and frivolous, the essence of summer.

He's a good person, too. Maybe not always, but for a faery king, he was remarkably good. For someone who'd struggled since birth just to get to where he should've always been, he was remarkably kind. *And he's here for me.*

She leaned her head on him and tried to follow the movie. They'd been doing that a lot, just being near each other late at night. She couldn't sleep, and unless she was at Grams' apartment, Keenan was awake the moment she was. She wondered if he was awakened when she was at Grams' too. She hadn't asked. She just started spending more nights at the loft.

Grams didn't comment. She could see the pacing energy that filled Aislinn as they moved toward Solstice, and Aislinn's despair at Seth's absence became too much. *You need to be where you feel more at peace, sweetie,* Grams had said, *and that's not here with me right now. Go to your court.*

Being with Keenan was a weird mix of comfort and longing. He was true to his word in keeping a marked distance, treating her solicitously but not pressing her. The only times he was overtly affectionate were their late-night movies. They'd watched more than a dozen by now.

The movie that night wasn't funny or action-filled but a romance of sorts: an indie film about street musicians falling in love while they both belonged elsewhere. The music and the message were perfect, poignant and heartbreaking. The combination spoke to her, reminded her not to cross lines that would do irreparable damage all around. *Lust isn't reason enough.*

But as Keenan stroked her hair absently while they watched *Once,* it didn't feel like lust was all they had.

Sometime during the movie, she must have drifted off to sleep because when she looked up the screen was black. She had shifted so she was lying with her head on a pillow in his lap, but Keenan was still running his hand over her hair as he had been when she'd been watching the movie.

"Sorry." She blinked and looked up at him.

"You needed sleep. It's a compliment that you trust me enough to rest here."

She blushed and then felt foolish for it. It wasn't like she'd never woken up with friends. She'd crashed at Carla's place and at Rianne's and even at Leslie's before things had changed so much. Waking up beside Keenan—*okay*, on *him*—wasn't a big deal. She looked outside. Dawn was just breaking. He'd been holding her while she slept for hours. Before she could say anything, Keenan stood.

"Get changed." Keenan pulled her to her feet as he said the words.

"For?"

"Breakfast out. Meet me downstairs." Then he departed before she could ask anything or find words to tell him she appreciated his helping her feel secure enough to rest. She scowled at the door he'd left through. His distance during daylight hours made her feel awkward. On the one hand, she appreciated his keeping to his word not to pressure her, but on the other, it made her feel guilty. Once upon a time, he'd promised her that her wishes would be as his own. Despite his moments of telling her that what *he* wanted was different, he'd kept true to that. For not the first time, she wondered if she could've loved him if her heart wasn't already given to Seth.

She was so tired of wondering, of doubts, of worries.

Getting a decent night's sleep helped, but worrying over the same thoughts she'd been having for months didn't. Putting those thoughts away, she went to her room and got ready.

Downstairs, Keenan was waiting by the Thunderbird. They didn't take the car often, so she was a little surprised.

He seemed nervous. "No questions yet."

"Okay." She got in and watched the sky brighten as he drove them out of town toward farmlands she'd been to on rare school field trips and even rarer photo excursions, when Grams could be convinced that she would follow the rules about the faeries. Back then, trips to dangerous expanses of iron-free nature were exceedingly rare. Now, it was safe. The crowds of faeries in the fields and among the trees weren't a danger to her.

Keenan pulled into a gravel lot. A battered wooden sign, hand-painted and fading, proclaimed PEG & JOHN'S ORCHARD. On the other side of the vast and mostly empty parking lot stretched apple trees in long rows. As Aislinn looked, all she could see were branches and leaves and apples.

She'd never seen so many healthy trees. Even from this distance, she could see the ripening apples that clung to their strong branches.

When she got out of the car, he was already at her door.

"This is it, the orchard where . . ." She wasn't sure she wanted to finish that sentence.

Keenan didn't hesitate to say the words, to put the weight of it out there in front of her. "I brought one other person here, but"—he took her hands in his—"you're the only one who's ever come knowing what it means to me. I thought we could have breakfast here."

"Can we walk first? So I can see it." She felt shy. It wasn't a casual thing he was offering her—not that anything between them had ever been casual. This was his private space, though; bringing her here was a gift.

He let go of her hands and got a cooler out of the car. After taking her hand again, he led her across the uneven lot. The crunch of gravel under her feet seemed loud in the empty air between them.

At the edge of the lot was a patch of grass. A dark-haired girl wearing sunglasses sat on a chair behind a table covered in baskets. An old cash register sat on the table. She looked at Keenan suspiciously. "You're not usually back so soon."

"My friend needed to come somewhere special," he said.

The girl rolled her eyes, but she motioned at the baskets. "Go on."

Keenan gave her a blinding smile, but her dismissive look didn't alter. Aislinn found herself liking the girl for her instinctive mistrust. A pretty face didn't mean someone was harmless, and Keenan, for all his kindnesses, could be ruthless.

Aislinn let go of Keenan's hand and took a basket from the table.

"Come on." He led her under fruit-heavy branches, away from the world. *All I need is a red cape.* She felt childhood panics rise up for a moment: venturing into the woods where faeries lurked was never safe. Grams had taught her that. Little Red had found danger because she went away from the safety of steel. *He's my friend.* Aislinn pushed aside her twinge of mistrust and looked at the apples hanging overhead.

Casually, as if it wasn't unusual, she took his hand again.

He said nothing. Neither did she. They walked hand in hand, wandering among trees he'd nurtured even when Winter held dominion over the earth.

Finally, they stopped in a small clearing. He set the cooler down and released her hand. "Here."

"Okay." She sat in the grass under a tree and looked at him.

He sat beside her, near enough that it felt unnatural not to touch him. She shivered even though it was warm. The loss of his hand meant that the warmth that had been zinging between them had receded.

"This was my haven for years when I needed a place that was just mine." He looked lost then; clouds flickered in his eyes. "I remember when they were saplings. The mortals were so determined to make them thrive."

"So you helped."

He nodded. "Sometimes, things just need a little attention and time to grow." When she didn't reply, he added, "I was thinking last night. About things. About what you said before . . . when I kissed you."

She tensed.

"You said you wanted complete honesty. If we're to be true friends, that's what we must do." He ran his fingers through the grass between them. Tiny wild violets sprouted. "So here we are. Ask me anything."

"Anything?" She plucked at the grass beside her, enjoying the strength of it. The soil was healthy; the plants were strong. She could feel the web of tree roots under them. She thought about it, what he was offering. There weren't many things she could think to ask, except . . . "Tell me about Moira. You and Grams are the only ones I can ask."

"She was beautiful, and she didn't like me. Many of the others . . . Almost *all* of them"—he grinned—"with a few exceptions, were pliable. They were eager to fall in love. She wasn't." He shrugged. "I cared for each of them. I still do."

"But?"

"I had to become what they wanted to help them love me. Sometimes that meant adopting the fashion of the day, their newest dances, poets, origami . . . finding out what they liked and learning about it."

"Why not be yourself?"

"Sometimes I tried. With Don—" He stopped himself. "She was different, but we were talking about your mother. Moira was clever. I know *now* that she knew what I was, but at the time I didn't."

"Did you . . . I mean . . . I know you seduced . . . I mean, it's . . ." She blushed brighter than the apples above them. Asking her friend, her king, her maybe-something-more if he'd slept with her mother was weird by any standard.

"No. I never slept with any of the Summer Girls when they were mortal." He looked away, obviously as uncomfortable with the topic as she was. "I've never slept with a mortal. I kissed some of them—but not her, not Moira. She treated me with contempt almost from the beginning. No amount of charm, no gift, no words, nothing I tried worked."

"Oh."

"She was sort of like you, Aislinn. Strong. Clever. Afraid of me." He winced at the memory. "I didn't understand it, but she looked at me like I was a monster. So when she ran, I couldn't follow her. I knew she'd have to come back when she became a Summer Girl. I knew she wouldn't accept the test, so I let her go."

"And what? Waited?"

"I couldn't un-choose someone once she was chosen." Keenan looked sad. "I knew she was special. Just like you. When I realized that you were the one, I wondered if she would've been my queen if . . ."

"I've wondered too." She realized they were whispering even though the faeries that she'd seen in the orchard weren't anywhere near. "Or if I'm this because she was changing when she had me."

"If I'd have done things differently—brought her back—how many things would've been different? If I'd known she was pregnant, you would've been raised by the court. You wouldn't have resisted if you'd grown up with us. You wouldn't have been so involved with mortals."

She knew exactly what mortal involvement he was thinking of, but she couldn't consider even for a heartbeat that
her life would've been better without her mortal life. Loving
Seth was the most perfect thing she'd known, and his love
would be the only true love she'd ever know. That wasn't
something to wish away, even now when her heart ached.
Of course, saying all of that to the faery she was tied to for
eternity wasn't something either of them needed.

"I'm glad you didn't know," she said.

"That year while Moira was away, pregnant with you,
I spent all the free time I suddenly had trying to convince
Don to forgive me." He looked wistful. "Some nights she
would deign to sit with me. We went to a revel together . . .
and . . ."

"Does it get easier?"

He glanced at her. "Does what get easier?"

"Losing someone you love."

"No." He looked away. "I kept thinking one of her rejec-
tions would be the one that stopped hurting, but it was
when she didn't reject me that it hurt worse. I thought that
we had a few years, but now . . . He's gone, Ash, and I can't
not be around you. You're my queen. I can't *not* be drawn to
you. If I could set you free somehow and make Donia my
queen, I would, but I can't. And if there's a chance that you
and I might become more, I will be here with you."

"And Donia is . . ."

"Not something I want to discuss right now. Please?" He

held Aislinn's gaze and said, "I need time before I can talk about her."

"So we try to figure out how to be happy with what we do have," she added.

It wasn't love she felt, not like she felt for Seth, but there was friendship. There was longing. She could convince herself it was enough. If this was to be her future, she could do it. Loving someone meant being hurt; choosing passion with a friend was safer. Maybe it was calculating, keeping her heart safe, but it wasn't only selfish: it would make their court stronger. It made good sense.

She didn't want to fall in love with anyone else—not that she wanted to tell him that. *How do you tell someone that even though you'll be together for centuries, you don't want to love him?* Keenan deserved better.

They sat there, talking about the courts, faeries, stories from their lives—just talking. Finally, he paused. "Stay right here," he said. Then he vanished.

She leaned against the tree, content for a change, at peace with her world.

When he returned, he had several apples he'd plucked from a tree. "These were almost ripe the other day. I knew they'd be perfect today." Keenan knelt on the ground beside her and held an apple out, not to give it to her but for her to bite. "Taste."

She hesitated, but only for a moment. Then she tasted it: sweet and juicy. He had made that happen, brought these

trees to strength when the world was trapped under ice. A
few drops of juice trickled down her chin as she bit into the
fruit, and she laughed. "Perfect."

He ran his thumb across her skin and brought the apple
juice to his mouth. "It could be."

It's not. It wasn't real. It wasn't enough. *He's not Seth.*

She backed away, trying not to see the hurt in Keenan's
eyes.

CHAPTER 26

Niall stood scowling in Sorcha's sitting room. Shadows radiated from him, strands of darkness extending from a black star. He didn't move, even though the temptation to strike out was obvious in the clenching of his hands. "You've made a mistake, Sorcha."

Slowly, far more slowly than she'd approach any faery other than Bananach, Sorcha crossed the room to stand in front of him. She didn't stop until the hem of her skirt was atop his boots. "I do not make mistakes. I make reasonable choices. I chose to make him mine."

"He was not yours to take," he said. The handmaids of the abyss spun and faded into tongues of black flames as Niall gripped her arms. "The other courts might let you take the Sighted ones without consequence, but I'll fight for this one. I'll not let you take any of the halflings or Sighted ones that are mine to protect."

"You stand in Faerie and think to tell me what will be,

Niall. Is this really what you consider wise?" Around them, the room faded away until it was just the two of them in a wide-open plain. "My will is all that matters here."

"Perhaps you might want to remember which court once held equal sway in Faerie?" He stared at the space beside her. His brow furrowed in concentration, but it worked. The Dark King smiled as an obsidian mirror, shadows made solid, reached up from the dry earth at their feet. It wasn't much, but it was *there*.

The tempting cadence of Niall's voice revealed his pleasure as he remarked, "I might be new to *this* court, but I watched you well once upon a time. I learned more of your secrets than I've told anyone."

"Do you threaten me?"

"If I must." Niall shrugged. "I can bring my court here. I can take him back. Being the Dark King gives me the right to rule equally in Faerie."

"It would be foolish. I"—she took a small breath and the world around them shifted—"would crush you if you stood against me. You are a babe."

"There are people worth fighting for."

"We are partway in accord there: Seth is worth much. Fighting me is not the right answer." She gestured around them. They stood in an austere temple. Niall's obsidian mirror was flanked by ornate pillars. In the space behind her an altar heaped with carnage stood large. She didn't need to look to know it was there. "Is that what you'll offer Bananach? Your foolhardy compliance? You come here and behave impudently. Why do you think she brought him to me? He was a sacrifice to start her war."

"Seth is not a sacrifice to start *or* avoid war. He is not disposable."

"I know," Sorcha whispered, not in fear but because sharing truths wasn't something she did lightly. "I will keep him safe, as you would realize if you were thinking clearly. Should Bananach—or *anyone*—strike him, they strike me."

Niall paused at that declaration. The anger fled from his face. "Ash . . . Aislinn . . . does not know where he is. Yet. If she learns that you've taken him, she'll come here."

"Her king will not tell her." Sorcha knew that Keenan, that all of the faeries who were thinking clearly, knew precisely where Seth was. "It is not my responsibility—or of interest—to tell her. Nor is it yours, else you'd have done so."

Sorcha held out her hand.

Niall, still the gentleman, took her hand and directed it to the fold of his arm. "What game are you playing, Sorcha?"

"The same one I've been playing my whole life, Gancanagh."

For a few moments, Niall said nothing. Finally, he turned to face her and said, "I want to see Seth. I need to hear from him that he is well."

"As you will. He has been resting for the past several days. When I think him ready, you may see him, but not before. He is mine to protect."

"What did you do?"

"What needed done, Niall. That's what I always do," she said. Their courts might exist to oppose each other, but that didn't make them true enemies. It was about balance. Everything was. On occasion she might have even tipped the scales to assure that the Dark Court was nourished enough to stay healthy—never too healthy, of course, but strong enough to serve its function. That was what Faerie required, and although she was not their monarch while they were in the mortal realm, she still was the Unchanging Queen.

"Was his oath freely given?"

There was such hope in his voice that she almost wished she could lie to Niall. She couldn't, though. "It was. I do not tempt and misdirect, not like you."

"I've never tried to tempt you, Sorcha. Even when I thought you might be the answer I sought."

"More's the pity," she murmured as she left him to find his way to his room. He was a worthy king, one who could bring the Dark Court back to what it could be, but he wasn't a threat to her court, not today, not yet. In time he would be, but Niall wasn't truly there as the Dark King. He was there as Seth's friend, which meant he'd not abuse her court or her good will on this visit.

When Seth woke to find his queen standing in his room, his first reaction was gratitude: she'd saved him from mortality, given him a gift beyond words. Nothing he could do would be too much to repay her. She was stretching as she stared at the garden outside the window. It looked like the move of someone who had slept uncomfortably. *Which is nonsense.* The High Queen had no reason to be staying near him in any uncomfortable position, but Seth still looked at the muted green chair that sat near the window.

Sorcha didn't turn to face him. Instead she pushed open the windows and reached outside to twist several blossoms off. "You've been unaware for six days," she said by way of greeting. "Your body had changes to accept. This was easier for you."

He stretched. He felt almost as bad as when he woke in the hospital after the last Winter Queen had almost killed him. He was sore, weak, and surprised that he'd slept—*or been unconscious*—for the worst of it.

"But I'm not just a mortal now?"

Sorcha smiled. "You were never 'just a mortal,' Seth. You're an anomaly."

He quirked a brow, which made him increasingly aware of a screaming headache that was growing worse by the moment. "I was a mortal."

"Yes, but you matter in ways that you don't see."

"Which are?"

She walked over and handed him a washcloth from a basin beside the bed. At first, it looked like she was going to wipe his face, but she held it out. "The cold will help your head."

He laid it over his eyes for a moment. It smelled minty.

"Will I feel miserable the entire month I'm mortal?"

"No." Her voice was soft. "But your body is trying to understand the extra energy that's coiled inside you. Your senses will be different as a faery. Your gifts will be startling. The knowledge that most faeries are born possessing is being woven into your unconscious mind. If you were just to stay here, it wouldn't feel like this. The process could go more slowly."

"Woven?"

"With a few threads from Olivia's starlight. It makes things quicker, but it stings a bit."

He lifted the edge of the cloth from over his eyes to glance at her. "A bit?"

She had moved back to the window and was tearing up the blossoms she'd collected. "And the faery's essence that you received is stronger than most. That too makes the change more challenging. . . . I've done what I could to ease the pain."

The tone of her voice was very different from what it had been when she'd spoken to him before. Her expression was sculpture-stiff, but she was vulnerable. *Fragile.*

Seth sat up and stared at his new queen. "You've given me everything. Because of you I can be with Ash. I can be there for Niall. I can survive being in their world."

The High Queen nodded and her look of worry receded. "Few faeries will be strong enough to be a threat to you," she said. "I've made sure of that."

"Why?"

"Because I chose to."

"Right . . . so that month here . . ." Seth hated bringing it up, but right then all he wanted was to see Aislinn. "Do the six days unconscious and my first few days here count too?"

"Yes." Sorcha poured steaming water over the blossoms she'd plucked.

"So twelve of my thirty days are over?" He rolled out of bed and was briefly amused as she turned and quickly threw a robe at him.

"Yes." She poured the blossom tea and handed him a cup. "Drink this."

Seth didn't even think to hesitate. He *couldn't*. His queen had given him a command: he obeyed. He swallowed the vile drink, and then he scowled. "That . . . I just . . . I couldn't tell you no."

She smiled. "You're *mine*, Seth Morgan. You'd give me your heart if I ordered it."

She owns me.

He'd watched Niall, Donia, Keenan, and Aislinn with their faeries. It wasn't like this. He hadn't thought it would be like this when he'd sworn fealty. *Is it different because this is Faerie? Is it her? Me?* He scowled at her. "I didn't know."

She walked back to stand in front of the window again, once more keeping her distance from him. "If I choose to, I own your will, your body, your soul. Would you have changed your answer?"

"No," he admitted.

"Good." She nodded and stepped from the room into the garden. "Bring another cup of tea."

She didn't ask him to follow, but he knew that he should. It was expected.

Barefoot, wearing pajama pants and a robe, carrying a cup of disgusting tea, he followed Sorcha into the garden with no hesitation. She was his queen: her will was all that mattered.

He had to walk faster than he liked in order to catch up. "So I'm what? Your pet? Your servant?"

Sorcha's look was bemused. "I don't keep pets. Faerie isn't as twisted as it looks from out *there*"—she made a vague gesture toward a faraway stone wall—"we are civilized in my court."

"You own me. I'm not seeing how that's civilized." He sipped the noxious tea. "It isn't like that for other rulers."

"No?" She made a moue of confusion and then shrugged. "I am different. *We* are different."

"But I'm a faery when I'm out there?" He suddenly needed to have her confirm it. The weirdness of her being able to steal his will had unsettled him.

"A strong faery. A faery few will be able to overcome. You are *different*, but yes, definitely a faery." She looked away from him, staring at a bench that seemed as if it was carved of ivory. It was surrounded by tiny winged insects that shone like fireflies. They moved in a blurring arc and vanished.

"Okay. In *here* I'm a mortal. So what am I to do? Do I just lie about?" Seth hoped that his being a faery wasn't going to make him turn into someone who parsed words so oddly. Conversation with many faeries was infuriating. Sorcha was no exception.

She gave him another tolerant look—as if he were the one being difficult. "You will do what mortals have always done for us: you will create."

"Create?"

"Art. Music. Verse." Absently, she ran a hand over the bench. The patterns on it re-formed under her touch. "Everything you need is available here. Whatever medium. Whatever palette. Find inspiration and create something amazing for me."

"So my price for immortality is weeks spent here doing what I enjoy doing?"

"Just"—she gave him a calculating look that he had seen on other queens' faces—"don't disappoint me. I will have your passion in your creation, or you won't leave."

"No." Seth's temper piqued, and he took a step toward her. "A month per year. That is the deal."

"A month of *fealty* in Faerie was the deal. If you are to truly serve me, you will give me true art. Nothing offered to fill the surface only. True art. True passion." Her tone grew gentle then. "Rest today, Seth. Tomorrow, I will return."

There was something hidden in her voice, but before he could ask any questions, a gray stone wall on the opposite side of the garden path opened. Devlin emerged from behind it.

Sorcha gave a sad smile to Seth that confused him. "A

mortal shouldn't be allowed the autonomy and influence you've had. Three of the four courts have been touched by your will. Balance needs to be reestablished. You are out of the natural order and so must be nullified in some way. It is in everyone's best interests."

Seth suppressed a shudder as he looked from the High Queen to the waiting faery. Seth had believed that the worst of the faeries belonged to Niall these days, but as he looked at the placid expression on Devlin's face, he wasn't so sure.

The monsters don't always look like monsters.

Devlin gestured for Seth to precede him through the stone doorway, away from Sorcha, and Seth had to wonder just how far the queen's lackey would go to "nullify" something she declared out of order.

CHAPTER 27

Sorcha came to Seth's room again the next day—and the three that followed. She'd stay all day, for countless hours while he worked. They spoke of life and dreams, of philosophy and art, of music he'd enjoyed and theater she'd seen. They walked in the garden. And sometimes, she simply sat quietly meditating or reading while he painted or sketched. Seth couldn't imagine being away from her. If not for missing Aislinn, he could see himself staying in Faerie. Out there, he had no real purpose, no direction, no family. He lived only for Aislinn. In Faerie, he existed to create Art. He felt whole for the first time he could remember, at peace and sure of everything. He'd come seeking immortality, but what he'd found was more valuable.

Happiness. Peace. Home. It was tinged with an unending ache for Aislinn and a new sorrow that he'd be leaving Sorcha at the end of the month. His choice to be a faery had given him everything he'd sought—and other gifts he hadn't dreamed he could ever have.

The thought of leaving Faerie was frightening.

He channeled those emotions, desires, and fears into his art. Mostly, he'd been painting. The room was littered with half-finished canvases. He tried to work with the metals that had appeared in the side room as well. He'd completed a few tolerable things, but nothing worth her—nothing that met his goal.

"Seth?" Sorcha was beside him. "Are you able to pause for a bit today?"

"For?"

She smiled and wiped a bit of paint from his face. "You have a guest, dear."

Guests. He couldn't leave, but he could have guests if Sorcha allowed it. His heart was thundering. "A guest? Ash? She's here?"

"Not her." Sorcha sounded almost sad as she said it.

The Dark King appeared out of nothingness behind Sorcha. "I see my advice was completely ignored," he said.

Seth embraced Niall. Aside from seeing Aislinn, nothing else could please him as much as seeing the Dark King. He stepped back and said, "You were wrong."

Niall laughed. "More arrogant already . . . you've been spending time with the wrong court, little brother."

The High Queen's tense expression relaxed ever so slightly. "I'll leave you to roam with Niall then. I'll be in the dining hall after." To Niall, she only said, "Return to

me when you're ready to talk about other matters. May-
haps we can discuss regrets. . . ."

Seth couldn't help but watch her as she left. He could
count the heartbeats between each movement. He had: they
never altered. The rhythm of her motion was one of perfection. When her hand lifted to open the door, it was with
the same arc each time she reached out. If he measured the
distance, Seth knew she'd match it with precision. Today
though, she hesitated for a heartbeat extra on several steps.
The beat of her movements was imprecise.

"She's upset," Seth said.

"What?"

Seth explained the counting and added, "Like music.
Her song is not as it always is." He glanced at Niall. "You
unsettle her."

Niall's gaze went to the doorway through which Sorcha
had left. The flickering dancers surged forward as if they
would step from his eyes to pursue the High Queen. "It's a
natural antipathy."

"Perhaps she would be pleased by your attention. If it
would please her, maybe—"

"I don't know if you realize it or not, but your sudden
devotion to her is creepy." Niall shook his head.

Seth bit his lip ring, thinking the words over before
he answered. "My closest friend rules the court of nightmares. My girlfriend is the embodiment of a *season*. I'm
not sure you can really call this 'creepy.' Sorcha makes me

feel peaceful. I like it."

"There are going to be consequences."

"I made the right choice. This is what I want."

Niall shook his head. "Let's hope you're still saying that later."

Seth walked over to the window that led to his garden. He pushed it open. "Come on."

When Niall followed, Seth resumed speaking. "I find a different sort of peace in Sorcha's court. It's taken years of meditation to reach the calm I had before, and it felt like it was going to slip away every time I saw Keenan's influence growing stronger . . . but in one moment, one promise, complete peace. One month a year with her and I can have everything I need. Out there, I will be as you used to be—with faery weaknesses and faery strengths. I can be with Ash forever. I can be there for you forever. Don't you see? It's perfect."

"Except for the month here. Just come with me. I took you into my court's protection and . . . my court is the one that balances hers. We can take you home now."

"I *am* home, Niall. Aside from missing Ash—" Seth stopped himself. "Why do you know I'm here but she doesn't?"

"Seth . . ." Niall dropped his gaze.

"What?"

"Keenan hasn't told her. He knows. *Everyone* knows."

"Except her." Seth swallowed the words of anger and fear that rose up. Panic wasn't the answer. He was in Faerie; he had peace; and he'd have forever with Aislinn. "Why?"

"Come home with me," Niall repeated. "We can go to her."

"Keenan is taking advantage of my absence." Seth said the truth that Niall was avoiding. *"Already?* I've only been here a few days. Thirty days without me isn't going to change everything."

Devlin appeared in the path in front of them. "Tread carefully, Niall. Sorcha will not be pleased if you say what you would reveal." To Seth, Devlin said, "Sorcha requires that you do not pursue this matter."

And just like that, Seth was unable to continue the conversation. "I believe we need to talk about something else."

"Is that what you *want*? Give me the word . . ." Niall glared at Devlin. "Think, Seth. If you choose to, you can resist her wishes. It's harder with her. Harder in Faerie, but I know you can—"

"She's my queen, Niall. I want what she wants. She gave me the world."

"Do you have any idea how disturbing you are?" Niall's expression was raw. "You're my *friend*, Seth, and you're vacant."

"I'm not vacant. I'm just"—Seth shrugged—"at peace."

"I think I should go."

"It would be best. I have work yet, and she is oddly possessive of my attention. There's a door you can use." Seth gestured toward a thorn-hidden doorway in the distance, one of the openings from Sorcha's demesne into the mortal world.

"Be safe."

"I am. I'm happy here. She knows things. Everything makes so much more sense when she explains it." He let his thoughts wander to the late-night conversations they'd been having in the garden. Philosophy, religion, so many things were clear when he spoke to his queen. Then—brimming with art and passion and epiphanies—he'd return to the studio she'd given him and create until he could barely stay upright.

"Later, once you're away from Sorcha, we need to talk. Come see me when you are home? You *are* coming home, right?"

"I am coming back. Aislinn is on the other side of the veil." Seth reached out to clasp Niall's forearm. "But I will only discuss what Sorcha permits. Even when I am not here, I'll honor my vows to my queen."

"I'll see you when you come home—and are yourself again." Niall turned away.

Seth walked a few moments longer, and then he returned to his art. A little more than two of his four weeks were over in Faerie. Soon he'd be able to see Aislinn.

CHAPTER 28

More than four months had passed since Seth left. There were no calls or messages from him, nor was there any news from Niall. Skirmishes between Summer and Winter Court faeries happened more and more. Dark Court faeries attacked the increasingly vulnerable Summer Court fey, who were weakened by Aislinn's inability to move forward. Choosing to be happy was far easier to say than to do. She and Keenan were in a stasis of sorts, and their court was suffering for it. They sat side by side in the study as guards shared reports from around Huntsdale and beyond. It wasn't a new event, but the tone was worse yet again.

"The Ly Ergs grow bolder every day," a glaistig reported. She was not as disappointed by this as most Summer Court faeries would be, but the glaistigs were mercenaries. The hooved faeries roamed all of the courts, hiring on for trouble at times, living as solitaries at other points.

Keenan nodded.

Aislinn felt her court face lock into place, a mask to hide her worry.

Beside her, Keenan squeezed her hand. Sunlight slipped from his palm to hers. *Comfort but not enough.* He let her stay quiet as guards reported troubles, as if she were fragile. *I am.* She felt like that some days, that she was nothing more than spun glass that would shatter if she moved the wrong way.

Then Quinn spoke. "When Bananach was out and about, the guards looked in her nest. There's no evidence that Seth was ever there."

"What?" Aislinn's slight grasp on calmness fled. Hearing Seth's name so casually tied to Bananach's was bone chilling.

Keenan held tighter to her hand; he was an anchor tethering her to some semblance of stability. "Quinn—"

"No evidence?" Aislinn tried to keep her voice steady, and failed. "What do you mean?"

Quinn's posture didn't shift. He stayed focused on her although the other guards shifted anxiously. "She's the carrion crow, my Queen. If she'd killed him, there would be evidence. Neither blood nor bone there is his—"

"Enough," Keenan snarled. He kept her hand in his and pulled her closer to him.

Aislinn felt as much as saw a shimmer of fog uncoiling in the room. "No. I want to know." She looked over and caught Keenan's gaze. "I *need* to know."

"I can deal with this, Ash," Keenan spoke in a low voice,

feigning privacy. "You don't need to hear if there's . . . unpleasantness."

"I need to," she repeated.

He stared at her silently for several breaths before saying, "Continue."

Quinn cleared his throat. "There were strange things. A shirt of yours"—he paused as he stumbled over the words and glanced at Keenan—"hers, our queen. A bit of the pet serpent's shed skin. A book of Seth's."

"Why would she have any of that?" Aislinn had begun to accept that he'd simply left her. Now, with Seth's things at Bananach's nest, she wondered if she'd been completely wrong.

Keenan looked at the guards, at Quinn. The Summer King was angry. "Leave us."

The guards vanished amid murmured chastisements to Quinn. After turning his back on the departing faeries, Keenan pushed the coffee table away and knelt on the floor in front of her. "Let me handle this. Please?"

Aislinn rested her head on his shoulder. "I need to know why our things are there. He wouldn't go to her as a friend."

"Maybe he would. He *is* friends with Niall. Bananach is of that court." Keenan stroked her hair. "Seth's already accepted the Dark Court's protection. He was angry with me. We had words before, Aislinn. He told me that he'd use what influence he had to strike me if I . . . if I manipulated you."

"Seth?" She pulled back and stared at her king. "Seth *threatened* you? When? Why didn't you tell me?"

Keenan shrugged. "It didn't seem the right choice. You and I had talked. I intended to . . . Donia had forgiven me. I thought it would be unwise to tell you, and then he left and I saw no reason to upset you further."

"You should've said something. You agreed to not keep secrets from me." Her skin was steaming from the pulse of sunlight shifting angrily inside of her. Had he been anyone else he couldn't have touched her just then.

"But I *am* telling you," he said. "Quinn ought to have kept—"

"No." She pulled away. "Quinn was *right* to tell me. I am the Summer Queen, not a voiceless consort. We've discussed this."

"You're upset."

"War has my things. *Seth's* things. You're telling me Seth threatened you. Yeah, I'm upset."

"That was exactly what I didn't want. I need you happy, Aislinn."

She leaned back into the sofa cushions, putting distance between them. "And I need answers."

The Summer Court had searched all over. She'd had no signs of where Seth could have gone—until now.

"But it doesn't make sense," she said. "I met her. Seth's not . . . she's not someone he'd go with by choice."

"Really? Seth's closest friend is the Dark King. There are parts of your mortal that you aren't seeing. What was he like before you?" Keenan stared up at her. "Seth isn't an innocent, and the Dark Court is filled with temptations that have called more than a few mortals into their embrace, Ash."

"Aislinn. Not Ash. Don't call me that." Her heart ached. She hated the way it felt, how wrong it was to hear Keenan call her a mortal name anymore. *I am not a mortal. I am not that person now.* She was a faery queen whose court needed a stronger monarch. Other courts were as enemies, threatening from crossways she didn't understand. Donia was distant; Niall was resentful; both were secretive. The two courts that the Summer Court dealt with were closed off. And through that tension was the shadow of Bananach's proclamation that war was pending.

"If you want me to find out more, I could ask for an audience with Niall," Keenan suggested. "Unless you want to invite War into our home. . . ."

"No." Aislinn could still taste the smoke in the air when Bananach had spun her illusion in the park. "If we are on the edge of violence, I don't want her here. I'm trying to find a way to be the queen our faeries deserve, and bringing her to their haven is not the way. I can't just sit here doing nothing. She must know something."

"So what do you want, Aislinn?" Keenan looked wary. "Do you really want to put yourself in harm's way? Is that going to help? He wasn't happy. If he went with her, got ensnared in the temptations of—"

"Can we go to Bananach?" Aislinn thought she was

out of tears, but she felt the sting in her eyes as she tried not to cry. "If she hurt him—"

"We don't know if Seth was there socially or if it was something else. Let me—"

"If she hurt him"—Aislinn began again—"I won't ignore it. If she'd injured Donia or me, you wouldn't ignore it."

Keenan sighed. "I can't risk our court over a single mortal, Aislinn."

"It's my court too," she reminded him.

"Even if she took him, you can't attack *War*."

"Have you ever tried?"

"No."

"Then don't tell me I can't," she said. If Bananach had taken Seth and killed him, Aislinn would figure out how to exact revenge. She had eternity.

"You'd risk our court for this?" he asked.

"Yes. For someone I love? Without a doubt."

Keenan sighed, but he didn't continue his objections. "Let's go to the lion's den, my Queen."

Accompanied by a full platoon of guards, the Summer King and Queen made their way to Bananach. After the way Aislinn had fallen during her visit to Donia and the way she and Keenan were both debilitated the last time they confronted Niall, Aislinn wondered if they needed still more. Entering the Dark Court, the court of nightmares—the home of the Gabriel Hounds, of the carrion crow—no matter how she phrased it, it sounded like an unwise plan.

But Bananach might have answers.

Aislinn didn't ask how Keenan knew where to find Bananach; she was too frightened to think beyond the possibility that she was walking into the court of a faery who was decidedly hostile toward their court—and into the presence of the epitome of war and bloodshed.

Keenan led her across Huntsdale to a condemned ruin with blacked-out windows. This wasn't a bright, airy loft like their home or an aging mansion like Donia's. Even the air outside the building felt dirty. It made her cringe, like being naked in front of a crowd of lecherous strangers.

Fear. Pure, raw fear. They were in the right place.

As they walked up to the door, Keenan scowled. He didn't pause or knock. He slid the door open and strode inside. He looked ready to strike someone.

Rage.

"Keenan!" She grabbed his arm. "We need to talk to them. Remember? That—"

"Ash-girl, you've finally come calling."

Aislinn looked upward. Bananach was perched on a rafter like a nightmarish vulture. Her feathers were expanding as she sat there, building themselves into sweeping wings that would span two body lengths if they were spread wide. With a crackling sound, she fluttered those wings, stretching them.

"You are good to me," Bananach crowed. She dropped to the floor in front of them. "Come now. The Dark King will be irritating if I keep you to myself."

Aislinn started, "We're here to see you. I need to know—"

Bananach's hand clamped over Aislinn's mouth before the sentence was finished. "Shhh. Mustn't ruin my fun. No more speaking from you if you want speech of mine."

Aislinn nodded, and Bananach pulled her hand away, scratching furrows into her cheek in the process.

They followed Bananach into a gutted concrete abyss. A sickly smell, like burned sugar and musky bodies, lingered in the air. The floor was sticky underfoot, so that each step was accompanied by a squelching sound. Aislinn had the almost irrepressible urge to run. She kept her arms close to her body in an attempt not to touch anything or anyone. They weren't all misshapen, but many of the faeries seemed ill made. Others looked closer to what she was accustomed to but were equally frightening.

Red-palmed Ly Ergs grinned, too wide, gleeful in the funereal atmosphere. Vilas turned their gray gazes on Aislinn and Keenan. Jenny Greenteeth and her cluster of nightmarish kin spoke softly, like gossips at the gate. Spreading a cloud of fear, the Gabriel Hounds moved like sentinels throughout the crowd.

Aislinn looked back at their own guards. They were fine for individual skirmishes, but a full-out war would be devastating. The Summer Court wasn't ready for fighting, not truly. The Dark Court was wrought of violence, among other things. This was their domain.

"Do you like it?" Bananach whispered. "How they want to eat you alive? You took away the last king's mortal. You make the new king mourn for both of his mortals."

"*His* mortals? Seth is my—" Aislinn started.

But Bananach crowed. Her shadow-wings stretched out behind her and she dragged her talons over Aislinn's arm in a feigned caress. "Pitiful little ash-girl. I wonder if he mourns falsely. Pretending to blame you for taking the boy?"

In front of them, Aislinn saw a shadowed tableau. Unlike in the park when the image had looked real, this was an obvious illusion hanging in front of them. A battlefield spread out of the image. The ground was ravaged. Faeries lay broken and bloodied. Shades of the dead drifted in the smoke from funeral pyres. Mortals were tangled in the mix—horror-stricken and mad, dead and empty.

In the center of the carnage was a table of sun-bleached bone. Skulls were stacked high for legs; ribs and arms and spines were woven together with sinew to make the flat of the table. Bananach sat at the head of the table—and Seth was stretched out on it in front of her.

The shadow Bananach in the image caught Aislinn's gaze and said, "If I were queen, I'd eat his entrails at my table just to make you ache." Then she plunged her talons into Seth's stomach.

He screamed.

It's not real. It's not real at all. But the war faery's earlier words made Aislinn's fear grow. *Is this a "what-if"? Is this what will happen if I make the wrong choice?*

Keenan pulled her to him. "It's not real, Aislinn. Look away. Look away *now*."

The image shattered then as one of the Vilas spun through the room. Her delicate shoes, held to her feet with silver chains, made an unpleasant clattering noise as she moved across the cement floor.

"It's an illusion," Keenan said. "Seth is not here."

"Are you so sure, little kingling? Can you be sure of anything?" Bananach reached out and laid her hand over the site of Aislinn's now-healed stab wounds. "Stirrings, beautiful stirrings that will bring me my violence . . ."

Aislinn had to remind herself that she was not a mortal to be daunted so easily. She put her hand on the raven-faery's taloned hand. "Do you have Seth? Did you take him?"

"What a good question," Niall said.

The Dark King had come up behind them. He paused beside Bananach. "Well?"

"They were in my nest; they are in your presence. The mortal isn't here. But *you* know that. . . ." She leaned on his shoulder and let her wings curl forward to embrace him. Her wings were still shadowy, not fully tangible, but they weren't illusory anymore.

"Don't." Niall walked over to a throne on a raised platform. Unlike the Summer and Winter Courts, the Dark Court actually had a dais. The Dark Court embraced a bizarre mix of old-fashioned manners and disturbing perversities.

Aislinn walked forward several paces. Keenan stayed by her side. Some of their guards followed; others scattered into the room—not that they would be very effective in this crowd. Bananach was not the only threat: throughout the room were Ly Ergs, several glaistigs, the Hounds, and Cath Pulac. Aislinn shuddered at the sight of the feline faery. Like the great sphinx in the desert, she typically only watched.

Why is she *keeping company with the Dark Court?*

Aislinn and Keenan exchanged a glance as they took in the faeries who were sitting in Niall's presence. Bananach's whispering of war seemed far more frightening when they stood in a den filled with promises of fear and violence.

Niall lounged in his chair and watched them with a mixture of amusement and derision. "Why are you here?"

"I need to know what happened to Seth. Where he is. Why he's gone." Aislinn wasn't sure what she was to do. *Do queens curtsy to other rulers when they come seeking favors?* She would. She'd beg if it meant finding Seth. "I thought Bananach might answer questions."

Faeries laughed raucously at that.

"My Bananach?" Niall grinned. "Darling? Do you suppose you could answer the Summer Court's questions?"

The raven-faery was suddenly beside the Dark King; she gripped his neck like she'd strangle him.

Niall didn't react. "They have questions."

"Hmm?" She had drawn blood and was watching it trickle down Niall's throat.

"Questions," he repeated.

The room stilled as Bananach looked around and said, "My war comes. Wars need lambs and cinders."

Her wings solidified as everyone watched her.

"Unless you ruin it all, we are where we must be." Bananach kissed Niall and whispered, "We shall bleed, my King. If we're lucky, you might even die horribly."

Then she took flight. Aislinn clutched Keenan's hand as she passed them in a blur.

Once Bananach was gone, Niall made a gesture of dismissal. "You have the only answers you'll find here. Go now."

There were more answers to be had. Aislinn was sure of it. Niall knew something more. He cared too much about Seth to be this dismissive if he didn't already know what she wanted. *He wouldn't be this calm if Seth were dead.*

Her resolve broke. "Tell me what you know," she begged. "Please?"

The look Niall gave her was akin to the disdain he'd had when they'd argued at the Crow's Nest. The stillness that had accompanied Bananach's mad muttering held. When the Dark King broke the silence, he said, "I know that *you* are why he is gone, and I don't know that you deserve his return."

"He's okay, though?"

"He is alive and physically unharmed," Niall confirmed.

"But . . ." Aislinn felt simultaneously better and worse.

Seth is safe. It was just the one pain then, the one that had been weighing on her. *Seth left me and is not here by choice.* "You know where he is. You've known . . ."

The room was full of faeries who were staring at her as she fought not to break down in grief, or perhaps rage. They licked their lips like they could taste her feelings. Vulgar and hateful, these were the faeries she'd feared. They were nothing like her court.

Beside her, Keenan tensed. He extended a hand. She took it. "Will you tell him I—"

"I am not your messenger boy." Niall's scorn was chokingly thick. His faeries giggled and whispered.

She started toward the Dark King, but Keenan tugged her back.

"No. Come closer, Aislinn," Niall beckoned. "Come kneel before me and ask for the Dark Court's mercy."

"Aislinn—" Keenan started, but she was already walking toward the Dark King.

When she reached him, she dropped to her knees at his feet. "Will you tell me where he is?"

Niall leaned forward and whispered loud enough for everyone to hear, "Only if *he* asks me to."

And to that, Aislinn had no answer. She kneeled on the dirty floor and lowered her gaze to stare at the Dark King's boots. If Seth didn't want to be in this world, what right did she have to try to force him? Loving someone meant letting them be who they were, not caging them.

Maybe he didn't tell me good-bye because he knew I would try to make him stay. His last message had been that he'd call, not that he would come home to her.

She stayed there, kneeling, until Keenan led her away.

CHAPTER 29

Sorcha would rather be with her mortal in the garden; however, Devlin had insisted they speak. They walked through the halls, not beside each other but with him not quite a half step behind. It was only enough distance that she would notice. At a casual glance, other faeries would not see it. The swish of her skirts and measure of her step were so predictable that Devlin could time his movement to match hers. After eons together, he could predict every move in the Unchanging Queen. *And I loathe that.* She wouldn't speak that into their world though.

Her brother had existed almost as long as she and Bananach had. He was a tether between his sisters, an advisor to Order, a friend to War. Of the three, he found his the least appealing position, but Sorcha would gladly have traded fates with him. He had a freedom of choice that she lacked. Bananach had freedom but lacked a firm grasp on sanity.

"Forgive my questioning, but what good can come of

letting him leave here? Keep him or kill him. He's just a mortal. His going there will complicate matters. The other courts will quarrel."

"Seth is mine now, Devlin. He's my court, my subject, *mine.*"

"I could remedy that. He introduces risks that are dangerous. Your caring for him is . . . untidy, my queen." Devlin's tone was even, but even didn't mean safe. His devotion to order was often bloody: murder was merely another sort of order.

"He is mine," she repeated.

"He would be yours in the earth too. Let the hall take him. Your affection is causing you to act oddly." Devlin caught her gaze. "He inspires you to forget your tasks. You spend all of your time with him . . . and then he'll go to their realm, where you won't walk. If he doesn't return to you or if War kills him, I fear that you will be irrational. There are solutions. You can still control this situation. Kill him or keep him here where he is safe."

"And if that's what Bananach wants?" Sorcha paused to look in at Olivia. The starscapes she was painting were perfectly wrought—equidistant pinpoints of light with sporadic glimpses of randomness. The touch of chaos in the order—art required that. It was why true High Court faeries couldn't create.

Devlin stayed silent as they watched Olivia string stars on celestial spider-thread, weaving a frame to anchor bits of eternity for a few brief moments. If envy weren't so untidy,

Sorcha suspected she'd feel it in such moments. Devlin, for his part, was in awe. Consuming passion fascinated him, and Olivia was consumed by her art. She had only the barest tie to the world, moving through it like a breeze. She spoke, but never while she worked, and rarely when she thought of work.

Sorcha stepped back into the hall.

When Devlin followed, she told him, "I want Seth to have his freedom, but to be kept safe over there. I want him observed when I'm not with him. I need this, Dev. I've not asked for anything like this in all of forever."

"What do you see?"

Sorcha didn't like to talk about the arcs she saw in life-threads. They were rarely predictable, only temporally true, and always fluid. Each choice made the whole pattern shift and refine itself. Like Bananach's far-seeing, Sorcha saw what-ifs and maybes. Bananach only looked to those that would help her further her goals; Sorcha's vision was wider.

"I see his thread woven in mine," she whispered. "And it has no end, no knots or loops . . . and it shifts even as I speak. It blinks in and out of forever. It chokes mine; it fills in my own where it looks as I had died. He matters."

"Murdering him before this emotion clouded your logic would've simplified things."

"Or destroyed them."

Devlin frowned. "You're keeping something from me."

When Sorcha opened her mouth to reply, Devlin raised a hand. "I know. You are the High Queen. It is your right.

All is your right." For a strange moment, he seemed almost affectionate as he gazed at her, but then he spoke, "I will keep him safe over there, but you must tuck this emotion away. It is unnatural."

The faery who had been her counsel for longer than either of them could quite recall seemed to have only the court's needs in mind.

As I should.

But as she returned to business, she wondered if Seth would like her private garden and what art he would make for her before he left.

Every day, Sorcha came to Seth's quarters and listened to him talk, and when he wasn't working, she spent hours showing him as much of the breadth of Faerie as she could in their limited time. He'd miss her when he left. Much like when he'd known Linda was leaving, he felt a dull ache at the thought of going months without her company. It was a maudlin truth, but he suspected he'd admit it to her all the same.

Today, when she walked in, the High Queen had a pensive mien; her moonlight eyes sparkled with cold light so very different from Aislinn's sunlit looks.

Soon I'll see the sunlight again. He smiled at the thought of being with Aislinn, of telling her what he'd seen, of revealing that he'd found a way to have forever with her. He wanted to bring her to Faerie with him. *Maybe Sorcha would agree to let Ash stay with me during that month. Or visit.* He wasn't sure he was ready to ask, not until he talked to Aislinn, but even if they couldn't work that out, one month out of each year was a small price. He'd gained eternity with Aislinn in exchange for a few short months.

Sorcha didn't speak. She simply walked to the window and opened it, letting in moonlight and the thick scent of jasmine. It was day, but in Faerie, the skies shifted at Sorcha's whim: she apparently felt it should be night just then.

"Good morning," Seth murmured. He had been up working on another painting. It wasn't right, but something would be. It drove him, the pressure to capture something perfect, something ideal, and give it to her—a gift to one queen to pay the fee to return to another. What he felt for Sorcha was oddly like what he'd felt for Linda. He wanted her approval. He wanted her to look at him with pride.

But right then, Sorcha extended a hand, and he offered her his arm as expected.

"Manners, Seth. Women always appreciate a man who treats them with manners." Seth's father was at the mirror fastening the stiff white collar of his dress blues at the time. The military dress uniform seemed to turn his father into a different person, with a straighter spine and sharper moves. It also turned Linda into a different person. Seth's mother sat beside him, stroking his hair absently and gazing adoringly at her husband.

"Manners," Seth repeated obediently as he snuggled into her embrace. He might be in the fourth grade now,

but he wasn't going to turn down one of his mother's rare moments of cuddling. There was no doubt that she loved him, but she wasn't usually affectionate.

"Do little things to let her know that there's nothing and no one in the universe that matters more than she does when you look at her," his father said as he turned from the mirror. He held out a hand to Linda, who smiled and came to her feet. She was still in her housecoat, but her hair and makeup were already done for the night out.

As Seth watched, his father kissed her hand as if she were a queen.

His father's lessons on life weren't always clear at the time they were given, but they were invaluable. Seth tamped down on a surge of longing for his family.

Beside him, Sorcha was silent. She'd led him to another hall and approached one of the numerous tapestries that hung on the walls. Faded threads made the palette more muted than it must once have been, but age didn't detract from the beauty of the scene. Sorcha herself was depicted in it, surrounded by courtiers in various positions of attentiveness. Couples danced in what looked to be a formal way. Musicians played. But it was apparent that everyone in it was gazing at Sorcha, who sat regally observing the tableau. The real Sorcha—who looked much the same as her rendered image—pushed the weighty fabric aside. Behind it was yet another door.

"It's like a rabbit warren around here. You realize that this"—Seth pushed the aged wooden door open—"doesn't look like it belongs in the hotel at all?"

Laughter like the peal of crystal bells escaped her lips. "The hotel is a part of Faerie now. It doesn't quite conform to the rules of the mortal realm. It conforms to my rules. The whole of the mortal realm would too if I chose to linger there."

Outside the door was a different walled garden. A path wound into the heart of it as if to invite them to yet another world. The garden walls looked as though they were made of stones fitted together with spatial understanding in lieu of mortar. Flowering vines crept over those crumbling walls; their blooms burst out of crevices in erratic patterns.

"It's a bit chaotic for you, isn't it?"

Sorcha shook her head. "Not really. This my private garden where I meditate. No one comes here but me or my brother . . . and now you."

And as they walked, the stones in their path realigned themselves, the blossoms assumed a predictable pattern. It was surreal—even after all he'd seen. "Not in Kansas anymore, are we?"

"Kansas?" Her forehead furrowed. "We weren't in Kansas to begin with. That state is—"

"Things are weird here," he amended as he led her around an uneven flagstone.

"In truth, things make sense here." Sorcha trailed fingers over the plain-looking blossoms of the night-blooming jasmine. "Appearances are deceiving."

"The art is almost done." He was anxious that she like it. *Only a few days left.*

"I look forward to the unveiling." Her tone was light, but amusement lurked under it. "Unveilings are interesting. It's a moment of clarity. . . ."

"Sorcha?" He caught her gaze. "What's up?"

"I need to explain the 'catch' in the deal you made."

Seth's nerves weren't too jangled yet, but he suspected that they were about to be. "I was hoping I'd done well."

She squeezed his arm. "I've been making contracts since before your mortal records even existed. You knew the dangers and still stood firm."

"So I was a fool?"

"No, you were what mortals often are: blinded by passion." She let go of his arm and leaned her face closer to the jasmine. It made a shivery sound as it extended itself to her. Moonlight, from inside of her, illuminated her skin.

"What is it?" His heart thundered as he started to turn the words over in his mind. He'd warned Aislinn about making a deal with a faery king, but then he'd done much the same. Fear built in his chest as he waited—and evaporated when Sorcha turned her face to look at him.

Glamour to soothe me.

He knew it even as calm returned to him like a cool breeze on too-hot skin. Sorcha smiled and turned her face back to the jasmine.

And he waited, watching her—*my perfect queen*—enjoy the simplicity of her gardens. "Don't do that. Don't influence my feelings."

The calm breeze fled.

She straightened and stepped back on the path. "A month in Faerie with me is what you bargained."

"It is." He offered her his arm again.

She put her hand back in the crook of his arm and resumed walking. "Time moves differently here than in the mortal realm."

"How much differently?"

The rhythm of her steps was unchanged as she said, "A day here is six days there."

"So I've been gone more than five months?" He said the words slowly, trying to make sense of what Sorcha was revealing: he'd been away from Aislinn for almost half a year while Keenan was at her side. They'd been alone together—while she was already half enthralled by Keenan—for longer than he and Aislinn had officially dated.

"You have."

"I see."

"Do you really?" Sorcha paused, bringing their walk to a stop again. "She'll feel your absence much longer than you'll feel like you're away."

"I get that." Seth tugged his lip ring, pondering for a moment. Another surge of fear rose up inside him. Would she think he'd left her for good? Would she worry?

Would she be angry? *Have I lost her?* He wasn't going to give up now, not when he had come so close to having everything.

Sorcha darted a doubtful glance his way. "You could stay here. I can keep you safe. You're happy here. . . ."

"I could stay on the *chance* that things there are wrong?" He smiled at her. "I didn't get this far with her or with you by giving up on what I want. Fortune favors the bold, right?"

"Keenan knows you are here. Niall told you that."

Seth wasn't as calm as he'd like; there was a dark pleasure in the fact that Keenan's deceit would be revealed. It didn't entirely assuage the pain at the idea that Aislinn could've fallen in love with Keenan. "He'll need to answer for that when Ash finds out. Won't he?"

The idea of her with Keenan sickened him. *But we have forever. He had his one and only chance.*

"If she is gone from you, you could come home. You will always have a home with me." Sorcha didn't press the subject, but he knew her well enough to understand that what she was offering wasn't a minor thing for her. It wasn't something he'd ever thought he'd have, and right then, it was a great comfort. The only other person he'd thought he could count on was probably drifting further away. Risking Aislinn's love was not a price he'd have willingly chosen, but he hadn't thought he'd gain so much either. Faerie was nothing if not unexpected.

"I'll miss you," he said. He wasn't particularly inclined to hide his emotions, not from her. "Even if I don't come running back to you, I'll miss you."

With the same casual gestures she used in most of her movements, Sorcha let go of his arm and pretended to examine a blossom-laden vine. "That's to be expected."

"And, you, my Queen, will miss me."

The blossoms held her attention, and she lifted a shoulder in a dismissive shrug. "I may need to see how you adjust to that world as a faery."

"It would probably be wise." He wanted to bring her gifts, find perfect words, something to let her know that he valued her affection, that his missing her was no small thing. He moved closer. "Sorcha? My Queen? I would stay with you if not for loving her . . . but I wouldn't be here except for loving her."

"I know." She brushed his hair from his face.

Sorcha felt it when Devlin entered the garden. Her brother wasn't near, but she could feel his steps on her soil. This wasn't just any garden in Faerie: it was her private home, warded well. Few faeries could enter it at all; only one could do so at will.

"I should go back," she murmured.

"Fine." He stepped away from her, seeming hurt for reasons she didn't understand.

"Are you angry with me?" Strange that it mattered, this mortal child's opinion. It did, though.

"No." He gave her a curious look then, as calm as one of her own faeries. "Can I ask you a question?"

"For exchange?"

He grinned. "No. I just want an answer that only you can give me."

"Ask." She glanced up the path to assure that her brother was not approaching. She suddenly didn't want him to hear this conversation with Seth.

"This kindness you show me . . . What is it?"

She paused. It was a fair question. The answer was one he could ponder while he was away in the mortal realm. Perhaps it would even convince him to come back sooner. "Are you sure that's the question you want answered? There are other things you—"

"I'm sure," he murmured.

"I am the High Queen. I am without consort"—she held up a hand as he opened his mouth to say something, and then she continued—"or child."

"Child?"

"Children are a rare gift in Faerie. We live too long to have many young. To have one—" Sorcha shook her head. "Beira was a fool. She had a son, but she let her fear that he'd be like his father rule her. She kept her own affection bound away from him but for strange bursts of kindness he didn't see. Had she done otherwise, Keenan wouldn't have been a Summer King but . . ."

"Her heir."

Sorcha nodded. "He was born of sun and of ice. Beira's fears made him not hers."

"And you?"

"I have no heir, no consort, no parent. If I had a child, though, I'd visit him if he wanted my . . . meddling." She hadn't spoken this to anyone. It was irrational, this desire to have a real family. She had Devlin. She had her court.

And one very disturbed sister.

It wasn't enough. She wanted a family. Eternity with no true connections made sense; it helped her keep her focus. The Unchanging Queen had no business wanting change— but she did. "I want a son."

"I'm . . . honored." Seth didn't look aghast at her words. He paused, and he lowered his voice to say, "I have one mother who gave birth to me as a mortal, so she's been stuck with me because of that, and since you gave me a second birth, I guess that kind of means you're stuck with me too."

She felt warmth in her eyes, maudlin tenderness that made her leak tears. "To be remade means someone giving you of themselves. To be remade strong enough to with-stand the dangers of that world and of my affection meant having a strong faery make that gift. I wanted you to be strong."

Admitting what she'd done wasn't her intention either— at least that was what she'd told herself when she'd made the choice.

He was following her implications, though. "Did a

faery lose immortality for this?"

"No."

"What was the cost? The exchange?"

"A bit of mortal emotion and a little vulnerability." Sorcha kept her voice low too. Devlin might be trustworthy, but that didn't mean he respected her privacy fully. Her brother was as protective as Bananach was destructive.

"You did this?" he whispered.

She nodded slightly.

He had something like awe in his eyes as he looked at her. "Will you visit me?"

"I would come to check on you."

"Right." He embraced her, hastily, but still an embrace—a sudden, impulsive *hug*.

It was a kind of heaven she hadn't ever felt before.

Then Seth added, "Tell me who I'm allowed to speak to of this or bind me."

"Niall. Irial. They may know if you choose it. Niall already knows, I suspect."

"Aislinn?"

She'd known that question would come if Seth learned the truth, but she'd not known that it would come so soon. Careful of the words, Sorcha told him, "If you believe that not telling her will endanger your relationship irreparably or if you are ever so injured that you need me. Beyond that . . ."

"But Irial and Niall?"

Sorcha was pretty sure that she wasn't doing this maternal thing entirely right. *Already*. However, she was starting it with a child who was far from a true infant. She trusted her instincts, not logic, not well-pondered thoughts. "Irial has been in love with Niall for centuries. Niall cares for you and will keep you safer in that world, so I won't keep this from him. If he knows, I'll allow Irial to know as well. They've had enough troubles between them that I won't add a new one. I want them to be at peace with each other. That's why the mortal girl they love is not here with the other Sighted ones."

"You're far kinder than you admit."

"The mortal taint—" she began but stopped herself from that attempt at a lie. "I really should see what Devlin has come to tell me."

Her son leaned in and kissed her cheek. "You *just* became 'tainted,' and Leslie's been free for months."

"That was a gift to . . . someone who was once my—" Sorcha stopped. Her cheeks were actually burning. She was *blushing* on her own, fully in control of herself, with no Dark Court faeries near. She liked it.

"Mothers don't often tell their sons such things," Seth quipped, "so I would rather not hear."

It was positively endearing.

"Niall will help keep you safe in that other place you will live," she added hurriedly. "I could—"

"You should still come check on me. I will miss you."

Seth held out his arm to accompany her back to the end of the path where Devlin now stood.

"I will come then." She put her hand in the fold of his arm, and together they walked forward.

CHAPTER 30

As the next month passed, Aislinn didn't speak of what had happened in the Dark Court. Each time Keenan had tried to discuss it, Aislinn had fled. Hearing that Seth had chosen to leave her was like having the hurt made new again. She didn't want to touch that feeling, so she doted on her court. She acted lighthearted. She danced in the street with Tracey. She coaxed plants to strength all over the city. The earth and her faeries flourished under her attention. After a couple weeks of her being the epitome of an attentive queen, even the most cautious of her faeries believed she was fine.

Except Keenan.

But tonight was the monthly revelry, and after tonight, he would know that she was going to be fine too. It was Autumn Equinox, and she'd mourned Seth's loss longer than they'd been a couple. She couldn't spend eternity like this. He'd made his choice; he'd left her world, chosen not to be a mortal trying to love a faery. He'd turned his back on what she was, on what they had.

Choose to be happy. She'd spent almost six months mourning. *Let him go.*

Aislinn walked across the street to their park. Somewhere inside her she remembered that it was odd to own a park, but nestled next to that thought was the awareness that faeries had been staking territories for longer than mortals had walked the earth. Tonight, the oddity of what she was faded under the one truth that she could hold to: *I am the Summer Queen.*

Keenan stood waiting. He was her king, her partner in this strange world. Without mortal eyes watching, he was utterly himself—sunlight made solid, promises made tangible.

He knelt before her; his head was bowed as if he were her subject. And tonight, she wasn't objecting. Tonight, she wanted to feel powerful and free—not like her heart was being laid bare and sorrow was eating her alive. She was the Summer Queen, and this was her court. This was her king.

"My Queen."

"I am," she said. "Your *only* queen."

He still knelt, but he looked up at her. "If you choose that . . ."

Around them, faeries waited as they had last autumn when she was a mortal. This time, though, she understood the stakes far better. She stood, a faery queen, in her park at the end of summer, and her king knelt before her. She knew what she'd be choosing—a chance at being fully his.

Keenan held out a hand, an invitation he'd given her at every faire. At every turn he put the choice forward for her. And, at each faire, she'd taken his hand, but she'd kept herself back from him.

"Will you start the revelry . . . with me?" he asked. The question had become rote, a ritual that started a night of dance and drink, but the almost imperceptible pause was not routine.

"I can't promise forever." She took her king's hand.

Keenan stood and pulled her into his arms. As they began to move across the ground, soil warm under their feet, he whispered, "You already gave me forever, Aislinn. I'm asking for a chance at right now."

She shivered in her king's arms, but she didn't pull away. And this time, she welcomed it when he brought his lips to hers. Unlike that first time—at the faire that had changed everything—or the other two times he'd stolen kisses, she had no excuses: she was not drunk, angry, or caught off guard. She let herself enjoy the feel of his lips open against hers. It wasn't the tenderness that she'd shared with Seth. It wasn't the pressure Keenan had included in his earlier kisses. It was new and bittersweet.

She felt her hope and his joy spread like a tempest through their court. Flowers blossomed everywhere they touched the earth. This was what they'd lacked: the promise of happiness. *It can be enough. It has to be.* Then, the world spun away, or maybe they were the ones spinning.

She wasn't sure. Summer Girls twirled by, blurs of vibrant green against shades of copper and mahogany skin as their flowering vines slithered over their barely clad bodies, and for an unexpected moment, Aislinn didn't like how close they were to Keenan.

I have no right.

He pulled back only for a breath and whispered, "Tell me when to let go."

"Don't let me fall." She held tighter. "Save me."

"You've never needed saving, Aislinn." Keenan, her friend, her king, held on to her as the Summer Court danced dizzily around them, like spirals radiating out from their combined sunlight. "You still don't."

"It feels like I do." She felt tears slipping down her cheeks; as they moved in ever-faster turns, she saw the violets spring from the soil where those tears splashed to the ground. "I feel like . . . I feel like I'm missing a part of me."

"Would you feel that way if . . ." His words faded away.

"If it were you who left me?" Her voice was as soft as she could make it.

"It was selfish to ask. Forgive—"

"I would," she whispered. She closed her eyes against the tears—or maybe against the confusing emotions on his face. They matched the tumultuous feelings inside her. Even with her eyes closed, she knew that she was safe as she moved at impossible speeds through the crowd. Keenan had her in his arms, and he wouldn't let her fall.

If I'd met him before Seth . . . She hadn't, though.

Aislinn kept her face against his chest and told him, "I want to be sorry that you're apart from Donia, but I'm not."

Keenan didn't comment on bringing the subject up just then. "I've only truly loved a couple of times, Aislinn. I want to try loving you."

"You shouldn't lo—" Her words froze on her lips.

"That would be a lie, my Queen." His voice was gentle, even as he rebuked her. "One hundred eighty days, Aislinn. Seth's been gone for one hundred eighty days, and I've watched you try to pretend it doesn't hurt for every one of them. Can't I try to make you happy?"

"For the court."

"No," he corrected. "For you and for me. I miss your smiles. I waited for centuries to find my queen. Can we try this? Now that he's . . ."

". . . left me," she finished. She caught his gaze, let herself forget that there was anyone else around, and stood still. The faeries spun around them. It was just them in the center of a maelstrom. "Yes. Make me forget everything but right now. That's what the Summer Court is—not logic, not addiction, not war, not calm or cold. Make me warm. Make me not think. Make me anything but this."

He didn't answer; he just kissed her again. It was still like swallowing sunshine, and she didn't resist. Her own skin began to glow until any faeries not of their court would've had to turn their faces away.

There was earth under their feet, but she didn't feel it.

She didn't feel anything but sunlight chasing away everything that hurt inside of her. They moved through the park, flowers blossoming at their feet. She could taste the sunlight like warm honey on Keenan's lips.

Like every other revelry, she felt drunk on the dance and night. This time though, when morning came, her feet weren't touching the ground. She was in Keenan's arms, carried from the park and from their court to the side of the river where they'd been after the first faire. There was no picnic, no carefully planned seduction. It was just them along the riverbank.

When they had their monthly revels, they weren't sensible, but they also weren't vulnerable. Even War herself wouldn't cross them tonight.

Aislinn stayed in his arms when he sat down alongside the river. The cool water rolled over her feet and calves, like tiny electric pulses on her skin. It balanced the warm earth that they sank into as their combined sunlight turned soil into slick mud. And she shivered—as much from the river's touch as from Keenan's.

Some stray thought whispered that she was on the ground in a formal dress, but she was Summer—frivolity, impulsivity, warmth. *It's what I am. With him now.*

"Tell me when to let go," Keenan reminded her again.

"Don't let go," Aislinn insisted. "Talk to me. Tell me what you feel. Tell me everything you don't want to admit."

He grinned. "No."

"Treat me like a faery queen then."

"How so?"

She sat up and knelt beside him.

He stayed where he was, resting on the muddy bank, watching her.

Aislinn thought about the day they stood in the street and he'd let sunlight fall onto her like raindrops. Like so many other things since becoming Summer Queen, she understood now how to do that, but she'd not been able to experiment before. "Like this."

Every pleasure under the sun was hidden in the droplets of sunlight that fell from her skin to his. Faery magic was what she wanted to share with him. It was what she was now, and she didn't have to worry that she would hurt him as she would a mortal.

If Seth weren't human . . .

But if he hadn't been human, she'd never have had his friendship or love. If she'd still been human, she wouldn't have lost it either. But Keenan wasn't human, and neither was she.

Not now, not ever again.

She caught Keenan's gaze and gave him the words he'd given her: "I want to try loving you. *Make* me love you, Keenan. You've convinced so many others. Convince me. Seduce me so I don't have to hurt anymore."

She leaned toward him, but Keenan stopped her. He shook his head.

"This"—he gestured between them—"isn't love. It's something else."

"So . . ."

"Slower. Falling into bed . . . or riverbanks . . . isn't going to make you love me." Keenan stood up and held out a hand. "You're my queen. I've waited nine centuries to find you and almost a year more to reach this moment. I can wait a bit longer for the rest."

"But . . ."

He leaned in and kissed her softly. "If you're finally going to try to let yourself love me, we're going to date."

"We sort of *have* been."

"No." He caught her hands and pulled her into his embrace. "We've been trying very hard *not* to date. Let me show you our world. Let me take you to dinner and whisper temptations. Let me take you to ridiculous carnival rides and symphonies and dances in the rain. I want you to laugh and smile and trust me first. I want it to be real love if you are in my bed."

She paused. Sex seemed far easier than dating. They were friends; they had a spark. *Sex isn't love, though.* Keenan wanted a real chance. That meant something more than sharing her body.

"My solution was easier," she muttered, "and quicker."

He laughed. "After nine centuries, I was willing to accept whatever terms you set, but if we're going to try being together, I don't want any doubts. If you don't love me but still want to be . . . with me, I'll settle for that, but I want a chance to have it all."

"And if Seth . . ."

"Comes home?" Keenan pulled her closer and kissed her until the glow of sunlight shining from both of their bodies was blinding.

Then he promised, "That's up to you. It always has been, hasn't it?"

CHAPTER 31

Sorcha didn't weep when she came to see him that last morning. Sorcha looked at the paintings he'd done for her, and she looked at him.

"They aren't good enough," Seth said. "None of them are, not really."

"Would that I could lie to you," she murmured. "But they are wrought of passion. I'd be selfish if I refused to let you leave."

She walked around the room examining canvases she'd seen already.

"*They* aren't good enough, but this is." He opened his hand, and there in the center of his palm was a perfectly rendered cluster of silver jasmine blossoms. It was far more delicate than his other metalwork.

Sorcha's eyes teared up. She stroked a fingertip over the silver petals. "It is. It's exquisite."

"I didn't want to give you what you expected"—he

pinned it to her dress with a shaking hand—"so I worked on it when you weren't here."

She laughed, and since there were no witnesses to her foolishness, she leaned forward and kissed his cheek. She'd seen so many mothers do that, but the simple gesture had never quite made sense to her. Objectively, she'd understood—maternal affection was a biological imperative. It caused the mother to feel tenderness toward her progeny, keeping the smaller, precious creature safe. It was all very reasonable, but as she pressed her lips to her son's cheek, she wasn't feeling logical. It didn't feel reasonable. It was impulsive. It was something she wanted to tell him but found that she didn't have words for.

"It's perfect." She glanced down at the pin, and while the impulsiveness was riding her, she blurted out, "I don't want you to leave. What if they harm you? What if you need me? What if—"

"Mother." He smiled, peaceful and so very beautiful to her. "I'll be a faery. Under the Dark Court's protection, beloved by the Summer Queen, made strong by your gift. I'll be safe."

"But Bananach . . . and Winter . . . and . . ." She actually felt her heart beating uncomfortably fast. She'd known she'd feel something when he left, but this degree of worry and sadness was unexpected. "You could stay. We'll send Devlin to fetch your Summer Queen to us and—"

"No. I'm not going to ask her to abandon her court for me." He led her to the seat that looked out into the garden where they'd walked. She sat down, and he sat on the floor beside her feet.

"I need to go. I want to go. It'll feel like a breath, and I'll be back . . . *home*," he assured her.

"I think I might hate your other queen right now." She scowled.

Actual tears were building in her eyes. It was a simple physiological reaction; logic explained it away. The tears still fell.

"And I'm afraid. If my sister hurts you, I'll . . ." She took a steadying breath. "Bananach is not to be trusted, Seth. Not ever. Never go with her anywhere again. Promise me you'll stay away from her. She has only one goal—violence."

"So why did she bring me to you?"

Sorcha shook her head. "In order to provoke someone. In order to get me to make a choice that would allow her to lay blame at my feet. I don't truly know. I've spent eternity trying to guess her next move. It's always about machinations for another war. I am left trying to make the right choices."

"Did you make the right choice this time?"

"Yes." She stroked his face. "Whatever happens next, this was the right choice."

"Even if war comes . . ."

"The alternative was your death." She swallowed a sob at the thought. "When you left with her there were two paths you could've ended up on—this one or left dead for your Summer Queen to find. Either Niall's court or mine would have been thought responsible. Perhaps Winter. War would have had her wish."

It felt strange to talk of such things to anyone other than Devlin, but her son would have a voice in her court when he was ready. He could be fully faery if she wanted it so, but that would free him to leave her. Their bargain made him need to stay with her. *If he was fully faery, would he remain over there?* That wasn't something they needed to discuss. He wouldn't ever be High King: she was eternal, the Unchanging Queen. He would, however, be an influence, a voice, a power. He would stand equal to Devlin. Sorcha wondered how well both her son and her brother would accept that.

Seth didn't speak; he merely waited, patient as befit her son.

"If I keep you here, the likelihood of war is still strong. Sooner or later, Keenan would be unable to hide where you were. Aislinn would try to bend my will to her wishes. She is not strong enough to do that, and I would not"—Sorcha paused, weighing the words carefully—"react well. If your beloved came seeking retribution, I'd nullify the threat."

"You'd kill her."

"If discussion wasn't effective, yes. I'll eliminate anyone who threatens what I love. Or who I love. If Aislinn came against my court, I'd have to stop her . . . although I'd regret that you'd mourn." She wondered, briefly, if this mortal change inside her would be for the betterment of her court or not. She felt emotions driving her actions; she felt tenderness for her son that was tinged with loss and fear. Such untidiness was not of the High Court. *Will it change my court?* It didn't matter. She might have changed, but . . . the thought was one that had no completion. *What does it mean when the Unchanging Queen changes?* Sorcha shook her head. Pondering thusly was illogical. What was simply— *was.* She and her court would adjust. *That* was logical.

She spoke her next words with a finality that felt like a vow: "I won't allow Aislinn or Bananach or anyone else to take you from me. I won't allow them to endanger my court or my son."

And she knew as she said it that her court would come second to her son should the choice be before her. Somewhere inside she wondered if this was precisely what Bananach had intended, but that too was immaterial. After centuries of small victories back and forth, Sorcha knew enough to realize that every choice would echo through the tapestries of time. Her choices would change her sister's warmonger-ing; Bananach's actions would shift to counter those ripples; so it had been for centuries.

"Is it acceptable to say I'll worry too?" He looked young as he asked her. "I don't want what you gave me to make you vulnerable. I didn't think . . . I want you safe. If Bananach is such a threat, she should be stopped. Some in the other courts are friends to me. If I can keep you safe—"

"Children aren't to worry about their parents, Seth. I'm fine." Sorcha affixed her court smile, giving him what reas-surances she could offer. "I have been fighting her since I first existed. The only thing new is that I have a child to protect now. You are a gift. She just didn't realize that when she brought you to me."

He nodded, but worry was still plain in his eyes.

"Come," she said. "Let us see what you need to pack."

Aislinn sat in the study, curled into Keenan's embrace with a discomfort she couldn't quite erase. Tavish had given them approving glances as he'd shooed the Summer Girls away. The loft was peaceful, and she knew that her decisiveness was responsible for it. She dared a glance at him. This was it: her future. One way or another, they were bound together.

"... after lunch?"

"What?" She blushed.

He laughed. "Would you like to do something after lunch? A walk? A film? Shopping?"

"Yes?"

The look he gave her was new, or maybe just the openness of it was new. "Formal? Dine in? Picnic? Go to New York for pizza?" he added.

She scowled. "Now you're just being foolish."

"Why?" He moved around so he was facing her. "You're a faery queen, Aislinn. The world is yours. A few moments and we'd be there. I'm not a mortal. Neither are you."

She paused. The words she wanted to say weren't there. There were no reasons not to. *I am not a mortal.* She took a deep breath. "Can you figure out this dating thing? I've dated one person and . . ."

He brushed a soft kiss over her lips. "Be ready in an hour?"

She nodded, and Keenan left.

I can do this. The step from friendship to love isn't that far. It hadn't been with Seth. She forced thoughts of him away. He was gone, and she was moving on with her life.

CHAPTER 32

As Seth stepped through the moonlit veil, the world around him changed. It wasn't as simple as going from the peace and perfection of his mother's side to the harsh and jarring mortal world. In that single step, he was changed. The bargain he'd made was manifest. Seth was not mortal on this side of the veil: he was fey.

The world shifted under his feet. He felt it, the thrum of life that burrowed and nested in the soil. Wings from a far-off egret sent gusts of air that swirled into the currents in the sky.

Sorcha took his hand in hers. "It's strange at first. I've watched the mortals in the Summer Court change. Let the difference find its place inside you."

He couldn't speak. His senses—and not just the same five he'd had before—were flooded. As a mortal, his understanding of the world was restricted to a basic comprehension. Now, he knew things that had no physical sensory

source. He could feel what was in order. He could feel the
rightness of what was and what should be.

"Do they—*we*—all feel like this?" His words felt too
melodic, like his voice was reflected back through some fil-
ter that was softening sound.

She paused, her hand still holding his. "No. Not so fully,
but they aren't my children. You're the only one who is
that."

When he glanced over at her, he saw her through his
changed vision. Tiny moonlit chains like silver filigree
stretched between them in a net that wasn't visible to him
when they were in Faerie. He reached for the net. "What is
this?"

He could touch it; even as he realized it wasn't tangible,
it felt weighty in his hand like chain mail, heavier than it
looked.

"No one else will see it." She caught his free hand in hers.
"It's *us*. You're of me, as if I'd borne you myself. You share
my blood. It means you'll see things, know things . . . I
didn't know how to tell you."

"'See things'?" He looked beyond her to the white sand
beach where they stood. He didn't think it was *seeing*. He felt
things: crabs scuttling in the sand, seagulls and terns' feet
touching the earth. Absently, he walked toward the edge of
the sea. As the water brushed his feet, he felt the life teeming
in that water—animal and faery. Selchies mated somewhere
to the east. A merrow argued with her father.

Seth concentrated on not-feeling it, not knowing.

"It's not seeing," he told Sorcha. "I feel the world. It's like the whole time I thought I was alive, I was really barely conscious."

"That is faery. More so because you are mine. The Hounds create fear. Gancanaghs create lust. That's what they feel." She led Seth away from the water to a bit of worn rock. "You'll feel all that and other things too. A few of us can feel all of it, but some things will be stronger. Niall feels lusts and fears more truly. You'll feel rightness, logical choices, pure reason."

Seth sat beside her on the rocky outcrop and waited.

"The seeing part is different." Her gaze was wary, but her voice was unwavering. "My sister and I have far-seeing. She chooses to see the threads to pluck to create disorder. I choose to focus on the inverse. But they are *all* only possibilities and connections. You must remind yourself of that."

"Because I'm yours." He hadn't thought about any traits beyond longevity and strength when he sought this bargain. "This is all different because I'm your son."

"Yes. You will have some . . . differences from other faeries." She squeezed his hand in hers. "But when the seeing becomes too much, you will have time to be not-this within Faerie. You can return to me anytime and enjoy being mortal; you can escape from being a faery, from being of my blood."

"What all will I . . . I mean, what other changes . . ." He struggled to make sense of this added gift—*curse*—as he struggled too to make sense of the flood of information from the world around him. "I see possibilities."

She held tight to his hand when he thought to pull away. "Your own threads are less clear. It is only be others' threads you see. It may be only sometimes. I don't know how much of me you carry inside."

He lowered his head and closed his eyes, trying to block out everything but Sorcha's words. The sensory differences dulled to a distant din, but silvered threads of knowledge stretched out like roads he could follow with his mind. He would Know things if he let himself—and he didn't want to. Knowing without the power to change things was enough to make him feel unstable. He wanted to fix the conflict between the two merrows. He saw their threads. The girl was going to leave in anger. Her father would mourn because her death was likely after she left.

"How do you endure this?" he whispered.

"I change what I can, and I accept that I am not omnipotent." She stood before him and looked at him intently. "If you weren't able to be this, I wouldn't have chosen you. I can't see what you'll do now; too much of my essence lives in you. I know, however, that you are quite capable of anything you want to be. You are someone who will slay dragons, who will do feats worthy of ballads."

Seth realized that the gift Sorcha had given him was so much larger than he'd guessed. He had a purpose, a true purpose, out here as well as in Faerie. In Faerie, he created art for his queen mother; in the mortal world, he knew the things that could be set right. He could be her hand of order in this world if he had the skills to do so. "I don't know how to fight or politics or *anything*. . . ."

"Who are your friends?" she prompted.

"Ash, Niall . . ." He smiled as understanding dawned. "Niall knows how to fight. Gabriel and Chela are all about fighting. Donia knows all about politics. So does Niall. And Ash. So do the Summer Court guards . . . I can learn part of what I need from all three courts."

"All *four* courts," Sorcha added. "But you don't have to do those things. You don't have to become a hero, Seth. You could stay in Faerie, create art, walk with me and talk. I will bring us poets and musicians, philosophers and—"

"I will. Every year I'll come home to you . . . but this"—he kissed her cheek—"is my world too. I can make things better for the people I love. For you. For Ash. For Niall. I can make both worlds safer."

They sat silently for a few moments. Seth thought about the merrows who quarreled under the water.

"If the kelp strands were snarled as if by a storm, woven too tightly for the daughter to leave—" He stopped as that very thing happened. The merrow daughter was frustrated, but she turned back to her home.

Before he could comment, Sorcha pulled him to her in a quick embrace and said, "I need to leave. Go to your Aislinn. Find your place, and if you need me . . ."

"I do need you," he assured her.

"Call, and I'll be here." She gave him a look that was one he'd seen often on his father's face when he was younger—worry and hope. "Or you can come to me. Anytime. Devlin will assure your safety as well . . . and Niall . . . and . . ."

"I know." He kissed her cheek. "I remember all the instructions you gave me."

She sighed. "There's no stalling it, is there?"

With a small gesture, she bent space to open a doorway into the park across from Aislinn's loft. Sorcha was silent as Seth crossed the veil into the park.

He'd had the Sight before, so seeing the faeries who loitered in the park was not surprising. Aobheall was shimmering in her fountain; she paused as Seth appeared before her. Rowan guards stared at him. Summer Girls stopped mid-dance.

"Well, aren't you unexpected?" Aobheall murmured. The water around her froze, droplets held in the air like tiny crystals.

Seth stood, speechless as the differences in perception assailed him. Aobheall's voice was unchanged, but the pull to reach out to her was gone. There was no charm in his hand. Reality was different. *He* was different. The earth breathed around him, and he could feel it. The sighs of trees were a music that wove among the seeming silence of no one speaking to him.

"You are like us," Tracey whispered. "Not mortal."

She walked toward him with a sad expression that was

common for her, but as far as Seth saw it, not warranted by the circumstances. Tears filled her eyes. She hugged him. "What have you done?"

For the first time since he'd met any of the Summer Girls, Seth was not affected by her touch. He didn't feel the temptation to hold her longer or feel the fear of her injuring him in her forgetfulness.

He released her. "I've changed."

Skelley took Tracey in his arms and held on to her as she began to sob. Other Summer Girls wept silently.

"This is a *good* thing." Seth felt stronger, more alive, and sure of his choices. "It's what I want."

"So did they," Skelley said. "That's why they weep. They remember making that same foolish sacrifice."

Aobheall didn't frown or weep. She blew him a watery kiss. "Go see our queen, Seth, but know that life as a faery isn't as kind as you thought. She had to do what was best for her court."

The pressure in Seth's chest, the fears of what else had changed, grew. He hadn't felt that unease so strongly when he was in Faerie with Sorcha. There, he had calm. There, he had certainty. Now, he was walking into his beloved's home, hoping that what he'd built with her was still strong enough to be saved.

He didn't speak to the guards he passed; he didn't knock. He opened the door and walked into the loft. She was there. Her cheekbones were more obvious, as if she'd lost a bit too much weight, and she sat much closer to Keenan than she had before. She was smiling, though, looking at Keenan, who was midsentence.

Everything stopped as Seth came into the room. Keenan didn't move away from Aislinn, but his words and gestures stilled. Aislinn's smile vanished, replaced with a look somewhere between amazed and unsure. "Seth?"

"Hey." He hadn't been so nervous in months. "I'm back."

There were so many emotions racing through her expressions that he was afraid to move, but then she was across the room and in his arms, wrapped in his embrace, and in that moment everything was right in the world. She was crying and holding on to him.

Keenan stood, but he didn't cross the room. He looked furious. Small eddies of wind lifted around the room. Sand bit Seth's skin. "You're not mortal anymore," Keenan said.

"No, I'm not," Seth acknowledged.

Aislinn pulled back and looked at Seth. She didn't let go of his arm, but she stepped back. "What did you do?"

"I found an answer." Seth pulled her closer and whispered, "I missed you."

Keenan didn't say another word; he was almost mechanical in his movements as he walked past them and out the door.

Aislinn tensed as he passed, and for a moment, Seth wasn't sure if she was going to go after Keenan or stay with him. "Keenan? Wait!"

But the Summer King was already gone.

Donia knew it was him when he knocked at her door. Her spies had told her that Seth had returned to the mortal world as a faery. Keenan's arrival was inevitable.

"You knew where he was." She needed to hear it. They'd spent too long with half-truths. The time for such tolerances was past. "You knew Seth was in Faerie."

"I did," he admitted. He stood just inside her doorway and looked at her with the same summer-perfect eyes that she had dreamed of for most of her life and silently asked her to forgive him, to tell him something to make it all right.

She couldn't. "Ash is going to find out."

"I've ruined everything, haven't I?"

"With her?" Donia stayed at a distance, not touching him, not approaching. It was what she had to do. He'd given her words of love and then abandoned her to romance Aislinn. It wasn't unexpected, but it still hurt. Now he'd come seeking comfort. "Yes."

"And with you?" he asked.

She looked away. Sometimes love wasn't enough. "I think so."

"So I am left—" he broke off. "I've ruined everything, Don. My queen is going to . . . I've no idea what this will do to my court. I've lost you. Niall hates me . . . and Sorcha cares for Seth, the mortal—the *faery* I . . ." He looked at her. The sunlight that usually shone so brightly when he was upset had all but faded from him. "What am I going to do?"

He sunk to the floor.

"Hope that some of us are kinder to you than you've been to us," she whispered. Then, before she could soften again, she walked away and left the Summer King kneeling in her foyer.

Chapter 33

As her fey started filtering into the room, stealing glimpses of Seth and whispering things she didn't want to hear, Aislinn led Seth to her room and closed the door. It was the only room in the loft that was just hers, so it was the only place she could think without feeling like she was in *their* space. The loft was their home now. It had changed. She had changed.

Seth sat on her bed and watched her, patient as he'd always been. He'd changed too, not just what he was, but *who* he was.

The words wouldn't come. She'd thought them, spoken them to him in scenarios she played out in her mind, whispered them in the dark as if he could hear her. Now, they weren't there. She wanted to tell him she hated that he'd left her, that she was devastated that Niall had known where he was but she hadn't, that she'd thought she'd never be whole again, that she'd never love anyone else the way she loved him, that it hurt to breathe when he was away. She didn't know how to say any of that, not now, but there was something she had to tell him. "Keenan and I are . . . were . . . dating."

Seth crossed his arms over his chest. "Which means?"

"It means I told him he could try to make me . . . love him. That I was willing to give us a chance. . . ." She hated that he was looking at her like she was the one who'd messed everything up. He'd left her. He'd stayed away. He hadn't even called. She flopped down on the bed. "What was I supposed to do?"

"Have faith in us?"

"You *vanished* without any explanation and were gone for *six* months. . . ." She tucked her feet up under her. "I thought you weren't coming back. You left me without a word . . . after refusing to talk to me." She wasn't sure if it was temper or sorrow that was welling up inside of her. "You vanished."

"How long?" he asked.

"What?"

"Until you were with him? How long did he wait, Ash?"

She had never been truly angry with him, not once, but right then she would've gladly struck him. After six months of being worried and hurt and afraid, she finally felt the anger she hadn't allowed herself before.

"You left me." The words were bitten off.

"I had a chance to get to the faery who could give me forever with you. The timing sucked, but—" Seth stopped.

"I didn't know I'd be gone so long. I'm sorry it happened that way. I saw a chance. I took it."

"I waited. We sent faeries to look for you. I tried to talk to Niall . . . to Bananach. I waited for six months." She clasped her hands together to keep from gesturing.

They'd never had a fight; they'd never had a reason for one either.

She looked down at her hands until her temper stilled. "I thought you had abandoned me. Niall said—"

"The Dark King who's pissed at you told you something that made you doubt me, and you believed him." Seth crooked his brow.

"There was a girl in the background . . . in the voice mail . . ."

"Bananach. War. She took me to—"

"You left with *Bananach*? What were you thinking?"

"I was thinking it was worth the risk if it meant forever with my faery girlfriend." He spoke very softly. "I was thinking that being with you was worth the risk. She took me to Sorcha, and I made a deal so I could be in your world the whole way, so I'd be strong enough to not need guards and babysitters, so I'd be able to be around for you forever."

"And the cost?" She was afraid. She was a faery—and apparently he was too, now—but faery bargains weren't renowned for their fairness.

"A month with Sorcha every year."

"You were gone *six* months."

"I was with her for a month. In Faerie." He looked at her with a plea to understand, to agree that he didn't make a mistake. "Niall told me she was the one who could make me this. No one else was willing to help. It was only thirty days for me. I didn't know that it was longer for you."

"So every year . . ." she prompted.

"I leave for what feels like a month to me and six months to you."

"For the rest of your life."

He nodded.

She tried to make sense of his being gone, of his being around for eternity. It didn't make sense yet. He was hers, but at what price? Her heart raced as she thought about what he'd sacrificed. "And when you're there, is it awful?"

"No. It's almost perfect. The only thing that kept it from perfection was that you weren't with me." He looked enthralled as he spoke. "Faerie is incredible, and my only task is to create . . . and that's it. I walk in the gardens. I think. I create. It's amazing there."

"And . . . Sorcha?"

The expression on his face was one of tenderness and of longing. "She's perfection too. She is kind and gentle and wise and funny although she doesn't admit it. . . ."

"Oh." Her stomach twisted. He found eternity, but he'd found a queen as well. Aislinn wanted to not feel jealous, but she'd be worried for months and he'd been off falling for another faery queen. "So when you're there, you're with—"

"No. It's not like that at all." He scowled. "She's my

queen, my patron, a muse. It's like having a family, Ash. She's the mother I never . . . not that Linda doesn't love me . . . but Sorcha is . . . she's perfect."

They sat there silently for a while until she couldn't stand it anymore. "So now what?"

He shook his head. "I don't know. We figure out how to make it okay?"

But it was very much not okay. He'd risked it all to find forever with her, and she'd had so little faith in what they shared that she'd fallen into Keenan's arms.

It's where she was headed already.

He looked at her and admitted to himself that maybe it wasn't his mortality that had stood in the way, but someone else. As long as she was the Summer Queen, she'd be with Keenan. They'd have their revelry and their meetings and their late-night arguments.

And I just destined myself to watch them do this for decades, for centuries.

"Did you sleep with him?" He waited, needing to hear her say it, needing to know.

"I thought you were gone, and I didn't want to love anyone else . . . and he's my friend . . . and I care about him and—"

"So that's a yes?" His heart sounded like it was thundering in his ears.

"No . . . He turned me down." She looked like she was going to start weeping. "I just wanted to stop hurting. I

felt empty, and the court was weakening from my . . .
wallowing."

"I love you." He pulled her to him and kissed her the
way he had dreamed of when they were apart. She didn't
resist at all. It was almost like it had been before, but how it
was before wasn't good enough anymore. He'd been patient.
He'd been willing to not feel jealous of Keenan because he'd
believed that Keenan would be around to love her after he
had died.

With effort, he stopped kissing her. "I don't want to
share you with him. Not anymore. I'm not going to die. I'm
not going to be so easily broken now. And I'm not going to
watch him look at you the same way I do."

"I can't walk away from my court."

"Or him." Seth could see the threads of possibility. There
were paths that twisted and looped. There were possibilities
he couldn't see, which meant that he was in them. In others,
though, she was with Keenan.

"He's my king," she whispered.

"I know that, but . . . 'king' isn't beloved or lover. It can
be, but it doesn't have to be." Seth stopped short of telling her what he could see. Now wasn't the time. "I need to
know that he's not the one you want."

"I love *you*," she said.

"Tell me you don't feel any love like this"—he brushed
his lips across hers—"with him. Tell me you can be
around him and not feel like it's romantic. If he's your
friend, that's fine, but that isn't all he is. It hasn't been for

months . . . long before I left."

She stared at him, but no words came.

"I'm a faery too. I can't lie. But I can tell you that there is no one else—faery or mortal—that's shared my bed since I fell in love with you. I've not even considered taking anyone there. There's no one in my life but you. I don't want anyone else either. At all. Just you. Forever."

"What am I to do?" she whispered.

"Start by seeing him for what he really is."

"Which means?" Her voice rose, and her expression grew tense.

"He knew where I was, Ash." Seth kept his tone gentle. He didn't want to hurt her, but he wasn't going to help Keenan hide his deceits. "Niall knew where to look. So did Keenan. He's been around long enough to think to check in Faerie."

"But he couldn't. Maybe he—"

"Ask him." Seth shrugged. "He knew where I was. Donia knew. Niall knew. Bananach took me there. Everyone knew. Ask your guards to tell you. Ask the Summer Girls. They might not volunteer it, but if you ask them straight out, they'll answer you."

"So you think they *all* knew"—she folded her arms over her chest, hugging herself—"and *no one* told me? How could they do that?"

"What would you have done if you had known where I was?"

"Come to Faerie and rescued you."

"Your court isn't strong enough for a war, and you were in the midst of summer, impulsive and passionate. If you'd come, it would have been a disaster—which is why Niall didn't tell you. And Donia . . . I suspect she kept silent out of love for Keenan. She wouldn't want to see his— *your*—court broken, even though he's hurt her." He caught Aislinn's gaze. "But your court? Is that why Keenan didn't tell you? Or did he have other reasons as well?"

"He saw me falling apart. My whole court did. They *knew* how much I hurt." Aislinn wept. "He knew and . . . Why?"

Seth hated that he had to hurt her even more, but this was the issue she hadn't dealt with. "Tell me you won't forgive him. Tell me you aren't trying to figure out *right now* how it was somehow not as awful as it sounds."

Aislinn looked at him silently. Her face was tear-streaked.

"You forgave his manipulations over making you his queen. You forgave his manipulations that cost your court Niall's support and almost killed Leslie. And right now, you're trying to pretend he wasn't manipulating you again." Seth wanted her to interrupt him, to tell him he was wrong.

She didn't.

"You trust him. I don't know if it's a queen and king thing or if you're just trying to see the good in him. He's not good, though. He'd have had me killed if he thought it served his purpose. I get that. Niall does. You need to see him for who he truly is. For me, for your court, and for yourself."

"He's my *partner* for the rest of eternity."

"No, he's a coworker. I'm your *partner*"—he kissed her forehead—"for eternity if you want me. If he's your king, your friend, your coworker, that's all fine. I don't want to keep you to myself with no other people—or faeries—in your life, but I don't want to share your heart, especially not with someone who keeps hurting you. If you want to be with him, tell me. If you want to be with me, tell me that. You need to figure out what you truly want, Ash. Come find me when you're ready to tell me that I'm the only one."

And he left. It ripped some part of him to pieces, but he wasn't going to wait around hoping for scraps from Keenan's table.

CHAPTER 34

After Seth was gone from her, Sorcha stayed alone in his rooms. She wasn't quite ready to deal with Devlin or court matters or much of anything. Truth be told, her only desire just then was to follow Seth and help smooth over whatever conflict he found when he went back to the Summer Queen. Aislinn might've been mortal once, but she was the epicenter of summer, a season of heat and frivolity. Sorcha knew Keenan well enough to know that the once-mortal queen would've succumbed to his charms.

"How very mawkish, sister." Bananach came in through the garden door. Her shadowy wings were solid now. "Are you pining for your mortal pet?"

"He's under *your* king's protection. Not my pet and not mortal out there." Sorcha didn't deign to look at her sister. Now more than ever, the High Queen must appear Unchanged—but she felt the change. Despite War's presence, Sorcha felt almost in control of her emotions for the first time in an eternity.

"Precious! All the more access to twist his thoughts then." Bananach picked up one of Seth's paintbrushes and sniffed it. "Shall I tell you what he'll find upon his return? Shall I whisper to you of the ash-queen's weeping and wailing?"

Sorcha tilted her head and gave Bananach a bland smile. Inside, her heart was aching. The Summer Queen was probably no better than any other Summer Court faery—such a tempestuous, fickle lot.

"Why would that matter to me?" she asked.

"Because she will blame you. Because Seth Morgan's changing and returning has left Winter and Summer even more at odds. Because Darkness gnashes his teeth about the consequences of your actions, my dear sister." Bananach crowed the words as she punctuated each statement with miniature sword strokes in the air, brandishing Seth's paintbrush like a weapon.

"Niall knows where Seth was and why. I was honest with him—as I had been with the last Dark King." Sorcha stood and stepped around her sister, leaving the close quarters and trying to draw her sister's unpleasantness away from Seth's room.

As Sorcha moved past, Bananach snapped her jaw like the animal she was—brutish and crude.

"I've no use for your games, Bananach." The air in the garden was refreshing as Sorcha drew long breaths, letting her sister think she still needed space from her, feigning the discomfort she'd always had when War was in her presence.

For the first time, the discordant ripples weren't touching Sorcha. She still knew they were present, but she was inured to it.

Because I chose Seth to be my son. The touch of his mortality made her something new, not in balance with Bananach now. *After all these centuries, I have changed.*

The raven-faery wasn't pleased. She gripped Sorcha's arm. "Do you truly think I have no other pawns in play?"

"I am sure your machinations are vast." Sorcha brushed her hands over a cluster of jasmine blossoms and leaned closer to inspect the leaves on a small hawthorn bush. "When you aren't lost in bloodlust, you are formidable."

Bananach cocked her head and made a small satisfied sound before saying, "I can be stalled, but Reason always slips, and I wait. And when you stumble, when the regents over there are not wise, I will have my blood."

"Maybe."

Bananach let out an ugly caw. "Always. In the end, I always get my blood. One day it will be yours I wear like rouge."

Sorcha snapped a branch from a shrub, offering Bananach false proof that she'd become so unsettled that her temper slipped out. "Even in your deepest fits of madness, you won't forget that we are bound. You don't know what my death would mean for you any more than I do."

"It will mean that I am free of your wearisome logic." Bananach's wings fluttered in an erratic beat.

"If you thought it so simple, I'd have been dead long

ago." Sorcha squeezed the branch under her hand until it cut into her palm. Then she dropped the splintered wood and held up her hand. "Your blood and mine have been the same since we have first existed. Unchanging. If we are the same and you kill me, will you die too?"

Bananach glared at her. She snapped her beak. "Perhaps I should find out," she hissed, but she didn't advance. She stood watching.

The garden was silent. No more words were spoken for several moments.

"War is patient, sister mine. You hide here with your dusty tomes and empty art. The Unchanging Queen. Tedious. Predictable. I will move the pawns . . . and you will make small choices that do nothing to stop the inevitable." Bananach's drums of war rose to a deafening volume that echoed through the whole of Faerie and into the mortal world. "They watch each other with mistrust. The fighting comes soon. I *feel* it. I'll wait . . . and you will be as helpless as you always are when I am out there stirring trouble."

"You'll not have war this time," Sorcha told her. It wasn't a truth but an opinion.

"Why? Will you come after me, sister? Will you bring Faerie into the mortal world to hunt me?" Bananach crooned. Ravens that did not belong in Sorcha's garden flocked down around Bananach; vermin crawled from the earth like a writhing gray carpet; and Bananach stood with her wings outstretched. War was coming unless something significant changed.

Sorcha remained silent.

"Come after me. Bring chaos to their world," Bananach taunted. "Come protect your pet."

"You will not touch him." Sorcha stepped closer to her sister. "Summer and Darkness will strike you. I might not be able to stand against you, but I will send every faery I have to strike you. Come against him, and I will see you dead."

"And if killing me means your death?" Bananach tilted her head curiously.

"So be it." Sorcha kissed War on the forehead. "You've lost this battle, sister mine. There will be no war."

Bananach paused. She stared into the distance, but didn't share her visions of destruction. She smiled in horrific glee. "No, I've not lost yet."

Then she strode away through the garden with her entourage, and in her wake were charred footsteps and bleeding flowers.

EPILOGUE

Seth walked into Niall's home. Niall hadn't ever wanted him to be there, but that was before. *When I was mortal.* Things had changed.

No one stopped Seth. He was a declared Friend of the Dark Court, welcome among them, protected by their last breaths if necessary.

"Brother," Niall said as Seth approached the dais.

The throngs of Dark Court faeries watched openly. Seth saw threads of Ly Ergs and glaistigs woven together. Then the picture blurred. *Bananach. My aunt.* Seth couldn't see her threads, but he felt her somewhere in the world.

"I need your help." Seth didn't bow, but he lowered his gaze respectfully. He was a faery now, and chosen brother or not, Niall was still king.

"Say the word. If it's not against the good of my court"— Niall sat straighter in his throne—"I'll always help you."

Seth looked up and caught Niall's gaze. "I'm the High

Queen's own. For eternity, I'll spend a part of my life with her in Faerie. I'm the Summer Queen's beloved. But it is *your* help I need now. Sorcha's made me faery and given me gifts. I would do what's best for her now."

"Supporting the High Court's need for order is *not* what's best for the Dark Court," Ani said from somewhere to his left. The half-Hound, half-mortal girl had dreams of chaos that her king and court restricted.

"Neither's protecting the Summer Court's pet," grumbled one of the thistle-fey.

Protectively, Chela moved closer to Seth.

During the long pause, Seth stared only at Niall—whose threads were so myriad that that they might as well be invisible. The Dark King waited, hopeful in a way that he didn't even realize. If Seth couldn't see so truly, he'd believe that Niall's raising his hand was a casual gesture. It wasn't. It was both fearful and excited. "Tell me what you want."

"To train with Gabriel's Hounds. Sometimes setting things to order requires blood." Seth let his gaze drift across the assembled Dark Court fey and then back to their king. "I need to know how to defend myself and to wound others. I need to know how to hunt. Will you help me?"

"It would be an honor," Niall said. "If the Hounds agree?"

Gabriel laughed. Chela smiled. Faeries grinned and nodded.

Seth did bow then. He saw the threads of possibilities all around him. As long as he didn't tell them that it was

Bananach he intended to hunt, he'd find much help here.

"Welcome home, brother." Niall stepped forward and embraced him. "This change suits you well."

It did. Seth had a purpose now. *And a chance at eternity with Ash.*

356740492058443